GETTING TO Grace

Lee Barber

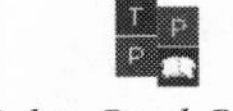

Relax. Read. Repeat.

GETTING TO GRACE
By Lee Barber
Published by TouchPoint Press
Brookland, AR 72417
www.touchpointpress.com

ISBN-13: 978-1-952816-27-7

Editor: Jenn Haskin
Cover design by David Ter-Avanesyan/Ter33Design
Cover image by Ioana Catalina E/Shutterstock.com

Visit the author's website at leebarber137.com

First Edition

Printed in the United States of America.

For Velma Marie Loveless Barber who, rumor has it,
always wanted to write a book.

Chapter One
1955

THE DORM ROOM DOOR opened and crashed against the wall. Grace's head snapped up.

"Welcome to your new life!" Deirdre stepped in and flicked her wrist, sending a rolled-up newspaper that flew end-over-end.

The paper bounced in the middle of the bed where Grace sat propped against the wall, her legs folded lotus-style on the white chenille spread. She reached down and uncurled the classified section of the Columbus Dispatch. "What new life?"

"Look at the job listings." Deirdre rummaged through her side of their tiny shared closet.

Searching until she spotted an underlined ad, Grace cleared her throat and read out loud, "Manager for developing rural arts community. Must be organized, sensible, able to manage projects large and small. Must love art, literature, and music, and must start immediately. Experience not required. Salary includes room and board." A phone number followed.

"I like you, Grace," Deirdre said as she sloughed off her black jacket in favor of her red, wool cape. "For a brainy girl, you pack a lot of pep in that short, lovely body of yours, but you're not happy here. Do something about that." She gave her cape a flourish. The cloth whirled around her nearly six-foot frame.

"Meeting tonight?" Grace asked.

"You bet. The workers will rise!" Deirdre made a grand exit, thunking the door against the frame as it shut.

The sudden sound of solitude thrummed in Grace's ears, broken only by the tromping of Deirdre's leave-taking and her booming voice as she greeted another dorm resident in the hall. Then, silence. Grace stared at the ad for another full minute, until her gaze drifted to the window. Outside, undergraduates trudged to and from academic buildings, their feet dodging slush left from yesterday's spring ice storm. She looked back down at the classified section.

Why in the world would she leave mid-semester? True, her grades had slipped this year, and Deirdre wasn't the first to notice that Grace's mood had, too. Grace thought she was over that. The first year of college had been everything she'd imagined, until Sarah ordered her to stay away as long as Richard was "in the picture." Without her older sister in her life, all the old feelings came back, loneliness, loss.

Re-rolling the newsprint and laying it on her pillow, she picked up the book by her side and opened it.

"It is not death that a man should fear, but he should fear never beginning to live," she read aloud. She'd been reading that passage by Marcus Aurelius when Deirdre returned from lunch.

Ice pellets pinged on the window. Grace looked outside to see students holding books to cover their heads, running toward doors. She closed her book again. Deirdre had said Grace wasn't happy. Grace hadn't been genuinely happy for a long time. Part of her died along with her parents. Did she fear beginning to live again?

Staying in college should feel full of hope, moving toward something that held meaning. But even when it didn't, a reasonable person would know to not give up on what could help secure an interesting job, financial independence.

On the other hand, why not? Happiness wasn't everything, but without at least a little, what was the point? School no longer held her interest, and it would always be there later when, and if, she decided to return. She lay the book on the bed, picked up her change purse and the rolled-up newsprint, and headed for the pay phone down the hall.

THE NEXT DAY, Grace drove a borrowed Buick, a beastly green machine in need of a tune-up, the longest distance she had ever travelled alone, about ninety minutes worth of miles. An hour earlier than expected, she passed a sign that read, "Welcome to Wood Grove, Ohio, Population 3,137, and Growing!" She eased her foot off the gas to let the car slow as fields gave way to houses.

"*What am I doing here?*" spun through her mind. Unable to place her feet back on the foundation of yesterday's decision, she had no idea how to answer that question, and yet, here she was, and early, to boot.

A sign on the right caught her eye. The car slid neatly into an angled parking spot in the middle of the four-block downtown. Grace pushed open the heavy car door and stepped out onto the pavement. The street was empty, Wood Grove's population either at work or in school, where she should be.

Right now she should be discussing Marcus Aurelius in her literature class. There, in his writing, that's where she'd found the inspiration to push herself out into the world. She wanted to retreat, but soldiered on, rolling his thoughts over in her mind, allowing his ancient wisdom to guide her steps away from the car, onto the sidewalk.

Through the front window of the G. C. Murphy Company Five & Dime, Grace saw a lunch counter extending halfway to the back of the store. Pictures of banana splits and milkshakes decorated the mirrored wall behind rows of glasses, stacked plates, scoops, cups, and cones. She pulled open the smudge-free glass door.

Inside, the air smelled like new clothes, candy, and comfort. She aimed for the empty round red vinyl stools stretching from one end of the counter to the other.

"Have a seat," the man behind the counter said. "Lunch rush is over, so you can have your pick. I'm Hank."

Grace chose one that placed her in the middle of the row. "I'll have a Coke."

"Coming right up." Hank flashed a wide smile, grabbed a glass, and filled it first with ice, then brown soda from a spigot. "Enjoy!" he said as he placed the glass in front her.

She watched him return to a sink topped with soap suds. He was an older man, maybe in his forties, but he plunged his hands into the water with the enthusiasm of a child at play.

Hank seemed to like what he was doing.

Sweet bubbly acid burned Grace's throat. Hank whistled Yankee Doodle. Was he actually fulfilled, satisfied, working behind a soda fountain? What made him so happy? Could she be happy working at a job like that?

The front door opened. Footsteps clicked across the tile floor, stopping at the stool just beyond her. Grace glanced down at a battered brown suitcase placed on the floor beside her and heard the young man order a Coke. Without moving her head, she noticed the folded hands he placed on the counter. His skin appeared smooth and tanned, like he had been working in the sun, which surprised her. Ohio lacked sun, particularly between November and April.

"Hello," the young man said, quietly enough that she knew he addressed her. "I'm Sam."

Hank placed another Coke on the counter and returned to the sink.

"Grace," she said.

"Excuse me?" Sam asked.

"My name is Grace."

Sam laughed. "Oh! I thought you were telling me to say grace before drinking. Catholic school will do that to you."

"Yes," Grace said.

"Sounds like you know what I'm talking about," he said.

She glanced at him. His thick black hair curled on the ends. "I have twelve years worth of knowing what you're talking about," she said.

"Did you go to school around here?" He sipped his drink.

"Dayton," she answered.

"That's west of here," he said, turning his head toward her. His skin appeared to be so smooth she wondered for a second if he wore makeup, but that would be absurd.

"And a little north," she said.

"Home of the Wright Brothers." He swiveled his stool in her direction. His eyes, blue like the sky, were spaced halfway between the top of his head and the bottom of his chin. She had never seen a more perfect face.

"And Charles Kettering," she added.

"I've heard of him." Sam sat up and squared his shoulders as he swiveled more, until their knees almost touched. "He invented the electric self-starter."

"Yes, he did," Grace said. Sam was handsome, and knowledgeable, too.

"Do you like history?" he asked.

He leaned his elbow on the counter to face her full on and she nearly shrank away from him, but something kept her in her place, which at the moment was so very close to him.

"I like history," she said. "Knowing history helps me understand the present."

He smiled. Her stomach dropped.

"A brilliant answer," he said, swiveling back to sip his drink. "Are you a student?"

She hesitated. "I've completed a year of college and now I'm interviewing for a job."

“Why the change?” he asked.

She considered how to answer, finally settling on, “I needed something different.”

He swiveled her way again and cocked his head to the side. “Interesting. I always thought finishing college paved the way to something different.”

“Maybe for you, it does.” Her tone sounded insolent, even to herself.

His head jerked back a little.

Grace wondered if she’d offended him.

He grinned. “I hope you finish your degree, Grace. You have a very fine mind.”

She turned away, a blush fire burning up her neck and into her cheeks.

“Sam!” A voice called from the direction of the front door followed by approaching footsteps. “Already breaking the hearts of our fair young Wood Grove maidens, I see.”

A chill ran across Grace’s back as the second young man passed behind her. In the mirror, she watched him shake Sam’s hand and clap him on the back before turning his attention to her.

“Or perhaps you are not a Wood Grove maiden. I haven’t seen you around. I’m Skip, Skip McKay.” He held out his hand.

Skip McKay’s hair was slicked back with so much oil she could see evenly spaced trenches where the comb had plowed through. His hand was warm, sweaty. “You’d be a lot prettier if you smiled,” he said.

He held her hand for too long and only dropped it when Hank walked over and said, “Now don’t go bothering this young lady, Skip.”

Grace folded her hands in her lap.

Hank reached in front of Grace for her empty glass. “Go on and leave her alone, Skip, or I’ll tell your parents you’re driving away our tourists.”

“Just being friendly,” Skip said, unapologetic, cocksure. He turned away from Grace. “Hank, meet my friend, Sam. We were roommates at Ohio State.”

"Nice to meet you, sir," Sam said, extending his hand toward Hank as he stood up on the other side of his stool. Sam's impeccable manners seemed out of place, more suited for a large city or a fancy restaurant. Grace watched as Hank seemed to size up the younger man before leaning across the counter to shake his hand. He nodded his head as he replied, "Nice to meet you, son."

Almost before Hank had finished his sentence, Skip said, "C'mon, Sam. We've got ground to cover." He picked up Sam's suitcase, brushing against Grace's thigh. As he walked behind her, he leaned toward her ear and whispered, "I hope I see you again, Sweetie." She could feel his breath on her cheek.

Sam met her eyes before following his friend. "Nice to meet you, Grace. I hope whatever you do, you use that mind of yours."

"You, too," Grace replied before she could catch herself.

"Oh, I intend to." He grinned and walked backwards toward the door. "'Every now and then a man's mind is stretched by a new idea or sensation, and never shrinks back to its former dimensions.' Oliver Wendell Holmes said that. I intend to continue to stretch my mind until the day I die."

Skip grabbed Sam's arm and pulled him toward the door. "No professors here to impress, buddy. Let's go."

When the two young men were through the door, Hank leaned down. "I have a daughter who graduated with Skip. She's in Cincinnati now, working for an accounting firm. Smart girl, took after her mother. I wouldn't let that boy close to my Ruby."

Through the plate glass window, Skip waved as he climbed into the driver's seat of a convertible, the front half of which lay in shadow while the sun's rays flamed off the gleaming red metal of the back half. He gunned the engine before backing the car out of the parking space. Sam raised his hand to wave from the passenger side, but Skip's takeoff slammed them both against their seats and the car disappeared beyond the window. Grace turned to look at Hank.

"That other boy," Hank said. "He seemed like he might be an upstanding young man, but what he's doing with Skip McKay, I don't know. That Skip is a dog." He tipped his head to Grace and walked away.

Grace liked dogs. She wouldn't discredit them by the comparison. Skip McKay looked more like a weasel to her.

She turned back to the window and looked at the empty parking spot.

The world seemed wider than twenty minutes ago. Grace had always done well in school, but no nun had ever commented on the "fineness" of her mind. Not even her father, her number one fan, had offered such a profound compliment. She put her money on the counter and walked to the door. Before leaving, Grace glanced back at the stool where Sam had been sitting.

Typically unmoved by good looking boys, Richard being the exception, she noted a small feeling of disturbance in her reaction to Sam. Disturbed because she liked her reaction, a mix of being ready to engage alongside an odd shyness rarely experienced by her, which felt like disloyalty. Was it okay to be attracted to others when you were committed to one? Still, meeting Sam seemed fortuitous, perhaps a harbinger of the many good things that could happen even in places like Wood Grove.

With a determined step, she moved toward the car, its faded surface a striking contrast with how she would present herself to the man who answered her call yesterday. For Mr. Nicholas Mason, writer of novels both famous and infamous, she would shine. She would be her best version of herself. She would show him she was the best person for the job, and when he offered her the position, she would say, "Let me call you tomorrow." She would take her time and think about what was best for her.

Sam's eyes flitted through her mind, initiating a little blip in her stomach. She chuckled as she admonished herself with an inner voice sounding like Sister Morgan. "*Rein yourself in, young lady. You have an interview in a few minutes.*"

A mile out of town, Grace spied a rusty mailbox with "Mason" painted on the side. Turning into the rutted lane, she could see an enormous three-story house rising from a knoll. There were no other farmhouses nearby, only empty fields backed by dense woods. She parked in back, between the house and a brick carriage house, her insides tense with fear, or excitement; she couldn't sort out which feeling seemed truer.

A man trotted out the back door. He appeared to be in his mid-thirties, tall and thin, his uncombed hair sticking out in all directions, glasses perched on top of his head. His face, though flawed, matched close-enough the polished photograph on the book jacket lying beside her.

Taking a deep breath, Grace opened the car door, and stepped out.

"Welcome! I'm Nick." His voice gripped her first, then his hand caught her elbow, as he guided her over the uneven ground. "You're so young! How old are you?"

"I'm nineteen," she said, stumbling on a rock. "How old are *you*?" Why was he asking? She was old enough.

"Thirty-five," he said and laughed as he helped her stay upright. "An old man."

Grace removed her elbow from his hand as she regained her balance, smoothed her black-and-white striped skirt, and walked toward the house.

Her host passed her to climb three steps and open the half-unhinged screen door. "I'll have this fixed as soon as possible," he said. "Pulled it loose when I tripped coming into the house last week. Nearly broke my neck." The tone of his voice communicated pride and joy more than caution.

She climbed the wooden stairs and crossed the threshold, registering shock as her feet stopped moving. She'd never been inside a building that displayed such deterioration.

A table, its barn red paint worn away in patches, rested on lopsided legs. On her left, a foot away from the wall, sat a stove, its oven door hanging open and burners missing. Ancient grease layered what once had been a white surface. An open door beyond the stove revealed a huge pantry, it's shelves empty.

To her right, the kitchen sink, gray from having enamel scrubbed away over the years, displayed a deep orange stain that spread out from past drips of a long-gone faucet. Empty cabinets with missing or broken doors lined the available space around the sink and on the wall opposite the back door.

Time and utter neglect had painted these fixtures on a canvas of torn wallpaper, broken windows, and a filthy floor, the scuffed linoleum missing altogether in places to reveal a black surface beneath.

An odor, something old, wet, and rotten hung in the air.

Two doors on the far wall offered escape.

"It looks rough," her host said, "but I've already had the major work done. Plumbing, electricity, the roof, all in good working order."

"The plumbing?" Grace looked at the sink.

"The pipes and drains," he said. "All of the fixtures will be replaced."

He touched her elbow again to guide her across the floor to the left-hand doorway in the wall opposite the back entrance. As she passed through, leaving the stench behind, she saw a wide hallway that ended with pillars on the right and left. The dark wooden pillars were joined at the top by a horizontal ladder of ornate rungs hanging a foot down from the ceiling. Beyond that, an elaborate front entryway. Side windows flanked a massive front door. To the left of the door, a thick bannister curled away from a set of steps going up and then turning to a staircase she couldn't see because it ran toward her.

The hallway walls, too, combined bare plaster with pieces of wallpaper that hung on, but unlike the hopeless state of the kitchen, there was a calm in the air here, the sense that this elder house had withstood its calamitous past.

"You said you were a student," Mr. Mason said. "What are you studying?"

"English," Grace replied.

"Ah," he said. "The degree for people who can't decide what they want to study."

Surprised, she said, "I read that you majored in English."

"Exactly!" He threw his hands up in the air and brought them down to perch on his cocked hips. "I speak from experience."

She almost smiled.

He guided her through the rest of the house, expounding like a salesman on the "outstanding" features of stained glass, lofty ceilings, and crown molding. He needn't have bothered. The place was palatial from her perspective; she was sold.

Four large bedrooms and one oversized bathroom consumed the second floor. The entire third floor was one open area, floored, with banks of windows on all four sides. "I keep wondering how they used this space," he said. "Maybe *costume* balls." He pronounced the word with an exaggerated "u."

She imagined him dressed as an English dandy, with tights or sleek pants, a blue velvet waisted coat, a ruffled shirt and top hat. He'd fit that role.

They descended from the third floor to the first in silence. When they once again stood in the massive hallway, beside the front door, her host said, "I think we'll need to put another bathroom in there." He gestured to the smallest room off the main hall. "There's only that one, upstairs."

Grace stepped around the hallway, peering up the stairs again, looking out the glass on the front door. Reflected in a side window, she saw her host cross his arms as he leaned against the stair banister, studying her.

"Who built this place?" she asked before wandering into the grandest room on the first floor. Featuring two fireplaces separated by a picture window with a half-moon-shaped stained-glass cap above, she imagined one might fit up to fifty, maybe even a hundred people in a room that size. This had never been a home for humble farmers.

Her host stepped up to her side. "A distant relative of mine built it in the early 1900s. She and her husband managed to keep it afloat during the depression and lived here until the late forties."

Grace and Sarah had recently closed on the sale of their parents' home. With Grace in college, and Sarah living in Columbus, they saw no need to maintain it. "Why didn't they sell it when they moved?" she asked.

"Their health failed. They moved back to Cincinnati. I don't know the whole story. I barely knew her."

Grace returned to the hallway.

"She died last year," he added. "Left me the house and some land. I don't know why."

Grace looked at him.

He smiled and shrugged. "I guess she liked me."

Turning away from his boyish face, Grace understood why this distant relative might have liked him. His manner matched the charm of his writing. Though Nicholas Mason's novels had been banned in her home, she read them anyway, when she was fourteen. The characters fascinated her. Grace might have liked discussing them with her father, but her mother had labeled them "filth," so Grace had enjoyed them on her own, away from the house. She wandered past her host and continued down the hall.

"What do you think so far?" he asked. She jumped at the proximity of his voice, right behind her left shoulder.

"It's big and it needs work." She did feel a bit shy in his presence, but not too shy to tell him what she really thought. "A lot of work."

"But think what we can do," he said. He walked in front of her and swept out his arm. "Poetry groups, writing workshops, play productions." He swatted at a straw sticking out of the woodwork around a doorway, then pointed to a bird's nest on the ledge above the inside of the front door. "I think we have a few audience members already."

Picking at bits of loose wallpaper, Grace walked up and down the hall. She had no experience with fixing up houses, but she could see past the thick dust on the wooden floors and the cobwebs drooping dark and heavy in the corners. She yearned for the room across the hall from the gigantic living room, the one not destined to become a bathroom, the one with the bay window.

The idea of poetry, prose, and plays inspired her.

She took a deep breath and exhaled as she turned to face Mr. Mason.

"You say you want a manager. What exactly do you mean?"

He assumed a serious expression, eyebrows knit together and raised. "Do you know how to handle a checkbook?"

A sweet memory flashed through her mind, her father showing her how to mark off cancelled checks, add new deposits, sum uncleared checks and subtract them from the new balance. "Yes," she said. "I know how to manage a checking account."

"And do you know how to organize yourself, you know, take a bunch of tasks and actually accomplish them on time?" he asked.

"Yes," she repeated. Her father had once called her the family's "air traffic controller." By the time she was twelve, her parents relied on her to manage vacation plans. At sixteen, she arranged her parents' funeral, wrote the obituaries, and spoke with the attorney as her sister wept.

"And can you handle difficult situations, difficult people?" he asked.

"Yes," she said again. Though three years her senior, Sarah had been too distraught, so Grace had identified their parents' battered faces. Later, when the judge had tried to put her under his jurisdiction, she insisted she would be fine with Sarah. Grace arranged for the priest to speak on their behalf, and she firmly coached Sarah into an almost adult-like demeanor for the final hearing. Grace could handle difficult people, difficult situations.

"Well, that's what I can't do!" Mr. Mason threw up his hands. "I missed a meeting with my agent last month, again. I forgot to pay the phone bill and they cut me off for a few days last week. And I detest difficult people. They take too much time. It detracts from my ability to create. I need someone to manage things for me."

She scanned the hallway one more time, then set her eyes on her host. "Your ad said room and board included. How much would I be paid?"

"Minimum wage to start with, plus bonuses when appropriate."

"For a forty-hour week?" she asked.

"Roughly," he said.

She looked around one more time. The possibility of real independence, adventure, rushed in and washed away her earlier plan to deliberate before deciding. "I want to do this, Mr. Mason."

"You do?" As his eyes opened wider, the skin on his forehead wrinkling into a soft washboard.

"I want to do this," Grace said, again. "I'll go back to school and pack my stuff. I can start the day after tomorrow."

"Don't you have to talk to your parents?" He sounded incredulous.

"My parents are dead," Grace said, with enhanced assurance, the way she'd learned to reply in debate. "I don't have to talk to anybody."

In the few seconds he hesitated, she hoped he would not offer condolences or ask what had happened to them. She never again wanted to say the words, "Killed in an accident caused by a drunk driver." She wanted to move on with her life.

Nicholas Mason had either read her thoughts or lacked the social grace to express what passed for caring. "Well, then, great!" He beamed. "What's your name again? I forgot."

She stood as tall as she could. "You never asked. My name is Grace. Grace Baxter."

"Welcome aboard, Grace Baxter!" He shook her hand and followed her outside, opening the car door while expressing his gratitude, his good fortune, and his confidence in knowing all along the right person would apply for the job.

As she fit the keys into the ignition, he hung one arm on the open door and stooped to be level with her face. "You're sure about this now?"

"I want to do this, Mr. Mason," Grace said. She kept her tone firm, resolute, and her face passive. Her mother had trained her well. Smiling can be seen as a form of flirtation. Until Grace knew she could trust him to be a gentleman, she would be all business with Mr. Nicholas Mason.

He stood tall and spread out his arms. "Great!" he said, then leaned back down and whispered, "But you have to call me Nick."

"I'll be here on Wednesday," she said. "I'll call you when I know what time my bus will arrive."

"Fine! Fine! I'll pick you up." He clipped the words, clicked his heels, and closed the door.

She backed the car making a sharp turn and put it in drive to move forward.

As she drove away, she heard him call, "Have a safe trip!" In the rearview mirror, she saw him waving goodbye with both arms.

The next forty-eight hours would be madness. Grace wondered if she would have time to sleep. She would see Richard as soon as she returned to campus. Then she would pack her bags. Tomorrow she would meet with the registrar to withdraw from school. Finally, she would call Sarah. That would be a dreadful call. There was no way around it.

On her way back through Wood Grove, she passed the G.C. Murphy Company Five & Dime and remembered Sam. Perhaps she would run into him again. She smiled as she remembered his comment about her "fine mind." Had she been a character in one of Mr. Mason's novels, she might have commented back about Sam's fine face, his thick luscious hair, his charm. The thought made her smile even more.

That was the kind of woman she wanted to be. The kind of woman who met men on an equal basis, person-to-person. Like Katherine Hepburn in *The Philadelphia Story*, or better yet, like Susan B. Anthony in real life.

The thought made her giddy.

Chapter Two

THE CONVERTIBLE SAILED along like a yacht on smooth water. After two days on the bus, Sam would have preferred going straight to the house, but Skip insisted on a long drive in the country. Sam leaned back and rested his arm across the top of the seat.

He had been in Wood Grove once before, when he and Skip were juniors, and had fallen in love with the town. With a little imagination, one could transform the town into a perfect setting, the townspeople into interesting characters with less predictable lives.

Tree, field, telephone pole, wire, cow, farmhouse, barn, fence, horse—the rural blur rushed past his half-open eyes. Sam let it lull away worries, weariness. When they finally returned to the edge of town, Skip slowed the car and the engine's roar. "How do you like her?" he asked.

"Classy chassis. Planning on some backseat bingo?" With Skip, Sam fell right into the old fraternity lingo. He never talked like that in Denver.

"Now don't go mocking my baby." Skip patted the dash. "She deserves respect, man. This chariot is reserved for someone special and she's no bingo babe."

"Someone special, eh?" Sam asked.

"I'm asking her to marry me next week."

They passed two young women and Skip honked his horn. Both women smiled and waved.

"Tell me about her," Sam said.

"I bought her from a dealer in Cincinnati. Cherokee red. Man, she's got horsepower! I've had her up over a hundred already."

"Not the car, Skip." Sam laughed. "The girl. Who's the girl?"

"Oh! Mary Sue. She's a beauty. More horsepower than anybody else in the county."

Sam leaned forward and turned so Skip could see the "*What?*" on his face.

Skip laughed. "Her dad owns Arabians."

"Sounds like good money and good breeding." Sam settled back into his seat, arms crossed.

"Oh, yeah." Skip drew out the words. "Mom and Dad are over the moon. Her parents…." He cleared his throat and wagged his head. "Not so much."

"What's that about?" Sam asked. Skip was a stand-up guy, a college graduate, and came from a good family. His dad was an attorney, for goodness sake. What possible objections could the young lady's parents have?

"Like my own parents," Skip said, "they are a bit disappointed with my career choice."

"You're only twenty-four and you own a used car lot! That's something to be proud of!"

Skip laughed. "They'll come around. My parents have almost forgiven me for not following you to law school." He flicked his wrist and pointed his thumb at Sam. "You would have been the perfect son for them."

During their senior year, Sam had watched Skip move through a painful process of admitting, first to himself, then to Sam, and then to his parents, that he had no intention of continuing on to law school. With a surprising lack of jealousy on Skip's part, his father, Stewart McKay, had turned his attention to Sam as successor to the family law practice passed down through two generations.

"They can't wait to see you!" Skip pulled into the driveway of his parents' home.

Nothing had changed. The edged lawn and groomed flower beds awaited spring growth. Shaped shade trees and a home maintained-to-perfection proved those pictures on magazine covers were real. Everything he had ever wanted lay before him. Someday Sam would have a house like this, a family like this.

"And we're here!" Skip turned off the engine.

Before Sam could step out of the car, the back door banged open. Out dashed a wild display of arms and legs. Skip's little sister adored Sam. She always had.

When Skip and Sam were first roommates, during their freshman year, Mr. and Mrs. McKay brought Gloria to visit. She took to Sam immediately, following close, reaching for his hand, asking, "Why's your last name so weird?" "Do you have a sister?" "Why are you so tanned?"

Mrs. McKay had tried to apologize, but Sam waved her away and patiently answered every one of Gloria's questions. "It's Spanish." "Yes, her name is Maria." "My skin is this color all year round because some of my ancestors were from Mexico."

Nearly two years had passed since he'd last seen Gloria, at his graduation. She was twelve now. He stepped out of the car and gave a quick, brief hug. "Look at you, Miss McKay. All grown up and ready to take on the world."

"You have no idea!" Gloria said. She linked her arm in his and guided him to the back door. "I am learning all about how much I hate books! Talk to her, Sam. Tell my mother to let her people go, me being the person she needs to free from the bondage of boredom."

"I don't know, Gloria." Sam smiled down at her. "Some of my best friends are books."

"No." She moaned. "Be on my side. Make it stop."

Sam stifled a laugh. As soon as they were in the kitchen, Gloria dropped his arm and continued walking without him, shoulders drooping, one menacing look back at her mother.

"Sam!" Mrs. McKay wiped her hands on her apron, placed them on Sam's shoulders, and kissed his cheek. "Good to see you. We're all so happy you're spending your spring break with us." She wore pearls. Her perfume was White Shoulders, his own mother's favorite.

Mr. McKay appeared at the door to the dining room and strode across the kitchen. As usual, he wore a suit and tie. "Good to see you, boy. How's Colorado treating you?"

"Fine, sir. All is well in Colorado."

Mr. McKay pumped Sam's hand with his usual vigor. "And your family is doing well?"

"Yes, sir," Sam replied as Mr. McKay released his hand. "They're all healthy and happy. They send their regards."

Sam played with his class ring, rolling it up to his knuckle and flexing the joint so the metal dug into his skin, penance for the guilt of his little lie. Instead of warm regards to the McKay family, his parents had sent him off with silent, longing faces. His father had been counting on Sam to help with the garden. His mother wanted him home again so she could watch him eat the food she prepared. Their needs seemed so simple, but they didn't line up with Sam's life anymore. Had they ever?

"Come on in and sit down." Mr. McKay put his arm around Sam's shoulder and guided him to the dining room.

Over the next hour, roast beef and mashed potatoes filled Sam's stomach as the conversation nourished his soul. To live in a family where people talked about their leadership in the community, broader politics, even current literature, that was his dream. The feast ended with vanilla ice cream melting over warm apples and cinnamon in a flaky crust. Afterward, Skip hurried away to return to the car lot. Gloria slunk back to her room to read. Mrs. McKay shooed away Sam's attempt to help clean up.

"You go on, Sam. Mr. McKay wants to take you to the office for the afternoon. I'm just so happy you came to visit." She hugged him around the shoulders one more time as she walked him to the back door.

Sam thanked her, aware of how he carried her scent with him now, and followed Mr. McKay out to his car.

"We're all so happy to have you here, Sam," Mr. McKay said as they started down the driveway.

"Yes, sir. I'm happy to be here, too." He glanced back at the house to take in the white siding, black shutters, and picket fence. Sam would have his own house on the edge of town, he was sure of it, but Stewart McKay might work for another decade or two. In the meantime, Sam expected his internship site in Denver to make a lucrative offer. The future appeared to be a steady climb.

The office of Stewart McKay, Attorney-at-Law, occupied the first floor of a downtown building, in the block past the Five & Dime store. Sam had received a Saturday tour on his first visit with the McKay family, when the office was closed. Today Mr. McKay's secretary greeted him. She asked, "Can I run out for coffee for anybody?"

"Yes, Lois," Mr. McKay said. "Pick up some coffee at Handels. And while you're at it, why don't you run over to the Five & Dime for a few of those chocolate bars you brought in the other day. Gotta keep up my stamina." He laughed as he patted his bulging belly.

When Lois smiled, Sam noticed her teeth were discolored. Her hair, streaked with gray, lay tight against her skull, twisted into a bun at the back of her head. She might be in her mid-to-late forties, but she could have been in her seventies for all Sam knew. After she left, he asked, "How long has Lois worked for you?"

"From the very beginning," Mr. McKay answered. "You have to have a secretary who can get the job done without making the wife jealous." He winked at Sam.

The implication jarred, but Sam smiled back anyway.

Mr. McKay put Sam to work reading current journals. After he finished, they discussed a few key articles. Sam helped organize files related to estate planning, then proofread the paperwork related to a will. The pace was pleasant. The clients who arrived to see Mr. McKay treated Sam with a reserved reverence. The coffee wasn't half bad.

"I could get used to this," Sam said to Mr. McKay before leaving for the day.

"That's the idea, my boy." Mr. McKay clasped his shoulder. "I'm counting on that."

Sam declined the offer of a ride home. He knew Skip was having dinner with Mary Sue and he had already told Mrs. McKay he would eat in town. He held Mr. McKay's briefcase as the older man locked the office door, and waved goodbye as Mr. McKay pulled away in his blue Cadillac, this year's model. Sam's father had always sworn he would buy a brand-new car before he died. Sam shook his head. His father would never have the money to do that.

The temperature had dropped since earlier in the afternoon. Sam zipped his jacket and turned the collar up to warm his neck. Hands shoved in pockets, he left the downtown area and eased along the streets of small-town Midwest America, mesmerized by scenes playing out in windows with shades up and curtains open.

A woman shook her finger at a man who looked up at her, sipping from a brown bottle. Why was she angry? Did the man drink too much? Was he rude to her mother?

Children ran through a living room. Where were their parents? In the kitchen preparing a meal together or in the bedroom, having a spat about how much money she spent at the grocery store?

A man lay with his head against the back of a chair, scratching the head of a German Shepherd. Did he live alone? Was he lonely?

Screen doors banged. Dogs barked. A motorcycle growled far away.

Sam breathed deep, his thoughts slowing. This was the best he'd felt since his unforgivable behavior with Elena Hernandez.

“Alcohol and women are the downfall of many men,” the priest had said when Sam went to confession. He told Sam to say a few Hail Marys and to stop being so hard on himself. Sam had wanted to challenge the priest, to explain that being hard on himself was the only way he knew to succeed, but instead of arguing, he’d walked away, head down, soaked in sin.

Here in Wood Grove, Sam started to feel buoyant, worthy again, as if the town reflected his value, his goodness. Back on Main St., he passed a group of teenage girls who giggled and blushed when he smiled at them.

“Who’s he?” the little redhead asked her friend.

“He’s staying at Gloria McKay’s house,” her friend answered.

They were past him now and Sam’s smile grew broader.

Being a celebrity in a small town required little more than being seen as slightly different, in a positive way. Yes, he could definitely get used to life in a place like Wood Grove.

Treating himself to dinner at Handels, the one restaurant in town, Sam inhaled a plate of beef and noodles. On the walk back to the McKay house, he wished he’d eaten more slowly while at the same time craving a piece of the pie he’d spied in a revolving glass case. He would have a future where he could eat at Handels every day of his life if he wanted to. He kicked a rock and sauntered after it. Wood Grove made him happy, satisfied, perhaps even a little sanctified.

The porch light welcomed him back to the McKay house. *Help yourself to a snack*, encouraged a note written in even, flowing cursive.

Sam went straight to his room and switched on the light.

A book lay on his pillow. *Pride and Prejudice* by Jane Austen. Sam read the enclosed note written in uneven print, the first letter of every word capitalized. *Mom Made Me Read This. I Shouldn’t Have To Be The Only One To Suffer, s*igned *Gloria,* with a heart by her name.

Sam locked the bedroom door, stripped to his underwear, climbed between the sheets, and opened the book.

"*It is a truth universally acknowledged, that a single man in possession of a good fortune, must be in want of a wife*," he read aloud.

Sam was a single man in search of a good fortune. Someday, he would be in want of a wife.

Elena's face came to mind. He hadn't spoken with her since that night. She'd been asleep in the morning and he'd snuck out of her apartment like a thief. In a way he had been a thief, though she a willing victim, pushing him to go to the bar, to drink one more, and then another. She had suggested her apartment. She had put on the music. She had asked him to dance.

Memory became fuzzy after that. Who led the way, to the couch, to the bedroom, to the point of no return? He should have stopped himself. That wasn't how he'd imagined his first time. Surely the same was true for Elena.

Earlier feelings of reprieve dissolved. Sam pushed Elena out of his mind but couldn't push away the remorse that kept returning no matter how many Hail Marys he repeated.

Sam looked back at the novel, seeking distraction, anything to soothe that scorching sense that at the end of his life he would burn in hell for all eternity. He knew the book's plot but had never read it through. When he arrived at the scene of the first dance, where Darcy shuns Elizabeth, he thought about the girl he'd met earlier in the day.

Grace seemed like the kind of girl who would laugh at a man who acted like Darcy. Sam wondered if he would ever see her again. Considering his behavior with Elena, maybe Grace was better off not running into guys like Sam a second time.

Chapter Three

ON THE DAY AFTER her first visit to Wood Grove, Grace's bus arrived at the drop-off point on time, but Nicholas Mason did not. Grace waited for an hour, on a small wooden bench in a corner, because the attendant was nice enough to offer space in the already cramped gas station.

A man in a suit came in to buy cigarettes, and a woman with a child used the restroom, but for the better part of an hour Grace sat alone, pretending to be absorbed in her novel. There was no escape. She had never felt more isolated, not in her entire life. Finally, she decided to walk, in a biting wind, to the big house where she hoped to find a warm and welcoming reception.

Thirty minutes later, the last few steps were sheer torture. She had loaded her suitcases with books because they brought a sense of security, stability. Now she cursed her version of stability. Did it have to be so darned heavy?

As she hefted the suitcases up the last step and through the door to the kitchen, her employer looked up from a stack of papers on the table. "Sorry I forgot to pick you up. Guess we need to buy a clock."

He might have offered to help, but he didn't. Grace pushed the door closed with her foot. Turning back to the papers, he said, "Leave your suitcases there by the door. I'll load them in the car later."

She lowered the bags to the floor, waiting for recognition that she had walked the entire way from town, that she must be tired and cold and ready for something warm to drink.

"I rented a place for you in town," he said, without looking up. "Change your clothes. Some guys from town are coming to help. We'll start tearing off the front porch this afternoon. The wood's all rotten. Gotta replace the whole thing."

Without a hint of the nervous tension clutching her belly, Grace planted her feet on the scarred, worn floor, and said, "We're not starting any major projects on the outside of the house until the kitchen is in good working order." She hesitated, then added, with exaggerated diction, "Nick."

His head raised to attention.

She waited to be fired before she'd even begun.

But he only smiled very slowly and said, "Okay, Grace. You're in charge."

"Okay, then." She picked up the suitcase with her work clothes, walked to the room with the bay window, set the heavy case down in the middle of the room, shut the door, and took a deep breath. Her shoulders ached. Her hands were numb. What had seemed like a dream floundered in reality.

The entire place was a mess! Including this room, top to bottom. Cream wallpaper covered the ceiling. Why would someone wallpaper a ceiling? The more pressing question, though, was how would she remove it? The walls, too, papered with weary green swirls, begged for attention. It all needed to come off.

Once solid and defining, the woodwork appeared weak with nicks and blemishes. The floor, gouged in places and scratched wall-to-wall, offered another opportunity to review not only the immense amount of work required, but how little Grace actually knew about how to repair this old house.

The phone rang twice, and two beats later Mr. Mason knocked on the door. "You have a call."

Only two people who mattered to Grace had the number.

She had seen the phone yesterday, in the dining room between the kitchen and the living room. She headed there as Mr. Mason disappeared into the kitchen. The receiver lay beside the base unit on a small table. She picked up the receiver and brought it to her ear while standing. There were no chairs in the room.

"Hello?" she said.

"I talked to Donald last night and he, too, thinks you're making a terrible mistake, and not only for you." This was not the voice Grace had hoped to hear. "Donald says scandalous behavior on your part could reflect badly on me. I mean to marry him, Grace."

"Hello, Sarah. I arrived safe and sound." Grace hugged one arm to her chest as the other gripped the phone.

"Besides the possibility of ruining my chances with Donald, what would Mommy and Daddy say? They would be so disappointed."

"Daddy would understand," Grace said.

"How can you possibly think that?" Sarah spit back. Grace knew exactly how Sarah looked. She had seen her sister's face grow red and splotchy many times.

"Remember when he took us to the museum?" Grace asked. "He talked about how art can be used for good or evil. Mr. Mason wants to do something good here, Sarah. Daddy would be proud."

"It's bad enough you're dating a Negro," Sarah said, her voice rising in both pitch and volume. "Now you're leaving school to live with a man you don't even know. I never thought a sister of mine would turn out like you."

Grace persevered. "In Mr. Mason's latest book, his main characters are a mixed-race couple, and that book topped the best-seller list." Surely Sarah would calm down now and understand.

The pace of Sarah's voice only quickened. "I blame Sister Catherine for this, Grace. She filled your head with ideas about the church's obligation to right the wrongs of society. You do that through charity, Grace, not through throwing away your future on people you shouldn't even be associating with. You misunderstood Daddy, Grace. You be nice to people like that, but you don't *date* them."

Grace gave up. She stopped listening and practiced the breathing technique learned in her Eastern Religion class last fall. Inhale into belly, hold, blow out through whispering lips. Repeat. She focused on the air moving over the hairs in her nose, filling the space in the back of her mouth, her ribs expanding.

Finally, Sarah fell silent.

Grace waited, unable to find words that would convince her sister.

"Grace!" Sarah snapped. "Are you still there?"

"I'm here," she said. "Look, Sarah. I know you don't understand, but—"

"Nobody understands, Grace," Sarah said. "Nobody who matters understands. You were supposed to be the good one. You made the good grades. You went to mass. And then Mommy and Daddy had to die. And you started listening to Sister Catherine, and reading all those books, and thinking, thinking, thinking. Stop thinking so much. Do the right thing. At least finish college. Marry a nice boy. You're never going to be a nun, now. I know that. But you can at least stop being crazy. Will you stop acting so crazy?"

Grace clenched her jaw and pressed her lips together. She wanted Sarah to understand. "I…"

"You know what, Grace? Forget it. Do what you want to do. I'm done with you." The phone clicked and Sarah was gone.

Grace sighed and hung up the phone. Sarah had been more fragile since their parents' deaths. The thought of losing her, too, seemed unbearable. Grace steeled herself against the pain and walked into the hallway.

"Everything okay?" Mr. Mason called from the kitchen.

"Yeah, fine," Grace answered. She returned to her room and opened the suitcase. The shirt and pants she used for her fall painting class lay on top. The shirt had been her father's. She wrapped herself in the memory of his arms and moved to the window where she dropped down onto the seat and scanned the view. She could see the carriage house, the fields, the woods, and near the road, scraggly bushes.

A doe wandered into the yard not five feet from the grimy glass of the bay window. Grace held very still. The doe raised her head to meet Grace's eyes. They stared at each other until a car backfired on the road and the doe leapt sideways, bounding across the driveway and disappearing around the side of the carriage house. Grace gushed, "Wow," and froze in wonder, breathless for a moment.

A bird lit on nearby tree. The wind scuffled leaves across the ground. The beauty before her clarified Grace's decision. She repeated the same question she had been asking herself since deciding to take this job. "What do I have to lose?"

Behind her, loud voices moved down the hall.

"Yes, sir," a deep male voice said. "We sure can clean up that kitchen and make it look brand new. It might take up to a month. Do you want us to start on the porch after that?"

"All in good time, my good men," Nick replied. "Let's clean out this kitchen today, shall we?"

The voices faded and Grace heard the door to the kitchen close. She looked at her suitcase lying in the middle of the room and remembered the labor of carrying it this far. Her shoulders still ached; her hands, no longer numb, were sore now.

Strength would come.

After changing into her work clothes, she stepped into the hallway and turned right. Marching into the kitchen, she watched as two sweaty men with rolled-up flannel shirtsleeves wrestled the stove out the back door. When the door shut behind them, she turned to her employer. "Show me how to take off the wallpaper."

He rummaged in a toolbox on the floor and handed over a wide putty knife and gloves three sizes too large. "Should be fairly easy," he said. "The glue's come unstuck, for the most part." He demonstrated by tugging at a loose seam on the kitchen wall and ripping off a swath of faded pink and green flowers.

After fetching a ladder from the carriage house, she worked through the rest of the morning, and into the afternoon, scraping up from the lower corner to the ceiling and across the wall to reveal gray-white plaster in the room with the bay window, her room now. A pile of crunchy paper grew around her feet.

Mr. Mason splattered praise as he passed the door, calling out, "You're amazing! Look at you go!"

Every so often, she would look back at what she had accomplished, take another breath, and refocus on the wall in front of her. For the first time in two-and-a-half years, Grace fell back into her body. Her shoulders relaxed. She could sense the bottoms of her feet resting on the cotton socks she wore inside her sneakers.

She had made a good decision. She could learn how to manage new and bigger projects, as she had learned how to remove wallpaper. She could do this, she thought, but then doubt returned and a gnawing sensation gripped her stomach. She realized she hadn't eaten since breakfast.

The next time her employer sailed by with a cheerful validation, she called out, "I'm hungry."

He returned to the door. "Oh! Right! Break time! How about taking the car into town and picking up some groceries?"

She pushed herself to a standing position to receive the key he dangled in front of her. He dropped the key into her hand, reached into his back pocket, pulled out a wallet and extract several bills, laying them on top of the keys.

"What do you want?" she asked.

"Anything," he said. "Beer, wine, bread, cheese."

Grace rolled her eyes, collected her coat, and followed him into the kitchen. He veered right, disappearing into the large pantry. She could hear his steps dashing up the back stairway to the second floor. She didn't hear any other noises in the rest of the house and thought maybe the workers, too, had knocked off for the day.

Tomorrow she would ask about a work schedule.

More familiar now, the drive into town offered a chance to start thinking about what could be explored in the near future. She parked across from the library, anticipating her first visit, but looked down at her pants, barely suitable for the grocery.

The library could wait for another day.

Grace headed for the A&P wishing she'd at least brushed her hair or checked her face for dirt or bits of paper with glue. Nobody seemed to notice her. Was that a good thing? She wasn't sure.

Even though the grocery store smelled a bit like food gone bad, everything in Wood Grove came bathed in the aura of newness. The canned goods aisle appealed as never before. The meat counter held promise. The vegetable and fruit section beckoned. Grace noticed the ease with which her basket moved through each section, slowly filling up, until she remembered they had no refrigeration, nor a working stove, and she retraced her steps, returning almost everything in the cart.

By the time she reached the checkout line, she had enough to feed two, for one meal, with some left over. Sliced salami and turkey, a hunk of yellow cheese, a loaf of white bread, and a head of lettuce. Two red apples rolled among the rest of the food. She had splurged on a small jar of mustard. She would have to plan meals for each day, which had not been mentioned in her job description, and which she did not plan to continue for long.

Kitchen renovation and managing a cook could not happen soon enough.

After placing her bag on the passenger seat, she walked around to the driver's side.

A voice called, "Grace!" from across the street. The young man from the lunch counter, Sam, waved from the library steps. He jogged across the street, stopping a few feet from where she stood, her hand still on the door latch.

"Hey," he said. "How's that new job working out?"

His smile hugged the muscles in her back and spread a slow warm feeling into her rib cage which reminded her of the sloppy stained shirt she wore. Thank goodness she had her coat on.

"Good!" she said, smiling back, thinking maybe she should smile a little less, but unable to.

He glanced down at her pants. "Looks like some heavy labor there."

"Starting renovations." Why hadn't she changed her clothes before leaving the house?

"What exactly is this job?" He shifted the two books in his hands to an under-the-arm carry and shoved his hands in his pockets.

"Just a job. What are you reading?"

"Just some books." He bunched his shoulders up to his ears. "I'm freezing out here. Want to get a cup of coffee?"

"I should be getting back."

"It's just a cup of coffee," he said and grinned.

She was thirsty. And she hadn't planned on actually starting to work today at all. One cup of coffee wouldn't take too long.

They crossed the street together and went down a few blocks to Handels, a place advertising burgers, home cooked meals, and fresh baked pies. A bell on the door announced their arrival. The smell of grilled meat made Grace's mouth water.

After they sat at the counter, Sam ordered two coffees.

"So," he said as the waitress walked away. "Tell me about this new job."

"Not much to tell," Grace said. Why did he keep asking? "I'm more interested in your books." She could see now he had selected two by Barbara Cartland. "My sister reads those. Do you like them?"

"I don't know," Sam said. "I haven't read them yet."

"Why pick them?" she asked.

"They're the librarian's favorites. I told her I wanted something like Jane Austen, but more contemporary."

"Why?"

Sam shrugged his shoulders. "I haven't read many women writers."

Grace looked again at the books. "I think you'll be disappointed in those."

The coffee arrived and she cupped her hands around the warm, white ceramic.

He pushed the novels to the side and sipped his coffee. "You've read them?"

"I've read a few, enough to know books like that would have me living my mother's life. I want more." Sam seemed puzzled, but Grace pushed on. "I like reading classic literature."

"For pleasure?" he asked.

Again, Sam appeared to be puzzled. She had no reason to want to please him, and yet she did, but that didn't stop her from risking the appearance of impertinence. "Why else?"

"For an assignment," he said. "I don't think I've ever picked up Aristotle for pleasure."

"Try it sometime," she said. Now she sounded like a snob. She bit her lip.

"What do your parents think about you quitting school?" he asked.

"My parents are dead," she said, and then, not because he'd asked but because she wanted to tell him, "Car accident when I was sixteen. I only have a sister and she thinks I'm crazy. She wants me to be a nun." Why had she said that? Sam made her feel a little crazy.

"Are you?" he asked.

She looked at him. He continued to smile at her.

“No,” Grace said. “But my sister might be. She reads those all the time.” She gestured to his books.

Sam laughed. “I’ll bear that in mind.”

Grace sipped her coffee and studied the pattern on the counter. Being around men often confused her. Was she supposed to say what she thought or say what she thought they wanted to hear?

“You’re an interesting girl, Grace,” Sam said.

Sam didn’t seem to mind hearing what she thought, which made him a most interesting young man, but she wasn’t going to say that. “Tell me about you, Sam,” she said. “What have you done since finishing college?”

“I’m a third-year law student,” he said.

“A law student?” Dating a law student would impress Sarah. The thought ignited a sense of disloyalty to Richard. “And what do your parents think about that?” Grace asked.

“They’re disappointed I didn’t choose priesthood.”

Startled, she looked at him. His smile was gone.

“So we’re both disappointments,” she said.

“It seems we have that in common.”

This had to be the most unusual conversation Grace had ever experienced. Monday morning she had been a bored college sophomore without direction, and today, only two days later, here she was, sitting in a diner, talking to a young man whose honesty and vulnerability were beyond anything she would have imagined from one so handsome that to look at him made her ache inside. She couldn’t wait to tell Deirdre.

“I have to go,” Sam said. “Thanks so much for sitting with me.”

Grace stood and took her change purse from her pocket.

“No, please,” Sam said. “Let me pay.”

“Okay, but next time, I’ll buy the coffee.” Saying that made her confidence, her courage, blossom.

"Deal." He held out his hand and Grace offered hers, unprepared for the shock that travelled up her arm when her palm touched the smooth surface of his skin.

She took back her hand, brushing her hair behind her ear.

On the way out, he held the door for her, the bell tinkling again to announce their exit.

"Let me walk you to your car," he said.

"Only if you're going that way."

"Actually, I'm not," he said.

"Then let's say goodbye here." She headed to Mr. Mason's car. "See you around, Sam."

"You, too, Grace."

She wanted to look back but forced her eyes forward, her employer's car her beacon. She scanned the road before crossing, opened the door, slid into the driver's seat, and fit the key into the ignition. Only then did she search the street scene in front of her. Sam was gone.

When she arrived back at the house, Grace found a note on the kitchen table. *Napping. I'll eat later.* Grace made two sandwiches, wrapped her employer's in the paper bag from the store, and devoured her own.

She returned to her room, energized by the food, and the coffee, and her interaction with Sam. She worked until the light from the window faded. Dropping the putty knife into a pile of curled paper, she decided she had done enough. She was ready to end the day and find her bed, wherever that might be.

Worried she might have to wake Nick, she tried the kitchen first. Finding him there, leaning against the counter and eating his sandwich, came as a relief.

"This is it?" He held up his half-eaten sandwich. "No beer?"

"I don't drink beer," Grace informed her new employer. "And I'm too young to buy anything but three two."

Her employer laughed. "What the hell is this three two anyway?"

"Lower alcohol content," Grace said.

"I know, dear," Mr. Mason said. "But what the hell is that about? I mean, what's the point?" He laughed again and finished off his sandwich. "Luckily, I have one left." He reached behind his back and brought forward a tall, slender, brown bottle. "Chilled this one in the stream that runs through the woods." He picked up a silver opener and popped the top off.

Grace watched him hold up the bottle for a long drink. She sighed and gave a quick, disapproving shake of her head. "We'll have to shop every day for food until we have a refrigerator, and we need supplies. Do you want to come to town with me tomorrow?"

"Have to work on revisions. I'll be busy for a few days. Can you handle that?"

Grace nodded. "I'll take the car. I'll need money."

"You can take my checkbook. Do you cook?"

"Only when I have to. We'll talk about that later. And, Nick?"

He peered at her over his beer.

"We need help. Lots of help."

"No problem!" He waved the beer bottle in the air. "I have money. You tell me what to do and then make it happen."

"Right." Grace picked up her apple and bit into it as she headed for the bay window.

Twenty minutes later, she found her employer sitting at the lopsided table in the kitchen, reading a book. She handed the shopping list to him. She watched his eyes move from top to bottom.

He ran his hand through his hair and returned the list. "Do it. By the way, here's the address for the room I rented." He pulled a piece of paper from his shirt pocket and placed it in her hand. "They're expecting you. Nice older couple, and by that I mean older than me, much older." He took a checkbook from his back pocket and slapped it on the table. "Keep receipts. My accountant will have a cow if you don't."

The image of a man with a ledger giving birth to a full-grown cow flashed through her mind. Mr. Mason could say the oddest things. "How are you going to get back into town to sleep?" she asked.

"I'll be sleeping here. Had a bed delivered this morning."

She stopped short of saying she, too, could stay here, but a house in town sounded nice, clean, orderly. "Okay. See you in the morning."

Grace lingered for a moment, waiting for him to look up again. When he didn't, she walked back to her room.

A note lay on top of the largest suitcase.

Remind me to call my agent tomorrow. If I forget to eat, shove some food in my face. And any time my wife calls, tell her I'm out.

"His *wife*?"

Picking up the case, she returned to the kitchen to inform Mr. Mason she would not be telling his wife anything untrue, but the table was empty. Grace carried the case out the door, heaved it into the back seat, and returned for the smaller one.

With the address for her sleeping room pressed between her lips, and the steering wheel gripped in her left hand, she thrust the key into the ignition with her right hand. As the engine turned over, she turned over in her mind how the note shed a whole new light on the situation.

Maybe Sarah would relax a little knowing Mr. Mason was married, though it sounded like he and his wife weren't getting along. She wouldn't tell Sarah about that. Maybe Richard would feel better, too. He had been shocked when she told him she was leaving school. He said the idea of her being alone in the house with a man she didn't know scared him.

"Men are snakes," he'd said.

"Or weasels," she'd said, and they had continued to come up with increasingly dangerous animals until they were both laughing, and it all ended with Richard pledging his determination to trust her, no matter what.

Funny how knowing Mr. Mason was married also made Grace feel better. The next time she saw Sam, she would tell him about her employer and her new job. She wondered what Sam would say, if he would caution or encourage her. Surely her attraction to Sam would fade over time, as attraction inevitably does—at least that's what her mother had said—and Grace needed a few friends around town. Hopefully, Sam would be one of them.

Chapter Four

FANTASIES ABOUT HIS FUTURE life dominated the highlights of Sam's week in Wood Grove. At least once a day he walked to the empty field chosen for his dream home. He'd spent enough time in Mr. McKay's office to visualize himself in the chair behind the desk with some idea about how his days would unfold after he assumed the practice. All of that and he'd still had time to read a novel a day. Life couldn't be sweeter.

"I can't believe you're leaving tomorrow morning." Mrs. McKay served a bowl of soup, setting it on the starched blue placemat. Steam from sliced carrots, peas, celery, and green beans floating in chicken stock curled around Sam's nose.

"Can't you stay another week?" Gloria asked. "You could take me horseback riding."

"This will be our last meal with Sam," Mrs. McKay said. "His bus leaves so early in the morning, you won't even be awake yet." She ladled soup into Gloria's bowl. "And he's been busy with matters more important than taking young girls horseback riding."

"I'm sorry, Gloria," Sam said.

Mrs. McKay covered Sam's hand with her own. "You don't have to apologize. Gloria's much too forward with her requests." She removed her hand to ladle soup in her own bowl. "Mr. McKay and I have a dinner meeting tonight. You'll have to fend for yourself."

"Mary Sue and I are going out." Skip chewed bread around his words. "She wants to celebrate our six-month anniversary."

"Isn't that sweet?" Mrs. McKay smiled over at her son.

"You hardly paid attention to me at all." Gloria's lower lip came forward as she leaned her forearms on the table, puppy-eyes on Sam.

"Young girls who don't listen to their mothers should not expect special attention from anybody." Mrs. McKay cast a knowing look on her daughter before carrying the pot of soup to the kitchen door.

Gloria glanced at her father, still hidden behind his newspaper, and stuck her tongue out at her mother's back. Sam pressed his lips together and opened his eyes wide. Gloria's eyes darted from Sam to her plate. He could see how she tensed her face, swallowing laughter.

They all ate with little conversation. Skip excused himself first. As he exited the dining room, he called back to Sam, "I acquired a new vehicle this morning, low mileage, and for you, a good price! You can drive yourself back to Denver."

"Car's not in the budget," Sam said, but the back door slammed on his words.

"That boy never learned how to shut a door properly," Mr. McKay said. "He comes and goes like a hooligan. Maybe Mary Sue will knock some sense into him." He wiped his mouth with his napkin.

Mrs. McKay stood and began to whisk away the dishes and utensils. "You may be excused, Gloria."

Gloria slid out of her chair and stepped toward the kitchen door.

"Not that way, young lady. You are grounded until you finish *Persuasion.*"

"Ah, Mom," Gloria whined. She turned and moped her way toward her bedroom.

"She's not performing up to her potential," Mrs. McKay said. "Her grades are only average. I know she can do better."

Sam started to suggest maybe Gloria needed some time off, but he checked himself. Maybe Mrs. McKay was doing for Gloria what someone should have done for his brother, Hector. His parents had always indulged their younger son. At sixteen, Hector seemed out of control, more interested in cars and girls than schoolwork or helping his parents. If Hector would help out more with their parents, less burden would fall on Sam. Mrs. McKay was the better parent. He could learn from her.

"Let me help you with the dishes." Sam stood and reached for the bowls she carried.

"Absolutely not. It's almost time for you and Mr. McKay to return to the office." Mrs. McKay, her face uncompromising, turned to carry the dishes to the kitchen.

Sam clasped his hands. "Thank you for another wonderful meal."

"Oh, Sam," she said, softer now. "I wish all young men were as considerate and polite as you."

Sam didn't know what to say.

"C'mon, son." Mr. McKay stood. "We have a full afternoon ahead of us."

Sam smiled at Mrs. McKay as he followed her husband through the kitchen and out the door.

The afternoon was much like the other days Sam had spent in the office. More of Lois's obsequious service, more journals, more articles, a few clients.

After sending Lois home early for the day, Mr. McKay beckoned Sam to the row of seats in the waiting area, across from Lois's desk. "Sit over here, Sam."

Sam sat on the heavy wooden chair. Mr. McKay sat in the chair next to him, facing forward. He leaned over, his elbows on his knees, and started talking.

"I want you to know how much I have enjoyed your company this week. I can see you are going to be a fine attorney someday and you know

I would like to see you here, in this office, after I retire. But whether or not that happens, I want to talk with you about something that will affect you no matter where you work."

Sam leaned forward and rested his elbows on his knees, listening.

"I'm sure you don't know this," Mr. McKay said. "But when my grandfather arrived in America, way back in the 1800s, his last name was not McKay, no sir, and he did not come from Scotland. My grandfather was from Poland." He turned his head and looked at Sam.

Sam nodded. "Poland. No sir, I did not know that."

Mr. McKay looked back at his hands. "Well, it's true. He was from Poland and his name was Aleksander Wojciechowski. That's Aleksander with a 'ks,' not an 'x,' and I don't even know if I remember how to spell his last name." He turned and looked at Sam again, smiling.

"Yes, sir. That would be hard to spell."

Mr. McKay again looked at his hands. "Well, Sam. The point is, to me and my family, you're Sam, and we don't really care where your grandparents came from, but the folks around here can be a little funny at times. Folk in other places can be funny like that, too. My grandfather changed his name to Alex McKay. He didn't have much education at the time, but he was a smart man." Mr. McKay turned again. "Do you hear what I'm saying to you, son?"

"You think I should change my name." Sam looked at his hands.

"Yes, officially. Folks come in here and see that name on your law degree, no telling what they're going to think or if they're going to trust you. Wherever you go, son, you're going to find more success with a name that is easier on the tongue." He clapped Sam on the back and stood.

"Yes, sir." Sam stood. "Thank you, sir."

"Now go on out of here. You deserve some time off, too. Go have some fun."

"Yes, sir." Sam collected his belongings and walked out into the late afternoon to head up the street.

The idea of a name change wasn't new. Sam, himself, had been considering the idea since he was six years old and switched to the Catholic school in the white neighborhood. He'd received plenty of taunts from the more bullying boys, but instead of letting them ruin his school day, he'd learned to parry with humor, tact.

Still, he ached to fit in, and so he'd suggested to his mother one day he be allowed to change his name to something more "normal."

"Sam Carver," he'd suggested.

She'd replied mostly in English, with unexpected passion and a firm, "No."

"Don't ever let your father hear you say that, mijo," she'd said. "Be proud of your name. Be proud of who you are." He would never forget the look in her eye.

He never mentioned the idea again, but it lived on and flitted through his mind at times.

Stewart McKay thought a name change made sense. Even after all these years, Sam was sure his mother would not agree.

Climbing the steps to the library, head down, Sam almost collided with a young woman skipping down.

"Hello, Sam." Grace stood on the steps, smiling.

Seeing her shoved all worry aside. Some men might find all those freckles unbecoming. Sam found them adorable.

"I owe you a cup of coffee," she said.

She had no idea how good that sounded to him. "No time like the present," he replied.

"Did you need to find more books today?" she asked, following him back into the library.

"Returning these," he answered as he pulled out the two books tucked under his arm.

"How were they?" Grace asked.

Sam put the books on the counter. "Less disappointing than would meet your standards, I'm afraid."

Grace laughed. "I find that very discouraging."

Sam found her delightful.

He held the door on the way out and she breezed in front of him, sweet and fresh and feminine. Thick, long, blonde hair billowed across her back. She must have had it pulled up the last time. He would have remembered how it moved when she walked.

He followed her out the door.

"Shall we go to Handels?" she asked.

"Sure." He stepped up to match her pace.

"How's the job?" he asked, remembering how she had dodged his question the first time. What could it be?

"I'm a manager," she answered without hesitation. "I've been hired to help manage an arts community. We're at the beginning of the project. The house still needs major renovation. That's what we're doing now." She walked a fraction of a step in front of him.

"Arts community? What does that mean?" He sped up a hair.

"We're gathering a group of people who want to make art a central part of life."

"Are you an artist?" he asked.

"I'm the manager," she said.

She seemed taller than he remembered.

"Where is this happening?" he asked. Wood Grove was small, but the downtown had a number of two- and three-story buildings.

She opened the door at Handels and the bell continued to tinkle as she waited for him to enter.

"I would have opened it," he said.

"I know." She let go of the door and moved past him.

Sam followed the scent of her hair and sat beside her at the counter.

"Two coffees, please," she said to the waitress. "Do you want anything else, Sam?"

"No, thank you," he answered.

The first time he met her, she had worn a dress. Black and white skirt, white blouse, with saddle oxfords. The second time she wore work pants with paint on them. Today she wore baggy tan pants, a sweater the color of dark coffee, and brown leather shoes with laces. Her lips were rosier. He detected other subtle differences in her face. She had on makeup.

"Why are you looking at me like that? Is something wrong with my face?" She touched her fingers to her lips.

"Not at all. You look nice." He hadn't meant to make her self-conscious. "Are you working with a group of people?" Sam asked, hoping to put her at ease.

"Right now, one, the owner," she said, her hand reaching for the cup offered by the waitress. "Thanks," she said.

"You're welcome, honey." The waitress put another cup in front of Sam.

Sam thanked her and turned again to the refreshing young woman beside him.

"He hired me first," Grace continued, "but we'll add on staff and residents over time."

"Residents?" He sipped at the coffee. *Too hot.* He put it down on the counter to cool.

"Yes, some people will live on site. Me, and a cook, a maintenance man, a few others, and the owner, of course."

"Where is this community?"

"In the first house west of town. It sits back from the road, on a small hill."

"I've seen that house," Sam said. "The land around there is picturesque, like a postcard."

Grace nodded. "It is beautiful. And you should see the house. The third floor is all one room, maybe even designed to be a ballroom."

"And you're out there by yourself with the owner?" She had referred to the owner as "he." Grace was much too young and attractive to be alone with a man in a house on the edge of town. Nobody would hear if she called out for help.

"I'm staying in town until the house is ready. But after that, yes, I will live in the house."

"If you were my sister, I'd be concerned." More than concerned, he would forbid her. Maria would listen to him, even if she didn't like what he said.

"The owner is Nicholas Mason, Sam," Grace said. "He's not going to do anything unsavory. He has his professional reputation to protect. Have you ever read his books?"

"No, but I will now." He poured a thin line of cream into his coffee and sipped again. One minute shy, the next minute opening doors, ordering his coffee, and talking like a much more mature person. Was Grace a girl or a woman?

They warmed up to other topics as the coffee cooled, each sipping and chatting in turn.

When their cups were nearly empty, Sam suggested a refill.

"I'm sorry, I can't," Grace said. "I have errands to run."

She paid before Sam could stop her, but he opened the door this time. When they were both on the sidewalk again, he said, "I'm so glad we ran into each other again." Her eyes were green, the pupils dilated.

"Me, too. I hoped I would." She hugged her arms.

He started to offer his coat, but instead asked, "Would you like to go to a movie tonight, Grace?" He didn't want this to be the last time he spoke with her before leaving. There was a theatre in a nearby town. Surely Skip could loan a car to him.

"Thanks for the invitation," she said, looking down, "but I'm busy tonight. My friend, boyfriend actually, is coming to visit. I'm headed to the library now. We're meeting there shortly."

The hiccup in his thought process startled Sam. He knew he found her interesting, but he hadn't realized how much she attracted him. He stepped back in his mind. "Your boyfriend is a lucky fellow. I hope you have a good evening and I wish you great success with your new job."

"I hope to see you around," Grace said.

"Not much chance of that. I'm going home to Denver tomorrow."

"I assumed you lived closer."

Confused by the disappointment in her voice, which seemed to match his own, Sam held out his hand. "Nice meeting you, Grace… I don't know your last name."

"Baxter." She took his hand and grasped it. "And yours?"

Sam balked for only a second before saying, "My name is Salomon Sanchez del Cielo, but Sam Cielo will do."

"What a wonderful name!" Grace said, her eyes lighting up.

"Yes," Sam said. "I agree." If taking over Stewart's practice required changing his name, Sam would decline. He didn't want to be like his parents, but he would not dishonor them in any way.

"Nice meeting you, Sam Cielo." She smiled one last time and walked north, toward the library, without looking back.

Sam turned south, walking at a brisk pace.

Why did Grace having a boyfriend matter so much? Prior to hearing she did, he hadn't thought of her like that at all. He walked hard, his shoes pounding the asphalt as he left the town border. He knew the sun would set early and he wanted to be back within the safety of streetlights before nightfall.

He passed the house with "Mason" scrawled on the mailbox. Now he understood why the pile of discards in front of the old carriage house had been growing over the past week. The job Grace had described sounded risky. Off course for a young woman with such promise.

A minute later, Sam stopped to survey the empty field he had claimed on his first visit to Wood Grove. He hoped to someday build a large home there. He leapt across the drainage ditch to walk the perimeter of the land as he designed the house in his mind.

Inside the front door would be a hallway leading to the kitchen at the rear of the house. On the right, a living area with a sofa, chairs, coffee table arranged near the front window. A dining room table at the far end of the room. The left side of the hall would have a stairwell going up and beyond the stairwell, his office, tucked away from the commotion of his happy family. A wife and three or four children. Maybe a dog. Maybe two.

Upstairs, a master bedroom with its own bath and three additional bedrooms with another full bath. Outside, a garage to the rear, maybe one big enough for two cars. There would be a vegetable garden in the back, flowers in the front. His parents would visit. Maybe they would move to Ohio, help out with the kids. He could build another house down the road for them. The late afternoon light waned.

On the trip back to town, Sam stopped on the road in front of the three-story house where Grace worked. Little chance she'd be there when he moved to Wood Grove. She'd be long gone by then, far too intelligent, too adventurous, to be trapped in a limited job. He wished he'd asked if he could write. He'd probably never see her again.

In town, he slowed his pace, looking in the windows of stores that had closed at six. Streetlights came on. Sam jogged across the street, stopping to prop his shoe on the curb to retie it.

Muddy work boots stopped in front of him. Sam raised his head to a large belly hanging over stained work pants. As he lowered his foot to the street, he stood and took in the whole man, tall, with rough stubbled cheeks. The man didn't acknowledge Sam's presence, instead concentrating on something behind him, something that made the man's eyes squint and his mouth turn down.

"Hey, Salt and Pepper," the man shouted.

Sam turned to see Grace and a lanky black man link arms and head to the intersection. Sam stepped up on the curb, close enough to smell alcohol on the man's breath and tobacco wafting from his clothes.

The man shouted again, louder this time. "Hey, Salt and Pepper, why don't you go back to wherever you came from?" He turned toward them and took a step.

Sam froze for a moment, unsure, then placed himself between the man and his line of sight on the couple. "Hey, buddy, can I bum a cigarette?"

The man looked down, blood vessels visible on his nose, and put his hand to his pocket. "Sure, no problem. What's the world coming to, eh? Can't believe I'm seeing that shit around here." He handed an unfiltered Camel to Sam.

Sam took the cigarette and slid it into his jacket pocket. "Thanks so much. I'll save this for later." He hoped Grace and her friend would pick up their pace as he scrambled in his mind for a distraction. "Say. Can you tell me where to find Skip McKay's car lot?" he asked.

The man did an about-face, pointed, and slurred his way through the directions. "You go down there for about two blocks, then turn right and go another block, then turn left and it's on the left. No, wait a minute." He laughed. "We're on Main Street. Head straight down there." He pointed again. "It's about a quarter mile down there, on the way out of town."

Sam glanced over his shoulder and saw the couple disappear into Handels. "Thanks, buddy." He clapped the man on the shoulder.

The man turned to look up the street. "Hmm, where'd they go? Goddamn N—"

"Thanks again for the help," Sam said. "And the cigarette. I'll pay you back."

"You don't have to do that," The man searched the street again.

"I think you were headed down there." Sam pointed south, away from Handels.

"Yeah." The man took a wobbly step in that direction. "Now where was I going?"

Sam walked north. When he reached the corner, he glanced back. The man continued to stumble away, in the opposite direction. Sam turned and jogged across the intersection. When he entered the front door of Handels, the bell on the door announced his arrival.

Grace and her young man sat opposite each other in a booth, looking at menus. Sam approached them, saying, “I wanted to apologize—”

The young man’s head snapped up as he glared, his grip tight on the menu. “Maybe your friend out there should be the one to apologize.”

“Richard.” Grace put her hand on her companion’s arm.

Assuming the posture he’d honed as a teen, solid and firm, Sam stood ready, but not aggressive. His mouth had always been his best defense. “He’s not my friend—” Sam began, but the waitress arrived, her face haggard, her words clipped.

“Are you ready to order?” She smacked her gum as she pulled a pencil from behind her ear and pointed it at her order pad. “Sir.” She glanced at Sam. “Are you going to sit down here?”

“He was leaving,” Grace’s boyfriend said. He left no room for argument or explanation.

Sam looked at Grace. She looked down at the table. He glanced at her companion. The young man glared.

Feet heavy, Sam walked out the door and through the rest of the business district before coming to residential streets that now seemed less welcoming, cold. Doors were shut, curtains drawn. Why hadn’t Grace stood up for him? Could she really think the drunk had been his friend? He never wanted to be seen as aligned with anyone who acted like that guy, especially not by someone like her.

The McKay house, too, stood dark and empty. More than likely, Gloria had been shipped off to a friend’s house. Her parents wouldn’t have trusted her to stay home alone. Sam walked through the quiet kitchen and hallway without turning on any lights until he reached the guest room where he switched on the light beside the bed. He picked up a notebook and pen.

"Dear Grace," he started. The more he wrote, the better he felt. He wrote until his hand hurt, wrote some more, and finished with, "Your friend, Sam." Sitting back against the pillow, he read through the entire letter, tore it into tiny pieces, and threw them in the trash can by the chair.

Why was he wasting his time on a girl he'd never see again?

Sam needed to focus on women who would be like Mrs. McKay someday. He needed a modern, yet traditional, woman who would bear healthy children, create a comfortable home, cook delicious food, and serve, by his side, as a leader in the community. She would be pretty, yes, but far more important, she would be intelligent, and strong-willed, and why did he keep seeing Grace when he thought of his future wife?

He looked at the bits of white paper in the trash can, reminiscent of the first seven letters he'd composed to Elena before leaving town last week. He'd finally settled on short and simple, extending his heartfelt apology for any way in which he'd imposed himself on her and expressing hope they could remain trusted colleagues and friends. He'd dropped the letter off with the doorman at her apartment building right before heading for the bus station.

Prudence outweighed passion, and even preference at times. The lesson he'd learned from Elena could not be forgotten, ever. Sam had no room for mistakes in his life. He would not write another letter to Grace.

She probably wouldn't have read it anyway.

Chapter Five

AFTER SAM LEFT, Handels started to fill up. Two men in business suits sat at a booth opposite Grace. The man facing her seemed intent on catching her eye, a hardness etched into his expression. She ignored him and leaned toward Richard, determined to let nothing mar the one evening she would have with him for many weeks to come.

The last four days had been turning points for both of them.

Richard had been offered a job by his internship, a small company in Columbus. He would start full time in June, after graduation.

"Oh, Richard," Grace said. "I'm so happy for you." Columbus. Not so far. They would be able to see each other, if he wanted to. She did.

"I had an offer in Cleveland," he said. Had he chosen Columbus to be closer to her? "But I think the company in Columbus is going places. They're considering a partnership with a similar company in New Jersey."

She smiled and squeezed his hand.

"And—" he gathered up both of her hands, playing with her fingers "—I did like the idea of being closer to you."

There, he'd said it. Grace grinned, unable to hide her happiness. Sarah had tried to train her younger sister to play hard-to-get, but the lessons never took. Richard was the only boy Grace had ever dated, the only boy she'd ever wanted to date. Why should she hide her feelings?

The bell above the door tinkled for the third time in a row. Grace's countenance fell as she saw Skip McKay walk in, followed by a plump young woman with bouncing brown curls. Skip turned toward Richard and Grace, shook his head, and swung back toward the still open door. "C'mon, Mary Sue, I'm not eating in here with that."

The young woman seemed confused until she turned and froze, her eyes darting from Grace to Richard. "Oh my," she said as Skip commandeered their exit and the door shut behind them, silencing the rest of the young woman's words.

Grace clasped her glass of ice water.

"You can't let it get to you," Richard said. "That makes them win."

"How can you ignore it?" she asked. "That guy outside scared me. 'Salt and Pepper.' I'd never heard that before."

Richard put his hands behind his head, leaned back, and smiled. "I prefer 'Herb and Spice.' You be cilantro and I'll be coriander."

Grace grimaced. "I hate cilantro. It tastes like dishwater."

"I didn't know that. You be any herb you want, I'll be the root." He grasped her hand again.

"Helping me study for Botany exams last fall has come in handy. That was smooth—" she hesitated "—but really, Richard. He scared me. What makes men act like that?"

"Alcohol, for starters, and because they know they can. Nobody stops them."

"Here you go." The waitress was back, plucking plates from a round tray, and plunking them on the table. "Need anything else?"

"No, thank you," Richard said.

A sad little sandwich sat in the middle of Grace's plate, barely grilled and containing only a two-inch square of processed cheese in the middle. She patted the top piece of bread and smiled at Richard. His roast beef, mashed potatoes, and green beans were slopped against each other in the middle of the plate. She wanted to believe the cook merely lacked presentation skills, but she couldn't afford naiveté. Not anymore.

Richard acted as if nothing was amiss. Unfolding his napkin and laying it in his lap, he nodded to Grace. She did the same.

"Mm-mmm!" he vocalized after trying a bite. "A bit too much salt for my taste buds, but nothing a little pepper won't fix." He covered the food with a light sprinkling of black flecks.

Other conversations in the restaurant died down for a few seconds, but then picked up again as Richard and Grace ate, their eyes locked in rebellious joy.

When they finished, Richard left a two-dollar tip, which exceeded the cost of their meals, and they walked out with their heads high. He looked up and down the street before walking Grace to the car, his arm around her shoulders, their pace just shy of a trot. Once in the car, Richard instructed Grace to lock her door as he locked his own.

They sat in silence for a minute before Richard started the engine. As soon as the car was in motion, Grace realized she had been holding her breath. She let it out slowly. "Go south," she said. She wanted Richard to see Nick's house, to understand the dream that brought her to Wood Grove.

The town seemed less friendly now. She thought about the evening, about Sam, Skip, and the substandard presentation of the meal. The small liberal arts college she had attended welcomed all kinds of people: Deirdre, who preferred women professors and talked about how females should rise to positions of power, including the presidency; people from other countries with darker skin who spoke English with heavy accents; boys and girls like Richard, from larger cities, on scholarship. Deirdre had applauded Grace's choice of boyfriend. And nobody on campus had given them a hard time when they held hands or walked arm-in-arm. She'd forgotten what it was like outside that little bubble of scholarship and freedom.

"You know the guy who came into the restaurant to apologize?" she asked. "His name is Sam."

"You know him?" Richard asked.

"I've run into him a few times. We've talked briefly. He seemed like such a nice person."

"You can't tell the nice ones from the ones who will stab you from behind. You always have to watch your back."

Downtown gave way to a few houses and scattered businesses, then fields and wooded areas.

"It's the next driveway," she said as they neared the house.

Richard slowed and turned the car into the drive.

"There was a girl in high school who dated a black boy from another part of town," Grace said. They drove past the pile of kitchen cabinets, stove, and sink, all jumbled together on the ground. She had arranged to have it hauled away but the men couldn't come for another week.

"And?" Richard asked.

"She was sent away to live in another state with her aunt."

"High school can be harsh," Richard said.

"Nobody can tell me what to do," Grace said, crossing her arms. "I'm on my own now. I intend to keep it that way. I will date who I want to date, when I want to date them."

"Who else are you planning to date?" Richard parked the car and turned off the engine.

"Only you, for as long as you'll have me." She put her arms around his neck.

"I've never felt this way about anybody before, Grace."

She kissed her agreement, loving the soft warmth of his lips and the scent of his skin. He'd given up aftershave after she told him she preferred the scent of people to perfume. "You're perfect for me," Grace whispered in his ear. Soft whiskers caressed her cheek.

He pulled back. "I am asking you to save yourself for me, Grace. I propose we look forward to being engaged in a year or two, when you're a little older."

“I like that proposal.” She kissed him again, then pulled away and opened her car door. “Come in. I want to show the house to you. We’ve been working hard already but there’s so much to do.”

“Is Mr. Mason here?”

She ignored his hostile tone. “Nick drove up to Columbus.”

“So it’s ‘Nick’ now?” Richard asked.

“He insisted.” She tugged at Richard’s arm saying, “C’mon,” as she guided him through the back door and into the kitchen where she turned on the overhead light.

Naked plaster, exposed pipes, and a stripped wooden floor had left the kitchen a big empty box. Grace walked the perimeter, describing her plans. “There will be a sink here, a stove here, refrigerator here, and cabinets here, here, and here.”

“Are you going to learn how to bake?” Richard asked.

“No. Not. Ever,” she answered.

He laughed.

“The ceiling will be white, the walls buttery yellow, and the floor black and white diagonally placed tiles.” Grace lifted a corner of folded cotton cloth lying on the floor. “Mrs. Cavanaugh, the woman I’m staying with, said she would teach me how to make cafe curtains.” Soon this cloth would hang at the windows, starched and stately, sporting red apples, purple grapes, rosy peaches, yellow pears, all entwined with green vines on a white background with tiny black polka dots.

“You’re going to sew them yourself?” Richard asked. “I’m impressed.”

She pulled Richard’s arm, flipping on lights as they progressed forward, stopping first in the great room with the fireplaces and stained-glass window. He expressed appropriate awe. She beamed.

Together, they explored the rest of the house, Richard peeking in rooms and climbing the staircase slowly as Grace jabbered on, determined to sell the project, desperate to win Richard’s approval. “I know it looks rough. Nick had the roof, plumbing, and electric repaired before I came on board." She listed the accomplishments of the past three days, in order, ending with, "I have to help Nick learn how to stick with a plan. I can't manage properly if he keeps changing his mind. One minute he says okay to yellow, the next minute he wants blue, then he's back to yellow."

"And why is it you think you can help him, Miss Baxter?" Richard asked.

"My father told me the best leaders place high importance on people and projects. I'm teaching Nick to do that. He keeps insisting only people matter. I keep telling him, 'Having a plan and working through it step-by-step is also vital.'"

They were on the second floor now.

"Sounds like you're the one in charge." Richard opened the door to an empty bedroom, switched on the light, and peered inside.

"Nick said that to me, too. But really, he's the decision maker."

Richard stopped to look out a window facing the moonlit woods behind the house. "How much land did you say he owns?"

"About two hundred acres, mostly wooded and not on the road, except for where the house sits."

"That man has some money!"

"I told you, he inherited the house and land, but yes, he does have money. Of course he does. He's a famous writer."

"So you've said." Richard yawned and moved on down the hall, stopping at Nick's room. They stationed themselves outside the open door, the interior of the room lit by a lamp on a table beside the four-poster bed with books strewn across crumpled sheets.

"And is he going to have enough money to fix up the house?" Richard turned her around and pulled her into his arms. "To pay you?"

She lay her head on his chest and listened to his heartbeat. "I already opened a bank account downtown. And he pays for the food. He says that's part of the agreement, guests included. Nick said you can have all the food you want, whenever you visit. And you can stay in the guest room, when it's ready."

"And you trust him?" Richard pushed her away far enough to look down into her eyes. "He hasn't tried any funny business?"

She smiled. "You're jealous."

His eyes, and his tone, darkened. "I am concerned about you."

She hugged him again, "Thank you for worrying about me, but no, no funny business. I'm not a child, Richard. I know how to take care of myself."

"Okay, Miss Baxter." He positioned her by his side and they walked with arms linked as she guided him toward the staircase to the third floor. "You keep me posted. If he tries any funny business, I'll bring the boys down here and we'll take care of him."

Grace laughed. There were no boys. There used to be. Richard had grown up in Cleveland, in a neighborhood where the boys ran in gangs who kept track of each other, watched out for each other, took care of each other. But he'd left all of that behind when he enrolled in the engineering program. The boys were only in his mind now, though he still seemed to derive a sense of power and security from the mention of what once had been.

The tour ended with the two remaining rooms on the first floor. "This one…," Grace said as they walked into the room nearest the front door. "This one will have a bathroom for men and one for women and a place to hang coats." She pulled Richard back toward the kitchen and made a sharp right turn into the room with the bay window. "And this one will be mine!" She pointed out her plan. "I want a desk there, and plants there, and a rug here, and a small couch there, and a bed there."

Richard nodded and hummed his support. "I like your plan." He hugged her again and kissed the top of her head. "So, tell me a bit more about this Nick guy. You said on the phone he's married."

Grace pulled Richard to the seat of the bay window as she explained. "Nick said their families go way back. He and Natalie were thrown together and expected to be a couple. When they graduated from college, their parents started planning the wedding. Nick said he never gave it a second thought, like he never knew he had a choice."

"Like royalty."

"I guess so." Grace hadn't thought of that, but Richard was right. Nick's story rang of generational obligation with all the glory, and the sacrifice, of privilege. She and Richard sat facing each other, his arms crossed. She wanted him to soften toward Nick. "Both families are part of the Chicago elite," she said. "That's what Nick called them. He said things were okay at first, but then he started publishing and doing book tours. Natalie got uncomfortable and became a 'nagger.' That's what he said."

"So he left her?" Richard asked.

"He did invite her to come, and their son, too, of course."

"He has a kid?" Richard looked like he'd taken a bite of bad food. "He left his wife and a kid?"

Grace tried to tamp down his rancor. "I wasn't very comfortable about it either, but Nick talked about how suffocated he felt in Chicago, how he feels liberated living here, how it helps his writing. And he really did invite them to come. I heard him ask her again this morning, on the phone."

"I don't trust him, Grace. A man who leaves behind his wife and kid?" Richard pulled her close and she again rested her head on his chest. "You can't count on a guy like that."

"What have I got to lose? I did a pros and cons list and the pros won. If he doesn't come through with enough money to make this happen, I can find another job. I will have gained some job skills…."

"Stripping wallpaper?" Richard interrupted.

"Stripping wallpaper, being an assistant, standing on my own two feet."

"Seems to me like you do a bit too much on your own already." He tapped her leg with his foot. "How are the nightmares?"

“Maybe a little better.” She lifted her head from his chest and gazed at the pocket on his plaid shirt. A loose thread hung from the outside corner. “I had a bad one last night. When I woke up my Mom was lying beside me, bleeding from her nose and mouth.” Grace’s pulse increased; her breaths became shallow. “Then I really woke up and realized it was a dream.”

Richard put his hands on her shoulders. “Grace, maybe you should tell a doctor.”

“What’s a doctor going to do, Richard? Say I’m crazy? You’re the only one I’m telling. It helps when I tell you.” She moved toward him, slipping her arms around his waist. “Thank you for being my friend.”

He bent his head and Grace anticipated a long stretch of attentive, tender kisses, but the back door banged and they drew apart like teenagers caught necking on the couch.

“Hello!” Nick sang out. “Honeys, I’m home.”

“Nick’s back,” Grace jumped up.

“I assumed,” Richard said, his voice so dry it sucked up any hope for happy introductions.

“We’re in here,” Grace called out. She pulled Richard off the window seat and guided him to the hallway.

The kitchen door swung open and Nick burst through. “I bear gifts!” He stopped, a bottle of wine brandished in each hand, and cocked his head to the side. “You’re black!”

“I am!” Richard stepped forward. “Is that a problem?”

Grace blushed. What could Nick be thinking? She grabbed Richard’s hand and held tight.

“Come with me,” Nick said as he headed across the hall.

Richard looked down at Grace. She shrugged her shoulders and pulled Richard forward. Nick strode into the living room and placed the wine soundly on the mantle.

"Not a problem at all, just a surprise," Nick said. He turned and extended his hand to Richard while looking sideways at Grace. "You didn't tell me."

Richard dropped Grace's hand and reached out slowly. Grace watched as he endured a solid arm pump from Nick.

What a night! First the drunk guy, then Handels, and now Nick! Telling Nick about Richard being black had never crossed her mind. Why would it? She expected him, of all people, to understand. As had become her habit in the past week, she planted her feet on the floor and asked, "Nick, are you expecting to fill this place with white artists, white patrons, whites only? Because that's not the kind of life I want."

Richard squinted his eyes and examined her with an expression of concern. Nick furrowed his eyebrows and jutted out his chin as his head dropped closer to his chest, his gaze burrowing into her. Grace's cheeks burned hotter but she bit her lower lip and stared back at him.

Nick recovered first. He stood up straight and shook his shoulders, his face relaxing. "Well, Grace. That's good to hear, because that's not the kind of life I want either." He reached back and picked up a bottle of wine, waving it in the air. "Let's have a toast, to new friends, and a colorful life."

"I don't drink," Richard said.

"You know I don't either," Grace muttered.

"That's okay!" Nick announced. "I brought Coca Cola!"

They toasted with soda and wine in jelly jars, Grace's face cooling, her heartbeat slowing. Nick lit a pile of wood in the fireplace and the three of them sat cross-legged on the floor, Richard's hand on her knee, while Nick told story after story about his college years. Finally, he asked how Richard and Grace met.

"We had a class together…" Grace started.

"And we had the same last name," Richard continued.

"Something clicked," Grace said. "That's it. End of story."

"I'm sure there's more to the story," Nick said.

Nick hadn't earned the right to more details. The memory of his earlier behavior still smoldered. Grace shrugged her shoulders and bit her lip.

"What are you studying?" Nick asked, turning to Richard.

"Engineering," Richard answered.

"Engineering? Why not acting? Don't you think so, Grace?"

"He's going to design better cars," Grace said.

"Let the ugly guys design cars," Nick said. "A face like his should deliver lines that make the most hate-filled hearts ache for a better world. Look at him, Grace. His face is classic, the next Sidney Poitier. You and I, we're more like Thelma Ritter and that guy on my wife's soap opera. He plays, oh, what's his name?" He snapped his fingers three times. "Can't remember the character, but the actor is a guy named Don Knotts. Fish Face. You and I look more like Thelma and Fish Face."

Richard shifted his legs. Grace touched his thigh. The fire popped. Nick drank another glass of wine. The freshest reason for irritation faded. Weariness settled over Grace. For her, the evening had ended an hour ago. She watched the flames dance across the log, her breath deepening as her mind again reviewed the week.

Here she sat, Richard beside her, with a famous writer. In the past week, she had been hired for a job, moved to a new town, stripped wallpaper until her arms ached, had coffee with a most handsome law student, and welcomed her boyfriend for a visit. Becoming an adult exhausted her.

Nick yawned first. "Us ugly old guys need our beauty sleep. You young ones can keep the fire burning." He stood, stumbled once, regained his balance, and leaned down to pick up the nearly empty bottle.

After Nick retreated to his room, Richard asked, "Do you really want to work for this man?"

She snuggled her head onto his shoulder. "He's not so bad. He drank too much."

"I'll say." Richard blew a raspberry. "I'm Poitier and you're Ritter."

"Do you even know who she is?" Grace asked.

"I can, in fact, picture Thelma Ritter. There's no comparison. She's much prettier than you."

Grace moved away and punched his arm. Richard howled and pulled her to the floor, wrestling until she kissed him. He stopped kissing before she was ready, but pulled her in close, his arms around her while the fire cracked and sizzled. She let herself melt into the moment, wishing it could last forever.

"I have to go," he said. "I told Stan I'd have his car back by midnight."

"You won't make it back in time."

"He'll understand."

She walked him to his car. Richard put his arms around her again as she shivered. "Now go on back in the house," he said. "You're freezing."

"Drive safely," Grace said. "Write back and remember what you asked."

"I won't forget." He shut the door, turned on the engine, and waved once before crunching the tires over the gravel.

She hugged herself hard as she watched his car move down the driveway and turn onto the road. When the taillights disappeared, she raised her head, wondering when she would see him again. The stars blazed above her: the Milky Way, Big Dipper, Little Dipper, and Orion, her father's favorite. Grace put her head down and aimed for the door.

Back in the house, she found Nick standing at the kitchen sink, in the dark, the faint glow from the fireplace barely visible through the open door to the dining room.

"Richard's gone?" he asked.

"He had to take the car back."

"I enjoyed him. You know, you're a brave young woman, Grace. I like the way you're handling your life."

Grace thought for a moment. "If you truly like the way I handle my life, then let me manage this project. Let me come up with a plan and lay out the timeline. I'll come to you for help, I promise, and you will always have the final say, but let me show you what I can do."

Nick put his head down for a long pause.

"Okay," he said, looking up. "But promise me one thing."

"What?" she asked.

"The next time you invite a boyfriend over, warn me ahead of time if they're, you know, something other than what one would expect from a young, innocent girl like you."

Grace rolled her eyes. In addition to being the most fascinating man she had ever met, Nicholas Mason could be rude, but he had agreed to allow her to plan the project, a huge concession on his part. Over time, she would assert that her love life was her own business, but that needn't start tonight, nor ever, come to think of it, because there weren't going to be any other boyfriends.

She was going to marry Richard.

Chapter Six
1962

PHONE PRESSED TO HER EAR, Grace waited for her sister to come back to their phone call. While waiting, she surveyed the one place in the world that had been her sanctuary, hers alone, for the past seven years, until yesterday.

Starting with her desk, paper piles neatly organized, she moved on to the window seat, plants hanging above, over to her quilt-covered bed, the oriental rug she'd found at a thrift store, a tall chest of drawers, and finally stopped at Polly's bed with matching chest.

Polly's furniture occupied the spot that, prior to yesterday, had contained a loveseat that now rested on wooden slats in the basement. For the time being, no more naps curled into the creamy brocade fabric, head resting on the armrest, the perfect height for Grace's neck and shoulder.

Shuffling noises came through the receiver. "I'm back!" Sarah announced. "Sorry I took so long. I had to sign for packages and wait for the delivery man to make two trips back to his truck to bring all the boxes. Now, where were we?"

"We moved Polly into my room," Grace said.

"That room is too small," Sarah said.

"We'll manage." Grace bit back the obvious. Her room, the room now shared with Polly, was huge compared to most standards, but probably only slightly larger than Sarah's walk-in closet. Grace never mentioned Sarah's wealth, nor the disparity in their lifestyles.

"Last time we talked you said you'd been having problems with your stomach. I have a new doctor. He says I need to stop drinking every day, but what does he know? A little wine after dinner never hurt anyone."

"My stomach's better," Grace said. Her stomach still hurt every day.

"Maybe you're feeling a bit crowded. I don't think I could share a bedroom."

Of course she couldn't. Sarah and Donald had their own bedrooms, and a third they called their "honeymoon suite," though they'd been married long past the honeymoon phase. Richard called it their "conjugal visitation location." He had visited Sarah's house one time, after he and Grace were married. He'd said, "Once is enough," and Grace hadn't argued. Donald had barely said a word through dinner and excused himself right after eating. The evening had been painful for everyone, it seemed.

"If your stomach starts hurting again, maybe you need more meat. Mommy always said if you don't eat meat every day, you won't have enough protein and you'll get sick."

"Maybe." Grace fiddled with the phone cord. She didn't like meat, but she also didn't have time to be sick.

"Fill me in on the rest of what's happening down there in Never-Never Land." Never-Never Land was Sarah's version of a kinder reference to the community in Wood Grove. She had more than once referred to it as, "The Loony Bin."

"John and Loretta moved upstairs," Grace said. "We all decided we wanted the dining room back."

"The black couple," Sarah said. "He's a handyman and she cooks?"

"They're active in the civil rights movement," Grace said. "But, yes, they also provide those services here." Sarah seemed to have no idea of their significance in Grace's life. In Loretta, she had found a kindred spirit. In John, a best friend.

"I always forget about the civil rights stuff," Sarah said. "Maybe because it has nothing to do with art."

"Art affects everything; everything is affected by art." They'd been over this before. Grace had grown tired of explaining.

"Speaking of art," Sarah said. "Did I tell you Donald bought the most exquisite necklace for me when he was in Paris? Wearable is my favorite kind of art."

Turning her left hand in the desk lamp, Grace watched light bounce off the small diamond Richard had placed there on her twenty-first birthday. Nestled beside the engagement ring sat a plain gold band. Sarah was right. Jewelry was a form of wearable art. Grace's ring set expressed the simplicity of her marriage to Richard. He lived and worked in Columbus and she in Wood Grove. They saw each other at least twice a week and they'd never lost the fresh feeling of being together, every moment precious.

"So John and Loretta took Polly's room upstairs and she moved in with you," Sarah said. "Polly's the other black one, the prim, proper one who teaches high school English."

"Would you stop?" Though she understood Sarah's lack of experience regarding issues of race, Grace still had a limit for how much she could tolerate.

"How else can I remember them?" Sarah asked. "I think in categories. Black white, male female. My therapist says its normal."

Untangling her phone cord, Grace moved to the window. April showers had left puddles on the ground. Fran and Peter walked the paved driveway toward the road. They had both taken the week off. He looked even taller and thinner when he stood by his short, round spouse. "Do you remember Peter and Fran?" she asked.

"They both work in Columbus," Sarah said. "He's some kind of newspaper guy and smells like tobacco smoke."

"He's an illustrator," Grace said.

"And Fran is the pear-shaped secretary?"

"Fran works in administration at the art college." Grace watched Fran leave Peter's side to pick up something in the grass. Probably a twig or acorn she would collect in a jar holding dried flowers. Fran liked to place jars like that around the house. "And our newest community members are Max and Elizabeth."

"Oh! I remember him," Sarah said. "He's that Jewish sculptor and she's his nude model."

"And a dancer," Grace said.

"He's dark in mood," Sarah said. "And she's like a puff of air."

"That's one way to describe them." Grace couldn't help but smile. Sarah displayed such insight at times.

"I am never going to remember them all, Grace!"

"Visualize the second floor in your head," Grace coached her sister. "John and Loretta are on the same side of the hallway as Nick. Their bedrooms face east. Fran and Peter, and Max and Elizabeth, are in the bedrooms facing west."

"Which way is east?" Sarah asked.

"The front of the house, it faces the road."

"Which way is west?"

Really? Grace thought. "The back of the house, the side facing the woods."

"I'm terrible with directions," Sarah said. "Next time I come, I'll take the tour again, and I'll remember, I promise." The tinkling of ice against glass came through the line as Sarah paused. Grace heard her sister swallow before asking, "How's Richard?"

"He's fine," Grace said. "They offered him a promotion."

"How exciting! You must be jazzed." Sarah tried so hard to be hip.

"Not really," Grace sighed. "The position is located at the office in New Jersey."

"New Jersey!"

“Right,” Grace sighed again. “New Jersey.”

“Why so glum?” Sarah asked. “I’d hate to see you move, but think what fun that will be! When I visit, we can go into the city together.”

Fun for Sarah, sure. The subway, shopping, shows, she’d been there, done that, could afford to do it again and again. And she would, because she liked it. But Grace didn’t like shopping, and though she’d like to visit the museums and take in a Broadway show, she’d never let herself fully develop the desire because she didn’t have enough money. “I’m not leaving,” she said.

“What are you going to do if he takes the new position?” Sarah asked.

“I don’t know.” As it was, she and Richard pieced together their marriage with daily phone calls, most weekends at the Columbus apartment, and an occasional Wednesday night in Wood Grove. Richard living in New Jersey without her seemed impossible, but was it?

“You’ve done what needed to be done, Grace,” Sarah said. “You’ve gotten the community on its feet. Time for you to move on. You could go to school. Develop a career. You’re young enough.”

Sarah would never understand Grace’s commitment to the community. Grace would never understand Sarah’s ability to settle for doing little more than spending her husband’s money. “I don’t want to move,” Grace said.

“Being a wife means sacrificing, Grace.”

“I don’t want to be a wife like that.”

“There is no ‘like that,’ Grace,” Sarah said. “There’s only being a wife.”

Grace had no response to that. She’d never been able to define for herself what being a wife meant, but she was sure Sarah’s definition would not be a good fit. “Did I tell you Fran wants to direct the Solstice plays from now on?” she asked.

“I thought the plays were your thing.” Sarah’s surprise sounded genuine. She seemed to know that giving up the director position had been a sacrifice.

Sarah's surprise, in turn, surprised Grace, and pleased her. "Fran needs it more than I do now," she said.

"You're so generous," Sarah said. "You really would have made a good nun, but think for minute. Letting go of the play means you have one less tie to Wood Grove. Start packing. I think you're moving to New Jersey."

The tiny moment of shared understanding evaporated. "Listen," Grace said. "Loretta asked me to help with lunch. She has a meeting. I'll call again, soon."

"Okay. Bye, bye, honey. Love you." Sarah's voice always turned breathier, like their mother's had been, when they were signing off.

"Love you, too, Sarah." Grace hung up the phone and shook out her arms. Staying connected to Sarah took effort. After Grace's move to Wood Grove, her sister's rejection had lasted only a few weeks, but Grace still stepped with care. Sarah was all the family she had left, other than Richard. Grace didn't want to lose her again, not even for a day.

Moving out into the hall, Grace looked toward the front door. Lush green ferns cascaded down blue ceramic pots placed on pedestals marking the end of the hallway and the beginning of the entryway. Light bounced off the pots and the polished floors.

All of the floors in the house had been sanded, stained, and sealed by John. He had finished patching and painting all of the walls, too. Finally, the house had begun to live up to its potential.

Currently, a display of pictures by local schoolchildren graced the hallway. Polly had hosted an opening on Friday night. The children were thrilled to see their art framed and hung. The parents seemed to appreciate the free drinks.

Grace pushed open the swinging door and walked across the black and white tiled floor in the dark, quiet kitchen. Sarah still didn't know her sister well enough to catch the little lie. Loretta would never ask Grace for help with cooking. As soon as Loretta came on board, Grace made it clear that she was done with kitchen duty forever. Being so easily dishonest with Sarah made Grace sad, their connection requiring inauthenticity left her even sadder.

Descending the back steps, Grace's arms chilled through the stitches of her knit sweater. She skirted the row of cars parked along the driveway and stepped across the swath of grass which ended at the tree line. Over the years, she had cleared a path to the creek that cut through the woods about a quarter mile behind the house. Many years worth of decomposed leaves and sticks cradled her feet as she stepped onto the path.

She had seen pictures of the New Jersey office's urban location.

Her feet would strike only hard surfaces there, a place formed in steel and concrete.

There would be no paths to clear in New Jersey, no creeks to explore. There would be cars, endless roads, tall buildings, and taller expectations. She would be Richard's wife, no longer the wife living elsewhere with a house full of people who were "interesting" or "odd" to some, "dangerous" to others.

She would be the wife anticipated to produce the first child while promising the second and discussing the third. The other wives would invite her to parties where they would talk about recipes and kitchen devices and hairstyles and clothing. She would be expected to cut her hair. She was not going. Sarah would never understand.

Stumbling on a rock, Grace swore. Forget New Jersey. She was here, now, in this moment, in her beloved woods.

A bird darted across the path ahead of her. Fresh green burst through swollen tree buds. The wind rustled branches and chilled her even more. A drop of rain hit her nose. She surged forward, jogging a bit, then walking with a long stride, pumping her arms, keeping her eyes on the path to dodge slick spots. The tension in her neck and shoulders eased.

This is what she would not be able to do in New Jersey. She would not be able to live.

Two men appeared a short distance down the path, advancing toward her. The signs that forbade trespassing had been effective over the years, except for an occasional teenager or two from town. Grace usually felt safe. She slowed her pace, finally recognizing one of them.

"Ugh, him," she muttered out loud.

He wore his signature sweater, the beige sleeves, side panels, and midline zipper separated by two straight columns of brown suede cutting his body into stripes. She had seen him one day, recently, in the doughnut shop and noticed stains on the suede, oily drips from a past meal. As usual, he had bared his teeth, his version of a smile, with powdery sugar around his mouth and masticated dough trapped in his gum line.

Skip McKay made her gag.

Skip walked forward, hands gesticulating at the end of manic arms, as he half-turned toward his companion. The companion seemed to notice her approach, his eyes full ahead now. There was something familiar about him.

Grace took a deep breath and lengthened her spine. No longer concerned about the seclusion of her circumstance, she merely wanted to pass them as quickly as possible and resume her solitary walk. Her stomach clenched into a soft fist.

Now Skip looked ahead, raised his arm, and shouted, "Hello, Grace!"

She could no longer hope for a quiet, polite passing on the path.

She sighed.

"Grace!" he said again as they neared. "Let me introduce you to your new neighbor!"

The man with him wore gray pants, nice cut, and a black leather jacket, expensive, with a black fedora. Under the hat, thick black hair framed dark eyes and a warm smile. And then she recognized him.

It had been seven years.

Her heart beat faster. The fist of tension around her stomach tightened.

The two men stopped, and Grace halted a few feet away from them.

"Grace Baxter, this is Sam Cielo. He's moved to town to take over my father's law practice," Skip said. "And he's purchased the land bordering the property here. He plans to build a house there. I've been telling Sam about you and Nick and the marvelous things you're doing for Wood Grove."

Skip must not have remembered their first meeting at the lunch counter.

"Hello, Grace." Sam said.

"Nice to meet you, Mr. Cielo." She barely looked at him. "I'm sure we'll run into each other again. It's a small town."

Grace skirted around them and continued toward the creek without looking back. When she calculated they must be out of sight, she looked back and saw they had all but disappeared down the path.

Turning to the side of the path, she bent over and threw up.

Standing again, sweat forming under her arms, she contemplated yesterday's meals. Nothing to make her sick like this. Maybe a late spring virus. Again she reminded herself she did not have time to be sick.

Her heart calmed and her body resumed a state of equilibrium. She walked on.

In a few short minutes, Grace climbed onto the smooth comfort of the boulder she claimed as her own. She lay on the surface, listening to the sound of the water moving over the creek bed.

Sam seemed different, a little heavier, more mature. She never expected to see him again. She remembered their first meeting, later sharing coffee, teasing him about the books he read, and the last time, the unfortunate incident outside Handels. Grace hadn't known what to do, the whole situation confusing and Richard reacting with such certainty. She should have insisted Richard listen, given Sam a chance to explain. Surely he hadn't been with that nasty drunk guy, the first of many to sling racial slurs.

So he was back, and planning to build next door. She'd pushed Nick to buy that land, but he wouldn't budge. If they had to have someone living so close, Sam seemed like a good bet. Someday she would have a conversation with him. She would apologize for Richard's sharpness that night, for her passivity. They would be cordial neighbors.

After an hour on the rock, Grace returned to the house, refreshed, no longer worried about New Jersey. She would simply tell Richard she wasn't going and the logical choice would be for him to stay in Ohio. Any increase in salary associated with the new position would be offset by the higher cost of living on the East Coast. If Richard needed a change of scenery, they would take a vacation. He would see the sense in her thinking. He would agree with her and that would be that.

She went to her room and lay on her bed, surprised by the exhaustion that crept over her. Maybe she did have a bug. She napped, read, and slept again.

Voices across the hall awakened her. Grace dragged herself out of bed and went to the bathroom down the hall to freshen up, holding a warm cloth over her face, brushing her hair into submission. Her stomach still felt off, but the tantalizing aroma of lunch drew her to the dining room.

Nick sat at his usual spot at the head of the table. Grace slipped into the chair on his right.

"Judge Wright ordered the desegregation of elementary schools in New Orleans last week," John said as he forked a salmon patty onto his plate. "These look delicious, Loretta."

"It's about time. I think we have the Catholics to thank for that." Max received the platter from John and passed it on to Elizabeth. "They do look good, Loretta, but I'm not in the mood for fish tonight."

"Don't get me started on the Catholics," Nick said.

Fran loaded her plate with mashed potatoes. "George Poage died."

"Who's he?" Elizabeth asked.

Fran handed the potatoes to Peter. "Darling, let's go to New York to see *Inherit the Wind.*"

"Starring Ed Begley," Elizabeth chimed in.

"Oh! I want to go, too," Polly said. "Let's go together."

Grace chewed slowly as she listened to the members of her growing community explore the latest in politics and art, talking over each other, passing the patties, potatoes, vegetables, and bread, requesting more wine, interrupting, arguing, laughing.

Putting herself in Sarah's place, Grace could see how a visitor might be overwhelmed.

The phone rang. Nick leaned back and picked up the receiver.

"Hello? Oh, Hello, Richard… yes, she's right here…we're eating… no, she's already out of her chair, heading to her office."

The dining room noise faded as Grace closed the door to her room. When she picked up the receiver, she said, "You can hang up, Nick. I'm here."

The dining room noise coming from the other extension ended with a click.

"Hello, darling," she said. "You're calling early. Is anything wrong?"

"Paul called me into his office today," Richard said. "He said he needed an answer. I'm taking the position in New Jersey."

"What?" She was confused. She had already worked this out. She hadn't had time to tell him. "I thought about it today. I wanted to talk tonight."

"There's nothing to talk about," Richard said. "I told him, 'Yes.' What I want to know is, are you coming?"

"What? Where?" Did he want her to drive to Columbus tonight?

"New Jersey, Grace. You are moving to New Jersey with me?" It was question, a command, and a plea, all at once.

"Wait." Her thoughts banged against the wall of his clipped tone. "Let's talk about this."

“I don’t need to talk about it,” Richard said. “I made my decision. I told Paul. I’m taking the position.”

She hesitated. “How are we going to see each other?” Heat rose in her belly, her chest, her head. “I guess we could work something out.” Flying was expensive. She hadn’t planned for this, but there had to be a way to make it work.

Richard sighed. “It’s been three years, Grace. I thought by now we’d be living in the same place, building a life together, creating a home for our family.”

She could barely breathe. “I thought you would be here by now, living in Wood Grove.” The words came out whispered, weak.

“I accepted the transfer, Grace. I’m moving to New Jersey. Three other people in my team agreed to join me there. Tim, Bart, and Donna. Their families are moving with them.”

He sounded so distant now, almost cruel.

“Donna?” Lovely, caramel-toned, widowed mother of two young boys. Grace had watched Richard play baseball with Donna’s boys at company picnics. He adored them.

“Let me know if you change your mind. Otherwise, I think it’s time we hire a lawyer.”

“A lawyer?” She woke up. “Why do we need a lawyer?”

“Let’s stop kidding ourselves, Grace. This isn’t a marriage. If you’re not moving with me to New Jersey, I want a divorce.”

Chapter Seven

AFTER SEEING GRACE in the woods, Sam spent the morning at the car lot warding off Skip's attempts to sell a car to him.

"How are you going to get around?" Skip asked, his high-pressure tactic bordering on condescension.

"I'll walk." Sam had no intention of going into debt for something he could very well do without. Sooner or later Sam would buy a new car, and he supposed he should buy it from Skip, though he might prefer a Cadillac, but a Buick would do. He'd think about that later, after he settled in, established himself in town, recouped his savings account. Buying the land had taken a chunk of money.

Finally convinced he couldn't wrestle his old friend into a deal, Skip clapped Sam on the back and said he'd be ready when Sam came around. "I'll bring your bags to the house. Don't let Dad work you too hard. See you for dinner!" Skip moved on to real customers.

Sam eased himself into being in Wood Grove as he walked slowly up the road to the office. He'd left everything behind, sold or given away the furniture he'd collected, and arrived with only the clothes he could fit into two new suitcases. He wanted to start fresh. Thank goodness the McKays were willing to provide a place for him to stay, "for as long as you want to be here." He couldn't ask for better friends.

The door to Stewart's office required an extra tug to open. Sam would buy some sandpaper or a plane to fix that. Stepping into a darker, dingier version of what he remembered from his last visit, he smelled something stale in the air. Dust particles danced in a ray of sunlight filtering through a blind slat. A sweater hung unevenly from the back of Lois's empty chair. He made it no further than her desk when Stewart walked out of his office and launched into a spirited monologue.

"Welcome, my boy! I've been thinking about how the world has changed since I opened my practice. Let me tell you." Stewart paced to the end of the waiting area and turned to face Sam.

Hand extended, Sam stepped toward the aging attorney, saying, "Good to see you, sir," but Stewart shoved his hands in pockets and paced past Sam to Lois's desk where he turned and returned to the other side of the room.

"Divorce rates spiked following the end of the big war," Stewart said. "I worked night and day, but all those unhappy couples paid off my mortgage! The divorce craze has waned, but don't worry, son. The pendulum will swing." Stewart stopped, his legs spread slightly, raising his right hand in the air. "What goes down—" his hand scooped toward the floor "—must come up." His hand swooped back up toward the ceiling.

Leaning against the edge of the desk, Sam crossed his arms and legs, watched, and listened.

Stewart approached the desk, his eyes wild, his hair sticking up in several places. "Sooner or later divorce will rise again and that's what will pay off the mortgage on that house you plan to build." He slapped Sam hard on the shoulder and laughed, his face reddening as he collapsed into a long coughing fit. When it ended, Stewart mopped his forehead with a white handkerchief.

"Are you okay, sir?" Sam asked.

"Oh, sure, I'm fine." He paced again. "Land deals, there's your bread and butter right now." He stopped in front of Sam again. "You jump on helping people make a nice profit off selling their land, maybe to someone who wants to build houses or a commercial business. You'll be lining your own pockets while assisting the county with economic development. You're part of a small system here, Sam. Everybody counts. You're in the big time now."

Sam ignored the contradiction and acquiesced to the finger poking his chest.

The door to the street opened. A small, bent woman crossed the threshold. She juggled a handbag and an umbrella. Beneath the plastic rain hat, gray hair pulled tight against her scalp. Sam took the umbrella from her hand.

"Thank you," she said, without looking up.

"A two-hour lunch, Lois?" Stewart's voice boomed. "You're late again."

"You told me to come in at three," Lois said. "I'm early."

Stewart waved her off and walked into his office, beckoning Sam to follow.

Sam tried to make eye contact with Lois, to offer silent support, but she kept her head down.

The rest of the afternoon revolved around Stewart's reminiscence, interrupted by short naps. There were no clients.

By five, Sam had assessed the situation, which Lois confirmed as he prepared to leave for the day, Stewart again snoring at his desk.

"Today is a particularly bad day," she said. "He's really been quite ill."

"Can he get the job done?" Did Sam have a responsibility to report Stewart to the Ohio bar?

Lois allayed that fear when she declared, "I make sure everything goes well. On his good days, he is as he always was." In her warm, honey-coated voice, Sam heard more than respect. He wondered about her life and what she would actually lose when her Mr. McKay no longer sat on the other side of the wall.

Sam turned away from her, knowing he would have to work night and day to learn as much as he could before Stewart's good days disappeared altogether. Sam's father had warned him. "It's too good to be true, mijo. Slow down. You have a good job already." But Sam had trusted Stewart McKay, trusted him more than he trusted his own father. And the land had been available, the land he'd picked out for his perfect home, in the perfect town, with the perfect job. Damn, he'd always been a sucker for the seductive promise of a happy ending.

"Thanks, Lois. I'll see you in the morning." Sam closed the door behind him, again thinking of what he needed to fix the place where it kept sticking, and stepped out into the late afternoon, the sun hiding behind diffuse clouds.

"Sam!" Arms wrapped around his torso and lacquered hair brushed rough against his cheek. The woman pulled back and Sam could see, beneath the teased bangs and chin-length hair, the round face of Gloria McKay.

"Gloria! Good to see you!" He hugged her back. The last time he'd seen her, she was fourteen. She'd grown into an attractive twenty-one-year old woman. "Picking up your Dad?"

"No." She linked her arm in his and held it close as she moved down the sidewalk. "I heard you were coming. It's so good to see you. When did you arrive?"

"Early this morning. Skip picked me up. He said you weren't living at home anymore. What are you doing with yourself?"

"I work at a restaurant down in Chillicothe."

"And you live there?" he asked.

"With a roommate. She works at the bank. Two young single women." She raised her hand to waggle it in the air. "Wild times."

Sam laughed with her. She didn't appear to be too wild.

"Any plans for the future?" He thought about his own sister. Maria had gone to college and now worked at a hospital. The pay wasn't the greatest, but a nurse could always find a job.

"I plan to work on Thursday, Friday, and Saturday this week," she answered. "And then do my laundry. Big plans." She hugged his arm tighter.

"Why not college?" he asked.

She hesitated. "I didn't even finish high school, Sam."

He stopped short. "What?" They were at the entrance of a small city park. "What do mean you didn't finish high school?"

She shrugged her shoulders. "Just didn't finish."

In the middle of the park, benches lined the perimeter of a gazebo that provided shade for some picnic tables. Sam guided Gloria toward a table.

"Why did you quit school?" he asked when they were seated.

"I was fed up," she said. "On the day I turned eighteen during my senior year, I got a job and never went back. I loved being on my own, making my own money, but I'm beginning to feel a little stuck. I don't want to wait tables forever."

"You could go back and finish," Sam said. "Night school. Your parents would help."

Her head dropped. "My parents kicked me out. Dad said he never wanted to see me again. They don't even invite me to holiday meals. They don't want me around."

"I'm so sorry, Gloria." Even when his brother, Hector, faced a possible jail sentence for a fight he'd started, Sam's parents helped as much as they could. "I had no idea. Skip didn't say anything."

She gave a derisive snort and lifted her head. "He wouldn't. I'm not worth talking about."

Sam pulled her to him. "Hey, don't talk like that. You're a good kid."

He felt her sink into his shoulder and let her rest there, sniffling.

Life in Wood Grove had certainly changed since his last visit. Should he go back to Denver and reapply to the firm? They were sorry to lose him, they'd said, and would take him back if he changed his mind. He had options. Sam settled onto the bench and watched the cars moving up and down Main Street.

“See that?” Gloria asked.

Sam looked up and saw a stooped figure, slow, tense, making her way up the sidewalk. “You mean Lois?”

“I caught them kissing once, when I was about nine. I wanted to surprise Dad, so I went into the office very quietly. Lois wasn’t at her desk. When I snuck around the corner, there they were, all tangled up, his hand sliding up her skirt.”

Sam’s suspicions confirmed, he asked, “What did you do?”

“I ran all the way home. He showed up a few minutes later, all out of breath. Must have seen me before I got out the door.”

“And?”

“Nothing. I went to my room. He never said a word to me about it.”

“You didn’t tell your mother?”

“I was afraid to.”

Sam didn’t ask for more details. As a kid, he wouldn’t have known how to respond, either.

After a minute or so, Gloria moved away from him and patted her hair.

“I still have your copy of *Pride and Prejudice,*” Sam said.

“You do?” She looked at him, her eyes shining, nose running. Sam fished a handkerchief out of his pocket and handed it to her. She blew her nose, then laid her head back on his shoulder. “Why did you keep it?” she asked.

“That book had a profound impact on me.”

“It did?” she asked.

“It taught me that a woman’s mind can remain unfettered, even when constrained by social convention.”

“That’s what you learned from that book?” Gloria asked. “Wow. I hated it.”

Sam laughed and squeezed her shoulders. “I know you did.”

DINNER AT THE MCKAY house that evening was a quiet affair, overcooked pork chops and canned corn. Nothing like Sam remembered from his previous visits. Hair pulled back with a brown band, Mrs. McKay put plates on the table and told everyone to serve themselves. Talk centered on neighborhood gossip and Mrs. McKay's complaints about not having enough help around the house. Skip's wife, Mary Sue, now occupied the seat formerly assigned to Gloria. Sam kept thinking of Gloria's red-rimmed eyes.

He looked at Stewart and Mrs. McKay. How could they treat their daughter like that? She should be here, welcomed as an important part of the family.

"Another glass of wine, please." Skip held out his wineglass to Mary Sue.

"Honey, I think you've had enough." Skip's wife glanced around the table. "That's your third one."

"I can handle it," he slurred.

Mary Sue took the wineglass and filled it from the bottle beside her plate.

Mrs. McKay held up her emptied water glass. "Put some in there for me, too, Mary Sue."

Sam had never seen Mrs. McKay drink. He and Stewart's wife had a long talk before dinner. Mrs. McKay informed Sam that her husband's medication affected his behavior. Sam felt certain he had seen evidence of that earlier in the day. She expressed little remorse about Sam being invited into the downward spiral of their lives. In fact, she seemed almost unaware of the rate or depth of decline in her spouse.

Stewart left the table and ambled toward the living room. Sam heard him drop into his easy chair. Soon the television blared.

Skip rambled on about his amazing year, the fantastic work crew he'd assembled, and the record sales they'd achieved. His sales were the best in the state, in practically the whole country, for a dealership that size. "I would be making a lot more profit, but I had to build up so slowly. Mary Sue's dad could've helped, but he refused."

"Now, Skip," Mary Sue chided him. "Don't start in on Daddy. He did offer to help some, but you wouldn't take it unless he gave you the whole amount."

"Why should I settle for less?" Skip hit the table with his fist. "I deserve that money as much as anybody." He leaned forward and stage-whispered to Sam. "It's going to be all mine someday, anyway. Mary Sue's an only child." He drained the wineglass and started to put it down on the edge of his napkin.

"Now stop that, Skip," Mary Sue took the glass before it toppled over. "What's Sam going to think about my daddy?" She smiled at Sam. "My daddy is generous and kind. And he owns half the buildings in town. I'll make sure he knows you're here. He'll want to make an appointment with you." She brushed breadcrumbs off Skip's pant leg.

"I'd love to meet him," Sam said.

"Do you have a girlfriend back in Denver?" Mary Sue asked. "I hope it's okay to ask such a personal question."

"Of course he does!" Skip shouted.

"Lower your voice, Skip," his mother said. "You're going to wake your father, or raise the dead." She giggled.

"Mama McKay, you are not accustomed to drinking wine. Let me make some coffee." Mary Sue gathered the plates and silverware before leaving the dining room.

"So do you?" Skip asked.

"Do I what?" Sam asked.

"Have a girlfriend in Denver."

"No." Sam brushed off the question. "Nobody special."

"Right," Skip said. "I'll bet you had the pick of the best, and all the rest."

"I didn't really have time to date," Sam said.

"Right." Skip cuffed Sam's upper arm. "You old devil."

"I put the coffee on, Mama McKay," Mary Sue said as she returned. She sat back down. "Are we having dessert?"

"Oh," Mrs. McKay put her hand to her mouth. "I completely forgot about dessert."

"Nothing to worry about," Sam assured her. "Dinner was delicious. Thank you so much."

"I like dessert." Skip sat back on his chair, sulking.

Mary Sue reached across the table and put her hand over Sam's. "I have a friend. Skip graduated with her from high school. She is a University of Cincinnati graduate with a degree in accounting."

Sam smiled. His friends were always trying to set him up.

"Her mother died when she was a kid," Mary Sue continued. "And she was an only child, so she had to move back to Wood Grove after her father had a stroke, even though I think she had a pretty good job at a major company."

"You're not talking about Ruby Valley, are you?" Skip asked. "She's smart all right, but dang she's ugly."

"Skip!" his mother said.

"Let me go check on the coffee." Mary Sue left the table again.

"You can go out with her if you like," Skip said. "But she'll only be the first in a long line of women you can try on for size." He finished with a wink. "Take, for instance, that Grace Baxter. Remember her from the woods yesterday? I would take her out in a heartbeat."

"You're married, Skip." Mrs. McKay examined her cuticles.

"I said, 'would,' except she lives with a bunch of commie-red weirdos, and blacks, next door to your new land."

"You said they added something good to the community," Sam said.

Skip snorted. "Salesmanship, Sam. Tell 'em anything to make 'em think you like 'em, you're a team. Close the sale, and move on. You'll need to learn sales, too, but instead of selling cars, you'll be selling yourself." Skip shook himself around the shoulders. "Brrr, I wouldn't want to be you."

Mary Sue appeared with a tray of steaming cups. "I brought some for everybody." She set the tray on the table and served the cups with sober grace.

"Tell me a little bit about your friend," Sam said. He raised his cup to test for heat.

"She's really funny." Mary Sue put her cup back down on her saucer. "Funny, and like I said, smart. She never got in trouble for talking back to the principal, because she did it with so many big words, I think he was afraid of her."

"She talks too much," Skip said.

"Your friend sounds nice," Sam said. "Find out if she'd like to have dinner with me."

Mary Sue blushed. "How sweet of you, Sam. I think you and Ruby will really hit it off."

Sam excused himself and carried his coffee to his room.

Ruby did sound interesting, but he'd suggested the dinner date simply to oppose Skip. Had he always been this way? Had they all always been as they were now? Skip rude, Stewart unfaithful, Mrs. McKay unhappy, and Gloria on the outs?

Sam put his coffee on the nightstand and sat on the edge of the bed.

Grace Baxter. She had been the silver lining in this gray cloud of a day. He never imagined he would see her again. He had sat right here and written a letter to her. She must be mid-to-late twenties now, still doing the same job that took her from her college studies. When he saw her in the woods, he'd wanted to tell Skip to get lost. He'd wanted to walk with her, renew their acquaintance, explain about the last time they saw each other.

Still freckled with a fresh face and those lovely green eyes, she had tried to hide it, but she remembered him.

What had life thrown at her?

Sam ran his hand through his hair.

She might be a reason to stay.

Chapter Eight

GRACE WOKE INTO A hazy fog, turned, and gazed into Richard's face, his eyes a dead blank stare, blood pooling on the pillow. Her eyes flew open and she shot up in bed, drops of sweat rolling down her side. Breath calming, her eyes adjusting, she could make out Polly's quilt-covered form and hear her breathing quietly. Grace slid out of bed, pulled a robe around her, and padded barefoot to the dining room.

Dialing their number in Columbus, she leaned her back against the wall and sank, her bottom finally hitting the floor, knees against her chest, feet snug against her buttocks.

"Hello?" His words were groggy. She had no idea what time it was.

"Richard? Thank God. I had a dream. I haven't had one in months." She pushed her hair out of her face.

"Please come with me to New Jersey," he said.

The words plunged her face into icy water. A wave of nausea rolled in. The grave-digging notion he would leave made everything a shroud of uncertainty.

"I can't, Richard," she said.

He was silent.

"Richard?" Her voice was a shadow now.

"I have to." His voice caught. His tears convinced her. He was going.

She clutched the phone and cried, silently at first, then big gulping sobs. When her emotions eased, and she could breathe with only minor hiccups of air, she asked, "Why?"

"I'm sorry, Grace," he said. "I thought we would finally agree on a place to live together. I never would have married you if I'd known we would end up divorced."

"But why?" she asked again. "Why do we have to get a divorce? We could make this work somehow. Even if we only see each other once a month, we can talk on the phone every day. I don't want to lose you. I don't want a divorce." She heard her own desperation, so close to out-of-control terror.

"I don't either. But what I don't want even more is this kind of marriage. I'm ready to be part of a family, have children, come home every night to someone."

Someone other than her? How could he choose another? He was hers, and she his. They belonged together.

"Grace, you really do need to see a doctor about those nightmares."

She couldn't speak.

"Are you okay?" he asked.

"No," she said, nausea building. "I have to go."

"Call me at lunch. We can be adult about this, work out a fair and equitable settlement."

"I have to go." She pushed herself to standing, hung up the phone, and hurried to the bathroom. After vomiting, she soaked her face with a warm cloth, grateful for Nick's decision to add a bathroom to the main floor.

Nick might be erratic, unpredictable, immature at times, but in the long run, he came through.

Natalie had finally divorced Nick last year. He went to Chicago to work out the details. A few weeks later, some papers arrived in the mail. Nick signed them and Grace delivered them to the post office. So business-like. Nick went on as if nothing had changed. Not at all what she anticipated.

Divorce. The concept seemed foreign when applied to her own life. Divorce meant alone. Unattached. She needed to be attached. She needed someone who would listen when the dreams happened, but Richard had been firm, and she knew he would follow through.

Grace tiptoed back into her dark room. Polly was already up, dressing for the day.

"I didn't turn the light on," Polly said. "I thought you might be sleeping. You're up early."

Switching on the overhead light and moving to her bed, Grace arranged the mound of sheets and blankets into a loose arrangement resembling "made." "Yep," she said. "I have a big day ahead."

"Anything special?" Polly asked.

"Every day is special," Grace answered. She could thank Nick for this well-honed ability to manage her disappointments and worries. Covering up his occasional wild streaks had become another unwritten part of her job description.

Nick didn't respond to life as most people would. His divorce had barely touched him, but when his publisher asked for a tiny revision of the third chapter, Nick went bonkers, threatening to dissolve the community and move to New York, live in a place where he would not be distracted by others. Only Nick would think he could avoid relationships by moving to a place where there were over seven million people. The thought made her smile. She might survive divorce after all.

Polly left the room. Grace sat down at her desk and pulled out a legal pad.

Richard had said she needed a lawyer. Sarah could help.

She wrote *Call Sarah about an attorney* at the top of the page. Thirty minutes later, she had a page full of questions and tasks related to the car, cash, investments, and household items she and Richard owned in common. He could have most of it; he had earned the money. She wanted the few things she had brought into the marriage: her parents' bed and matching chest of drawers, some paintings which had hung on the wall when she was a child, her clothes and bathroom accessories. Itemizing the list empowered her. She had named her terms.

At the end of the page she wrote, M*ake an appointment with the doctor*. Richard was right. It was time to address this issue of nightmares and she could use some help with the stomach upset, too. Her mother had often had stomach issues. Maybe it ran in the family. Maybe the doctor could help, at least with the nausea. But what could he do about the nightmares? She hoped he wouldn't simply label her, "crazy."

Grace waited until late morning to share the news with Nick. The others would learn about it soon enough.

"He's nuts to divorce you." Nick paced the floor of his bedroom.

Grace sat on the edge of his bed, all other surfaces being covered with clothes or books. Her feet dangled above the floor.

"I can't believe this." Nick continued to pace. "He's moving to New Jersey and wants to divorce you right away. Something doesn't add up. Is he seeing someone else?"

"No," she answered, but then, how would she know? Was he?

"This complicates everything." Nick threw up his hands.

How did her failure at marriage complicate everything for Nick? "I plan to stay," she said. "I want to keep working here. I need to help Fran with the Solstice play, at least for the first year. We only have two months. And there's so much left to do, so many projects we haven't completed."

She traced a line of thread on the quilt with her finger and remembered drinking tea with Loretta as she stitched. Loretta produced at least two quilts a year, sometimes seasonally. This one was a beauty, deep shades of green accented with blue, red, and coral in interlocking squares.

Nick sighed deeply and dropped down hard on the mattress beside her. She nearly bounced off the bed.

"The thing is, Grace, I've developed certain feelings for you."

Her finger froze and her breath stopped as she steadied herself. She turned to look at him.

He looked straight ahead, not at her, as he spoke, balling his fists and extending his fingers repeatedly as he explained. "I liked you very much from the first time we met, but you were so young. And then you brought

Richard here, which completely relieved me. I liked him. I didn't want to step onto his territory." He took a deep breath.

She crossed her arms. She didn't like being cast as anyone's territory.

Nick's hair curled over the top of his shirt collar and the rest of it lay in waves. He needed a cut. He needed a shave, too.

"And then you two were married which sealed the deal," he continued. "We were business partners, so to speak, even though technically I employ you, but I've never really thought of you that way. From the moment you decided to come here, I've thought of you as a partner."

He continued to look ahead and she turned to face the same direction. Three drawers in his dresser were partially open, a sock escaping from the top one.

Nick sighed again and turned toward her. She turned back to look at him.

"Grace, I think I'm in love with you. No, I know I'm in love with you. I want you to stay and I want you to be more than my employee, more than my business partner."

She could feel her face redden. She eased herself off the bed and walked to the dresser, pushing the sock inside and shutting the drawers. She turned and faced Nick, letting her back rest against the dresser, crossing her arms over her breasts. Her heartbeat increased. She raised her right hand to her face, biting the tip of her index finger for a moment. The pain sobered her.

"Nick," she said. "I wasn't expecting this." She clasped her hands in front of her, massaging the base of her palms together.

He sat on the edge of the bed, searching her face.

"I'm confused," she said.

"Of course you are, darling. This is new for both of us." He moved off the bed and crossed the space between them. "Take your time. You know I'm leaving for New York this afternoon. I'll be gone for a few weeks. Let it sink in. We can talk when I return."

"Okay." She walked to the door and turned back. "I need to take the car into town. I'll be back in time for you to leave."

“No problem.” He waved her out the door. “What’s mine is yours.”

“Um, okay. Thanks.” She walked the hall to the back stairway, her feet numb to the pressure of the floor, life becoming more unreal by the minute.

“WHAT DID THE DOCTOR say?” Loretta asked when Grace returned from town.

“I got bumped for an emergency.” She had been able to schedule an appointment that day, but had to then reschedule for two weeks ahead.

“Doctors are nearly useless, unless you cut off your arm and are bleeding to death. Then they come in real handy.” Loretta peeled a potato into one long slice of skin.

“You are an ace with a knife,” Grace said.

Loretta looked at Grace while continuing to peel. “Good skill to keep the menfolk in line.”

Grace smiled, but she knew the comment wasn’t meant to be entirely humorous. Before meeting Loretta, Grace had been unaware of how vulnerable some young girls could be.

“I’m so sorry to hear about Richard.” Loretta sighed and picked up another potato. “He will regret this decision someday.”

Grace had confided everything to Loretta after leaving Nick’s room earlier in the day.

“And Nick!” Loretta shook her knife at the wall. “Ooh, he is some panther stalking women in the woods. I wouldn’t trust him for all the fabric currently shelved in the stores of Cleveland, Columbus, and Cincinnati. And that’s saying something.”

“He’s not that bad,” Grace said.

“Sugar, he is like the honey that traps mosquitos. Don’t be a mosquito.”

Grace laughed. “A mosquito?”

"Don't get me wrong." Loretta's fingers maneuvered the knife with increasing speed. "I love the man. Love, love, love him. John and I would not have moved here if we didn't see the good in him and fundamentally trust him. But neither of us are young, single, naive women."

Grace picked up a chunk of raw potato and popped it into her mouth. "I'm not naive."

"Don't steal any more of these." Loretta pointed the knife at her. "I might cut off your finger." She gathered the peels and dropped them into a bucket. "You are naive, Grace, if you think you can trust him in the way he is asking you to trust him."

"It's a moot point." Grace snatched another chunk of potato when Loretta turned away for a moment. "I'm not even divorced yet."

She retreated to her room, leaving Loretta to her daily routine of cooking for nine. She seemed to love it. Grace would never understand.

"Divorce." She repeated it out loud when she was alone, the door closed. Every time she said the word, a heaviness fell on her arms and chest.

Grace had called her sister earlier.

"Divorce!" Sarah had echoed the word like a ricocheted bullet. "You're Catholic! Catholics don't get divorced, at least not easily."

After calming down a bit, Sarah had been kinder to Grace than anticipated. Sarah had also expressed a surprising amount of anger at Richard. Not what Grace had expected, at all. She thought Sarah might be relieved. Her sister had only jumped to her defense, proclaiming Richard the "dumbest" man alive. Grace didn't agree, but she liked her sister's protective defense, even though it was based on an inaccurate character attack.

As usual, Sarah had offered financial help. As usual, Grace had declined. Sarah had also agreed to come up with the names and numbers of the best attorneys in town. Grace had teared up with gratitude.

She sat down at her desk now and reviewed the long list she had made before dawn. Able to tick off today's tasks, she looked around the room, her ears thrumming with thoughts racing the same track over and over.

Richard is divorcing me.

Nick is in love with me.

Despair and elation. She wasn't ready to admit to Loretta, barely to herself, that Nick's declaration, though stunning, was not a complete surprise, nor altogether unwelcome.

Grace, too, had been attracted to Nick from the start, his physical appearance far above average. In addition to daily runs up and down the road, he engaged in random bouts of exercise, breaking away from a group meeting to perform a dozen push-ups, run around the outside of the house to the point of exhaustion, or race up and down the stairs, a wild grin on his face.

Though past forty, his body was trim, sinewy. Grace had seen how a few women in town looked at him. Funny how their interest had never made her jealous until now, when she knew he was in love with her. Would she worry about other women?

She stood, knocking a pen to the floor. What was she thinking? She was married to Richard. Twisting the ring on her finger, terror gripped her right below the ribcage. She needed to read something, escape into a story about someone else, where endings were predictable and happiness possible. A quick survey revealed none of the books on her shelves would do.

Grace shrugged her shoulders into her red and black plaid jacket and stuffed some money into the pocket. She wouldn't take the car again. She would walk to the bookstore, meaning she would not see Nick before he left for New York. She was too confused. She needed time away from him. She pulled her red knit hat, a gift from her old roommate Deirdre, onto her head, and wound a black knit scarf, a gift from Sarah, around her neck. Walking would be good. She left through the front door and didn't look back.

Chapter Nine

MAIN STREET IN WOOD GROVE soothed Sam. The stores bustled in the morning. The afternoons were slower, with school-age kids moving in packs, the girls a gaggle of skirts and bobby socks, the boys learning how to strut. He remembered those days. Though not carefree, they held promise. He had managed to hang onto some of that in himself for a long time, but the challenges he now faced threatened his resilience.

In the few days he'd been back, Sam had read through enough of Stewart's recent work to see the collapsing of a fine mind. Judging by the many misspellings, Sam had deduced Lois's eyesight was failing, too. The financial records revealed Stewart's practice as a complete shambles. Why had Sam taken Stewart at his word? If Sam stayed, he would have to start from scratch.

Walking back from lunch at Handels, he passed the last building on the block and almost collided with a plaid jacket coming around the corner. Sam reached out and ended up holding the person by the arms. Impact averted, he dropped his hands. The face lifted and Sam looked into familiar eyes.

"Hello," he said. "Funny how we keep bumping into each other."

She pulled her scarf down from her face. "Yes, funny."

"Nice to see you again, Grace." He offered his right hand.

She looked at his hand and offered her own. "Hello, Sam."

"Would you like to grab cup of coffee?" He needed time with her.

"No," she said. "I'm sorry. I can't today." She walked around him and on down the sidewalk, creating distance with a brisk pace.

"Damn," Sam muttered under his breath. He ambled on without glancing back. *She must think I'm a jerk.* He needed to talk to her, to explain.

"Sam!"

Ed Turnbull hailed him from the corner across the street. "My missus wants to know if you'd like to come to dinner on a regular basis. How about every Tuesday night at six?"

"Tell her I'd be happy to join you," Sam called back. "And tell her thanks so much for last night. I felt very much at home."

"She'll be happy to hear." Ed gave a final wave and continued on his way.

Seeing Ed lightened Sam's mood. Mary Sue had introduced them, appointing herself as Wood Grove's Welcome Wagon for the new attorney in town. "You need to meet everyone, Sam," she'd said. "They're going to love you!" How did Skip end up with such a sweet, thoughtful wife? Some guys had all the luck.

Ed's father had recently died and now Ed acted as mortician for Turnbull's Funeral Home. Funny that a mortician could be so jovial.

Last night had been pleasant. Mrs. Turnbull, Edith, served roast beef, potatoes, and green beans from last year's garden. Sam shared a few gardening tips he'd learned from his father. Four-year-old Pam Turnbull, a plump rosy-cheeked cherub, donned her lacy white tutu and performed ballet moves. The whole evening delighted him.

This is what Sam had expected from Wood Grove and the Turnbulls had delivered. Maybe he would stay. Eventually Grace would talk to him. She couldn't avoid him forever.

The afternoon continued its uphill climb after he returned to the office. Stewart had gone home early. Sam started to address the general chaos in Stewart's inner office when he heard the door to the street open.

Lois greeted someone and a voice replied, asking for him.

Sam brushed off his hands and slipped on his suit jacket. He straightened his tie before walking into the reception area.

"This woman wants to see you, Mr. Cielo." Lois pinched her lips and looked back down at her desk.

A dignified woman with mahogany-colored skin reached out her hand and said, "Hello, Mr. Cielo. I am Polly Drape. I teach English at the high school and I wanted to welcome you to town."

Lois looked over her glasses, her face a mask of white makeup and bright red lipstick.

Sam took Polly's hand and thanked her for coming.

Lois continued to eye them.

"Why don't you knock off early, Lois?" Sam said. "It's a nice day. Enjoy the rest of the afternoon."

Lois raised her eyebrows, reached down to bring her purse to her lap, and pushed her chair back. "I'll be back tomorrow," she said, more like a threat than a promise. She stood, gathering her raincoat and umbrella, draping both over her arm.

After the door closed behind her, Sam offered a seat in the reception area to Polly and sat down beside her. He didn't want her to see the disarray in Stewart's office.

"Again, thanks for stopping by. How can I help you?" he asked.

"In all honesty, Mr. Cielo, I think I might be able to help you."

"Call me Sam," he said. "And how might you help me?"

"First let me ask a few questions," she said.

Polly Drape quizzed him about his interest in education and young people, and about his willingness to serve in volunteer positions. He answered with as much clear thinking as he could, considering his life was upside down at the moment.

She sat forward and put her hands on her knees. "I am so happy to hear your values are the values we want to pass on to the children in our charge.

Some of the children come from families who work with us to educate the students. But there are so many who come from families where manual labor is valued over the ability to understand the history of our country and the world."

"A firm grasp of history is essential to democracy," Sam said.

"Exactly," she said with delight. "We want our community to turn out graduates who can lead this country in the manner of our current president. '*Ask not what your country can do for you. Ask what you can do for your country.*'"

"I couldn't agree more," Sam said.

"Those words and sentiments are what we want our students to carry with them, always. Yet, some of them can't even read. And some of them continue to live in the past, as if the Civil War never happened. I'm sure you can understand my meaning." She sat back and folded her hands on her lap.

Sam remembered Stewart's advice to change his name. This morning he had hung his law degree on the office wall, his full name on display for all who entered there. He knew it might cost him a few clients, but the world was changing, and Wood Grove would catch on, or catch up, some day, maybe even in his lifetime.

"May I ask about you?" he asked.

"Surely," she said.

"How did you come to teach here? I'm not seeing a large population of Negroes in the area." He hoped his bluntness wouldn't offend her.

"I appreciate your candor, Mr. Cielo," she said. "My family goes way back in this town. My mother was the housekeeper for Mr. Stewart McKay's mother. My mother helped raise Stewart when he was a boy."

Sam relaxed knowing he hadn't offended her. "So you know Stewart," he said.

"I do." Her voice came down hard on "do" and lifted as she continued. "My family saved all their money so I could have an education. When I graduated college, my mother went to the McKay family and asked if they would help me with a job. They pressured the school board to hire me." She laughed. "It didn't take much pressure. Three McKays sat on the board at the time."

Sam smiled.

"And you?" she asked. "How did someone with your last name end up in your position?"

Sam provided a brief biography.

She nodded as he spoke and when he finished, she said, "So it seems the McKay family has paved the way for both our careers."

"We do have that in common," Sam said. He chose not to mention he had been doing fine in Denver, but Denver was over now. Hanging his law degree on the wall had been his way of deciding. He would stay.

"It's a shame they are in such a state now." Polly lowered her head.

Sam chuckled. "So no more pussyfooting, huh?"

"Though he seems too young for it to be happening, it is no secret Stewart McKay is becoming senile," Polly said, lifting her head and looking Sam in the eye. "He has invited you into a situation which has become an embarrassment to his family and to the town. We need someone who will restore an aura of respect and dignity. The school board will vote tonight to unseat Mr. Stewart McKay. We would like you to assume his seat until the election."

Sam rubbed his head. "I'm honored you would think of me."

"We did our homework," Polly said. "The board researched your activity in Denver and found only positive reports of your work and behavior there. The board president asked me to talk to you on his behalf."

"Why did he send you?" Sam asked. "Why didn't the board president ask me himself?"

"I suppose he wanted to avoid any possible negative repercussions."

"And what about negative repercussions for you?"

Polly laughed. "There isn't much Stewart McKay could do to hurt me at this point. I learned how to handle him when I was growing up."

Sam waited for more, but she didn't offer. He didn't ask.

"I don't expect you to answer today," she said. "You can contact me at the high school or at my home, if you like."

When she told him her address, he said, "I just bought the land next door. Do you mind if I ask a few questions?"

She laughed and sat back in her chair, more relaxed than before. "Fire away. Better to hear it from me than the town gossips."

"Who lives there?" he asked.

Polly filled him in on the history of Nick's community. She talked about Nick's original idea and Grace's hard work to keep Nick moving forward. Polly highlighted the variety of projects they had completed, the plays presented, the art shows hung, the plans for Max's sculpture studio, and Grace's hope for adding buildings to accommodate overnight guests. She ended with, "Now Grace has nearly accomplished her dream of starting a foundation which will provide scholarships to low-income people for arts programs."

"The whole thing seems a bit odd," Sam said. "Is it working?"

"People are hungry for change," Polly said. "Churches have church camps. Corporations have retreat centers. Why not a center dedicated to the promotion of art education and appreciation? I think it's a marvelous idea, visionary, our little Chautauqua in central Ohio."

Sam wondered about the impact on his property. He wanted to make sure he would be able to maintain the peace and serenity of the setting. "Grace sounds ambitious," he said.

"She is driven."

"Why did you decide to live there?" he asked.

"Look at me," Polly said. "I love living here in Wood Grove, being close to my family, but there aren't many people here who…."

"Who understand and appreciate who you really are?" Sam asked.

"Exactly," she said. "I met Grace one day in the library. She has a mind for literature, poetry. Our conversation made me feel more at home in the very place I grew up. When she introduced me to Nick, I knew I wanted both of them in my life. When I met Richard, he clinched the deal."

"Richard?" Sam asked.

"Grace's husband." Polly laughed. "Little white girl like her with a tall handsome, black man by her side." Her speech took on a more relaxed cadence, not as clipped and artificially Midwestern as when she had first arrived. "That girl has power she doesn't even know."

"She's married," Sam said.

"As are Max and Elizabeth, Fran and Peter, and John and Loretta. Nick and I are the only singles, so far."

Polly stood. "Sam—" she reached out to shake his hand, back to professional and polished "—I so appreciate your time today. Please, stop by to visit, and please consider the invitation by the board. We need some new blood in this town."

Sam thanked her as he escorted her out the door.

As soon as the door shut behind Polly, he clucked his tongue and said again, "She's married."

He removed his jacket and resumed his efforts to bring order to the office. Grace was married, but he still felt a need to make things right with her. Someday they would be neighbors. Before that happened, he wanted to be able to at least think of her as a friend.

HE WORKED IN THE office until the clock reminded him to hurry over to Handels for his dinner date. Mary Sue had arranged for him to meet her friend, Ruby. As he stepped through the door of the diner, a young woman stood and waved him over.

"You must be Sam." She shook his hand before sitting again.

"And you must be Ruby." He hung his jacket on the chrome rack bolted to the side of the seats separating the booths.

"I am!" she said. A red satin ribbon held her bobbed auburn hair away from her face. Her red-and-white-checked dress pulled tight across her bosom, but seemed to have plenty of cloth at the waist.

"Let me tell you something right off the bat," Ruby began. Her eyes were large and blue, her smile wide and appealing.

Skip obviously didn't know how to appreciate women.

"I'm dating Hal Teck," she said. "I have no intention of dating two men at one time, so I did agree to have dinner with you, but I am not looking for anything else at this point in time." She picked up the menu and displayed it to Sam, pointing to an item. "Their cheeseburgers are the best."

Sam liked her.

After they ordered food, he asked questions. Skip had been right about one thing. Ruby Valley did like to talk. She talked about growing up in Wood Grove, going to school in Cincinnati, coming back home to care for her father, and her romantic first date with Hal.

The waitress delivered their cheeseburgers. Ruby and Sam dug in with no worries about first date decorum, cheeseburger juice dripping. They both laughed as they used their napkins at the same time to dab their chins dry.

Ruby continued her story about Hal. "We always liked each other in high school," she said. "But he thought I would think he wasn't smart enough, and I thought he would think I wasn't pretty enough." Her voice was musical, spirited.

"Are you happy living here now?" he asked. She had spoken with regret about leaving her job in Cincinnati.

"I don't really have a choice, do I?" she said. "There's nobody else to care for Dad and now that I'm dating Hal—" she grinned— "I'm happy."

"Are you working?" he asked.

"I work part time at Dr. Turner's office, being the receptionist and filing paperwork. It's okay."

An idea formed in Sam's head.

"Ruby, can you spell?" he asked.

"I went to state in the eighth-grade spelling bee," she said. "I lost on antediluvian. Can you believe that? My Sunday school teaching mother, had she been alive at the time, would have thrashed me." She smiled.

Sam doubted that Ruby Valley had ever been thrashed, or ever would be, by anybody.

He leaned forward over his clasped hands.

"Ruby," he said. "Can you type?"

Chapter Ten

THE TYPEWRITER CLACKED, *With Love and Appreciation*. Grace pulled crisp white paper out of the carriage, proofread, and signed it. She and Deirdre had been corresponding for six months about the idea of a foundation. Deirdre had taken the lead with a friend who was an attorney. Soon they would establish a tax-exempt, non-profit entity ready for charitable contributions. Folding the paper neatly in thirds, Grace creased each seam with precision and tucked the letter into an envelope.

Prior to seeing the doctor at eleven, she would have time for a few routine tasks. She slid her calendar closer, put a check beside *Finish the letter to Deirdre,* and added *Talk to Nick*.

Earlier in the day, Nick left a message with Elizabeth that he would arrive from New York in the afternoon. Elizabeth hinted at a surprise. Grace planned to communicate to Nick that she needed sufficient time to move through her divorce without too many expectations, or drama, on his part. Anyone could understand that, even Nick. So whatever surprise he had cooked up, it better not have anything to do with her.

The phone rang. Grace picked up the receiver and said, "Hello?"

"Put Nicholas on the phone." Always imperious, with no apparent attempt to regard Grace as worth the bother of civility, Natalie Mason was at least consistent.

"Hello, Mrs. Mason. I'm afraid Nick is out of town. We expect him back this afternoon."

"Where is he this time?" Natalie demanded.

"Arriving from New York," Grace answered in her best possible customer service voice. Over the years, it had become a game. The worse Natalie's behavior, the greater Grace's resolve to remain unaffected. A rolling stomach made that more difficult today. The doctor's visit couldn't come too soon.

"I need him," Natalie said, her voice breaking.

This was new. Natalie always demanded to talk to Nick without a hello or goodbye to whomever answered the phone. Grace waited, unsure how to respond.

Natalie sniffed once and her voice regained its officious rancor. "Tell him that his son needs him. Thomas is about to be kicked out of preparatory school. If Nick has any conscience at all, he will come to Illinois and help me straighten this out." She ended the call in her customary fashion, a moment of silence followed by a resounding click to signal the disconnect.

Replacing the phone in its cradle, Grace shifted on her seat.

His son needed him. Grace knew what it was like to be seventeen and need a father.

She wrote a reminder note to tell Nick that Natalie had called, and moved on to the next task of vacuuming the rugs in the great room. Someday, there would be a paid cleaning crew.

SHORTLY AFTER ELEVEN O'CLOCK, Grace stood at the window between the waiting room and the doctor's examining rooms. She submitted the filled-out forms to the woman on the other side of the window; the woman had introduced herself as Ruby.

"The doctor will see you shortly," Ruby said, her voice pleasant, bubbly.

A nurse came through the door and ushered her to the inner Sanctum where she asked Grace to stand on a scale, measured her height, took a blood pressure reading, drew blood, and directed Grace to a bathroom to pee in a cup. When she returned to the examining room, the nurse provided a gown and asked Grace to undress.

Grace willed herself to not vomit.

The doctor came in, unsmiling, efficient, and asked why she was there.

She described her nightmares and her stomach issues.

Without asking any more questions, he listened to her heart and probed her abdomen, which nearly did her in. She managed to not retch by poking the tip of her middle finger with her thumbnail, focusing on the sharp pain there.

The doctor left and she lay on the hard exam table, wondering if he would order more tests, provide a list of possible maladies, or tell her, "It's all in your head." Chilled now, the thin cotton gown offering no protection, she rose from the table and started to put on her socks when the door opened and the doctor stepped back in.

"I'm sorry," he said. "I forgot to say you could get dressed."

She sat in a chair shivering under the gown, still barefoot.

The doctor leaned against the exam table, smiling. "I think we have the answer to your problem, Mrs. Baxter," he said. "Hormone changes impact your digestion and can affect your sleep, too. Those nightmares will probably go away soon."

She'd been having the nightmares for years. Hadn't he listened to her?

"Let Ruby set you up with another appointment," he said. "If you have any problems, call right away. Congratulations! You're going to have a baby."

He carried his chart, and his triumphant grin, out of the room.

Grace put her head between her legs.

When she could sit up again without feeling dizzy, she dressed, her body wooden, her thoughts pushed into a tiny corner of her mind.

At the desk, Ruby's cheerful voice talked dates and times. Grace could barely respond. She would see the doctor again in a month. She walked out the door and headed back to the house.

The doctor must be mistaken. She couldn't be pregnant. Richard and she had been so careful. She'd skipped periods before, so last month's absence of bleeding hadn't raised any suspicion. She'd chalked up the stomach upset to something understandable, acceptable. Her father had an ulcer. She remembered her mother complaining of digestive discomfort at times. She'd thought maybe it ran in the family.

But if she was pregnant, would Richard still move to New Jersey? Would she want him to stay, knowing he would have left her?

They had met twice in the last two weeks, both tearful each time, and still he held his ground. The divorce was in process.

And then there was Nick.

Since his departure, she'd been struggling with his confession of love. Without Richard, Nick had started to seem like a logical choice. She did find him attractive, and she probably loved him. But Nick and a baby? Look how unreliable he had been for his first wife and son.

By the time she walked home, she had worked out nothing in her head, but had come to accept the doctor's diagnosis. That didn't ease her shock. Being hit by a bus might have been less complicated.

The ideated past floated in, her parents' heads banging together, then against the windows, and finally the dashboard. She had imagined it, dreamt it, but no one could say with certainty the sequence of events that occurred during those awful moments.

In a similar way, no one could pinpoint the occurrences that led to this thing growing inside her, when the sperm slipped through and fertilized the egg, another accident, unexpected, life-altering, but not awful. She could never think of new life as a bloody mess, not even when that is exactly how she would describe her entire existence at the moment: one colossal bloody out-of-control ugly mess.

Back at the house, Grace lay on her bed for hours, skipping lunch, appreciating every blessed moment nobody knocked on her door to ask for help.

She should be able to call Richard. His heart had been her source of help for so long, but that was over. She needed to not need him, not now, not ever. She heard the front door open, and then Nick's voice, answered by a softer, feminine sound. Grace would have to tell him about the baby. What would he say?

Feet moved to the door. Hand turned the knob. Legs knew which way to turn. Odd how knowing she carried new life left her feeling lifeless.

Nick's voice again. "I told you it was grand. And it will be grander. I promise."

A woman stood beside him. The woman was tall and thin, with beautiful reddish-brown skin, her shiny black hair pulled away from her face. Even in the midst of personal crisis, Grace thought of the community. *Nick's brought us an actress. She's young, but looks professional. This will be good for the Solstice play.* When Grace neared the end of the hall, almost stepping into the foyer, the woman threw her arms around Nick's neck and kissed him on the mouth.

"Yes, love. This is worth leaving New York, as are you," she said and kissed him again.

Legs stopped moving.

Nick locked eyes with Grace. When the woman detached herself from his face, he opened his arms and announced, "Welcome the newest member of our little family. This is Norma."

Norma turned and smiled, her mouth a wide dazzle of white teeth beneath high cheekbones. "Nice to meet you," she said and turned back to Nick. "Where's our room, cherie? I need to rest."

Nick gathered the suitcases and gestured to the stairs. "I'll show you." Norma headed up.

Before following her, he stepped toward Grace and mumbled, "Sorry about what I said before I left. Never should have crossed that line," then followed Norma up the stairs.

Grace returned to her office and shut the door.

Over the next hour, she stared at the ceiling, indifferent to Nick's betrayal. He was as Loretta had described, lovable when accepted for who he was, but never reliable as a life partner. Grace took a deep breath and settled back into her body which felt different now, kinder, warmer, wiser.

Sun broke through the late afternoon clouds. Her room filled with light. Grace left her bed and pulled on her jacket. She needed air.

The day had warmed considerably. Fran and Peter played badminton on the lawn without a net. Grace heard John's voice coming from the second floor of the carriage house. He and Max had made progress on the new studio, but they would be at it for weeks. Elizabeth wandered through the grass, close to the tree line, her open palm skimming the tops of taller weeds. Grace could hear her talking to herself, reciting lines from Shakespeare.

A voice called out. Loretta emerged from the doorway of the carriage house stairwell. She crossed the grass to the driveway and stopped, rubbing goosebumps on her bare arms. "Did you see Nick? He has someone with him."

"Her name is Norma," Grace said. "She'll be staying in his room."

Loretta raised her eyebrows. "How is that sitting with you?"

"You were right about him." Grace scuffed her toe on the ground.

"Oh, honey, I'm so sorry," Loretta said.

"It's okay." Grace kicked at a rock and sent it flying a few feet.

"You don't look okay."

"I saw the doctor," Grace said. "I'm pregnant."

Loretta drew in air sharply and let it back out with an, "Oh, my." She put her hand on Grace's arm. "What are you going to do?"

Grace kicked another rock. It hit the side of Nick's car and pinged off, leaving a mark. She looked at Loretta and smiled. "I guess I'm going to have a baby."

Loretta wrapped her arms around Grace and swayed back and forth with her. "What wonderful news. I've been holding on to a little secret myself. I'm going to have a baby, too."

Tears pooled in Grace's eyes. She would not be alone. She hugged Loretta back, hard. "Thank you for being here. Thank you."

"We're going to get through this, baby girl." Loretta left the hug but continued to hold both of Grace's arms as she looked into her eyes. "You'll see."

"Yeah," Grace pulled her arm loose and dragged her sleeve over her eyes. "We will."

She hugged Loretta again and walked toward the path leading into the woods. With a determined pace, she walked to the creek. Her feet snapped twigs on the ground. A robin flitted above. The earliest wildflowers had already peaked and waned, but the current show of Mayapples and an occasional Jack-in-the Pulpit thrilled her.

Pregnant.

Her pace quickened and her legs moved into an easy run.

Right at this minute, new life was forming inside her. A baby. Would it be a boy or a girl? Would it look like her or Richard? She could do this without him. Women raised children without men all the time, all over the world. And the truth was, she wouldn't be alone. She had Loretta.

By the time she reached the creek, her own heat forced off the jacket. Grace sat on her boulder, hugged her knees to her chest, and listened. Water rushed. The urge to celebrate grew as she kicked off her shoes. She removed her socks. Her soles met the cool hard surface of the rock. She was alive with a baby growing inside her.

She stood and unzipped her pants, letting them fall and pushing them to the side of the rock, then pulled her shirt over her head and dropped it beside her feet. She faced the water, feeling the air. She wanted more. She pulled her panties off both legs and dropped them onto her shirt. Then she reached behind and unclasped her bra, letting it drop.

Stretching her arms, with nothing between the sky and her skin, she breathed in as deeply as she could, blew out hard, and inhaled again.

She stood naked on the rock, swinging her arms from side-to-side and stretching them up. Nothing like this had ever happened to her, nothing this grand, this wonderful, this needed.

Gradually her muscles cooled and she reached down to grab her shirt. She pulled it over her head, stepped carefully off the rock, and pulled on her panties and pants. Something splashed in the creek. When she looked, she saw only ripples, probably a frog. She slipped back into her jacket, stuffed her bra in the pocket, and sat on the rock.

Leaves rustled behind her.

Grace jerked her head around.

Sam Cielo left the path and walked toward her. "Hello, Grace," he said.

"How long have you been there?" She pulled on her socks and shoved her feet into her shoes, covering as much skin as possible.

"I hope it's okay to walk here. I saw the signs, but I couldn't resist."

Would he appear to be so relaxed if he'd seen her naked? She finished tying her shoes. "We post the sign to keep out troublemakers." Good Lord, if he'd shown up two minutes earlier—

"I hoped I might run into you," he said.

"You did?" Grace picked a seed pod from her pant hem.

"I wanted to explain," he said. "That last time, at Handels, I was only trying to help."

"I know." She inspected the other hem. No more seed pods. "I'm sorry, too. I should have given you a chance to explain."

"Friends?" He stood beside her now, holding out his hand, his dark eyes warm, inviting.

Grace pushed herself upright and extended her arm. "Sure," she said. "Friends."

When he grasped her hand, she could have sworn the little blob of cells growing inside her belly pulsed, but that would be impossible. The sensation had to be her own.

"Can we grab a coffee sometime?" he asked as he let go of her hand. "Renew our acquaintance? Maybe your husband could join us."

Her insides froze. "We're both so busy," she said, thrusting her hands into the pockets. "That probably won't happen soon."

Sam's eyes shifted down and when he lifted them, they showed a kind of reserve that comes with age. He had changed, matured. So had she.

"I guess I'll be seeing you around," he said.

"No doubt." Did she sound curt? She didn't mean to.

He walked away and she watched until he disappeared down the path. Maybe someday they could be friends, but not now. She needed to hunker down with those she knew she could trust. Thank God for Loretta.

Grace waited for a few minutes before walking back to the house. The sky clouded over. The temperature dipped. She shivered inside her coat. Skinny dipping had occurred in that very spot many times, but never by herself. How foolish she'd been to take off her clothes when she was alone. What might have happened if someone other than Sam had come along? Her heart sped up. She increased her pace and pumped her arms.

This baby needed a mother who could keep herself and her child safe, secure, and situated in a stable home. She could no longer allow her life to be ruled by Nick's fancies, nor by fate. She needed a plan, something solid and substantial to guide her in this new role.

A cool breeze lifted her hair as it rustled through the trees, bending them eastward. Grace pushed on.

Being a mother would be a series of challenges and decisions. Grace knew how to face change.

A large bird swooped across the path and disappeared into the web of branches.

She had survived the loss of her parents. She would survive losing Richard. Nick's failure to mature would affect her no more. If confidence were made of cells, Grace's began to differentiate, multiply.

By the time she cleared the woods, drops of rain fell. The carriage house windows were dark. The grassy areas and driveways were empty. Grace saw no one as she made her way to her room. She closed the door behind her and sat at the desk.

As the evening meal's aromas began to swirl around her, Grace thought, typed, ripped up drafts, and started over, attempting to address all aspects of how life had changed since the appointment with the doctor.

Shortly before dinner time, she went to Nick's room and knocked on his door. He answered right away, his glasses on the tip of his nose. Peripherally, Grace could see Norma's form under his bedclothes.

"I need to talk to you," Grace said.

"I'm in the middle of something," Nick said without looking at her. He brought his hands up to embrace an unseen source. "God, I'm on fire. The words crackle and sear."

"Now," she said, her hands clasped, her feet connecting with the floor.

Nick looked at her for less than two seconds before flipping his hands in a display of exasperation, blowing up his imaginary source of inspiration. "Okay." He rubbed his head. "Give me five. Your office?"

"That'll work." Grace walked away.

He showed up in ten and walked in without knocking. "It must be important," he said. "You know how I hate to be interrupted."

Grace pulled her chair out from the desk and turned it around. "Have a seat."

Nick sat, legs spread, feet perched on the toes of his shoes, his hands on his knees, fingers tapping.

Grace sat on the edge of her bed, legs crossed.

"I'm pregnant," she said.

"Wow!" He lowered his heels to the floor. "Glad it's not mine!"

"Me, too," Grace muttered and cleared her throat. "I need things to change around here or I'm leaving."

Nick stood, hung his glasses on the front of his shirt, ran his fingers through his hair, and sat down. "Grace, if this is about Norma—"

"This is about me," she said. "I'm pregnant, Nick. Richard is moving to New Jersey. I've been working for you for seven years—"

"With me, Grace. You work with me. We've done this together."

She started again. "I've been working here for seven years and we are nowhere near where I thought we would be by now. The community still can't survive without ongoing investment from you. That has to stop. I need to know what we're doing has substance, sustainability, a future. If I can't count on that, I need to go."

She waited.

"I know I've been distracted at times." Nick stood, took two steps to the window, sat down on the seat there, crossed his legs, tapped his knee a few times, returned to her desk chair and sat down again. "I can't do this without you. This place is working for me. I need to be able to come back here to recharge."

She waited.

"Okay…what changes?" he asked.

"I need a raise," Grace said. "I need to know I can support myself and my child."

"What about Richard?" Nick asked. "Won't he be involved?"

"I want to know I can do this by myself."

Nick took a deep breath, his eyes traveling over the room. "I can't imagine this place without you."

She waited.

He looked at her, his eyes glistening. "What do you want?"

Her heart jumped when she saw his tears, but she refused to let her resolve be moved by his emotion. She pulled a folded piece of paper from her pocket. "The details are here. It boils down to this. If something happens to you, I want the foundation to be the beneficiary of this house, any additional improvements, and the surrounding five acres of land."

He pulled his mouth sideways and started to speak.

She silenced him with a raised hand.

"I want a cottage built behind the main house," she said. "Two bedrooms and a kitchen, with a wooden swing on a front porch."

He nodded. "You'll want to raise the child there."

"I want a business plan that includes the eventual erection of a dorm for workshop participants, an outdoor stage for plays, and a gazebo. We can't produce income if we don't have the space to do it." She had included everything on her wish list. The gazebo was a last-minute thought, in case he wanted to negotiate.

He looked down again.

Grace waited, still holding the piece of paper in her outstretched hand.

He looked up. "Okay," he said. "You deserve all of that."

Was there a note of chagrin in his voice? She hoped so.

He slapped his thighs and stood. "I'll see an attorney and have the paperwork drawn up. I think it's time we name this place. What do you have in mind?"

"I'll discuss that with the others and let you know." She waved the piece of paper with her notes, "Take this."

He took the paper, walked to the door, stopped, and turned. "I want you to stay."

Grace ignored the tenderness in his voice. "Call Natalie. She says that Thomas is in some kind of trouble at school. She wants you to go there."

Nick threw back his head, arms outstretched, and shouted, "Kids!"

His footsteps faded down the hall to trudge up the front staircase one step at a time.

Grace visualized her plan. Ten years from now, there would be weeklong camps in the summer, writing seminars, visiting artists, traditional folk artists, a series of plays, and weekend retreats throughout the fall, winter, and spring.

She and her child would live in the attic, a proper place designed to be warm in the winter and cool in the summer.

John, Loretta, and their child would live in the cottage.

Life would go on without Richard, and Norma would live with Nick until he tired of her, and Sam Cielo would build a house next door, and Grace would never, ever, risk being seen naked in the woods again.

Chapter Eleven

ON THE THIRD FRIDAY morning since his move to Maple Grove, Lois greeted Sam's arrival with, "Mr. McKay has an emergency appointment this afternoon with Mr. Nicholas Mason."

"I thought we had an agreement," Sam said.

"Please, Mr. Cielo." Cracks in Lois's makeup revealed dark circles under her eyes. "Mr. Mason said he only wants to make out a new will. Let me help Stewart with that. I promise, when we've finished with the will, I will leave quietly."

Sam hesitated. Since Ruby wouldn't start for two more weeks, Lois could save him a few hours of secretarial work. "I suppose there would be no harm in that," he said. "But only if I read the final draft."

"Yes, Mr. Cielo. I'll make sure you read the final copy before Mr. Mason signs. Thank you. You are being very kind."

"Let me know if you need anything." Sam knew his voice was gruff. He didn't want to be mean, but he had to be firm with her.

"I will." She smiled revealing a streak of red lipstick on her front teeth.

Sam walked into Stewart's office, picked up the folder with documents regarding the termination of Stewart's practice, sat down behind the desk, and propped his feet up.

The agreement with Lois stated Stewart would provide six months of pay for years of service. By the end of the year, Sam would pay another six months worth of salary to cover Lois until her social security payments kicked in. In exchange, Lois would maintain a sense of decorum in future communication about the McKay family, Sam, and her forced retirement. Lois had no pension and no family to help. At the same time, Sam understood she had managed to pay off the mortgage on her small house. She would be able to survive well enough.

Sam appreciated the role played by Mrs. McKay in negotiations. In a long heart-to-heart, Sam communicated his need for Stewart to bow out of the practice. Sam stated he would be assuming the vacant seat on the school board. Mrs. McKay expressed quiet understanding. She offered the downtown office, rent free, for two years in consideration of the pretense perpetrated by her family. They should have fully disclosed Stewart's condition to Sam before encouraging him to move to Wood Grove.

Mrs. McKay collaborated on the plan for Lois's dismissal, and then suggested that Sam find another place to live. Stewart could be unpredictable at times.

His wife kept Stewart away from the office most days. As far as Sam knew, his old mentor had not yet expressed any thoughts or feelings about learning that the end of his practice had been negotiated by his wife and protégé.

At ten o'clock, Sam left the office. Over his shoulder, he said, "I'll be back in an hour," put his hands in his pockets, and walked three blocks to the doughnut shop. Ruby waited there on the sidewalk.

"I have the key," she said. She opened the door beside the shop windows.

Sam followed her up the worn staircase. The walls were marked with black streaks, evidence of things moved up or down the stairs with little concern for their impact. At the top of the stairs, a hall stretched to the back of the building.

Ruby turned to the first door on the right and inserted a shiny gold key into the tarnished lock. Grime spread out from the knob for about eight inches.

"It's right over the shop," Ruby said. "It always smells like fried dough."

"And that makes it affordable," Sam said.

The door swung open. The efficiency was about what he had anticipated for the price.

Sam walked the perimeter, looking out two windows that faced the street and two that faced the building next door.

As promised, the aroma of glazed sweets permeated every corner.

"Wow," Sam said. "It's so clean in here."

"When Hal heard about your situation, he insisted we look at it first," Ruby said. "Then he insisted we clean it. We were up here until midnight last night."

"You didn't have to do that!" Sam said.

"There were perks." Ruby cocked her head toward the couch.

"Was it broken when you arrived?" Sam asked.

"It was only a kiss!" Ruby said, blushing. "But I'm telling you, he's the one."

Sam put his hand on her shoulder. "I'm happy for you. Please thank Hal for me. After I settle in, I'll have you two over for dinner."

"Hal said his parents have a nice foldout couch they don't need anymore," Ruby said. "They're happy to sell it to you for a good price. Hal and his brothers can deliver it."

Sam hadn't met Hal and already he felt indebted to the man, but the broken couch had to go. "Thanks for finding this place, Ruby."

"Really?" she asked. "It's small, and like I said, the smell."

"I can be happy here," Sam assured her. "That's all that matters." He moved over to the wooden table-for-two and leaned on it with his fingertips. He could see himself working there at night. It reminded him of the small place he'd shared with another law student when he was in school.

"Good!" Ruby said. "I have to get going now. Let me know if you need anything else."

"Just you, at your new desk, two weeks from Monday," Sam said.

"Looking forward to it!"

Sam escorted her out the door. She locked it with the key, which she then handed to Sam.

"Mr. and Mrs. Palmieri, the doughnut shop owners, are your new landlords," she said. "They said you can stay here now, and rent will start the first of May." They descended the steps with Ruby in the lead. "Do you want Hal to exchange the couches?" she asked.

"I hate to put him out, but yes, that would be great." Sam really did hate to accept help from others, but he needed a hand right now.

"No problem," Ruby said. "Hal likes to help. I have to scoot." She waved over her back as she walked away.

Sam shut the door to the stairwell. He disliked going backward even more than accepting help. He worked hard and expected to be able to maintain a tough independence with a steady climb up as a reward for his efforts. The apartment he'd left in Denver had been in a good building with a doorman. This would only be temporary, he promised himself.

Back at the office, Sam spent the rest of the morning combing through bookshelves, boxes, and desk drawers. He found unopened letters from 1959 and what might have been unpaid accounts dating back even further. Overwhelmed with the amount of cleanup required, and amazed no one had lodged complaints about Stewart, Sam decided to focus on one achievable task: the top desk drawer.

There he found a tangle of pencils, pens, paper clips, notes, chewing gum wrappers, half-eaten chocolate bars, and an unused condom. Sam wrapped the last three items in scrap paper and deposited them in the round metal trashcan. He would have liked to dump the entire drawer, but he was on a tight budget, so he separated the contents into organized piles, reviewing his situation.

His first month's rent for the apartment was due in a few weeks. He had enough money to make it through the next six months. After that, he would need a sufficient number of billable hours to cover Ruby's salary, the payments to Lois, and his living expenses. He'd been keeping regular office hours, to establish a routine for himself, and to be available in the unlikely event that an actual client showed up. He was, however, relieved to not be the lead with Mr. Nicholas Mason.

Everyone in town seemed to have an opinion about the people living in the big house next to Sam's property. Ed likened them to the people who generally congregated in places like Paris or New York. Skip referred to them as the products of "reefer madness," but he might not be a reliable informant. Ruby said Nick was a bit of a character, and though the others might seem like serious, career-minded people, she had always avoided them. She'd heard gossip about orgies, in the woods, at night.

Putting the last paper clip in the corresponding pile, Sam thought about Polly Drape's description of Grace Baxter as "driven." Richard, whoever he was, was a lucky man. Perhaps Sam had already met Grace's Richard. The pepper to Grace's salt. If that was the case, Sam hoped Mr. Pepper would be as forgiving as his captivating wife. The last thing Sam needed in town was an enemy.

One thing, however, was certain. At this point, Sam could not afford to risk any kind of real involvement with his future neighbors. The fact that Grace was married was a relief, knowing what he now knew about the community's reputation. He wanted to be on friendly terms, but he needed to be seen as someone with whom clients could entrust the intimate details of their lives. The opinions expressed thus far indicated that many townspeople were not in favor of whatever was going on out there in the house beside his land. Sam needed to steer clear.

He paper-clipped random notes together and put them back in the drawer. He would review all of them later. He threw away the remaining trash and returned the rest of the contents to the drawer, neatly separated, vowing to find something to separate the drawer into sections to maintain order.

Dusting the desk surface with his clean handkerchief, Sam congratulated himself on a job well done.

"One drawer at time, we are going to do this!"

"What's that?" Lois called out.

"Nothing," Sam called back. He rounded the doorframe while pulling on his suit coat. "I'm going out for lunch. Are you sure Mr. McKay will be here for his meeting with Mr. Mason?"

"Oh yes," Lois replied. "I spoke with Mrs. McKay and she assured me he would be here promptly at one fifteen. Mr. Mason is scheduled for two."

Sam opened the door to the street. "I'll be back by one."

AFTER A QUICK LUNCH, Sam returned to the office at twelve forty-five. Mrs. McKay delivered her freshly shaved and cologned spouse at one o'clock. Stewart seemed happy to reign over his office again with no comment about the recent changes. Whether this was by choice or because Stewart couldn't comprehend the changes that had occurred, Sam was grateful for the ease of the transition, thus far.

Lois doted over her boss, first running out for coffee, then appearing at the door every ten minutes, to ask, "Can I bring you anything?"

Stewart's mood was magnanimous: "No, my dear. But thank you for asking."

Sam listened to the same stories, with the same inflections, that he had heard countless times. Patience, he reminded himself. This will all end soon. Stewart deserved respect. He should end his career with as much dignity as possible.

By the time Nicholas Mason arrived, at two-thirty, Stewart was starting to fade. He seemed disoriented, having addressed Sam as "Skip" at one point and then asking, "What is it you're here for, son?"

When Lois directed Mr. Mason to the only seat in Stewart's office, Sam pulled another chair in from the reception area.

Lois's eyes lit up. "Will I be in attendance?"

"No," Sam said. "I will. Thank you very much. That will be all."

The look on her face indicated she understood his meaning. She was no longer needed. She retreated to her desk as Sam shut the door on the furious clacking of typewriter keys.

Sam turned back toward the business at hand, astonished to witness the incredible reawakening of Stewart McKay.

"Mr. Mason." Stewart stood and shook his client's hand. "Please be seated. This is my associate, Sam Cielo. He will be sitting in today. I understand you are in the market to update your will." And he was off. Stewart didn't skip a beat during the preliminaries. Like a well-rehearsed song, he sang every note to perfection. He laid out the basics of what must be included in a will, defined terms, and cautioned Mason to choose wisely in naming his beneficiaries.

Thus Sam observed the confounding shift in abilities that Mrs. McKay had described to him. "One minute he's completely out of it. The next minute he's as sharp as he's ever been," she had said. Sam hadn't believed her, but now that he'd seen it himself, he began to feel a new level of compassion regarding how difficult this must be for her, and for Lois.

Nicholas Mason seemed distracted, at one point taking a pen from his pocket and rolling it between his fingers, avoiding eye contact with the older man who was doing a fine job of providing sound legal advice.

Sam detected an herbal smell emanating from Mr. Mason's clothing, something not altogether unknown, and then he remembered. Some young attorneys at a New Year's Eve party, on the penthouse balcony of the firm's owner, passing a roughly rolled cigarette and offering it to Sam. His one experience with marijuana. It had made him feel good. A little lightheaded. On this point, Skip had been correct. Nicholas Mason smoked reefer.

Stewart finished explaining the basics and asked, “Do you have any questions?”

“I’ve been through this before,” Mason answered.

Sam found him impertinent. Stewart only smiled.

“The thing is,” Mason said, “Grace, my *manager*, is in a pickle, which is what she’ll probably crave soon.” He snorted a laugh. “Found out she’s pregnant and her husband wants a divorce.” He shook his head. “Kids. They tend to make life difficult.”

“Why is he divorcing her?” Sam asked.

“Hardly relevant, Sam,” Stewart said and frowned at Sam.

“Of course,” Sam said. He sat back. “I apologize.” What kind of mess had Grace managed to get herself into?

“Write up the will so that Grace inherits the house and surrounding five acres,” Mason said. “Leave the rest of the land and my estate to my son, Thomas. In the event of his death, it goes to my ex-wife, Natalie.”

“And in the event of Grace’s death?” Stewart asked.

“Oh, she won’t die before me.” Mason laughed. “She’s far too organized to do that.” He stood.

Sam rose from his chair. He wanted to take Mason outside and pummel him. How dare he make light of what must be a very difficult time for Grace.

“Fine, fine,” Stewart said. “But we’ll need names, addresses, identifying information for all of your holdings, deeds, et cetera.”

“Right,” Mason said. He rubbed his cheek. “I can’t very well ask Grace to supply that. She wants me to leave the house to some silly foundation.” He seemed to deliberate. “I’ll tell you what. I’ll give you the name of my cousin in Chicago. He manages my money and he hates my ex, so no worries about him telling her anything. He’ll give you all of that information. Are we done now?”

“Yes,” Stewart stood and shook Mason’s hand. “Thank you for coming in. Give that contact information to Lois and as soon as we receive what we need, we'll complete the necessary documents and call you back in to sign."

"Yeah, great." Mason slapped Sam on the shoulder on the way out the door. "Thanks, man."

After he heard the front door open and close, Sam went to the window and pulled down a blind slat with one finger. He watched Mason climb into a car and pull out into the street, nearly colliding with another car that screeched to a stop. Mason drove on as if he hadn't noticed.

Sam thought about the first time he'd seen Grace at the lunch counter. She was beautiful, hopeful, and bold. Now she was pregnant, soon-to-be single, and under the thumb of someone as thoughtless as Nicholas Mason. Even wonderful people could make complete messes out of their lives. Sam dropped the blind slat and looked down at the floor.

On the one hand, he wanted to help. On the other hand, he was happy to not be involved.

Given the complexity and uncertainty of his own situation, Sam would steer clear. He couldn't risk his own future on someone with a checkered past. He needed someone the town could see as unblemished, though it pained him to not be the one to save Grace from her mistakes.

He did like her.

Chapter Twelve

SARAH'S BREAKFAST TABLE sat in a nook overlooking the backyard. Grace stared out the window. A white privacy fence enclosed an oasis of masterful gardening in the midst of the historic urban neighborhood. Flower beds, laid out with precision, were immaculate. Red tulips and white narcissus bloomed, their sunny centers glowing.

"Does it kick?" Sarah asked. She tapped her fingernail on the side of her coffee mug.

"Not yet," Grace answered. "It's probably the size of peanut."

When Grace had called to tell her sister about the baby, Sarah cried. She'd always wanted a baby but hadn't been fortunate in that way. Grace knew her pregnancy provided what Sarah craved more than anything, a chance to feel like her future would extend beyond her death, a legacy of love.

Sarah promised to help in any way possible. Could she host a baby shower? Maybe two? One in Wood Grove and one in Columbus? Would Grace feel okay about a trust for the child? Something to ensure their ability to attend college and maybe a little more than that? Sarah's perspective seemed to be that Grace was having this baby for both of them. Grace wouldn't argue with that.

"Where are you, Grace?" Sarah put her cup down. "Earth to Grace," she sang.

"I'm okay."

Sarah placed her hands on top of Grace's. "You're more than okay. You're going to have a baby. The next year will be the most important year of your life, because you will be giving life to a brand-new human being. Mommy and Daddy would have loved this."

"I never thought I'd be doing this alone," Grace said.

"You're not alone. You have me, and Loretta. I want you to come and stay with us for the last month. Please. Let me take care of you."

"I'll think about it." Grace stood and took her cup to the sink.

"We have better hospitals here in Columbus," Sarah said.

"That's a selling point." Grace returned to the table and slipped her purse strap over her shoulder. "Thanks for being happy for me."

"Of course I am." Sarah accompanied Grace to the front door. "Call me when you get home."

"I will." Grace hugged her sister and trudged to Nick's car, dreading her next stop.

With light traffic, the drive took less than twenty minutes. She parked close to the curb, walked up the sidewalk, and entered the building. Their apartment was on the bottom floor, letter A. The mailbox door hung open, the glue on the door still visible from the label that used to be there: *Richard Baxter & Grace Baxter*. She used her key to unlock the apartment door and stepped in.

In the six weeks since accepting the promotion, Richard had wasted no time in finding a place to live in New Jersey. He cleared their apartment and packed her belongings before she'd had a chance to do it herself, which she would have preferred, but maybe this was better, like ripping off a Band-Aid.

Two boxes marked "Grace" sat by the door. Her furniture had been loaded onto a truck and would be delivered in a few days. Grace walked to the bedroom remembering the last time she had slept there with Richard, not realizing then that it would be their final time together.

She heard the door to the apartment open and returned to the living room.

Richard stood in the doorway, his hand still on the knob, his face tired.

"What do you need to talk about?" he asked.

She wanted to go to him, wrap her arms around him, give him the news with joy. Instead, she stood across the room and stated the fact of the matter.

"I'm pregnant."

"You're what?" His eyes opened wide.

"Pregnant," she said, again.

"Oh my God, Grace." He let go of the doorknob and brought his hand to his head. "I'm leaving this afternoon and you pick now to tell me that? How long have you known?"

She leaned against the bedroom doorframe. "What difference does it make?"

"Christ!" he sputtered and walked to the kitchen area, increasing the distance between them. "So are you coming to New Jersey with me now?" He leaned back on the counter, crossing his arms, covering his heart.

She almost smiled, tempted to point out the contradiction between the question and the manner in which it was asked, but she didn't want to fight with him. She didn't want to beg, or ask for support, or even care anymore. She wasn't cruel enough to keep his child a secret, but she had managed, with great and ongoing effort, to close her heart to him.

"I'm not staying," he said.

"I know that." Her voice was calm.

"What are we going to do?" he asked.

"You're going to New Jersey."

"And what about the baby?" He sounded desperate. She decided, again, to not care.

"I'm going to visit your mother as often as I can," Grace said, "so that she can know her grandchild and our child will have a connection to your family."

"What about me?"

"You will come back three or four times a year to visit until she, or he, is old enough to be with you, without me. At that point, I want you to be a more active parent. New Jersey in the summer. Ohio in the fall, winter, and spring. That's what we're going to do."

"Jesus." He looked down, rocking his head back and forth slowly.

She pushed herself off the doorframe, walked to him, and held out her right hand. "Agreed?"

He looked up, tears in his eyes, and pulled her into his chest, sobbing.

She melted against him, unable to escape the sea of sadness surging over her.

"I'm so sorry," he said over and over.

Mute, she could not only not console him, but lost all control herself, soaking the front of his shirt with her own tears.

When they parted, Grace rolled away from his body and leaned against the counter beside him, but not touching. They were silent for a long time, letting the separation sink in once again.

Grace spoke first. "I can't go to New Jersey. I have to stay here and finish what I started."

"The baby has to have a father," Richard said. "We can stay married."

"Either way, the baby's last name will be Baxter," she said.

"Yeah," Richard said, one harsh puff of air through his nose acknowledging sad amusement.

"You have to go." She pushed him away with a light shove.

"Yeah." He nudged himself off the counter.

She watched him walk to the door.

"I'll be in touch," he said.

"I know," she said.

BY THE TIME SHE ARRIVED back in Wood Grove, Grace had contained the sadness with thoughts of how the community could move forward. Nick had promised a solid future and that firmed up Grace's sense of her place in the present.

She carried the boxes into the house and placed them on her bed. As she started to open the first one, Nick appeared in her doorway.

"You have to find a part in the Solstice play for Norma," he said.

Grace looked back down at the box and pulled it open. "I told you yesterday, the play has been cast. There are no available parts."

"Change the play," he said.

"Fran is in charge."

"She'll listen to you."

"We're only a month away from the performance, Nick. You know how hard it is to get everybody here at the same time. We have rehearsal dates." She pulled out a stack of clothing and placed it on her bed.

"Include Norma, Grace. She's feeling very left out." His voice was stern now.

Grace looked at Nick. He stood in the doorway, frowning.

"Okay," she said and turned back to the box, removing some paperbacks. "I'll figure something out."

She heard Nick cross the room. He hugged her sideways, briefly, around the shoulders.

When he released her, she turned to him, and sniffed. "What's that smell?"

He grinned.

She turned back to the box.

"Norma likes it," he said. "She brought some with her. She says we can probably grow it around here."

"Absolutely, not," Grace said, without looking up. "No plants, no smoking in the house, and no driving while high." She would never tolerate anyone choosing to drive while impaired.

Nick hugged her again. "Okay, Sister Mary Grace of Order and Propriety."

She ignored him as he walked to the door. "Shut it, please," she said.

After the door latched, she turned and flopped down on the bed, her elbow hitting the stack of books beside her. She picked one up, remembering that she bought them at Wood Grove's used bookstore a few years back, something to read on her weekends in Columbus. She'd never had time to follow through with that plan. Opening the cover on Persuasion, she saw a large red heart framing a familiar name, *Sam Cielo.* Grace smiled. What a funny coincidence. She wondered who had written it.

AT LUNCH, GRACE SEATED herself at the far end of the table, opposite Nick. John told Nick about the progress he and Max had made on the new studio. Fran quizzed Elizabeth about details related to her dance career. Polly talked about her meetings with the new attorney in town. He'd agreed to take the open seat on the school board. Polly liked him, found him to be easygoing and like-minded. Grace wondered if Polly would also find him attractive. Who wouldn't?

A voice rose above the others. "You're mighty quiet down there."

Grace looked up at Norma. She sat on Nick's right, the seat formerly occupied by Grace.

"I thought you were the one in charge around here," Norma said. She brought a spoonful of soup to her mouth and held it there as she said, "The rule-maker. Sister Mary Grace of the Order to Maintain Proper-iety." She turned her eyes to Nick, grinning. He looked at Norma and frowned, shaking his head almost imperceptibly.

The other conversations died down. Grace took her napkin from her lap and put it on her plate. "That was delicious, Loretta. Thank you so much for another wonderful meal." She stood and picked up her plate. With the exaggerated friendliness she had learned over the years from her phone calls with Natalie, she asked, "Do you like the food here, Norma? Because we can always change the menu to suit your tastes."

Norma had already put the soup in her mouth. "Mm hm." She swallowed rapidly. "It's good."

Grace took her dishes to the kitchen, returned to her room, and opened the Austen book.

Thirty minutes later, a tentative knock interrupted her reading.

"Grace?" Nick called. "Are you awake?"

She walked to the door and pulled it open.

"I thought you might be sleeping," Nick said. "Natalie took naps when she was pregnant."

"What do you want, Nick?" Grace asked.

"We want you to come out to the dining room. We've been talking about a name for the community."

"You discussed that without me?" She would have used the word perturbed, if anyone had asked how she felt.

"We've come up with some ideas and landed on one that seems like the right choice. I mean, I like it. Will you come out?"

Grace laid the book on her bed and followed Nick across the hall.

Before opening the door to the dining room, he turned and said, "I thought Norma was a little out of line at lunch."

"She was only quoting you," Grace said.

"She's young. She will learn to not do that."

Grace shook her head and chuckled. How could Nick do that to her? He could be so darned annoying and inappropriate, but then say something that made her laugh. As she followed him into the dining room, she considered the benefits of loving him from a distance. He came off much better when viewed at arm's length.

The dishes had been cleared, but the seats were still full. Fran waved Grace to the head of the table. Nick sat to her right. Norma had been demoted to the far end of the table. She sat with a pouty look on her face, sipping from a cup she cradled in her hands, one knee drawn up to her chest. Her full skirt lay draped in such a way that her long, sculpted legs were bared.

"We came up with a list of ten possibilities," Nick said.

"Nine," Peter said.

"I thought there were eleven," Elizabeth piped up.

"Does it really matter?" Max asked.

"Oh for God's sake." Fran threw a wadded-up napkin at Peter and clipped his nose. "You all drive me nuts!"

"Nice shot!" Nick said.

Fran stood. "I'm running this meeting now. Grace?" She turned to the head of the table. "We deliberated long and hard."

"I was in my room for thirty minutes," Grace said.

Loretta shushed Grace. "If you don't let them finish, we'll be in here all night."

"Grace," Fran began again. "Before we move on to the naming of the community, we want you to know that we are all fully aware of your situation."

Grace had not expected this. She fidgeted in her seat.

"We know that Richard is moving to New Jersey, and we know that you are going to have a baby."

Grace glared at Nick. "I would have told them myself."

"I thought they should be aware," Nick said.

Fran continued. "Peter and I have never been inclined toward children. Max and Elizabeth have no interest, either. Polly says she would, perhaps, someday. You know John and Loretta are expecting, too, so great timing, you three!"

"Ole!" Nick shouted.

Leave it to him to turn the announcement of their pregnancies into a bullfight.

"We want you to know we only want you to be happy, but we're happy you decided to stay with us. We will help with your child in any way that we can." Fran's words were heartfelt. She had tears in her eyes.

Grace looked at each person around the table, passing over Norma. But for the newest one, they were welcoming, safe. Emotions surged. She wiggled her foot. She did not want to cry. "Thanks. I'm glad I'm staying, too."

"And now!" Nick jumped up. "Sit down, Fran. That was lovely, but we have an announcement to make! Drumroll, John."

John tapped out a drumroll with his fingers on the edge of the table.

"Peter?" Nick opened his arm toward Pete.

Pete stood and unrolled a banner of paper, four feet long, stretching it between his fingers. In large, ornate, black crayon-drawn letters, "GraceHaven" spread from one end to the other.

"GraceHaven?" Grace asked.

"It's perfect!" Nick said.

"It sounds very Christian," Grace said.

"Exactly!" Norma said. "That's what I think."

Grace ignored her.

"Why not ArtHaven?" Grace asked.

"I like that," Norma said. "ArtHaven makes much more sense."

Grace again ignored her. "GraceHaven. It's not about me, is it?"

"Of course not!" Nick said. "If it were about a person, I would have suggested NickHaven, but what the heck would that mean? Think about it. Elvis has his Graceland. I have my GraceHaven."

"You're not Elvis, Nick." Grace said.

"He's the Elvis of the literary world," Norma cooed.

Bile rose from Grace's stomach. She swallowed hard. "Let me think about it."

Norma uncurled her body and pushed herself off the chair. "I don't need to think about it." She moved around the table to Nick's chair and hugged him from behind. "It's awful. The only thing you're going to attract with a name like that is a bunch of tired old women looking for some afternoon embroidery sessions while studying their scripture."

Grace looked at the sign again. Norma hated the name. "GraceHaven," Grace said. "I accept."

"Hurrah!" Nick shouted. "Break out the champagne!" He moved away from Norma and headed to the door to the kitchen.

Norma began to move toward the door to the hallway.

"Stay to celebrate," Loretta called to her.

The younger woman turned, a wisp of vulnerability quickly vanishing from her face, replaced by her usual outer shell of self-possession.

"Take Nick's chair," Grace said. "He'll be too busy pouring to sit."

Norma returned, lowering herself into the chair as if it were a throne.

Loretta nodded "well done" at Grace.

Had she been asked, Grace would not have agreed to Norma's presence in their community at all. But since she seemed to be staying, Grace would do everything possible to embrace her presence, including a part in the Solstice play.

Theirs would not be a community of exclusion. GraceHaven would be a model for moving forward, through creativity, to end the ways in which groups and individuals were divided, no matter how difficult. Richard would not be a part of her future, but she had one. And at the moment, surveying the people who sat around the table, her future looked pretty good.

Chapter Thirteen
1975

NICK ASKED GRACE TO JOIN him in the living room and she had no reason to deny the request. She followed him to the new sofa and plopped down on the cushion.

"I'm fifty-five years old, Grace," he said. "I need to settle down." Nick lowered himself to the couch. "Norma wants to move out of our room and live in the dorm, with Grant. She and I have been together for an eternity."

"It's only been thirteen years, Nick," Grace said. "Hardly an eternity."

"Nearly as long as my marriage!" Nick said.

Grace stared up at the stained glass. Even after twenty years, her eyes still found new paths to follow in the lines of the lead and fresh appreciation for the swirls and bubbles in each piece of glass.

"I'm floored; never saw it coming." He sighed.

"That must hurt," Grace said. What could she say? Everyone else had seen the way Norma looked at Grant. Why hadn't Nick?

"Thomas wrote," Nick said. He forced most of the heaviness in his voice, forever the king of drama. "He wants to stop by with his kids and visit when they drive through to Washington DC this summer."

"How old are they now?" Grace asked.

"Melissa is eleven, Mark ten, and little Mallory is seven, I think. They're growing up and I barely know them. My own grandchildren, Grace, and I barely know them," he paused, "or my son, for that matter."

In the past, she would have consoled him, but not anymore. It was about time he faced the truth.

"Ah, Grace," Nick sighed more deeply.

She hoisted herself off the couch and held out her hands. "Come on, old man. Let's go eat breakfast."

He put his hands into hers. She had to dig in with her heels, but managed to stay upright as he made a show of barely being able to move. When he finally stood, she tried to drop his hands, but he held tight.

"Why didn't we end up together?" He looked at her with the expression commonly displayed with ads for charitable giving. "We would have been a fabulous couple. Is it too late for us?"

She laughed, squeezing his hands before releasing them. "You always feel better after you eat."

He followed her toward the dining room. When the phone rang, she said, "Go on. I'll be in shortly."

She left him without looking back, crossed the hall, and entered her newly decorated office. For the first years of her son's life, he and Grace had shared this as a bedroom in addition to office space. When Teddy turned six, she allowed him to move out to the cottage to share a room with John and Loretta's son, Stephen. For another six years, the room with the bay window had returned to being her private bedroom and the community office.

Now she luxuriated in the space around her, large enough to spread her arms and dance across the floor, which she'd done every single day since moving her bed to the third floor. She'd finally let go of the plan for a complete renovation up there. The corner she'd carved out for herself would do.

A breeze lifted the lace curtains in the window. The air promised rain.

"How's our Teddy?" Sarah asked before saying, "Hello."

"He wants to be an astronaut," Grace answered. "How was Australia?" She picked dead leaves off a hanging spider plant and laid them in a neat pile on the window seat.

"I liked New Zealand better. Tell me more about Teddy."

"He's good." Grace moved on to the ficus. "No growth spurt yet. He's still the shortest boy in his class. He and Stephen both finished seventh grade with high honors."

"That's my boy," Sarah said. "He's going to be a doctor some day. Or an engineer."

"He's going to be whatever he wants to be." Dusty memories of Sarah's disappointment about Grace's choices lingered. She would spare her son as much of that as she could.

"Trust me, Grace. He'll want to be a doctor or an engineer. And Stephen's parents? Loretta and John are good, too?"

"They're good, but you'd know that if you came to visit once in a while."

"I don't like driving down there by myself," Sarah said.

And yet her sister expected Grace to make the trip at least once a week. Sarah could be a bit of a diva. "Nick proposed again, sort of."

"You're kidding," Sarah said.

"Honestly, I'm worried about him," Grace said. "He's been so glum and now Norma wants to move in with Grant."

"You saw that coming," Sarah said. "Is she still giving you as much trouble?"

"She is what she is," Grace said. "I think she's seen me as competition in a game I don't play. Maybe she'll get over that some day."

"Or maybe not," Sarah said. "As long it doesn't bother you, who cares? My therapist always tells me to go with the flow."

"Whatever that means," Grace muttered under her breath. She'd be more than willing to not fight the current, as long as it flowed in a direction that made sense for everybody. She'd had to build more than one dam to control the flood of Norma's grandiose ideas. Having her housed in another building, away from Nick, would be a blessing.

"Everything else is going well?" Sarah asked.

"All good. Arthur and Ben have settled in."

"Arthur is the writer, tall, distinguished-looking, and Ben's the actor," Sarah said. "He sounds British."

"He's from Connecticut," Grace said. "They seem to be a good fit here."

"Any changes out in the dorm?" Sarah asked.

"Nope," Grace answered. "Fran and Peter are still out there with Max and Elizabeth, and Polly. After Norma moves in with Grant, the bottom floor will be filled, unless Polly wants a roommate."

"What does Grant do, again? His voice is sexy, like Sam Elliot."

"Grant is an administrator for a council that funds art programs in the state."

"You have a full house!" Sarah said. "If anybody else wants to move in, they'll have to live on the dorm's second floor."

"We save that for guests," Grace said.

With the third-floor project now abandoned, only the outdoor stage remained to be built. Nick had held up his end of their plan. GraceHaven had come to life.

"Our upcoming programs center primarily on women's issues," Grace said. "Consciousness-raising, assertiveness, self-defense, and, of course, art. Next month we're hosting a workshop on the writings of Mary Daly and Alice Walker. Have you read them?"

"No," her sister said. "Do any of those programs have you looking at your vagina in a mirror?"

Grace laughed. "I read about that. Would you like me to arrange something themed in that direction?" She sat in her desk chair.

"No, God no, thanks for the offer, but no." Sarah fell silent. Grace waited, comfortable with the quiet connection. Finally, Sarah said, "I'm proud of you, Grace, really proud."

"Thanks, Sarah." Grace leaned back in her chair and put her feet up on her desk. "How are things with you?"

"We're okay." Sarah's voice caught and went silent again.

Her sister's hesitation frightened Grace. "What's going on?"

Sarah's exhale was audible. "I guess I might as well tell you now. We've actually been back for a few weeks. Remember I told you that Donald's been feeling tired? It's cancer, Grace. It's bad."

"I'm so sorry," Grace said. She knew she should feel more concern for Donald, but her thoughts stayed with Sarah. "How are you?"

"I'm okay," Sarah said. "I haven't had any anxiety medication for months and I don't even feel like I need it."

"What can I do to help?" Grace asked.

"Be ready to help when I need you. Take care of Teddy. You two are my only family, other than Donald."

"We'll be there for you," Grace assured her.

"Mom!"

Grace put her hand over the receiver and called out, "I'm in my office."

Teddy rounded the corner, catching the doorframe with a dirt-covered hand. He walked rapidly to her chair and stood at attention in front of her. "I think I'm in trouble." His chubby, light brown face grimaced.

"I'm sorry, Sarah. I Can I call back later? Teddy needs me."

"No problem. I'll be fine. Kiss Teddy for me."

After she said goodbye and hung up the phone, Grace reached out to brush soft brown curls from her son's eyes. "What did you do?" Folding her hands in her lap, she listened.

"It was Stephen's idea," he said, looked at the floor, and started again. "Okay, it was my idea." He had never been able to lie, even as a toddler, when it would have been developmentally appropriate, according to the books she'd read.

"We were hanging out in the woods," he said. "And we decided... I suggested... that we explore the gardens next door." His little voice remained musical, though soon, she knew, he would shoot up in height, down in vocal depth.

"On Mr. Cielo's property," she said.

"Yes," he confirmed.

"I told you to never go over there." Sam had been cordial, but not inviting. Though he'd lived next door for seven years now, she'd never been in his house. But she'd seen enough from the road to guess he probably wouldn't welcome uninvited guests, especially those prone to throwing balls that might break ceramic patio pots or hanging bird feeders.

"I know, Mom, and I'm sorry, I really am, but the thing is, there were these berries, and they looked so good, and there were so many, and we, I, didn't think he would notice a few missing. But he came home as we were leaving, and he yelled, and we dropped the berries and ran. I'm sure he's going to call the sheriff or something." His voice faded and he stood with his head still down, eyes on the floor.

"You wouldn't have seen the berries and been tempted if you hadn't been where you were told not to go," Grace said.

"I know, Mom." A tear ran down his cheek.

"Thanks for telling me. I suppose I have to go talk to Loretta and John about this. Have you finished your homework?"

"No, ma'am."

Loretta had taught him to talk like that.

"Go get some lunch. As soon as you're done eating, take a bath and do your homework. I expect you to apologize to Mr. Cielo and do a few hours of work for him, to make up for the loss of his berries. Agreed?"

"Yes, ma'am." He raised his head and looked in her eyes. "You're not mad at me?"

“Teddy, everybody makes mistakes. The important thing is to learn from them. What did you learn today?”

“To not go into Mr. Cielo’s yard,” he lowered his head again.

“And what else?”

“To not steal berries.”

“And?”

“And to listen to my mother.”

“Go wash your hands and eat.” She pulled her son in and hugged him, breathing the scent of the woods in his hair. He would fly to New Jersey in a little over a week. She would miss him terribly, as she did every summer.

“I love you, Mommy.” He squeezed her tight.

“I love you, Cowboy. Now, scoot.”

He let go and ran out the door.

Grace flipped through her Rolodex for Sam’s number.

Contrary to Grace’s expectation of needing to calm her offended neighbor, Sam laughed and extended an invitation for dinner on his patio to talk about the incident. Grace agreed, her heart pounding.

The impact of that man defied reason. He and she were so different.

“DINNER? HE INVITED you for dinner?” Loretta asked.

“To talk about the berries,” Grace said.

They stood together on the cottage porch. After telling Loretta about Sarah’s news, Grace had communicated Teddy’s confession and her thoughts about an appropriate response. Loretta had agreed that whatever Grace worked out for Teddy would apply to Stephen, as well.

“So, dinner?” Loretta asked.

“Stop looking at me like that,” Grace said. “It’s not a date.” She had once made a confession of her own regarding her attraction to Sam Cielo. Perhaps she should have kept that to herself.

"My boy was there, too, and Sam didn't invite me over for dinner." Loretta's eyes twinkled. "What are you wearing?" She pulled Grace down to the porch swing.

"I don't know. What do you think I should wear?" Grace looked down at her bare feet. What did one wear to a meal on the patio to discuss such matters?

"Honey," Loretta paused, crossing her arms, and sitting back on the swing. "If you don't know what to wear, it's a date."

Grace's tummy fluttered. "It's not a date," she declared. No point in expecting this to be more than a neighborly invite. "Can Teddy stay with you this evening?"

"He can spend the night if you like." Loretta teased.

Folding her arms and retreating into the corner of the swing, Grace pretended not to hear. Loretta powered the swing with tiny rhythmic plantar-to-porch pushes. They rocked together without talking, bird and insect songs filling the air. Slowly Grace's leg unwound, her foot finding Loretta's lap for a massage.

After twenty minutes of bliss, Grace pushed herself out of the swing. "I could stay here all day, but I've got work to do."

"I'm sorry about Sarah's husband," Loretta said. "Tell her I'm praying for him, for both of them."

"I will." Grace waved as she left the porch.

"Have fun on your date!" Loretta called.

Grace ignored her.

SHE HAD AGREED TO BE at his house at five o'clock. He said he would serve dinner at five-thirty, allowing time for berry-theft talk before eating. She started dressing at three. After pulling every single piece of clothing she owned from the oak armoire and holding it up to herself in the mirror, she finally admitted out loud, "I think I have a date with Sam Cielo."

None of her clothes would do. Grace descended the two staircases as quickly as possible and headed to the dorm to see Fran, who, though a few sizes larger, chose fashions that would accommodate a smaller figure. She welcomed Grace into the efficiency she shared with Peter.

"Of course you can borrow something," Fran said. She rolled open the closet and started pushing through her apparel. "Not this, or this, or this, or this."

"Anything, really," Grace said. "Don't pick something too new. I'll feel horrible if I stain it."

"Nonsense," Fran said. "Everything can be washed these days. How about this?" She laid out a full black skirt and a black blouse with three-quarter length sleeves. "The skirt is long on me, but I think it'll hit you about mid-calf."

"Nice." Grace touched one of the colorful mandalas printed on the skirt.

"With these?" Fran added an array of silver chains that would lie under the collar, looping above Grace's bustline.

"Perfect! I have black tights and a teal shawl. Thank you, Fran." She hugged the shorter, rounder woman. "I owe you."

"Oh, Grace." Fran shook her head. "You do so much for us. Don't worry about it. Have a good night."

Back in her room, Grace brushed out her hair and clipped it away from her face. The length fanned around her shoulders, more brown than blonde now, but not sporting gray yet. Being thirty-nine, she checked often.

At ten to five, she left the house and walked down the driveway. The perennial beds under the large, carved sign for GraceHaven needed weeding. She would enjoy doing that some morning. The walk to Sam's took less than two minutes.

He greeted her at the front door with, "Welcome! You're right on time." He wore an apron, blue, like his eyes, and complimented Grace on her appearance.

“Thanks,” she said. She should dress like this more often. No wonder Sarah spent so much time shopping. Something other than jeans felt good.

Sam led her down a hallway, toward the back of the house. Through the doors on the right, she could see a living room that turned into a dining room at the end closest to the kitchen. Everything appeared to be light and inviting, not the dark paneled interior she had expected.

“Have a seat.” He waved her over to the table in the kitchen. While he finished prepping the salad, they talked about the strawberry theft.

“I want Teddy and Stephen to provide some kind of service to make up for what they picked.”

“Don’t worry about it,” Sam said. “Boys will be boys. Sounds like they learned their lesson.”

“I insist,” Grace said. “They will be over to apologize and offer some kind of manual labor to reinforce the lesson learned.”

“Okay, I’ll sentence them to a community service project.” Sam grinned as he reached behind his back to untie the apron. “Dinner’s ready. Would you like to eat here, in the dining room, or on the patio, as promised?”

“Here is fine,” Grace answered, happy with the way he put her at ease.

He served the salad. She noticed large sprigs of cilantro right away, but smiled and thanked him. He sat across from her and said, “Bon appetite.”

Gray strands streaked his hair. He smiled at her. She looked down at her salad. How would she navigate around the one herb she detested? Might as well get it over with. After the first few bites, she could almost forget the cilantro made all of the green, red, and orange vegetable bits taste like soap suds.

“How are things going at GraceHaven?” Sam asked.

“All is well,” Grace said. She described the upcoming programs.

Sam sat back in his chair. “Remember the first time we met?”

"I remember," she said. "You told me to finish college."

"I did?" he asked. "You've done well without a degree."

"Some days I wish I'd finished." She had acknowledged this to herself many times, but she'd never spoken of it to anyone else. She wondered if the motivation to say it out loud now was for her own benefit, or if she said it to please Sam.

When she asked about him, Sam said his was a rather dull story and she had probably learned about most of it through what was easily seen. He worked all the time. He hoped to retire someday to something a bit more creative.

That interested her and they talked about his literary preferences and his appreciation for visual art and theater. Grace learned they had much in common.

"Would you consider taking a part in one of our plays?" she asked.

He laughed and said, "No."

At the end of the meal, she offered to help clean up.

"No need for that," Sam said. "I unwind at the end of the day by tidying up."

"I need to get back," Grace said, because she couldn't think of a reason to stay.

Sam walked her to the front door. "It's late. I'll walk you home."

"I can walk alone in the dark." She wanted to retract the defensive tone.

"I'm sorry," he said. "I didn't mean to imply that you needed an escort."

He was too nice. Grace felt like a jerk. She held out her hand. "Thanks for dinner, Sam. We'll send Teddy and Stephen over next Saturday morning."

She had made it down the front steps when he said, "Grace."

She stopped and turned around.

"I really enjoyed being with you. Can we do this again, maybe next Saturday night?"

Yes! her whole self sang out. "Um, sure," she said. "What time?"

"I'll pick you up at six. Dinner and movie?"

"See you then." She turned and continued walking toward the road, a maniacal grin taking control of her lips.

She wanted to turn cartwheels and leap into a grand jeté, but forced her feet to stay on the ground and her legs to move at a moderate pace, wondering if he was still there.

At the end of the drive, she turned left and looked back.

Sam waved from the door.

Grace waved back.

She couldn't wait to tell Loretta. She had a date. A real date, with Sam Cielo.

Chapter Fourteen

SAM WALKED TO WORK on Monday morning. He hadn't felt this good in years. As he passed the doughnut shop, he remembered his years in the apartment above, saving every penny as he worked on a design for his home. At the same time, he'd rediscovered a passion for writing, publishing articles in law journals and popular magazines. Loneliness had never been a problem. Once Stewart left the practice, the townspeople embraced Sam with unexpected warmth. His life was good, and now he had a chance to get to know Grace better. What were his reasons for not being friendlier with her? He couldn't remember.

"Good Monday morning, Ruby." Sam took off his hat and shut the door behind him.

"Nice running into you at the theater in Chillicothe on Saturday night." Ruby grinned.

Sam sat across from her desk while he unbuttoned his jacket. "Spit it out, Ruby. Not that you need encouragement."

"I've never seen Grace Baxter appear to be so relaxed and happy. Usually she's all business." Ruby began talking like a robot. "Straight to the point, no nonsense, get the job done, and go."

"We had a good time," he said. "She's not like that at all." He stood, shed the jacket, hung it on the wooden rack by the front door, and extracted a newspaper from the pocket.

"Are you going to see her again?" Ruby asked.

"Yes," he answered. "Any changes to the schedule today?"

"No, sir," Ruby looked down at her desk calendar. "No cancellations, business as usual."

"Any word from that writer's conference in Vermont?"

"The one that asked you to lecture on—" she looked down at a note written in the margin of her calendar "—Not Sounding Like a Complete Idiot When You're Writing about Legal Matters in Popular Fiction? They called Friday afternoon to confirm receipt of your agreement to present and, yes, you may have table space to distribute brochures and business cards."

"Good!" Sam smiled. "I like Vermont. Sounds like a working vacation." He moved toward his office.

"Maybe you could invite Grace to go with you," Ruby said.

"Nice idea. Maybe I will." He walked into his office and shut the door.

Before he could take two steps toward his desk, the door opened. "Are you serious?" Ruby asked. "Do you like her that much?"

Sam turned and assumed his usual stance for these early morning check-ins, leaning back against his desk, legs crossed at the ankles, arms folded. "You sound surprised. Would me liking-her-that-much be a problem?"

Ruby assumed her usual stance, leaning on the doorframe of Sam's office, a thoughtful expression coming over her face. "She's so different from anybody you've dated in the past."

"Maybe that's what I like about her." He uncrossed his legs and moved around to the other side of the desk, signaling the end to this part of their morning routine. "Do I have your permission to continue to date her so I can see for myself how much I like her?"

"You have my permission to date anybody you like." She smiled and a dreaminess came into her eyes as she turned them upward. "Date them all until you find the one you like best. I am so lucky I found Hal when we were young enough to have a family." She looked back at Sam, "But it's not too late for you. You can still find your Hal."

"I don't want a Hal, Ruby," he said. "Right now, I only want to get to know Grace Baxter."

Ruby pushed herself off the doorframe. "And I only want you to find the right person. That's what I tell my boys. Date whoever you want, but save the good stuff for the one you want to keep forever. Hal and I were both virgins when we got married."

"I think Grace and I have both moved beyond that milestone," Sam said.

"I know that, Sam. I'm only saying, save something for the forever one. And hurry up! You're not getting any younger."

"Close the door, Ruby," Sam said, adding, "Please."

She tossed one more knowing glance before shutting the door.

Sam settled into the newspaper, reading about how Gerald Ford had tripped on some stairs. The article was written as if this might be the defining moment of Ford's career. Ruby didn't see Grace as the one for Sam, but she wouldn't come down too hard on him for dating the woman. Would others in town be as kind? GraceHaven had a questionable reputation. And though Sam's reputation was solid, the mercurial nature of public sentiment required vigilance. Sam didn't want his defining moment to be based on something as silly as who he dated, but like Gerald Ford, Sam had no control over the blindspots of others, and the good people of Wood Grove certainly had their share of blindspots.

Oh yes, this was his past hesitation regarding Grace. He remembered now.

He heard the front door open and muffled voices followed by a tap on the door.

"Yes?" he asked.

Ruby opened the door wide enough to slide through. She shut it behind her. "Gloria McKay is here. She says she needs to see you." Lowering her voice, Ruby ran her index and middle fingers down both sides of her nose. "She's been crying."

Sam closed the newspaper. "Tell her to come in."

Ruby opened the door to back out and usher in Gloria. After throwing a look of both concern and curiosity to Sam, Ruby closed the door.

Sam walked around his desk and guided Gloria to a chair. Mascara, washed down by tears, darkened the circles under her eyes. She dabbed at her nose with a sopping tissue. Sam offered a fresh one from the box on his desk.

"I'm sorry, Sam," she said. "I didn't know where else to go."

Sam knew Gloria probably didn't have anywhere else to go. Her father had died only a few years after Sam took over the practice. Mrs. McKay now lived with Skip and Mary Sue. Skip drank too much. Sam had tried to talk Skip into better choices, but Skip had called him a "boot licker." Sam had little to do with his old friend these days.

Gloria blew her nose on a fresh tissue. Sam held out the box again. She took another.

"Jasper has a girlfriend," she said.

Sam wasn't surprised. He had attended the small wedding for Gloria and Jasper. At the reception, a drunken bridegroom had fallen across the wedding cake. Apparently, marriage hadn't improved his behavior.

"I'm sorry," Sam said, sitting down beside her and leaning in. "You don't deserve to be treated like that."

"I know." Her voice broke as fresh tears flowed.

Sam held his posture, waiting for her to surface again.

She blew her nose. He placed the tissue box on her lap.

"Thanks," she said.

Sam sat back. "Are you still with him?"

"No!"

Sam nodded. "Okay."

“The thing is—” she took a deep breath “—we moved into a place that’s too expensive for me to rent on my own, and….” Her voice cracked, replaced by sobs.

Sam moved forward, patting her hand. “You’ll be okay. You can move, or find a roommate. If you need some money to make the transition, I can help.”

He would have done anything to help her feel better. With others, Sam had learned how to wait out the tears, to not get too involved. Gloria was different. He responded to her as he would to a sister.

“The thing is—” she said when she could talk again “—I’m pregnant.”

Sam continued to pat her hand, his own emotions subsiding as he reviewed the implications. She would need money, housing, stability, someone to help.

“Calm down,” he said. “Are you sure Jasper’s not coming back?”

“Oh, he’s not coming back!”

Sam liked seeing that little bit of fight in her. He patted her hand one more time, then sat back on the chair. “Don’t divorce him until after the baby is born. Now don’t get mad, but I have to ask. Are you sure the baby is his?”

Gloria pulled away. “Sam!”

He smiled. “I thought so, but I had to ask.” Sam stood and walked around his desk to sit in his black, leather, swivel chair. “You go home and start thinking about what you want to do. Come by my house tonight. We’ll have dinner and talk.”

“What do you mean, ‘think about what I want to do?’ I want my life to go back to how we were before I found out about his girlfriend.”

The whine in her voice didn’t surprise him. Like Jasper, Gloria had some growing up to do. “You’re past that, Gloria. You’re going to have a baby. You have to start thinking like someone who will be responsible for the life of another person.”

"How can I do that?" She slunk into her chair. "I won't have health insurance. I won't be able to work. I don't have anyone to help me."

"Stop it, Gloria." His voice was firm.

She looked up, eyes wide.

"You are not alone. Go to the restroom and pull yourself together."

Gloria stood like an obedient child and stepped out of Sam's office.

Sam opened his bottom desk drawer and pulled out a file. From the file, he extracted a few business cards and brochures containing information about local social service agencies and contact information for key providers.

When Gloria returned—tears dried, hair combed, makeup freshened—Sam gave the information to her with instructions about who to ask for and what to ask. Then he escorted her to the front door, reminding her to come to his house around seven. He gave her a brief hug before she walked out.

Ruby's eyes followed him as he walked back to his office. "Don't get too close, Sam. You're ripe for a midlife mistake."

"You watch too many movies, Ruby," he said.

AFTER SEEING TWO CLIENTS, and eating a quick lunch at his desk, Sam settled back into the newspaper. As he finished skimming the rest of the front section, the phone rang. The door to his office was open. He knew by Ruby's response that she would turn the call over to him. Rather than her normal mode of shouting to him from her desk, which saved her from having to walk five steps, she appeared in his doorway.

"There's a woman on the line. She asked to speak to you. Said she's an old friend." Ruby raised her eyebrows. "She sounds very sophisticated and I've never heard you mention her."

"What's her name?" he asked as he reached for his phone.

"Elena Flemming, but she said that you would remember her as Elena Hernandez."

Sam's eyes flew open and his hand stopped. He hadn't seen Elena since the end of his second year in law school. She had never really talked to him after their night together. When she didn't return in the fall, he noticed, but never heard where she'd gone.

Ruby acknowledged his surprise with a smirk.

He put his hand on the receiver and said, "Close the door behind you."

"Hmm," she said, and shut the door.

He waited until he heard the door latch, then picked up the receiver.

Elena's voice was the same, though a bit heavier. Life does that to you, he thought, as they accomplished the exchange of condensed life stories.

No, she didn't finish law school. She had married an old friend of the family and settled in Denver. Her husband was a developer. They had one child, a daughter.

No, Sam had never gotten married. He had a private practice in Ohio. He was happy.

"I'm surprised to hear from you," he said. "How did you find me?"

"Marguerite helped. She has many talents."

Sam dropped his head back as he remembered. "Marguerite. She's still with you?" He had never been able to figure out their relationship. Was she a companion or a bodyguard?

"She lives with us, yes. I asked her to find you and she did her magic. She's been a tremendous help over the years, especially with Randi, our daughter. She's thinking about transferring to Ohio State. I remember you did your undergrad work there."

Sam ran his hand through his hair. Something didn't add up. Why would Elena call after all these years because her daughter was transferring to his Alma Mater? Did she even remember what happened between them? Maybe not, they'd both been drunk out of their minds.

"We'll be in Columbus this weekend," she said. "I wondered if you would have dinner with us. Saturday night?"

He and Grace had planned to attend a play in Columbus that night. He would like to see Elena again, and he'd be happy to meet her daughter, but not at the expense of breaking his date with Grace.

"Could we make it another time?"

Elena hesitated. "Randi's busy all day with a campus tour and meeting some of the professors from the Engineering department."

"Good for her," Sam said. "More women should enroll in the sciences."

"I suppose so," Elena said.

"Maybe you and I could meet earlier in the day for lunch." He could meet Grace later. He didn't think she would mind driving to Columbus on her own. She had mentioned a sister there. Maybe she could have a visit with her, two birds, one stone.

Elena sighed. "There's no easy way to do this."

"Why's that?" he asked. There were many easy ways to flex a schedule so all tasks could be accomplished. If not, then no big deal. They hadn't seen each other in twenty years. What difference would it make?

Elena sighed again. "I don't know if I'm doing the right thing. Everything is a mess right now."

Sam shifted in his chair. If Elena needed help, he would certainly do what he could.

She sighed a third time, distressed, which was not at all like the Elena he remembered. "My husband will be furious when he finds out I've contacted you," she said.

"He would?" Sam asked. She remembered, all right, and she must have told her husband about Sam. He did not want to be placed in the middle of someone else's marital discord, especially over ancient history.

"I'm sorry, Sam. I should have contacted you years ago."

She shouldn't be the one to apologize. "You did nothing wrong, Elena. The fault lies with me. I'm so sorry. I never meant to cross that line."

"Sam, stop talking, please. This is hard. You don't understand."

"What don't I understand, Elena?"

"I should have told you right away. Randi is your daughter."

If behavior were a fault line, the pressured plates of good and evil shifted. Sam thought for a second he might actually be feeling the ground move beneath him. The edifices of social standing and community confidence he had erected over the years cracked, crumbled. He couldn't speak.

"Sam?" Elena asked. "Are you there?"

"Yes," he choked out and cleared his throat. "I am." He paused. "Are you sure?" And then, "Of course you are. I'm sorry." He sat back in his chair, heart pounding, breaking a sweat, and checked himself. No chest tightness. No left arm or jaw pain. No dizziness or nausea. "Why did you wait all this time to tell me?"

The story unfolded, Elena breaking into rapid Spanish at times. Their evening together had not been the mistake for her that it had been for him. She had planned for something like that to happen. In love for the first time, ready for her fairy tale to be complete, she had seduced him, thinking that once he had taken her virginity, he would automatically do the right thing.

"I appreciate your honesty," he said, his mind reeling.

When she woke in the morning and he was gone, she felt devastated. Marguerite came home, found Elena in a state, and wrangled the truth from her charge.

"So, she was a bodyguard for you," Sam said. His heart rate began to slow.

"A protector of sorts. She told my parents. They permitted me to complete the year, with the stipulation that I would have no further contact with you."

"That's why you wouldn't talk to me."

"I would have left them for you, Sam. But the note you sent before spring break, letting me know that you only wanted to be my friend, convinced me I had made a terrible mistake."

Sam wanted to challenge her, to declare that she should have told him, but he knew he hadn't been ready for marriage or parenthood twenty years ago, and he hated revisionism at all levels, so he remained silent, listening as she continued.

When she discovered she was pregnant, her parents stepped in and arranged a hasty early June wedding with Leo, ten years her senior, a good man who treated her well and never shamed her for what she brought to the marriage. But Leo's compassion had limits, and this had become all too apparent in the past year.

"At the end of her freshman year in college," Elena said, "Randi came home and announced that she had a girlfriend." Elena paused for long enough that Sam felt he needed to say something.

"How did you feel about that?" he asked.

"I was shocked, but unwilling to let that stand in the way of my love for her. Leo couldn't accept it. He gave her a year. He said if she didn't come back around to being the girl that he had always loved, he would disown her."

"Did he?"

"He wrote her out of his will in early May. She's heartbroken, Sam. Maybe he's punishing her for not being his biological daughter in the first place. I don't know."

Sam doodled on a notepad, to calm his nerves. "Does she know about me?"

"I didn't know what else to do. When Leo changed his will, I sat her down and told her. Was I wrong?"

He took his time answering. He could point out that now was a fine time to ask for his opinion about their daughter, but the past was past. "I think you did the right thing."

"Will you join us for dinner on Saturday night? Randi wants to meet you, but she's feeling shy and wants to meet in a neutral place."

"Of course I'll come," Sam answered. "Where and when?"

Chapter Fifteen

MONDAY EVENING, AFTER DINNER, Grace stood beside Loretta at the kitchen sink.

"You like him." Loretta handed Grace another pan to dry. "I haven't seen you this happy in a long, long time."

Grace ran the towel over the inside of the round saucepan and then dried the outside. "I do like him. He's how I remember from the first time I met him. He's warm and friendly and funny." She picked up a pan and ran the towel over the inside, then the outside.

"Grace, honey. You already dried that one. If I didn't know any better, I would say that you are acting like a woman in love."

Grace put the pan down and wiped the counter around the drainer. "I don't know him that well yet. Besides, I don't even know what 'falling in love' means. It sounds like a trap."

"Weren't you in love with Richard?" Loretta leaned her arm on the sink, dangling a lime-green, crocheted dishcloth from her fingertip.

"I was young," Grace said. She still ached sometimes when she thought of her ex-husband. Teddy had flown out yesterday to be with his father for the summer. Their son loved spending the summer with his father and stepmother. Donna's two grown children were in college now. She and Richard had two of their own, ages seven and three.

Richard had given to Teddy what she couldn't, a real family. But then, she had provided a different kind of family. John and Loretta were a second set of parents. Stephen was Teddy's brother in every sense of the word; the two of them were inseparable when Teddy was in Ohio. Polly took him to plays and poetry readings. Elizabeth had introduced him to exotic dancing, the PG version. Arthur had begun teaching him how to play chess and Ben ran Shakespeare lines with him. Grace had done all right by her son.

"Wake up." Loretta shoved another pan at her. "You're cramping my style."

Grace took the roasting pan and cradled it in her arm, running the towel over the shiny silver surfaces. She missed Teddy, but he would come back at the end of August. Would she still be seeing Sam? If she was, what would Teddy think about that?

After they finished cleaning the kitchen, Loretta retreated to the cottage. Grace wandered down the hall, looking again at the children's art on the wall. She had helped frame them, the skill levels ranging from stick people to fleshed-out portraits with eyelashes and nose hairs. In her favorite, an angry red monster with claws spread roared at a little girl. The child leaned toward the monster, chin up, fists clenched. Every time Grace looked at the picture, she wondered what monsters the little girl faced down in real life and sent a silent prayer to the artist, for continued strength and courage.

When she came to the end of the hall, Grace ran her hands over the ferns, noticing the way the leaves tickled her palms. Was she in love? It didn't matter. What mattered was feeling like a woman again. For the first time since Richard left, her body responded in ways that warmed her from inside. If her happiness required being with a man, then so be it. She liked Sam. She didn't need to apologize for that, or explain it to anybody, not even herself.

"Grace!" Nick came down the steps two at a time. "Great news! I just got off the phone with my agent. The novel sold! That makes 30. And there's talk about a movie script. Ha!"

"Congratulations."

"You know, I was feeling so low that I actually considered our neighbor's offer to buy the property. But now, no way! My life is going great. Not thinking I'll change a thing." He hugged her briefly around the shoulders and walked down the hall toward the kitchen.

"What neighbor?" Grace asked.

"That attorney, Sam Seesaw, Saylow, Swing Low, Sweet Chariot." His baritone voice echoed in the hall, fading as the kitchen door shut behind him.

A handful of fern fronds died in the crush of her fist.

Sam had offered to buy GraceHaven? When? And why hadn't he said something to her?

Whatever had been released in the euphoric aftermath of her two dates with the man dried up.

"Unbelievable," she muttered as she walked past the picture of the little girl and her monster.

Sam had no right to buy the project Grace had spent the last twenty years developing. To think that he would sit across from her at the table and act like he cared, like he wanted to know her. She wanted to rip something. She wanted to smash something.

She pushed through the door to her office. The phone rang.

Without thinking, she picked up the receiver and said, "Hello?"

"You sound mad," Richard said.

"Oh, sorry." Grace calmed her voice. "Is Teddy okay?"

"Yeah, he's great. Thanks for sending the presents. Donna always appreciates those little touches. She really likes you, you know."

"I like her, too." Who wouldn't? Donna was perfect. Donna had everything, because Donna deserved everything, which apparently Grace did not because she couldn't get past two dates without learning that the guy was a total—

"So Teddy's good," Richard said, his voice measured, strong. "But I did call to talk about him."

Grace sat down, forcing herself to pay attention. "Is Teddy okay?"

Richard assured her, again, that Teddy was fine. "He told me about raiding the neighbor's strawberries."

"No big deal," Grace said. "He and Stephen went over Saturday morning and apologized. The neighbor had him sweep the sidewalk or something." She didn't want to think about that neighbor at the moment.

"I think Teddy's little taste of vandalism might be a bigger deal, in the long run, if we don't nip this in the bud."

"Huh?" What in the world did he mean by that? "You've lost me, Richard."

"I think Teddy needs to be with his father more, Grace. I know we talked about letting him decide when he hits fourteen, but I think we should let him decide now."

"What are you saying?" He couldn't possibly mean what he was saying.

"Donna and I have been talking about this for the past year. When Teddy told me about the strawberries, I asked him how he would feel about spending more time in New Jersey. He's ready, Grace. If you agree, I'll send him back to Ohio for the summer, and this fall, he can start seventh grade here."

"Teddy doesn't want to live in New Jersey." Grace couldn't believe Richard would cook up something so preposterous. He had agreed. They had a plan. She had always assumed when Teddy turned fourteen, he would choose Ohio. Allowing him to decide would be a formality.

"He does want to live in New Jersey, Grace. We talked about it last year, but I thought he was too young. It was his idea. He wants to live here during the school year." Richard's voice sounded calm, reasonable. Grace wanted to drag her fingers down a chalkboard, the perfect score for this segment of the horror flick that had become the end of her day.

"Let me talk to him," she said.

"Are you okay?" Richard asked.

She forced a softer tone into her voice. "I am fine. Let me talk to Teddy."

"Okay."

The phone went silent and she took a deep breath, filling her abdomen, chest, shoulders and blew out slowly. The red monster receded. Grace unclenched her jaw.

"Hey, Mom." Teddy's voice sounded tentative.

"Hey, Cowboy," she said, amazed at how calm her own voice had become. "Daddy tells me you're thinking of a big change there."

"Are you mad?" he asked. She could hear the edge of tears.

"No, no, I'm not mad. Tell me what you're thinking."

She knew her relaxed tone had given her son permission and he launched into a long story about how he had spent the last year working on a pros and cons list about Ohio and New Jersey.

She could barely breathe.

"There are so many things to do here," he said. "When Dylan and Todd are home from college, they always take me to sports games, hockey, basketball, baseball. And sometimes I babysit for Derrick and Tyler, not for very long, but if Donna has to run out to the store or something. She pays me, too."

He talked on and on, to the point of breathlessness. How had she missed this? He had been thinking about this for a year, and she had been clueless.

Teddy finally inhaled and asked, "So you're okay with this? Dad said I would fly back this weekend and spend the whole summer with you and then come back here in August."

"Sure, Teddy, if that's what you want." Something broke inside of her.

"Cool! Let me get Dad back on the phone. Love you, Mom."

"Love you, too, Cowboy."

Richard's voice came back on the line, all business, talking flight times.

Grace couldn't feel a thing. She wrote down information, said she'd be there to pick up Teddy when he landed, said goodbye, and hung up the phone.

What cure was there for losing so much in the span of less than one hour? If only she drank, or smoked, or shot heroin. She needed a fix, all right. What fix was there for loss after loss after loss after loss? She had tried running in the past. She had a pair of special shoes in the closet. She slipped off her loafers. The sun would set in about an hour. Plenty of time to work off this need to punch the hell out of a bag, a wall, the face of the strawberry-growing guy next door.

Shoes tied, Grace left the house and took off at a slow jog, winding her way around the cars, between the cottage and the dorm, and into the woods. Fresh green leaves covered the undergrowth and most of the trees.

She ran all the way to the boulder and turned around without stopping, the air heavy, like her heart, her legs, her thoughts, her mood, her future.

"Ugh!" she tried to shout it out. "Blech!" She made every sound she could think of that matched how she felt inside. She ran back to the house, around the driveway, and down the road away from town.

She averted her eyes when she ran past the house with the bird feeders and too much cilantro. He was nothing to her again, as he always should have been. She had been foolish to let herself enjoy his company. Men sucked. Everybody sucked. She sucked.

She ran until her sides cramped and she had to hold them as she cooled down.

Shortly after turning to walk back to the house, Grace heard a car approach from behind. Looking over her shoulder, she saw a convertible, the top up. She knew who drove that car. He pulled up even with her and asked, "Can I give you a lift?"

"No," she said and kept walking.

"Are you sure?"

"I don't want a ride," she said, not looking at him.

"You're sure, now."

"I am sure. I do not want a ride."

"Really? Because you're looking pretty beat there. I don't mind if you sweat on my leather seats."

She stopped. Without looking at him, she yelled, her arms gesticulating for emphasis. "I said no, Skip. I had to say no three times. Why do I have to repeat myself? No means no. Stop following me, Skip. Stop looking at me and stop—" she whirled to face him and stopped yelling.

A small, gray-haired woman peered around Skip McKay from the passenger side of his car, a horrified look on her face. Skip's face looked puzzled, concerned.

"No, thank you," Grace said, and turned to continue down the road.

Skip's car eased away. She didn't look up until the sound of its motor faded away.

The sun had set by the time she made it back to Sam's driveway. She walked past without looking, but then turned around and headed to his house. She could see as she strode down the freshly resurfaced asphalt that the porch light was on, but there were lights coming from the living room windows. Unless they were on a timer, somebody was home. She rapped on the door three times and waited. The latch turned and Grace steeled herself, but instead of Sam, Gloria McKay opened the door. Would this day of McKays never end? Grace didn't know Gloria, but she knew who she was. Small town. Everybody knew everybody, at least by name.

"Is Sam here?" Grace asked.

"He's in the kitchen. Come on in." Gloria opened the screen door and Grace climbed the last step. She felt awkward now, with no rehearsed script, or even the hint of a plan.

She waited by the door while Gloria went to the kitchen. Sam emerged, drying his hands on his expensive-looking kitchen towel, white like a lie that is still a lie, with two red stripes.

“Hey,” he said.

Grace picked up on a new awkwardness in him. She flashed on the idea that he felt uncomfortable because Gloria was there. Were they having a dinner date? Of course they were. He probably dated several at once. Gigolo.

“I didn’t expect to see you tonight,” he said.

“Yeah, well, I needed to ask you something.”

“Sure,” he said, not looking at all sure.

“Can we go someplace a little more private?” she asked.

“Sure.” He flipped on a hall light and guided her to a room down the hall.

She hadn’t seen this part of the house.

Sam opened the door revealing a home office. Bookshelves lined the walls. He walked to his desk and turned over a legal pad so the blank cardboard back faced up. Turning back to Grace, he asked, “What’s up?”

“When were you going to tell me that you were trying to buy GraceHaven?”

“What?” His surprise seemed genuine.

“Nick told me you offered to buy GraceHaven.”

“I offered to buy the woods,” Sam said. “I want to make sure it remains undeveloped.”

And then she remembered. Nick had said that Sam wanted to buy the “property.”

“Oh,” she said, relieved that at least one disastrous turn of events had been righted. “Nick said something. I misunderstood.”

“Okay.” The way Sam said it seemed distant. When they had gone to dinner, he had been open, engaging, interested. Now he seemed far away.

She wondered again about his evening with Gloria.

"I'm glad you stopped by," he said. "Because I was going to call. I need to cancel for Saturday night."

"Sure," said Grace. She would be picking up Teddy anyway. "No worries. We can do it another time."

"Yeah, maybe," he said. "Well, the thing is, something's come up, several things actually. I'm sorry to say I'm going to be busy for a while and I probably won't have much time for anything other than work. Sorry. I had a good time being with you."

"No problem," Grace said, heading for the front door. "Sorry to interrupt your evening."

Sam stepped in front of her and made it to the door first. He put his hand on her arm as she reached for the screen door. "I'm really sorry, Grace. The timing's not right, but I mean it. I have really enjoyed our time together."

"Okay," she said. Why did he look so forlorn? She was the one being dumped. "No problem. I had a good time, too." She flashed a smile before taking the steps and sidewalk at a fast clip.

She could feel him staring at her back. Maybe this was best. She didn't want to be one of many. Maybe ending before they'd really begun was a good thing. They had never even kissed. At least he wasn't the scoundrel that, ten minutes ago, she had suspected him of being.

The evening ended on the porch of the cottage. Loretta's foot rocked the porch swing and her shoulder supported Grace's head.

"We'll have the whole summer with Teddy," Grace said.

Loretta patted her knee.

"I need to spend more time with Sarah now. Maybe that will be a good thing for both of us."

Loretta chuckled. "That must have been Skip's mother in the car with him. I can't wait to attend church circle this week."

"She goes to your church?" Grace asked, raising her head.

"Oh, honey, she doesn't attend my church circle, but she does attend the Methodist ladies' circle, and all the circles in this town are a tight network of information sharing."

Grace put her head back on Loretta's shoulder, burrowing in. "If they say anything about me, keep it to yourself. I don't want to know."

Chapter Sixteen
1983

GRACE HAD ALWAYS KNOWN that someday GraceHaven would have to weather its first death, but she never expected it to be someone so young, so dear to her. As Teddy turned the car into the drive that wound through the cemetery, he said, "I can't help thinking that if I hadn't moved to New Jersey, this wouldn't have happened. Or if I'd started with him at OSU last fall."

"Stephen's death had nothing to do with you," Grace said. "That young woman identified him and they held him in that cell without any medical care. The pneumonia killed him, Teddy." She still couldn't believe it. Boys like Stephen didn't rape girls and pneumonia didn't kill young people in 1983. The whole thing was inconceivable.

"That girl lied," Teddy said. "Stephen would never hurt someone like that."

Grace wondered if her son realized that how many times he had uttered those exact words in the past two days. Every time, she agreed with him, fiercely. Never once did she admit out loud what she really thought—that sex was complicated—and that males of all ages were often confused.

"He was a good boy," she said. She put the car in park and turned off the ignition. "Whatever happened, I will always remember his goodness."

She and Teddy walked together across the January-hard ground, their boots crunching down the thin layer of icy snow, to join the others at

Stephen's gravesite. The group huddled together as the minister said one final prayer. Loretta's knees buckled as the mourners said the last, "Amen." John held her up until she could stand on her own again.

Teddy asked to stay with John and Loretta while Grace headed over to the church. Grace agreed without hesitation. Teddy was to Loretta as Stephen had been to Grace, as if each boy had two mothers and each mother two sons. She drove the few miles back to town in quiet empty silence, death a frozen reminder that loss is life.

The parking lot at the Baptist church held only a few cars when Grace arrived. She parked in the back row and walked across the glistening asphalt. Each step started as a test, and she slipped twice, but managed to avoid falling. Once inside the church, she moved coat racks closer to the door and stood by to welcome the carloads that began to arrive.

"Please go through the buffet line and fill your plate. The minister will bless the food when all are seated," she repeated ten, twenty, thirty or more times.

When Teddy arrived, he told her that John and Loretta had gone straight back to GraceHaven. They were exhausted.

"Are you okay?" Grace asked. "You don't have to stay." She didn't want to stay. She wanted to go home and bury herself in a pile of blankets, but somebody had to be in charge.

"I'm okay," he said, and walked away to join a group of young people who had been his elementary school classmates, too.

Her feet ached from the night before. The visitation had been punishing. Grace and Teddy stood with the family at Stephen's coffin, receiving every attendee with as much shared solace as they could muster. Reflected in each face Grace found the same aloneness that held her apart from herself, and hence, others. They were all refugees from the comfortable place of thinking this could never happen.

Just as she decided she could leave her post, one more person opened the church door. Sam brushed ice from his arms before crossing the threshold. After placing his coat on a hanger and jamming it into the stuffed rack, he took Grace by the shoulders.

"How're you holding up?" he asked.

Six months after their first and only real date, he had started inviting her to dinner again, but she always had an excuse lying around in the broad category of, "too busy." After more than a few rejections, he stopped asking, but they had achieved a comfortable connection over the years. He'd been a reliable neighbor, once loaning his car when Grace's alternator went out and no other cars were available, and GraceHaven had sheltered Sam for a few days when a storm knocked out his electricity.

"I'm okay." She crossed her arms. "Thanks for coming. I know it meant a lot to John to see you at the funeral."

"Least I could do," he said.

"I need to go in there." She nodded toward the fellowship hall. "Duty calls."

"Grace," Sam said.

She waited.

"If there's anything I can do to help—"

"Thanks, Sam," she said. "I think we're covered."

For the next hour, Grace remained on her feet. She thanked Ed Turnbull, again, for the kind and compassionate way in which he managed the funeral arrangements. Fran and Peter offered to reschedule their trip to Florida. They were to fly out in the morning. Grace told them to go. Arthur left early, saying he didn't feel well. Max and Elizabeth took him back to GraceHaven.

Skip and Mary Sue McKay called Grace over to say how sorry they were about Stephen's death. Grace thanked them. Why were they even there? They didn't know Stephen. Skip took her hand, saying that he would do anything he could to help. Grace again thanked them both for coming and said she had to check on the food. Honestly. The man had approached her in the woods one evening last fall and made it clear he was available for whatever, whenever. She had pointed out the no-trespassing sign and asked him to abide by it. Why did Mary Sue put up with him? Grace hoped the answer was love, not money. No woman should be financially trapped into staying with a man like that.

Grace surveyed the buffet tables and watched as caterers removed large pans that now held only the remains of lasagna, salad, chicken breasts, bread. She thanked the workers, praising the quality of the food, the manner in which they had served. The church women had tried to vote down the use of a caterer, insisting they themselves donate the food, that being their tradition, but Grace had insisted otherwise. Instead, she'd asked them to spend time with Loretta, which they had done, around the clock since Stephen's death. Grace was sure at least one of them was at the cottage now, feeding Loretta whatever comfort their prayers could provide.

Teddy beckoned her over. He sat at the end of a table with Sam.

"Teddy's been telling me that he plans to transfer to Ohio State in the fall," Sam said. He stood to pull out a chair for her.

Cold penetrated her knit skirt and tights as she made contact with the metal seat. She looked at her son, his hair pulled back into a ponytail, a soft mustache growing on his upper lip. "You're sure you still want to do that?"

"I think I do," he said.

"Rutgers is a good school." She wanted him closer, but not at the expense of losing the advantages that Richard made possible.

"Ohio State is in the Top Ten Alliance," Sam said.

"I want to transfer," Teddy said. "I like the campus. The education department is highly rated. Plus I'd be closer to you. I'd like that."

"Don't do it for me, Teddy," Grace said.

"I think it's great he wants to be closer to you," Sam said. "My parents are in their seventies. I wish I was closer to them, to help more."

Grace turned to Sam. “So move there. You’re old enough to retire.” That would solve her problem with him. Out of sight, out of mind.

Sam’s blue eyes flashed for a second, in contrast with the easy laugh that followed. “I’m only fifty-two, Grace. Not ready to throw in the towel yet.” He looked back at her son. “You ought to consider law, Teddy. It’s a field that includes so many aspects of life, especially in a small town. Some days I feel like a litigator, social worker, counselor, and teacher all rolled into one.”

“That does sound interesting,” Teddy said.

Grace excused herself to join Loretta’s sister, who had caught Grace’s eye and signaled her over.

Charlene’s sweet perfume enveloped Grace as she slid into the empty chair. Charlene placed her hands over Grace’s, which were clasped on her lap, and said, “After all these years, Grace, I am happy we finally met, but what sad circumstances.” Her eyes teared.

“What took us so long?” Grace asked. She and Charlene had spent the previous evening sitting together at the kitchen table, drinking tea.

“I understand much better now,” Charlene said. “I used to think that Loretta and John had taken a step back in time, maintenance, cooking of all things, but I see now they actually enjoy being at GraceHaven. Loretta told me it keeps her grounded. I never understood what leaders they are in the work to truly emancipate our people, or how the community supports them in accomplishing such a rigorous schedule.”

Grace nodded. Undoing the rigor of that schedule had been one of her main tasks in the last week. John had provided a detailed list. She must have made a hundred follow-up phone calls after canceling meetings, rescheduling a seminar, making sure that each registrant was aware of the change, and refunding money when the new date didn’t work for them.

“You all have been so kind to us,” Charlene said. “Putting us up like that so we could be close to John and Loretta.”

"Are you comfortable?" Grace asked.

"Oh, yes," she patted Grace's hand again. "Please thank Nick for us. I can't believe he insisted on providing our meals so we wouldn't have to eat out."

"He would have been here, but he couldn't get away." Grace imagined Nick writing at his apartment in Paris. She could only imagine from pictures he had sent because she had never been to Paris. Nick was gone for months at a time now. She barely missed him.

"Tell me again what you do, Grace," Charlene leaned forward, her smooth dark skin shining with health and her eyes clear, kind, inviting. Grace knew Loretta's sister was a nurse, a director of nursing, in fact, at a small hospital outside of Atlanta. If Grace ever needed medical care, she would want a face like that on the provider.

"I clean," Grace said.

"Oh, you do more than cleaning." Charlene laughed.

"My title is manager, but my real job is doing anything that needs to be done, and that does include a fair amount of cleaning." The budget could afford help for the yard work and cooking but still didn't support a routine housecleaner.

"Well, GraceHaven is beautiful. I want to come back for one of your weekends!"

"We would love to have you," Grace said.

"Thank you for being such a good friend to Loretta." Charlene put her hand on Grace's arm. "She's going to need you more than ever."

"I think the needing-each-other is mutual," Grace said.

People started to leave. Grace broke away from the comfort of Loretta's sister to stand at the door. Slush covered the sidewalks. She cautioned people to watch their step, and made sure that older adults were accompanied by a strong arm.

Skip McKay pulled her toward him when she shook his hand. He clutched Grace's forearm with his other hand, leaning forward until she could feel his breath on her face. "Call us any time." Mary Sue stood a few feet away, clutching her purse, her face unreadable

Grace stepped back and removed her arm from Skip's touch. "Watch your step, on the way out, I mean."

After the lingerers had left, and the caterers were all packed up, Grace and Teddy rode back to GraceHaven together.

"Are you sure you want to come back to Ohio for school?" she asked.

"I am," Teddy said. "I've been thinking about it for a while, made a pros and cons list."

She glanced at him. He grinned at her.

"And it's not about me?" she asked.

"Not really," he said. "I miss Ohio. I miss being here with you, but that's about me, not you."

"And with Stephen gone?"

When Teddy arrived, he had spent the entire day in her attic room, looking at pictures of Stephen and remembering their early lives together, crying inconsolably at times.

"Being with him was only a part of coming back here. I miss you, Mom. I miss Wood Grove. Never thought I'd say that."

Grace smiled. "It does grow on you, doesn't it?"

She turned into the driveway. "You know I'd love to have you closer."

"I know that." Teddy sighed, pressing back into the headrest. "I'm coming back for me. I promise."

Once outside the car, Teddy said he was going to say goodnight to John and Loretta before turning in. He hugged his mother with a fierceness she hadn't felt from him since he was a little boy. She hugged him back and held on until he let go, then watched until he entered the cottage before walking into the house.

A large arrangement of Rainbow roses sat in the middle of the kitchen table.

"It's about time, Nick," Grace said. She picked up the card, expecting to read some inappropriate sentiment, even though he had selected an apt flower for the occasion. This storm, too, would pass.

Grace, Heavy hearts need a reminder. Take time to heal. The sun will shine again. Sam. She dropped the card and looked again at the roses, each one a collection of fuchsia, salmon, yellow, chartreuse, teal, blue, and purple petals. They matched the colors of the chairs placed around the white table. Perfect.

The phone rang. Grace headed for her office, looking back at the table as she walked to the door. No matter how much they filled the room with color and hope, they were still only flowers, fragile, and would wither soon. Nothing lasted forever. She left them behind and walked to her office.

Dropping into her desk chair, she picked up the receiver. "Hello, Sarah." Her sister had said she'd call at five.

"How did it go today? I would have been there if I could. I feel awful."

"You sound awful," Grace said. "It went fine."

"How are John and Loretta?" Sarah sneezed.

"I know it sounds trite, but they are as good as can be expected." Grace waited as Sarah blew her nose before asking, "How are you doing?"

"Horrible. I hate being sick. I feel so lonely when I can't get out."

"I'm sorry," Grace said.

"Not your fault. You can't be two places at once."

Since Donald's death, Grace had been the person to show up for Sarah in sickness and in health. Twice, Grace had spent the night in the hospital, sleeping on a cot beside the hospital bed, for Sarah's minor surgeries. They talked on the phone more than once a day, and had managed to take an annual vacation together for the past five years.

"How's Teddy?" Sarah asked.

"He's moving back in June and plans to attend OSU in the fall."

"He'll be living in Columbus? Marvelous!" Sarah's excitement stimulated a coughing fit. When she could talk again, she said, "I feel better already!" followed by another round of coughing.

"Go take care of yourself," Grace said. "I'll call in the morning."

Sarah agreed, hacking out a goodbye, and disconnected the call.

Grace dropped the receiver into its cradle and heard the back door bang open. "Mom!" Teddy yelled.

Grace bolted out of her chair and hurried to the hall where she met Teddy coming through the kitchen door.

"John's collapsed. Loretta called the squad. You have to come, now." Teddy's lips quivered.

"Calm down," she said. "Go to the dorm and get Charlene. She's in suite E." Grace put her hands on Teddy's arms. "Breathe, Teddy. Slow down and remember to breathe."

"Right," he inhaled. "Breathe."

"Exhale," she said.

"Right." He blew out, turned, and raced out the back door.

The light above the kitchen sink cast a warm glow around one side of the flower arrangement. Rainbow roses seemed even sillier now, romantic in a flimsy way that promised something that would never come. She pulled hard to close the back door and hugged her arms across her chest as she moved, as quick as she could, to the cottage on the other side of the driveway.

Chapter Seventeen

ON THE MONDAY FOLLOWING the funeral for John's son, Sam rose early and tapped the keys on his desktop computer for an hour followed by another hour of fast walking on the treadmill and lifting weights. He made it to the office by eight-thirty and sat at his desk, showered, shaved, as ready for the day as he could be.

Ruby arrived on time. She assumed her position in the doorframe.

Sam remained at his desk. "You look good this morning. New dress?" The light brown wasn't right for her, but the style suited her figure. Every pregnancy had added ten pounds. She had three kids.

"Hal bought it for me for Christmas."

"Nice," Sam said. He looked down at his newspaper.

"You doing okay?" she asked.

"Alive, alert, and ready for action," he answered.

"Did you hear the news about that boy's father?"

"Yes," Sam said. "Polly came over yesterday to tell me. I guess everybody over there's pretty devastated."

He sat back in his chair, lacing his fingers behind his head, feeling pretty devastated himself. He and John had talked "over the fence" many times since meeting at the border where Sam's property ended and GraceHaven began. The "fence" was a ten-foot-wide strip of trees and undergrowth that provided a natural barrier between the two properties. Sam and John had cleared some debris and picked up trash together as they chatted about their lives and doings about town. To John, their connection had probably seemed minor, but Sam felt like he'd lost a good friend.

"I can't believe that poor woman lost her son and husband in the same week."

"It's very sad." Sam lowered his hands and put them on the edge of the desk as he leaned forward in his chair, again looking down at his paper.

"You sure you're okay, Sam?"

Sam looked up. Ruby's sweet smile was gone, replaced with a look of concern.

"I'm good. A little tired, I guess."

"Gray days will do that to you," Ruby said. She shoved off the doorframe and turned to her desk. "Let me know if you need anything."

"I will." He'd let her know if he thought it would help, but Ruby couldn't give him what he needed, what he wanted.

He thought about seeing Grace at the boy's funeral, and then talking with her and her son in the church basement. She looked tired, sad. He would have liked to spend more time with her, offer consolation, be the friend she could lean on. He had been thrilled with their two dates and had only backed off because learning about Randi had blown his mind. By the time he realized what a mistake he'd made, Grace wouldn't go out with him again. And then he noticed that he never saw her with any man but Nick. She either had something going on with Nick all along, or she had taken up with him shortly after Randi's debut in Sam's life. Those two options were the only thing that made sense. Sam liked to think it was the former. That way, he'd never really had a chance.

He looked down at the paper again and started reading. An item on page nine caught his eye. Regarding the case of the alleged rape at a campus apartment, the article revealed that the student who died in jail was now absolved. Witnesses' statements revealed that Stephen J. Coffield had left the party earlier in the evening and another man was now implicated. At the time the article was written, the second man was in jail, awaiting arraignment.

Sam pulled his handkerchief from his pocket and blew his nose. Stories like that should never be printed, because stories like that should never happen. The world could be a cruel place.

The phone rang. Sam heard Ruby say, "Hang on, Randi." She called out, "Sam! Your favorite author is on the phone."

Sam folded his handkerchief and put it back in his pocket.

He picked up the phone and smiled as he said, "Hey, there. How's New York?"

Randi had moved to Ohio eight years ago and enrolled at Ohio State. Sam had suspended as many other activities as possible to establish a connection with his daughter. Nearly every weekend, they'd had dinner or gone to a museum, movie, or concert. After six months, she decided to quit school and try modeling, but by then their relationship was solid. Sam put her in touch with an old friend in New York who could introduce Randi to the right people. Randi's tall, thin frame and haunting dark eyes were perfect. She'd landed a modeling contract. Sam contracted with her for the author gig shortly after that. It was perfect for both of them.

"New York is cold!" Randi's voice was deep, like her mother's, but freer, more energetic. "Snow in the city is magical. Each flake has meaning, like the lives of the millions of people who share the island and surrounding boroughs."

Sam smiled. "Maybe you should try poetry."

"I have no time for that," Randi said. "I'm swamped. Thanks for sending the concert tickets. That was sweet of you."

"You're welcome. Wish I could join you, but I'm swamped here, too. Are you all clear to come to Ohio in March?"

"I can't wait to get back there! How many book signings are scheduled?"

"You have two in Columbus, one in Dayton, two in Cincinnati, and one in Wood Grove."

She laughed. "You are hilarious! Scheduling a reading for a used bookstore in your own hometown."

Sam smiled again. "It's good for the town. You'll be a big hit here."

"Okay," she stage-whispered. "How many people in town know that I share your DNA?"

"Two," he answered. "You and me."

"Thanks for keeping that between us. Dad would have a fit if he knew Mom had introduced me to you. In spite of how he's been acting for the past eight years, I want you to know he was a good father."

"I have no reason to doubt that, Randi."

She'd said that, or something similar, many times over the years. Sam admired her loyalty, even though he had no positive regard for Elena's husband. What kind of man disinherits a child for being gay? Only a complete asshole would do that.

They said goodbyes and promised to touch base soon. As he hung up, he considered that though he had no love for Leo Flemming, he did feel some measure of pity for the man, for what he had lost. Randi was a treasure. Sam congratulated himself on what he had with Randi, the perfect father-daughter relationship. He mentored her and she treated him like a beloved friend.

Ruby appeared in the doorway. "That sounded nice."

"Yeah," Sam sat forward. "She's doing great."

"Funny how your old friend shows up and her daughter becomes your number one literary client."

Sam opened his appointment book.

"I wonder sometimes if there's something more between you two," she said.

"Huh?" He looked up.

"Between you and the mother. You haven't seemed very interested in other women since she came along. I want you to know, whatever you're doing, I know it's none of my business, but you can talk to me about anything."

Sam smiled. "Thanks, but I already know that, Ruby. Elena and I are old friends. That's all."

"Okay," Ruby said. "But remember you can talk to me, Sam. It's not good to keep secrets. That's why men get high blood pressure. They don't talk enough."

"I talk, Ruby. Every day you and I talk. Go get yourself some coffee, will you? I'm all talked out right now."

She raised her eyebrows before walking away. Sam heard her put on her coat and the door closing as she left.

He sat back in the chair again, rubbing his face with his hands. Grace hadn't called to thank him for the flowers. Of course she hadn't. He'd heard she'd been with John when he died. Sam couldn't imagine what Grace must be feeling. He could send flowers again. How soon would be too soon?

He heard the door to the street open. "What did you forget, Ruby?" he called out.

"It's me, Sam," Gloria McKay answered.

Sam walked into the reception area. Gloria stood beside Ruby's desk, her belly popping through the front of her unbuttoned blue wool coat.

"Should you be out by yourself?" Sam asked. "The sidewalks are slick. You don't want to fall."

"Pregnant women do carry on with life," Gloria said.

"Is everything okay?" Sam asked.

"Yes, everything's okay, but I have a big favor to ask."

"Shoot," he said.

Gloria rested her hands on top of her belly. "Jasper has to drive a load to Florida. I'm afraid that he might not make it back in time if I go into labor. We only have a few more Lamaze classes. There's one tonight at six thirty." She squinted her eyes and asked, "Would you be our backup?"

"Backup?" Sam asked.

"Coach. In case Jasper can't be there. Will you be my backup coach for the delivery room?"

"Wow!" Sam said. "You mean while the baby's born?"

Gloria laughed. "That would be the point. My niece agreed to babysit for Stewie, so she can't help. Skip said he doesn't want to see my 'hoo-hah.' Mary Sue's afraid she might faint. I don't have anybody else to ask."

Sam didn't want to see Gloria's 'hoo-hah,' either, but he was sure he could make it through a birth without fainting. "I'd be honored," he said.

"Thank you." She threw her arms around his neck. "You're such a great friend."

"How's Stewie taking this?" Sam had provided babysitting for her firstborn many times.

She dug into her purse. "He's excited about being a big brother, but he's seven. I expect he'll get bored and resentful within two weeks." She pulled out a little black device, looked at Sam, and dangled it at arm's length. "Here."

Sam held out his hand to receive the object.

"I bought this pager for you," she said. "Carry it with you at all times and if it goes off, call me right away. I'll be in labor. If you can't get hold of me, go straight to the hospital in Chillicothe."

"Shall I pick you up at five-thirty tonight?" he asked.

"Sounds great." She hugged him again. "Thanks a million. I can always count on you." She opened the door and walked out.

"Be careful out there!" Sam called behind her.

Sam wondered how Gloria could risk another child with someone as unreliable as Jasper. Sure, Jasper had cleaned up his act. He seemed to have a steady income driving that big rig. And, by all appearances, he maintained the exterior of the house that Sam had helped Gloria purchase. But why hadn't the man married her again? For crying out loud, it seemed like the least he could do.

The office phone rang. He could let it go to the answering machine, but he was right there leaning on the edge of Ruby's desk. He picked up the receiver and said, "Law office."

"Sam? It's Grace. Thank God, you answered. I really didn't want to talk to Ruby. Can you take Teddy to the airport tonight? Arthur was going to, but he has some kind of bug now and I have to fly to Atlanta tomorrow and I'm not even sure I'm safe on the road right now. I'm sure you heard about John. I'm sorry to ask, but I really need help. Can you take him?"

"Slow down, Grace. No problem. I can take him. What time?" Sam asked.

"His flight leaves at seven," Grace answered.

He couldn't attend Gloria's Lamaze class and take Teddy to the airport at the same time.

"Sam?" she asked.

"Tell him I'll pick him up at five," Sam said. Better to get there early than risk missing the flight. Rush hour could be slow, and if anybody had an accident….

"Thank you," Grace said.

"What else can I do?" he asked.

"Nothing, that's all I need. Thanks so much."

He wanted to do more. "Anything, Grace, please, ask any time."

She thanked him again and said goodbye.

Sam put down the receiver and looked at the pager. He'd read enough about women in labor to know he could handle the birth without attending Lamaze training. Ruby could drive Gloria to the class tonight, and he would drive Teddy to the airport. Family life might not look like the dreams Sam once had, but he did have people he could count on, people who could count on him.

Some people with real families couldn't say that.

Chapter Eighteen

GRACE OPENED HER EYES to Loretta's peaceful face lying next to her on the pillow. She eased herself into a sitting position to watch the rise and fall of the quilt covering her best friend. Asleep and still breathing. That was a good sign.

Sunlight filled the room. What little sleep Grace had managed started right before dawn. The clock said eight. They would have to get moving. Grace slid out of bed and padded into Loretta's kitchen.

A note lay in the middle of the kitchen table. "Grace, Arthur's still sick. Ben and I will stay close by in case he needs anything. Sam offered to drive you to the airport. Sam will pick you up again after the return flight. I'll see you later. Call if you need anything. Hugs, Polly."

Grace lowered herself onto a kitchen chair and rested her head on her arms.

She would be in the car, with Sam, twice in one day.

He'd been attentive when he picked up Teddy last night. Before leaving for the airport, he'd asked: Could he bring over food? Were there calls he could make? Did they have someone to take over John's duties? If she gave a list to him, he'd be happy to do what he could. He knew how to maintain a house.

The offers were genuine, smart. She'd said she might have to take him up on a few.

When Teddy and she parted at the kitchen door, her son offered to stay, but she wouldn't have it. "Go. Finish the school year. Call any time. I'll be right here."

"I love you, Mom," Teddy said, with another long, strong hug.

She watched him walk to Sam's car, backpack slung over one shoulder, hair hanging loose and swinging side-to-side. Sam had opened the passenger side door like a chauffeur and Teddy had flashed a peace sign to his mother as he lowered himself onto the car seat. She had blown a kiss to her son right as Sam turned around to wave. Sam smiled and flashed a peace sign. Grace had smiled without thinking for the first time in weeks.

Her arms started aching from the weight of her head, but she was too tired to move. So much left to do; so much already done.

After Sam and Teddy left for the airport, Grace made final arrangements with Ed Turnbull for John's cremation. The memorial service would come later. Ed's compassion touched her deeply and she wanted to let herself fall apart, but she needed to keep it together until she was sure Loretta was safe.

When Donald died, Sarah had been stoic, maybe because his death wasn't a surprise. The loss of both Stephen and John had undone Loretta. She barely slept. She couldn't eat. Typically thin anyway, her weight plummeted. She looked anorexic. Charlene expressed concern that Loretta might not recover. Grace refused to share that concern. She had curled herself around Loretta's shaking, sobbing grief for three nights in a row, willing her friend to recover her hold on life, because Grace knew that she could, and because Grace needed her to.

It was going to be a long day.

"Hey."

Grace lifted her head.

Loretta stood in the hallway that separated the dining area from the two small bedrooms and bathroom. Gaunt and ghostlike, at least her voice still had some life in it. "What time is our flight?"

"Eleven."

"We'd better get moving, sister girl." She disappeared back into her bedroom and Grace moved away from the table, ready to face the day.

Sam picked them up at nine. This morning he didn't say much. He opened doors, carried bags, escorted Loretta with one arm around her back and the other holding her arm. Grace and Loretta shared the backseat. Before they had even covered the distance from GraceHaven into Wood Grove, Loretta laid her head on Grace's lap and slept with a light, even snore.

"What's the plan?" Sam asked.

"I'm flying with her to Atlanta. Her sister will pick her up at the airport. I'll turn around and fly back."

"Do you want me to fly with you?" he asked.

"No, there's no reason to do that. I'm sorry to have to bother you like this. Did you have to cancel clients?"

They both spoke with low, quiet voices. Loretta continued to snore.

"Easily rescheduled," he said. "I'm happy to help."

"Thank you." She looked out the window, watching naked, brown trunks and branches flow past the window. Every so often, a grouping or line of evergreens refreshed the view.

They made it to the airport before ten o'clock, with time to spare before boarding. Sam offered to park and stay with them, but Grace insisted on being dropped at the terminal. She slung both bags over her shoulders. Loretta carried a small, light cloth purse.

Sam hugged Grace around the shoulders before kissing Loretta on the cheek.

Loretta pressed the backs of her fingers against Sam's cheek. "Thank you. John always told me how much he liked you."

"I wish we'd spent more time together. He was a good man," Sam said.

Grace guided Loretta away before he could say more. She wasn't sure she could maintain her composure if Sam uttered one more kindness. As she held the door for Loretta, Grace turned back one time. Sam stood by his car watching them. She faced forward and walked Loretta to the ticket counter.

All checked in and having made it to the correct gate, they sat close to the boarding door. Loretta crocheted briefly. Grace watched the people.

A woman held her infant to her breast under the cover of a large shawl.

A man wearing a dark green suit held a newspaper close to his face.

Two young people in jeans and wool sweaters shared a candy bar.

"John would want us to carry on the work," Loretta said.

"Of course," Grace said. "There's no question of that." She had promised John she would do whatever it took to keep the work going, but she wasn't going to discuss that now.

As soon as they boarded the plane, Loretta fell asleep and slept all the way to Atlanta. Grace stayed awake, watchful.

Upon arrival, Loretta's family waited at the gate. Loretta hugged Grace weakly, saying she needed to lie down again, soon. Grace let Charlene take the lead in physically holding up her sister while dispatching her husband to locate a wheelchair. When he returned, Loretta allowed herself to be wheeled away. Before following behind her husband and sister, Charlene hugged Grace, thanking her, leaving behind the sweet scent of her perfume on Grace's coat and scarf.

While waiting for her return flight, and on the plane home, Grace brought the scarf to her nose and inhaled several times, remembering the strength in Charlene's touch, confident that Loretta would receive the best care possible, but also feeling abandoned herself. There had been direction, purpose, in the act of caring for Loretta. What would absorb Grace's pain now?

Sam met her at the gate in Columbus.

"I told you I'd meet you outside, where you dropped us off," she said.

"You look awful," Sam said.

"Thanks," Grace said.

He took her bag and slung it over his shoulder. "I'm taking you for food."

"No, Polly's cooking, I don't need you to do that."

She walked a step in front of him until they were outside and she had to follow him to his car.

When they were in the car, he said, "Sorry about what I said, but really, Grace, you look terrible. How much have you slept in the last week?"

She didn't answer. She had no answers. She shoved her purse between her head and the window.

He woke her when they were parked behind the main house.

She didn't want to wake up. She could have stayed in his car and slept for a week.

Wiping her mouth with the back of her hand, she thanked him, grabbed her purse, and opened the door.

He opened his door and moved in that direction.

"Stay in the car," she said. "I don't need help." She was out now, standing on the driveway.

He pulled his door shut.

She leaned down. "Thanks for taking me there and back. Don't worry about what you said. I know I look like shit. I appreciate the honesty." She smiled at him.

"Grace," he said. "I worry about you."

"Thanks, but don't." She shut the car door and walked into the house.

Dinner was on the table, homemade macaroni and cheese and a luscious salad. Norma, Grant, Benjamin, Polly, Max, and Elizabeth took their seats.

Grace sat at the head of table. Conversations were quiet. Grace answered questions but kept her eyes on the food, eating small portions, and thanking Polly. When she finished, Grace picked up her plate and started to rise from her seat.

Ben put his hand on her arm. "Leave it. We'll clean up tonight."

She lowered the plate back down to the table.

"Is there anything else we can do around here?" Max asked.

"I can cook!" Elizabeth said.

Max shushed her. Elizabeth sat back in her chair, mouthing, "I can."

Grace smiled at her. Elizabeth was such a lovable oddball. She didn't seem to lack intelligence, but did seem to lack social skills, her expressions nearly always unexpected, unless she was interacting with people under the age of five.

"We'll help in any way we can." Ben again put his hand on her arm.

Norma left her chair and went to the kitchen.

Grace surveyed the remaining faces at the table. "Give me a day to rest. I'll let you know at dinner tomorrow where we sit with maintenance and meal prep." Tears came to her eyes.

"Oh, Grace," Elizabeth said. "Don't cry. John came to me in a dream last night. He's with Stephen now. They're happy, really happy."

"Thanks," Grace said, and left the table.

As she walked into the hall, she heard Polly say, "Nick's flying in tonight. I'm to pick him up at the airport. Anybody want to ride with me?"

Grant and Ben volunteered to accompany Polly on her midnight run. When Ben offered to see if Arthur felt up to the trip, they started to debate about how many would comfortably fit in the car. The dining room door closed behind Grace.

She trudged up the two flights of steps to her room. John had either refinished, or supervised the refinishing of all of the steps, railings, and woodwork. She felt like she was touching his hands as she grasped the worn, smooth, curved support of the bannisters.

Though she'd been able to sleep in Sam's car, at home her body felt too wired to rest. Too many memories, she supposed. Sky and air might help. She put on extra socks and bundled herself in her fluffy coat with a fleece gaiter to cover her mouth, a matching hat, and two bulky mittens.

She gathered her yoga mat and the quilt Loretta had made for her, a pattern of violet, turquoise, deep red, and golden yellow.

She thought she might sit on the front porch by herself and managed to slip out the door without running into anyone, but saw Norma walking down the driveway, smoking.

Grace walked around to the back of the house. She often walked the woods at night. This night the moon lit her path. Her pace picked up speed and strength as she headed for the one place that might be, for Grace, most like the idyllic, soothing world that seemed to exist in Elizabeth's mind.

As she neared her destination, she could see someone standing on her boulder, but she wasn't afraid. She had seen Sam there before, many times.

He must have heard her approach, because he whirled his head around when she was still twenty feet away.

She walked up close to where he stood and said, "Move, please."

He stepped off the boulder. She unrolled the mat to make room for two. She sat on half, wrapped herself in the quilt, and said, "You're welcome to sit on the other half, but I'm not sharing my blanket."

As she settled onto the mat, crossing her legs and arranging the quilt so it created her own personal teepee, with only her face exposed, she felt him sit down beside her.

Ice had formed along the edges of the stream, but the middle still ran noisily, bubbling over the rocks.

Grace closed her eyes and listened to the sounds of the water, like bursting, like friction, like a small percussive band of drops playing an eternal tune that sound tracked birth, death, and everything that happened in between.

Grateful for Sam's silence, she didn't flinch when he rested his hand on her knee.

After a long period of meditation, in which her heart rate slowed and her thoughts calmed, she said, "You saw me that day I stripped and stood on my rock."

He removed his hand from her knee.

"I didn't mean to intrude," he said. "I was going to try to talk to you—" followed by a nervous chuckle "—but then you took off all of your clothes and I thought that something might be wrong with you, mentally, you know."

"I wondered if you were a pervert," Grace said. "Like your friend, Skip."

"Yeah, well, I'm not, but there are real perverts around, so you might want to watch getting naked by yourself in the woods."

"Haven't done it since," she said, "not that I need to be told by you."

He sighed. "We were having such a nice moment there."

A snarky reply rose to her lips but melted away when he put his hand back on her knee.

Her eyes shifted from contemplation of the stream and woods beyond, to softly closed and less blind to the dark and light thoughts that swirled in her mind.

"I am so sorry about Stephen and John," Sam said. "I wanted to say that in the car, on the way back. And I didn't have a chance to ask about Loretta. How was she on the flight?"

"She made it," Grace said. "But I don't know what's going to happen. She's a mess, Sam. Everything's a mess."

"I'm so very sorry, Grace," he said. "John was a good man. I meant it when I said I wish I'd spent more time with him. I feel like I lost something I never had."

She heard him sniff.

His unexpected sorrow cut right through the reserve that had been holding her together. A soft wail burst from her chest and she felt his arm circle her shoulders and tug her closer. She dropped her head against him and let herself cry until she was done.

One deep breath, accompanied by a surge of embarrassment, prompted her to lift herself away from him.

"Thanks," she said and took the handkerchief he offered.

She wiped her eyes and gave it back.

"Let me make some tea for you," he said.

Grace hesitated, turning to look at him for the first time since seating herself on the rock. He seemed so solid. Maybe she should stop resisting his invites. He'd been consistent over the years. A real friendship wasn't out of the question.

Words of acceptance were almost spoken when a funny buzzing noise sounded and Sam stood up, rattled, digging in his pocket. He pulled out a little black device and turned off the sound.

"Sorry," he said. "Gloria must be in labor. I'm Jasper's pinch hitter."

Grace nodded. "I take it this is your first."

"It shows?" He asked, chuckling.

"Just be there," Grace said. "She'll probably yell at you."

"Won't be the first time I've been yelled at by a woman," he said. "So, I really have to get going. How about dinner tomorrow night?"

She shook her head, "I don't think so, Sam."

"Why not?"

"Nick's coming back. We'll have so much to do. I'm going to be busy for the next few months."

"Aw," he said. "Nick."

Grace could see what he thought. She chose to not correct him. Let Sam think what he wanted. She was safer that way.

"Okay," he said. "Be well. You know where I am if you ever need anything."

"Thanks," she said.

He moved away from the rock.

She almost called him back, but checked herself. She was going to be busy for the next God-knew-how-long, and more to the point, she couldn't risk another round of falling in love and being discarded. She just couldn't set herself up for that kind of disappointment again.

He disappeared into the dark.

She took a deep breath and hugged the quilt around her knees.

Crying with him had been good. She might sleep tonight. She might dream of rainbows and roses.

Damn, she hadn't thanked him for the flowers.

Chapter Nineteen
1998

ONE-BY-ONE, THE STAINED glass above them backed by gray sky, each of the GraceHaven residents offered their piece of the eulogy. Grace heard myth more than memory. She had declined the opportunity to romanticize Nicholas Mason. She had said everything she ever wanted to say to or about him when he was alive. What could she possibly add now?

Loretta patted Grace's arm. "It's almost over, honey. After Norma, the minister will say a few words, and then there's only the eating to get through."

Brown skin sagged on Loretta's cheeks and darker crescents rimmed her tearing eyes. Beside Loretta sat her sister, Charlene. Charlene looked ten years younger than Loretta, though Grace knew they were only a year apart. Hard times will do that to you. Loretta had survived her losses, but the cost of living through them never went away.

Loretta would be seventy years old soon. Grace would be sixty-three in two months. Where the hell had her life gone?

She turned back to face forward. Rain pelted the windows behind the elegant reddish-brown woman who now stood at the lectern. "In many ways Nick was like a father to me."

Over the years, Grace had become immune to Norma's style, but today her words sliced through Grace's reserve. Nick hadn't been like a father to Norma. Nick had never been like a father to anybody, not even his own son. Nick Mason had never progressed much beyond the maturity of a typical three-year-old, testing to see how far he could go, coming back to touch Mommy's skirt for the courage to explore further, running back to hide his face in Mommy's lap when the unknown seemed too scary. The sick part was that Grace had played the role of Mommy for the past forty-three years. The thought rose in her throat, hot and acidic.

Norma's voice rang out. "I remember the first day Nick introduced me to the community…."

Grace would wager her small, precious savings account that she could remember the day with more accuracy.

"Such a great, great man. I wish that God would have taken me instead." Norma lowered her head as she left the lectern.

God could have both of them, as far as Grace was concerned. If Nick hadn't died in his sleep, she might have strangled him.

The minister approached the lectern and shook Norma's hand before she returned to her seat. He called for a moment of silence. Grace bowed her head, sinking into defeat.

The day after his death, Grace had searched Nick's desk and found the rewritten will, the one that would have fulfilled his promise to her, stuck between the pages of a short story, unsigned. A few phone calls confirmed the awful truth. There were no signed copies, anywhere. She balled her fist, clutching the black fabric on her knee, damning Nick's arrogant insistence that he couldn't be bothered with the details of life, damning her tolerance over the years.

"Honey, the minister is leaving," Loretta said. Grace smoothed her skirt as she started to move out of her chair, but somebody laid a warm hand on her shoulder.

"I'm so sorry about Nick." Sam's sea-blue eyes searched her face. What did he want from her? She had nothing to give.

"Excuse me." She slid from under his touch to follow the minister out the door.

Loretta followed close behind. "Why did you ignore him like that? Sam's been a good friend to you."

"He probably wants to buy the place," Grace said. "I wouldn't be surprised if this whole will business was premeditated, part of a plan to accomplish his long-held desire to extend his property. He'll open a bed & breakfast. Wait and see."

"You're talking crazy," Loretta said.

"Don't call me crazy." Leaving Loretta behind, she surged ahead to catch up with the minister, a young man with a full brown beard and black glasses. She intercepted him on the porch steps. He clutched his Bible against his chest.

"If you ever need anything…," he said.

"Thank you, I will." She thrust forward a check and crossed her arms.

The minister hesitated, stepped sideways off the last step and said, "I'll pray for you."

"We appreciate you coming. Have a safe trip home." Grace walked to the other side of the porch and faced the line of trees that separated GraceHaven from Sam's property.

Why had Sam even bothered to come? Guilt? Shame? She didn't really believe he'd done it on purpose, but Sam had to have some inkling of what the unsigned will meant for her. Nick's family had inherited everything. Grace was left with next-to-nothing.

She heard the minister's car start. He waved as he passed by. She raised her hand, not bothering to smile.

How could Nick not sign the will? She shivered, watching the icy rain turn to snow. She wanted to believe that Nick hadn't done it on purpose, either, but that would only mean he had been unconcerned about her welfare and she had allowed him to neglect her. She should have been more attentive. She never should have trusted him. She dug her fingers into her arms. Perhaps she had only gotten what she deserved.

By the time Grace returned to the gathering, she found that the caterers had hastily rearranged the chairs, lining them along the walls of the grand living room and replacing the furniture that had been stored in the office. She stood in the doorway and surveyed the people milling about.

Teddy sidled over and put his arm across her shoulders. “Mom.”

She reached for his wineglass. “Let me have a drink.”

“Drink it all. I was carrying it around for effect.”

He handed the glass to her. She reached behind his head with her free hand, gently tugging his ponytail.

“Where’s Aunt Sarah?” he asked.

“She went upstairs to lie down. She had a headache.” Grace sipped at the wine. When it hit her lips, she realized she hadn’t eaten since breakfast. “Take it back. I can’t drink more than that. Have you seen Elizabeth?”

Teddy took the glass and swirled the wine. “She’s behind the piano, dancing with Arthur.”

Grace caught a glimpse of Arthur’s white hair dipping up and down beyond the crowd gathered at the piano. “Arthur will take care of her.”

“You worried about her?”

“It’s only been six months since Max died and she’s been acting even more herself than usual. I think that warrants a little worry.”

“Yeah,” Teddy chuckled. “Elizabeth has always been a bit on the… let’s say *ethereal* side.”

Grace continued to scan the crowd, but she could feel Teddy’s eyes on her.

“What, Teddy?”

“What about you?” he asked.

“What about me?”

“Nick’s been dead less than a month. How are you doing?”

"I'll live." When Teddy didn't say anything, she asked, "Where's Judy?"

"She had to take Raven for a walk."

"Loretta?" she asked.

"She's in the kitchen. Charlene's with her. Driving here all the way from Atlanta was such a nice thing to do."

"What are they doing in the kitchen? That's why I hired caterers. Loretta's driving me nuts. She just won't stop."

"Relax, Mom. Loretta's doing what she wants to do. Everybody deals with death in their own way."

"What are you, an expert?" She hadn't meant to sound so cross. Teddy only pulled her closer and kissed her on the side of her head.

"How're you doing, Mom?"

She let her head rest against his chest. "I think we're okay." She flipped her wrist toward the couch facing the nearest fireplace. "Peter and Grant are over there reading the *New York Times*." Peter read over Grant's shoulder. Grant held the newspaper up and to the side, to accommodate both of them. "Fran's helping the caterers pick up used plates and glasses." Fran's dress clung to her hips, showing a distinct panty line. "Phil and Larry are having a great time at the piano."

Since their move to GraceHaven last year, Phil and Larry had proven themselves to be assets to the community. Both architects, they had a keen eye for design and weren't shy about pitching in with an opinion or hands-on help when needed.

"You-know-who's overplaying her role." Grace's eyes rested for a moment on Norma. She leaned against a mantle, a glass of wine under her nose, tears slipping down her cheeks. "I think we're okay," Grace repeated, this time with more conviction.

"I didn't ask about them. I asked about you." Teddy lowered his head until his cheek touched the top of her head "And how are you doing?"

"Haven't you been listening? Ben and Polly are on the couch with their heads together. Judy and Raven have been in and out all day. Judy has great plans for the landscaping. She wants to put in raised beds…."

"I don't want to hear any more about them or GraceHaven," Teddy said. "I want to hear about you."

Grace raised her head and bumped her son with her hip. "I am telling you about me. They are me. This place is me. This is what I live for."

She could see Teddy start to protest, but Polly and Ben appeared at his side and interrupted.

"We have something to tell you," Polly said.

Grace waited, forcing a smile. Polly looked at Ben, her mouth wreathed in more genuine lines.

"We're getting married," Ben said. His wrinkled face bunched together in a joyful grin.

Teddy took his arm from Grace's shoulder and pumped Ben's hand. "That's wonderful, Ben."

"Polly, I'm happy for you." Grace put her hands on the taller woman's shoulders and kissed her cheek.

"It was Nick's doing, really," Polly said. "Ben proposed to me the night after Nick died. We wanted to wait until after the memorial to tell you. I couldn't wait another minute!"

"We're both in our eighties now," Ben said. "I realized that any one of us might be next." He gazed at Polly. "I want to spend every moment with her for as long as I live."

Grace nodded, acknowledging what had been growing for decades. Polly and Ben had developed a sweet friendship. They sat beside each other at meals. He escorted her to events. She helped him practice his lines. This made perfect sense. Their friendship had evolved into love.

"I'm very happy for both of you." She hugged Polly and then Ben. "We'll have an engagement party. When's the wedding?"

"We'll talk about it later," Polly said. "Have you eaten yet?"

"No." Grace placed her hand on her abdomen, aware of a hollow feeling inside. "I've got to eat something before I faint." Kissing Polly's cheek, she excused herself to Teddy and Ben and headed for the dining room, happy to escape more of Teddy's probing.

When she reached the food table, she frowned down at the bowl left with only streaks of guacamole on the clear crystal surface. Grace started to whine to herself but stopped when two brown hands with perfectly manicured fingernails picked up the bowl while two brown hands with clipped nails filled the empty spot with a dish full of chunky smashed avocado, lemon juice, and garlic.

Before Grace could scoop some onto her plate, a thin, peach-colored hand, also sporting a perfect manicure, blocked Grace's spoon.

"I want some of that," Sarah said.

Grace pushed her sister's hand aside, but Sarah stood her ground. She managed to take two hefty scoops and drop them on her plate before Grace had a shot at it. Sarah dipped a chip, raised it to her lips, and munched down, her eyes closed. "Mmm, thank you God, and thank you, Loretta."

"How did you know I made it?" Loretta asked.

"Nobody prepares food like you, my dear," Sarah answered.

"Headache better?" Grace asked.

"Mmm," Sarah nodded as she chewed.

The two sets of sisters stood huddled by the table, three of them sharing cooking tips while Grace listened and ate.

The conversation shifted away from food. Charlene and Sarah, who had met earlier in the day, resumed a discussion of GraceHaven's situation.

"I can't believe he left you all high and dry," Sarah said. "Or maybe I can. I never did trust him."

"So he actually had the will drawn up and never signed it?" Charlene asked.

"I thought you had a copy." Sarah looked at Grace.

"I had an unsigned copy," Grace said, wiping the corner of her mouth. "He said he had an appointment to sign." She shrugged her shoulders.

"You should always have a copy of everything, with signatures," Sarah said. "I learned that before Donald died. Will, living will, power of attorney for healthcare, durable power of attorney. It wasn't cheap, but we got it done right."

Grace picked up a glass of wine from a tray on the table and drank half of it. "Yep," she said when she came up for air. "That would have been a smart thing to do." She drank down the other half and put the empty glass back on the tray.

"What are you going to do?" Charlene asked. "Can you rent from his son?"

"Maybe." A warm, pleasant feeling spread through Grace's midsection.

"Well, whatever happens, you two have each other." Sarah put one hand on Grace's arm and one on Loretta's. "Who knew we had such a dynamic duo in the family? Flying all over the country. Conducting tough conversations about race."

"I knew that," Charlene said.

"Well, I never realized how successful my little sister had become," Sarah said. "I'm proud of you, Grace."

"They are quite the team." Charlene beamed at her own sister.

"You two are starting to make me feel a little sick," Loretta said. "Charlene, will you accompany me back to my kitchen?"

"I would be honored." Charlene linked arms with Loretta. They disappeared into the kitchen.

"I wish she'd stay out of the kitchen," Grace said.

"People have their own ways of dealing with death." Sarah took a small mirror from her purse and examined her face.

"Everybody's an expert today." Grace picked up another glass of wine.

"Did you ever finish that renovation on the apartment over the garage?" Sarah asked, putting the mirror away.

Grace drank a large mouthful of wine. Max had outlived his use for the sculpture studio years before he passed. “We finished that last year. Our new groundskeeper lives up there with her dog.”

“I want to see it,” Sarah said. “I remember you had a very special designer working on it.”

“Yeah,” Grace said. She drank again. “Too bad Phil and Larry weren’t here during the design phase.”

“I’m sure it’s beautiful. May I go up and see it?”

“Find the young woman with the big black dog and ask for permission.”

“Okay with you if I leave after that? I want to get back before it’s too late.”

“No problem.” Grace set the wineglass on the table and hugged her sister. “Is Teddy sharing a ride back to Columbus?”

“We drove separately.” Sarah started to walk away, but turned and stepped back to Grace. “You look so tired. Teddy tells me you’ve been pretty cranky lately. Are you sure you don’t want the number for that therapist? She’s really good with trauma.”

Grace sighed. “I’m fine.” She picked up the wine again. “A few good nights of sleep and I’ll be back in action. I’ll figure this out, Sarah. Don’t worry about me.”

Sarah hugged her again. “Call me if you need anything.”

Her sister disappeared through the door to the kitchen. Grace stationed herself against the edge of the doorframe, pressing the hard surface into the muscles running up and down beside her spine.

A young woman stood against the wall at the other end of the room. Grace did now what she had avoided doing all day. She noticed her. Teddy approached the woman, offering a glass of wine. The young woman took it and smiled as she sipped.

She wore a navy-blue dress that fell below her knees, topped with a soft cream sweater with beads on the front. She had brown hair that brushed the tops of her shoulders. She might have been a co-ed at a women's college, circa nineteen sixty-five, but she wasn't. She was Mallory Mason, Nick's granddaughter.

Thirty years old, with an MBA, Mallory had arrived late last night. Via the brief interaction that Grace had been unable to avoid this morning, she had learned that Mallory Mason was not as benign as she appeared to be. The family had sent her to dismantle GraceHaven, and with an officious tone that could rival that of her grandmother, Mallory seemed like she might be up to the task.

With that thought weighing heavy, Grace scanned the rest of the crowd, deliberate in her decision to pass over Sam. He stood close to the doorway at the other end of the room. She knew she was being petulant. Loretta was right. Sam had been a good friend to them. Grace should probably give him the benefit of the doubt.

Her eyes darted back to him. He nursed a glass of wine as he, too, scanned the crowd. Yes, she should be nicer to him, more generous in her expectations. Even a little less rude would be an improvement.

She watched as Mary Sue McKay approached Sam and he embraced her with one arm. Skip joined his wife, his head bobbing and his arms wild. Mary Sue seemed refined, especially when juxtaposed with Skip's erratic movements and behavior. He still eyed Grace with the air of a hunter who would one day bring down his prey.

Grace gulped the last of the wine.

Skip deserved her wrath, but Grace knew she should act with more decorum toward Sam. She glanced at him one more time, taking in the way he seemed to dominate that part of the room. People do funny things, but people like Sam Cielo did not deliberately screw over their neighbors. The will was Nick's doing, not Sam's. He had never really done her wrong. She might even accept a dinner date to make up for her recent behavior, if he ever asked again.

Was that the wine talking? Grace looked at the drink in her hand. She had never downed two glasses of wine in such a short time in her entire life.

Skip and Mary Sue walked away from Sam. Sam caught Grace's eye and tipped his glass. She held up her wine and headed to the kitchen. She would be nicer to Sam, maybe even invite him to dinner first, maybe tomorrow. But right now, maybe she would have another glass of wine.

No maybes about it. That sounded like the right thing to do.

Chapter Twenty

AT LEAST SHE HAD acknowledged him. Sam watched as Grace disappeared through the door to the kitchen. She always looked good in black. Today a rosiness highlighted her cheeks and her mostly-gray hair hung in a thick braid down the middle of her back.

He remembered her grief after the deaths of Stephen and John, holding in everything until the dust settled. Earlier today, she had moved past him on her way to the dining room with her customary determination. Though Sam liked the way Grace always seemed to know where she was going, he knew she had to slow down at some point and allow the pain to rise up.

A young woman planted herself in front of him.

"Hey, Judy." Sam moved away from the doorway to shake Judy's hand. Her cheeks were pink. Her hand cold.

Sam and the GraceHaven groundskeeper had established a comfortable rapport starting late last summer and into the fall. As he and John had done so many years ago, Sam and Judy had met at the "fence" and worked together to clear weeds, pick up trash, and share ideas about gardening and landscaping.

"Been out in your garden yet?" Judy asked.

"Unfortunately, no," he said. "I had planned to this weekend, but the rain keeps coming down. Are you just in from outside?"

"I had to walk Raven."

Sam bent to pat the top of the dog's shiny, black head. "Does she go everywhere with you?"

"Almost everywhere."

"Come on over someday," Sam said. "I'll feed you lunch and you can help me with a patch of ground out by the garage. I can't decide what to do with it." He patted the dog once more. "She's welcome too."

"I'd like that, Sam."

"There you are." A petite woman with black leggings and tunic joined them. "Remember me?" She shook Judy's hand. "I think we passed each other this morning when I arrived. I'm Grace's sister, Sarah. And who do have we here?" She squatted to rub the dog's face. Raven licked her cheek.

"Sit!" Judy said in a clipped yet soft tone.

The dog sat, tongue in mouth, its soulful eyes on Judy.

"It's okay. I like doggie kisses." Sarah stood and faced Sam, holding out her hand. "I'm Sarah Gleason, and I'm sure that you and I haven't met. I would have remembered."

Sam shook her hand. "Sam Cielo. I live next door."

"Really? Grace never mentioned you. Is your wife here, too?"

"I don't have a wife," he said.

"Intriguing," she said.

Grace's sister wasn't subtle. With full makeup and short hair dyed blond, Sarah appeared to be nothing like her sister.

She turned to address Judy. "I am dying to see that apartment of yours. Mind showing me before I leave?"

"No problem," Judy said.

Turning again to Sam, Sarah smiled. "I hope we run into each other again."

"See you later, Sam," Judy said.

"Ladies." He tipped his head as they turned to walk away.

Sam watched them walk the length of the room and exit to the kitchen. Judging by the size of the rocks on Sarah's hand, she either had a professional career or had married well. He remembered Grace mentioning her a long time ago. Funny that Grace had never mentioned him to her.

“Hey, Sam, nice service, huh?”

Sam turned to shake Ed Turnbull’s hand. “Very nice, did you arrange it?”

“I helped the caterers set up the table and altar, had the memoriam cards printed, and brought Nick back from the crematory,” Ed said.

Sam nodded his head. “You did great, Ed. It’s going well.”

“I could have handled the crowd right in my funeral home, but they wanted to have it here. ‘Why not?’ I said. ‘You’ve got plenty of room and it’ll make you all more comfortable.’” He moved in closer “You’ve got to be flexible in this business. Most people choose to have the service outside of their home because they want to isolate death, put it someplace outside of the day-to-day. These people are different.”

Sam nodded in agreement. “That they are, Ed. They are different.” He looked around until he spied Grace over by the piano. She seemed engrossed in a conversation with a tall woman whose tendrils of red hair curled from beneath a high striped turban.

Indeed these people were different, but different in a way that appealed to him now. He’d been too careful when he was young. He sighed.

“Were you and Nick friends?” Ed asked, drawing Sam’s attention back to the here and now.

“We spoke a few times.”

“You lived so close to each other for so many years. Didn’t get along?”

“I think we had little in common,” Sam said. He remembered the first time he’d met Nicholas Mason and seen his flippant disregard for others.

“That surprises me, Sam. I always thought of the both of you as two peas in a pod.”

“How so?” What could Ed possibly mean by that? He had Sam’s full attention now.

Ed's face softened. He looked up at Sam as he mused. "You're both handsome, single, real ladies' men. I figured you got together on a regular basis to compare notes."

"You know me better than that." Sam crossed his arms, careful to not spill his wine. He was nothing like Nick with his legendary infidelity. Grace deserved better.

"That's too bad." Ed looked at the floor. "I could use some pointers."

Sam leaned back against the wall, finally understanding. "Ah, you're a little out of practice."

Ed's scalp and ears reddened. "Forty-two years out of practice. We would have celebrated our forty-third wedding anniversary in June."

Sam remembered Ed's contrition at Edith's funeral the previous summer. He also remembered Edith's delicious meals and the hospitality their family had extended as Sam played dinner guest for several years when he first moved to town.

"Why don't we go to lunch someday?" he asked, resisting the urge to put his hand on the widower's shoulder.

"That'd be great, Sam. I'll stop by your office next week."

"Do that."

Ed walked away and Sam peeked back toward the piano. Grace was gone. When had she slipped away?

Someone tugged on his jacket sleeve. Sam looked down at Elizabeth's soft smile. Her white hair curled around the gentle folds of her pale, unblemished skin.

"Hello, Sam. Nice to see you again."

Sam never knew how to take Elizabeth. He had often seen her flit around the property dressed in gauzy pinks, blues, greens, and yellows, like a pastel butterfly, even in the coldest weather. Grace had once said that Elizabeth was harmless but likened herself to an ecdysiast, an animal that sheds its skin, and that she had once worked as a high-end stripper in the era of burlesque, when Gypsy Rose Lee slinked and slithered across the stage to stardom.

Elizabeth might be harmless, but she exuded a primal kind of innocence—Eve before she bit the apple—that made Sam feel at risk of exposing too much of himself.

"Sam," Elizabeth whispered, "See that girl over there, talking to our Teddy?"

Sam followed her finger and located Teddy less than twenty feet away from them. He leaned toward a young woman who leaned back against the wall, one foot slightly behind her, her head down. A classic come-hither pose. Teddy said something to her and walked away.

"Yes," Sam whispered. "I see her."

"Grace doesn't like her. She hasn't said so, but I can tell."

"Why doesn't Grace like her?" Sam asked. Perhaps she was Teddy's girlfriend and Grace felt displaced. Her son had to be in his thirties now and Grace would have to let go sometime. Parenting seemed harder on mothers than on fathers, but he didn't really have the whole experience, so he knew his viewpoint was suspect.

"She's going to make us all move," Elizabeth said.

"How's that?" Sam asked.

"She's Nick's granddaughter."

"I see," Sam said. If only he'd been more rigorous as Stewart slipped out of the practice. If Nick had only signed that will….

"If we do have to move, perhaps I could move in with you," Elizabeth said.

Sam's head jerked a bit. "What did you say?"

"Or, perhaps not." Elizabeth smiled and drifted away.

"Couldn't help but overhear." Teddy Baxter clapped his hand on Sam's shoulder. "Don't worry. We'll make sure she has a place to go."

"Teddy." Sam clasped the younger man's hand. "I'm so sorry about that business with the will. How's Grace doing?" He knew they were close and Grace had only good things to say about her son. Sam had no reason to doubt her. Teddy seemed like a fine young man.

"She's good." Teddy paused. "Nobody else blames you, Sam. We understand that Stewart McKay drew up the will."

"What a fiasco, huh? It's a shame."

"She'll be okay. She can always live with me."

That would put her in Columbus. Sam might never see her again. The idea did not appeal to him. "You're looking spry for a public defender, Teddy. How do you manage to keep yourself out of the fray?"

"I run," Teddy said. "Every morning."

"Good man." Sam clapped Teddy's shoulder. "That'll keep you going for years. Can't be easy, your job."

"It's not. Most of my people are guilty as hell," Teddy said. "I don't fault them for their behaviors, but they are guilty."

"What do you mean?" Sam asked.

"I see a difference between guilt and fault. Those who are guilty of committing crimes must face the consequences, but flaws in the education and criminal justice systems often don't give some people a chance. Their options are limited. Crime works for them, until it doesn't."

"You can't blame the system, Teddy. People make their own choices, and parents have a huge hand in how their children turn out." He thought of Gloria and her kids. Sam did everything he could to keep the youngest, Mandy, in line.

"You can hardly fault the parents," Teddy said. "The same systems created the same problems for them that impact the current generation. We need massive change in this country."

"Change starts at home," Sam said.

"And in the House, Senate, and Supreme Court."

"Touché." Sam's own optimism had waned over the years, but he still fought the good fight. You do the best you can. Teddy was still young. He'd learn.

After a long exchange that ranged from international affairs to sports, literature, and restaurants in Columbus, Teddy said, “I see Mom over there. I should go check in with her.”

“Great seeing you, Teddy. Stop by some time when you’re in town.”

“I’ll do that.”

Sam watched the younger man move toward his mother. She glanced beyond her approaching son, made eye contact with Sam, and looked away far too soon.

He placed his wineglass on a side table and walked to the front door without saying goodbye to anyone. He could have stayed, deepened connections with those who lived in Nick’s community, struck up conversations with out-of-town guests, but he didn’t fit in with these people, never had. They would probably see him as a square peg with no place in their lives of many shapes, and they would be right.

Sam liked his life laid out in predictable, organized patterns. When he got home at night, his house was as neat as he had left it in the morning. Ruby claimed that he lived alone because that was the best way to ensure total control over his environment. Maybe she was right. The only problem with total control was a decided lack of company.

With Nick gone, would Grace be open to the company of other men? Sam crossed the wooden porch and trotted down the steps. What a thought. Nick’s ashes were barely cooled. She deserved more consideration. Sam pulled his collar up as an icy finger of air breezed under his shirt.

He’d go home, sit in the hot tub, and take a good book to bed. Maybe he’d watch his tape of the Bulls game later. Then again, he could go through those files in his briefcase. Reminded he had plenty to keep his mind occupied, Sam reassured himself he could beat down the rising tide of loneliness he had come to accept as a normal part of aging.

Chapter Twenty-One

GRACE COULDN'T REMEMBER the last time she'd stayed in bed this long on a Monday, or any other day for that matter. Teddy had come upstairs before dawn to say he was leaving. He planned to take Charlene to the airport before going to work. Grace remembered saying goodbye and then drifting off again to dream about Nick and Sam dueling at dawn in white robes with Star Wars light sabers on the front lawn. GraceHaven had been turned into a spa.

Her head felt like a bowling ball.

How in the world did people become alcoholic? This hurt too much to repeat. She dragged herself onto her yoga mat and moved through her usual routine twice before dressing and braiding her hair. No longer able to avoid the inevitable, and only because she had to pee so badly she feared a bladder infection, Grace left her safe little corner of the world and moved beyond the trifold screens to, as her father would have put it, "Face the music."

The bathroom was free. After relieving her bladder, which took the edge off the throbbing in her head, she brushed the fuzz off her tongue, clipped her nails, and tidied the medicine cabinet. Now she had no more excuses. She tiptoed down the stairs and emerged from the back stairwell where she found, to her profound relief, no one else in the kitchen.

White roses burst from a vase in the middle of the table. She read the card. *So sorry for your loss. My thoughts and prayers are with you. Sam.*

His thoughts and prayers? The phrase sounded old-fashioned and insincere, and the card wasn't even addressed to anybody in particular. Grace flipped the card back on the table and reached for a pitcher from the shelves on the back wall.

The smell of bleach hovered near the scrubbed sink. She filled the pitcher with water, took a glass from the cabinet, pulled a bowl of cut fruit out of the refrigerator, and carried the three items to her office. Once there, she put her breakfast on the side of the desk, turned on her computer, and alternated between writing, drinking, and eating, until she had drained the bottom of the last glass and finished off the last grape.

A pair of heels tapped down the stairs and stopped at her door.

"Come in, Mallory," Grace said without looking up. She saved her work and turned off the monitor before raising her eyes to the freshly showered young woman who now stood by her side.

Hair combed and pulled into a tight ponytail, Mallory wore a gold necklace and earrings, a white silk blouse, navy blue skirt, hose, and blue pumps. "Are you going to show me around today?" she asked.

"Dressing like that isn't necessary," Grace said. "We're pretty casual around here."

"Apparently that hasn't paid off for you, has it?" Mallory looked all business and sounded too much like her grandmother.

Grace gestured to the loveseat. "Why don't we talk about your plans first?"

"Okay." Mallory stepped over and sat on the edge of the loveseat, back straight, legs crossed at the knees, hands folded in her lap.

Grace took a breath, determined to approach the situation with calm consideration.

Mallory interrupted Grace's deliberation by saying, "Look, Grace, I don't like this any more than you do. My father has given me the authority to assume control of my grandfather's assets until they can be sold. We're happy to let you all stay here until you can find other places to go, but you need to know that from now on, I'm in charge."

Grace took a deep breath and counted to ten. The soft rhythmic pounding in her head kept time with her heartbeat. Tapping her fingers on the desk, using every bit of tact she could summon, and speaking in the tone perfected for her interactions with Nick's ex, she said, "May I suggest you allow me to continue to manage the community while you inventory the tangible property? When you have those assets in order, you and I can talk about the real estate."

Mallory seemed to deflate. "That might be a good idea" She shifted her eyes about the room. "I'll speak with my grandfather's attorney and get back with you regarding when I'll be ready to assume full control. Thank you for being thoughtful."

"We pride ourselves on getting along with each other around here," Grace said.

"Good," Mallory said. "We can talk later about setting up an office space for me."

"Sounds great," Grace said. "Now, let me introduce you to GraceHaven."

They trekked back up the two flights of stairs to the attic first. Grace's screened-off area contained her parents' bedroom suite, her mother's hope chest, and an armoire. "This is mine," she said. "Everything I own is either in this corner or in my office."

"Even the computer?" Mallory asked.

"Well, I guess you could say the computer was purchased for community business, so in that way it probably belongs to everybody." She might lose the computer, too? She wouldn't be able to afford another one and she'd just started feeling competent in using it!

The rest of the attic contained a maze of stored paintings, photographs, sculptures, and mobiles, all donations from artists who had lived there, or passed through over the years, a collage of art representing the history of the community.

"This is rather overwhelming," Mallory said, her voice low, quavery. "I suppose I should have it all appraised,"

"I suppose you should," Grace said. She didn't like how much she relished seeing the young woman falter. Weren't people in their sixties supposed to be working on acceptance, integration, wisdom? Grace was getting acquainted with a whole new bitter side of herself. She was too hungover to care.

They returned to the second floor, where they bumped into Ben, literally, in the hallway. Mallory reached out to steady him with her hand on his arm.

"You must be Mallory," Ben said. "How do you like our little oasis here?"

"I like it," Mallory said.

Her response surprised Grace.

"Arthur!" Ben called out. "Come and meet Mallory."

Arthur stepped into the hall, arms down, hands clasped. "Nice to meet you, Mallory."

"Hello, Arthur," Mallory said.

"We're delighted to have you here," Ben said. "If you need anything, any hour of the day, please don't hesitate to knock."

"I will. I mean, I won't... hesitate to knock." Mallory blushed and recovered with rehearsed precision. "Very nice to meet both of you. Ben, Arthur, if you need anything, please feel free to knock on my door."

So many cracks in that veneer and yet look at how she then gathers her wits and regains her demeanor. Grace couldn't wait to tell Sarah. Her sister would have ideas about how to handle this evil threat to GraceHaven.

Mallory continued down the hall; Grace followed behind in lockstep, looking back. Even Arthur grinned.

They passed through the ground floor and walked out the back door, stopping first at the door to the upstairs apartment in the carriage house.

“This is where Judy lives,” Grace said. “She’s the groundskeeper.”

“You hire somebody full time to mow the lawn?”

“Caring for the outside environment is more than mowing the lawn,” Grace said. “She cares for the trees, shrubs, perennial beds, annual plantings, including vegetable gardens, and pitches in with other maintenance, as needed. We all do.”

“What’s in the bottom of the building?” Mallory asked.

“The car, the riding mower, and various tools.”

“I won’t need the car since I have my own,” Mallory said. “Is there a place I can easily sell it?”

Grace winced. Nick’s car had always been her car. He rarely drove toward the end of his life. “Could we address the car later? We use it for business.”

“I suppose so.” Mallory swatted at an insect circling her arm. “Bees in April?”

“Probably not,” Grace said. Too bad. A little bee bite might take the sting out of this pretense. She knocked on the door and soon heard light footfalls on the stairs. Judy opened the door. Grace introduced the two young women to each other.

Judy invited them in and Grace followed up the stairs, noting the heaviness in her step, her face, her mind, musing that hangovers are aptly named because she felt like she’d been wrung out and hung over a fence to dry out.

“Grace designed it,” Judy said as she ushered Mallory through the door.

“It’s so dark,” Mallory said.

“Cozy,” Judy said.

“That’s a lot of brown,” Mallory said.

“I’m glad you didn’t paint it, Grace. I like the wood,” Judy said.

Grace raised her eyebrows. *Don’t worry about me, Judy. Mallory’s opinion counts for naught.* “Let’s move on.” Grace opened the door.

On her way out, Mallory nearly tripped on Raven. "Is she always so mellow?" she asked.

Judy lowered herself to one knee and stroked the dog's head. "Yes, unless she thinks somebody's getting hurt." She nuzzled the dog's snout, saying, "You don't like that do you, Raven? You don't like it when people are mean to each other."

Grace took the lead down the steps and across the paved driveway. She could hear Mallory behind, heels clicking. They passed the cottage.

"Who lives there?" Mallory asked.

"Loretta," Grace answered. "I think that she's napping. I don't want to disturb her."

"She introduced herself yesterday, at the memorial service," Mallory said. "She was very nice to me."

Grace forged ahead. Message received. *Loretta's nicer.* She'd heard it before.

She stopped in front of the gray, board-and-batten building that sat about twenty feet from the cottage. "This is known as the dorm. Built in the early seventies." Grace pointed to the stairs leading up. "We reserve the second floor for guests." She opened the door to the common area. British comedy aired on the television in the corner. Phil sat on the floor, Larry's head resting on his lap.

"Hey, you two, this is Mallory, Nick's granddaughter." Grace could hear the customer service tone slipping from her voice.

Both men stood and introduced themselves.

"Hey, Grace," Phil said. "Did you invite Mallory to our birthday party?"

"Phil's a bit freaked out," Larry said. "We're both hitting the big four-oh at the end of April. You have to come to our party. And bring a friend."

"Or two," Phil said.

"The more the merrier," Larry sang.

Mallory smiled. "What kind of artists are you?"

"Architects, dear," Larry said.

"You can chitchat later," Grace said. "We need to move on."

"Enjoy your stay, Mallory." Phil waved. "And come to our party!"

Grace walked to the door marked "B" and knocked.

"Come in!" Fran yelled.

Fran and Peter sat facing the glass doors that opened to the walled patio beyond.

"We're trying to decide what to plant this year," Fran said.

"I want you to meet Mallory, Nick's granddaughter," Grace said, with a low shout.

Fran stood and took Mallory's hand. "Oh, you look so much like Nick, dear. I should have guessed who you were when I saw you at the memorial yesterday. I thought maybe you had come with Teddy."

"Who's that?" Peter asked.

"It's Nick's granddaughter," Fran shouted at him, and lowered her voice to say, "He's too stubborn to get a hearing aid. Too many rock concerts."

"Nice to meet you," Peter waved and turned back to the patio view.

"Nice to meet you, Peter," Mallory shouted back.

"Peter was a commercial artist in Columbus and Fran is a highly skilled administrative assistant," Grace said, hoping to speed things up.

"And I perform in local theater whenever I can," Fran added.

"Local theater?" Mallory asked. "There's a group in Wood Grove?"

"I meant in Columbus. Other than the annual Solstice play, we lack live theater locally. You will be here long enough for the Solstice play? It's the highlight of my year."

"When is it?" Mallory asked.

Fran and Grace exchanged a quick glance.

"We generally shoot for sometime around the Solstice." Grace answered.

"Right," Mallory said, blushing for the second time.

Grace opened the door and ushered Mallory into the hall as goodbyes were said.

The door to apartment “C” was wide open. Polly invited them in. Grace introduced Elizabeth and then Polly. Mallory shook their hands.

“Polly is a retired art teacher and Elizabeth is a dancer and model,” Grace glanced at her watch. “Oh, look at the time. We need to wrap this up. I have an appointment soon.” She hurried Mallory back into the hall.

“How long before you kick us out?” Elizabeth asked.

“Don’t worry. We’ll be fine,” Polly said as she closed the door, muffling the rest of her assurances.

Elizabeth, the least reality-oriented of them all, seemed to have the best handle on the situation.

“Where will everybody go?” Mallory asked.

“I have no idea, Mallory. Everybody expected to stay here. We need time to adjust.”

“How much time?” Mallory asked.

“I don’t know,” Grace answered. Close to letting the lid pop off her pressure-cooked brew of grief, frustration, and worry, Grace checked herself yet again, moved on to door “D,” and knocked.

“Door’s open!” Norma yelled.

Grace and Mallory found Norma folding clothes out of a basket.

“Norma, I’d like you to meet Mallory, Nick’s granddaughter,” Grace said.

“Hello, Mallory.” Norma whiplashed a towel with a crack to snap the wrinkles out, folded it, and placed it on top of a pile of similar towels. “This must be hard for you, coming around and meeting all the folks that your Daddy is going to kick to the curb as soon as he can.”

For once in their relationship, Grace liked Norma, a little.

“Actually, Norma, that will be my job,” Mallory said. “But hopefully you’ll all find something at least slightly more accommodating than the gutter. It’s nice to meet you.”

Norma laughed. “You have your grandfather’s eyes, and his spirit. Welcome.”

The brief sense of kinship with Norma shattered. Grace wanted to spit.

"Grant's gone off with Arthur," Norma said. "I don't know when he'll be back."

Mallory said she'd make it a point to meet him later. Norma went back to folding.

As soon as they closed the door, Grace wiped her hands with a clap, saying, "And that ends the tour." She exited the building.

Mallory trotted to keep up. "Did Teddy grow up here?" she asked.

"He left when he was eleven." After the caterers wrapped up last night, Teddy said he'd been awake when Mallory arrived on Saturday. They'd met and then spent Sunday morning together before the memorial service. No wonder Grace had been able to avoid her. Teddy was a saint.

"Where did he go?" Mallory asked.

"New Jersey," Grace answered.

"Why?" the young woman asked.

Grace skipped up the steps and opened the back door. "Ask Teddy," she said, letting the screen door swoosh shut behind her. If only she had waited another week to adjust the pneumatic closer. It would have slammed.

Mallory stepped in behind her two seconds later.

Loretta stood at the sink, cleaning lettuce. She gestured to a photo album on the table. "Teddy suggested I show this to you, Mallory, to help you remember everybody."

"That was nice of him," Mallory blushed for the third time and sat down.

Taking a glass from the cabinet and moving in beside Loretta, Grace turned on the faucet and asked, in a low voice, "When did Teddy talk to you about this?"

"He called a bit ago," Loretta replied.

"He called, on a workday, with a special request to make nice to the person sent to sell off GraceHaven?"

"I can hear you, Grace," Mallory said. She turned the pages of the album one-by-one.

"I thought it was a nice gesture," Loretta said. "Shows a generosity of spirit."

"What kind of artist are you, Loretta?" Mallory asked.

"Oh, honey," Loretta answered. "I'm no artist. I have spent my life being active in the liberation of black people, first in the civil rights era, and now in the era of fighting racism as it has been institutionalized in policies and internalized in people."

"Wow," Mallory looked up. "Sounds impressive. I thought this place was for artists and creative types." She looked back down at the photos.

"Art is a liberating force," Grace said. "Liberation requires creativity."

Mallory turned one more page and stopped.

Grace looked at the picture. Stephen and Teddy, both age twelve, stood on either side of a small, blonde girl.

Mallory put her finger on the girl in the middle. She looked up at Grace, her eyes wide, and said, "That's me. I don't remember coming here."

Grace remembered. That was the summer she had one official date with Sam Cielo, the summer before Teddy moved to New Jersey for the entire school year.

After a few more page turns, while Grace slowly sipped the water, again regretting the third glass of wine, Mallory asked, "Who's that?" She pointed to a studio portrait of Teddy with Richard and Donna.

"That's Teddy's father and his stepmother," Loretta answered.

"His father is African American?" Mallory asked.

"Is that a problem?" Grace asked.

Loretta bumped her with her hip.

Mallory chuckled. "I thought his skin was dark because he'd vacationed in Florida or something," She smiled and chuckled again. "Actually, I'm relieved. I wondered if he might be my grandfather's son. That would make him my uncle."

Loretta snorted a laugh.

Grace pushed herself away from the counter. The sound of a loud vehicle rumbling down the driveway muffled her retort. Setting the glass on the counter, and without saying goodbye, she walked out the back door to investigate.

Jimmy Cardiff waved from the cab of a flatbed loaded with lumber. She'd forgotten. He'd said he'd be here to deliver on Monday morning. Jimmy was a prompt man.

"What's the lumber for?" Mallory asked.

Good grief, the girl was right behind her. Grace continued to walk, stopping about five feet from the driver's door as Jimmy came to a stop. The truck motor roared. "It's for the stage," she answered.

"What?" Mallory cupped her ear.

Grace directed Jimmy toward the open area in front of the gazebo.

"I'm going to dump it on the side of the driveway, Grace," Jimmy shouted. "Ground's too wet. If we drive on it, the truck'll really tear up your lawn."

Grace nodded and trotted beside the truck as Jimmy drove forward and stopped. He looked at her. She gave a thumbs up. Jimmy turned to the two young men sitting beside him. They jumped out of the other side of the cab.

Mallory stepped forward as the flatbed beeped its back-up warning and raised the truck bed. "What's it for?" she yelled.

"A stage," Grace answered as one end of the load slid to the ground with a loud bang followed by the sound of boards settling.

The two young men ran to place pieces of wood on the ground where the other end would fall.

The truck lurched forward and dumped the other end of the load. It fell, slamming down with a thunderous impact. The truck stopped.

Jimmy jumped down from the cab and handed a bill of sale to Grace. "Let me know if you need anything else, Grace. Sorry to hear about Nick. I always liked running into him at the bar. Great storyteller." He climbed back into the truck.

"Thanks, Jimmy," Grace called after him. She folded the receipt and put it in her back pocket.

"What is the lumber for?" Mallory asked a third time, anger enunciating each syllable.

"A stage," Grace answered, drawing out the long vowel sounds.

"Why wasn't I informed about this?" Mallory asked.

The other two men jumped into the passenger side of the cab and the truck rumbled down the driveway.

Grace turned and walked toward the house. "I guess I forgot to tell you, or ask you, or consult with you, or whatever it is I'm supposed to do with you." She was done in.

Mallory kept pace behind. "The first step would be communicating with me. 'We' are not building a stage. There is no 'we' operating here because I was not consulted. You are building a stage, without consulting with me, without even informing me of your plans. You are not in charge here, Grace. I am."

Grace stopped. Mallory positioned herself in front of Grace.

Grace glared.

Mallory glared back, but looked away first. She puckered her lips so her cheeks sank in and the muscles in her neck stuck out. "Who's paying for it?" she asked.

"We are," Grace answered. "We being the people who live here, the people who built this community. We have an account to receive rent, and pay for maintenance, utilities, and improvements that benefit GraceHaven."

"How much will the stage cost?" Mallory asked.

"About ten thousand dollars."

"Ten thousand dollars!" Mallory gasped.

"It's a good price." Grace's answer came out like a bullet. She stopped, took a breath, and continued in a less lethal tone. "The decision was made before Nick died. The carpenters would have built it last fall but there was too much rain, and then they were busy with more important projects. This is the first chance they've had to move on it. It has nothing to do with you."

"Are you kidding me?" Mallory sputtered. "My family now owns this property and all of the buildings on it. When that stage is built, we will own that, too. We don't want to own it, but my grandfather gave it all to us, which is why we own it. If you want to make decisions about the property, then buy it."

"I can't buy it." Grace shot back, every word a fresh regret. "I don't have that kind of money."

"Then find investors, Grace. That's what people do when they want something bad enough. They find the money and make it happen." Mallory sped away from Grace and opened the back door. It slammed shut behind her.

Damn that unreliable, worn out pneumatic closer! Grace stood in the yard, seething. Maybe she'd be better off with this place off her back.

"Grace!" Coming from the dorm, Norma closed the distance between them. "Why didn't you talk to me and Grant about a plan to organize a group of investors to buy the community?"

"There is no plan, Norma."

"Don't lie to me, Sister Mary Grace. I heard Mallory out here plain as day, you two talking about investors and buying GraceHaven. I want to know. Why weren't Grant and I invited?"

Reality came down hard. Grace had to decide. The choice was clear.

"Nobody's been invited yet. You'll be the first to know." Grace walked back into the house. She had a proposal to write.

Chapter Twenty-two

TOMORROW WOULD BE SATURDAY. Sam had sent a bouquet of flowers to Grace on Monday. Loretta had called on Tuesday to thank him and to say how much they all appreciated Sam's thoughtfulness over the years. She even made a point of saying that Grace, too, sent her thanks, and that she would thank him in person later, when things settled down. Had he really expected to hear back from her in less than a week? Well, to be honest he had, or at least hoped.

The clock above Ruby's desk showed five after three. "Go home early, Ruby," Sam said.

Ruby looked up from polishing her nails. "Really? I can stay and lock up at five."

"I can lock up. Go home and finish getting ready for that hot date with Hal."

"He's taking me to a dinner theatre for our anniversary."

She'd already told him more than once, but no point in saying that. "You two go celebrate your anniversary. Tell Hal I said hello."

"Thanks, Sam. I'll leave as soon as my polish dries."

Sam sauntered back to his desk.

The whole thing seemed odd. He had told the florist to put Grace's name on the envelope. Maybe he should have waited longer. Was he being obvious? If he had been with someone for decades and they died, how would he feel if a new someone made overtures so soon after the death? How long should one wait before throwing their hat in the ring?

"I'm going now, Sam," Ruby called from the outer room.

"Have a good weekend," he called back.

The door opened and closed.

Did Grace even want his hat in the ring?

Sam was aware that in the past he'd never questioned himself over women he invited into his life. If he liked someone, he asked them out. They usually said, "Yes," and the process began. Dates, flowers, months of happy bonding, more months of cozier togetherness, and then she would start dropping hints. He would be less attentive; she would break it off; he would move on. Case closed. He was tired of the whole rigamarole. He wanted to date Grace, to have a relationship with Grace, on her terms, whatever she wanted, though his preference ran toward close, intimate, permanent. He should have been stronger, braver, when he had a chance. The whole thing left him fearing something he'd never really known: defeat.

Going home held no appeal. A few months ago, Handels switched from being a diner to a bar that served pizza. He'd give it a try. Sam locked up early and walked down the street. Young people dodged him on the sidewalk; cars swooshed by; no one waved or said hello or looked at him. That was happening more often these days. The world belonged to the young, as it should.

The new door to Handels swung out with ease. Sam walked into garlic-onion-oregano-laden air, second only, in his opinion, to the scent of sautéed garlic, onions, and cumin. Plenty of empty booths were available, but he spotted a familiar figure sitting at the bar.

Sam claimed the stool next to the young man who had his hand on a half-empty glass and said, "Buy your next one?"

Teddy looked sideways and smiled. "What's new, Sam?"

"Not much. So? Up for another beer after that one?"

"I'm fine here."

Mandy McKay positioned herself behind the bar, facing Sam. "I wondered when I was going to see you in here. What can I do for you?"

"I'll have what he's having."

"You know I'm too young to serve alcohol," she said.

"Then get out from behind the bar." He took a peanut from the dish beside him and tossed it at her.

She caught it and dropped it into the pocket of her work apron. "Hey, Chuck," she called to the bartender. "Sam wants a Heineken."

The bartender set an uncapped beer on the counter in front of Sam.

Mandy leaned her forearms on the bar top. "Did you know Jeff and I broke up?"

"I'm sorry to hear that," Sam said.

"I thought you'd be proud. He broke up with me 'cause I wouldn't have sex with him."

"Good for you." Sam swigged the beer.

"He thought I was nuts when I told him I was going to hold out for marriage."

"It's not a popular stance these days." Sam set the beer back down on the bar.

"Tell me about it. I told you he'd dump me if I took your advice." She whipped a towel over her shoulder and walked away.

Sam took another drink of beer and explained without turning his head. "I've known her since she was a baby. Actually had the pleasure of attending her birth."

Mandy sailed past and threw a peanut at Sam. He caught it and put it in the clean ashtray. "How's work going, Teddy?"

"Work is the same. Too much to do for too little pay with inadequate help and overwhelming odds."

"Think you want to keep doing it?" Sam asked.

"I don't want to make a lifetime habit of it," Teddy answered.

"Ever consider moving back here?"

"And do what?" Teddy laughed.

"I'll retire someday."

Teddy turned to look at Sam.

Sam glanced at him before taking another drink from the bottle. "I'm sixty-seven years old, Teddy. I don't want to make a lifetime habit of this job either."

"Are you saying you'd consider having me take over your practice?"

"That's what I'm saying." He'd thought about it since the night of Nick's memorial. Teddy seemed like an affable young man. Sam had checked him out with some old friends in the Columbus area. Teddy had a gold-star rating, according to those who knew him.

"Why me?" Teddy asked.

"Why not? You know the town, the people. Your mother's here. Seems like a natural thing to do." Teddy was an obvious choice, and the more ties Grace had to the area, the less likely she would be to leave if GraceHaven folded.

"I haven't lived here for a long time," Teddy said.

"You were born here," Sam said. "That means a lot to people."

Mandy rang up a sale at the cash register and turned to Sam. "Mom told me to tell you she won first place in a contest with your enchilada recipe. She wants to split the prize with you."

"What did she win?" Sam asked.

"A weekend at a health spa."

"Tell her to take your father," Sam said.

"They separated again," Mandy said. "Didn't you know that?"

"No." He didn't know, but he wasn't surprised.

"She found some woman's phone number written on his underwear, in lipstick."

Sam flinched. Gloria tried, but Jasper would never be stable enough to be a good parent. Sam picked the peanut out of the ashtray and threw it back to Mandy. "Tell her to take you."

"Right." Mandy walked the length of the bar and disappeared into the kitchen.

"Your enchilada recipe?" Teddy asked.

"The secret's in the sauce."

"Apparently it's not much of a secret anymore." Teddy chuckled.

The doorbell tinkled and a woman's voice said, "Hey, Teddy."

Teddy stood to greet the young lady Elizabeth had pointed out to Sam at the memorial service.

"Glad you could make it," Teddy said. He introduced Sam to Nick's granddaughter.

"I've been meaning to contact you, Mr. Cielo." Mallory Mason offered her hand. "My father told me you were my grandfather's attorney."

Sam grasped her hand. "Nice to meet you, too, Mallory, but I'm sorry to say your father was wrong. Attorney Stewart McKay had some business with Mr. Mason, but my understanding is that Mr. Mason didn't follow through. Those files have been purged, I'm sure."

"Oh, my," Mallory said. "Well, I guess I'll have to find help elsewhere." Her shoulders slumped a shade.

"Can I get you something to drink?" Mandy asked.

"A Coke, please," Mallory said. "Would you like to join us, Mr. Cielo?"

"Yeah, Sam." Teddy encouraged him. "Come sit with us."

Sam picked up his beer. This beat going home to a solitary meal in a silent house.

Mallory slid into one side of the bench and Teddy sat beside her. Sam slid into the other side, facing them. Mandy brought Mallory's Coke and placed a peanut in front of Sam, batting her eyes at him before she walked away.

"I'm sorry about your grandfather." Sam held the half-full beer bottle with both hands.

"Thank you," Mallory said. "Kind of you to say that, but the truth is I didn't even know him." Mallory shrugged her shoulders. "I guess he simply wasn't a family man."

That was a fine understatement. Sam took a drink of beer, wondering if she had a clue about Nicholas Mason. "What have you learned about him since you arrived?" he asked.

"I've been reading his books. He was a great writer! I had no idea. And GraceHaven isn't anything like my grandmother described. The people are kind and funny and cultured. I don't think my father understands the nature of what my grandfather accomplished here."

"He didn't do it alone," Teddy said.

"Right, of course you're right." She lowered and shook her head as she spoke, her hair falling around her face, but not hiding the blood that rushed to her cheeks. "Anyway, I wish he'd done what was needed so the people who live there could stay."

Sam liked her. "Where are you from?" he asked.

The three of them spent the next hour eating pizza, talking about Mallory's hometown of Chicago, the advantages and disadvantages of small towns and large cities, and places they would like to visit. Sam could see an attraction between Teddy and Mallory. Though Grace and Nick had never been married, he thought about how it sometimes happens that families end up with double sets of in-laws, brothers marrying sisters, or vice versa.

As he finished the last wedge of pizza, Teddy asked, "So how's it going with the estate business, Mallory? How long do you think it will take?"

"I have no idea," Mallory said. "Like I said, I spent the week reading and talking to the people who live there. I haven't even started." She wiped her mouth with her napkin. "I guess I'm going to have to slog through the files stored in the basement."

"If I were you, I'd ask Grace," Sam said. "Generally, widows know far more about finances than they give themselves credit for."

"But they weren't married," Mallory said.

"A technicality." Sam took another drink of beer.

Teddy laughed. "Don't ever let Mom hear you say that."

"They were together for a long time," Sam said.

"Mom was never with Nick like that." Teddy sat up and put his hands on his thighs.

"She wasn't?" Sam and Mallory both asked in unison.

Teddy stopped smiling. "You both really thought that? Please. Give her some credit." He turned his head toward Mallory. "No offense, but your grandfather was a pain in the ass at times."

"They were never a couple?" Sam asked.

"No." Teddy shook his head. "Grace is nothing if not transparent. She would have told me. He almost snagged her once, but he proved unreliable. Mom doesn't fall for that a second time."

Sam's chest tightened.

"Say more," Mallory said.

"Well, for one thing," Teddy said, "Nick lured her away from college when she was nineteen and still grieving the loss of her parents. My aunt has strong feelings about that. Dad says after Mom moved to Wood Grove, he never had a chance. Nick took over her life. He made promises and he'd throw money at a project, but he left Mom on her own to develop it, manage it, and keep it going. He owed that place to her, morally, for all the years she invested."

Mallory was silent and Sam stunned. Grace had been available all these years?

Teddy turned again to Mallory, putting his hand on her arm. "I understand your position. You're doing the right thing, for your family. But don't kid yourself about Nick's part in GraceHaven. He might have funded it, but Mom founded and fostered it."

"So in your mind, it belongs to Grace, morally, at least." Mallory could have been defensive about that, but Sam only heard curiosity in her voice.

"Yeah," Teddy said. "And morality plus a couple of bucks will buy you a gallon of gas or two." He smiled. "Don't worry about Grace. She's had a lifetime of disappointments. She'll come out of this on top."

Sam raked his hand through his hair. "I think it's time I call it a night." He stood.

Teddy offered his hand. "Are you serious about what you said earlier?"

"As a heart attack—," Sam shook Teddy's hand "—and at my age, I don't joke around about heart attacks either. Give me a call. I'm in the book."

"Okay, Sam." Teddy's smile grew wider. "I'm going to call you."

"Mallory, thanks for inviting me to join you." Sam reached for his wallet.

"Let me pay for this one," Mallory said. "My treat."

"How about I pay for the tip?" He laid a twenty-dollar bill on the table. "Mandy's saving for college. She needs all the help she can get."

He moved toward the door.

"Sam!" Mallory said from her spot in the booth. "What are you doing next Saturday night, the 18th?"

"No plans," he said.

"There's a birthday party. Come hang out with us."

"That's a great idea," Teddy said.

Sam's chest relaxed. He visualized the great room, people, music, Grace, and then thought of Elizabeth, the way she had latched onto him at the memorial service, her funny suggestion that perhaps she could live with him.

"Mind if I bring a friend?" he asked.

"Please do!" Mallory said. "The more, the merrier."

"It's a date," Sam gave a two-finger salute and pushed open the door.

All these years, and she'd had been single. This time, nothing would stop him. He would get to Grace however she would take him, no matter how long it took.

Chapter Twenty-Three

FALLING TOWARD BLUE EYES, Grace could feel the warmth of his skin. He shook her shoulder and said, "Grace, wake up." Whirling toward his voice, hair covering her face, she raked her fingers across her forehead. The dream faded. Light from the stairwell illuminated a figure, breasts hugged snug against a shivering torso beside her bed.

"Teddy's sick," Mallory said. "He needs aspirin or something to bring his fever down."

Grace shoved the pile of blankets off, and sat up in the long-sleeved top, sweatpants, and thick socks she wore. "I'll take care of it." Pushing herself out of bed and onto the floor, she took three steps, opened the top dresser drawer, found her minor emergency kit, and put it into her pocket. She skirted around Mallory and made for the staircase, bare feet padding behind.

"What are you doing up?" she asked.

"He came to my room."

Mallory's footfalls followed Grace down to the landing. They left the stairwell and Grace stopped at the door to Nick's room. The nightlight in this hallway revealed that Mallory wore a thin, cotton pajama set.

"Go back to bed," Grace said.

"I want to come, too." Mallory quaked as she spoke.

Why in the world would the young woman want to help? Grace was too tired to argue. "Then put some clothes on. You're freezing." She walked down the hall into her son's room and entered without knocking.

He sat propped against his pillows, supported by the headboard. Grace put her hand on Teddy's forehead and asked, "Nausea?"

"I threw up a couple of times."

Feet padded into the room and assumed a position beside Grace. Mallory now wore jeans and a sweater, but no socks. The young woman continued to hug her herself, obviously feeling cold. Had she never heard of dressing for the weather?

Grace's attention returned to her son. "I have a homeopathic that might help and I have a bottle of Tylenol." She pulled the kit out of her pocket and extracted two bottles. "I think you'll be able to tolerate the homeopathic better. You might throw the Tylenol right back up."

"Give me the Tylenol." Teddy offered his hand, palm up. "I need water."

"I'll get it." Mallory walked to the bathroom, returned, and headed for the door, explaining, "I have to go down to the kitchen for a glass."

As soon as Mallory was gone, Grace asked, "Why did you wake her up? You should have asked me first."

Teddy sighed. "We sort of had a date last night."

"A date?" Grace asked. "She's only been here a week. You barely know her."

He sighed again. "That's sort of the point of dating."

Grace sat on the edge of the bed, silent, touching her son's forehead.

Mallory rushed back in, breathless, and held out a glass.

"I think he'll need some water," Grace said.

"Oh! Right." Mallory went into the bathroom. The sound of running water ensued.

Grace withdrew her hand and stared down at Teddy, challenging him. Teddy stared back, unmoved. Mallory returned to Teddy's bedside and handed the water to Grace, who gave the glass to Teddy.

He sat up to swallow the two tablets. "Thanks, Mallory," he said.

Thanks, Mallory? How about Thanks, Mom? Grace stood and looked down at her son. "I'm going back to bed."

"I'll stay with him." Mallory stepped forward.

That was unexpected and unnecessary. Teddy had grown out of needing someone to hold his hair back when he puked. He'd hung on longer than most boys, but a few years before he moved to New Jersey he'd kicked his mother out of the bathroom, citing the necessity of learning to be a man. Grace couldn't talk him out of it. He wanted to be all grown up. But if he was reverting back to earlier times, Mallory could have him. He could be a big baby when he didn't feel well.

"He'll want you to wait on him hand and foot," Grace said. "And he won't be nice until he feels better."

"I don't mind." Mallory dug her toe into the rug beside the bed.

On other hand, Teddy needed sleep, not someone distracting him with unnecessary TLC.

"I'd like you to stay, Mallory." Teddy sounded far more pathetic than required.

They were both adults. Grace was tired, and starting to feel cold. "Have at it," she said. "Let me know if you need anything." She closed the door behind her without a sound. No point in waking Ben or Arthur.

She climbed the stairs, turned off the light, and moved through the dark to her bed. Hadn't she raised her son to be more discerning? Mallory would not be a good fit for him. She would expect too much financially and too little emotionally.

Crawling back into bed, Grace remembered she'd been dreaming, a lovely dream. She tried sinking back into the images, the feelings, but nothing came, so she practiced tensing and releasing each part of her body, starting with her feet, and moving slowly up.

Her mind calmed, she drifted down the path, to the boulder, to a man.

For one lucid moment she knew she was starting to dream, and then she let go.

IN THE MORNING, Grace rose early. Sunlight poured through the windows. She pulled on black leggings for her bottom half, a teal velour tunic for her upper half, and a thick wool sweater for added warmth. Extra socks filled out her Birkenstocks. She was ready for the day. Considering her middle-of-the-night sleep interruption, an afternoon nap might be in order. She planned her day accordingly as she walked down the stairs to the second floor, thinking she should check on Teddy before breakfast.

The door to Nick's room hung open a crack. Grace pushed it far enough to peer in. If Teddy slept, she didn't want to wake him. The sight of Mallory, curled up and sleeping on her side, startled Grace. Still dressed in jeans and a sweater, Mallory faced the door. Grace pushed open the door further. Teddy lay curled around Mallory, his arm resting on her side. He was naked from the waist up, clad in pajama bottoms. The quilt lay crumpled on the floor.

Grace tiptoed into the room, picked up the quilt, and covered them both. She put her finger on Teddy's arm. His temperature seemed normal.

She left the room and shut the door behind her. The irony. In less than a week, Mallory Mason had managed to sleep with Teddy in a bed not twenty feet away from the bed in which Nick had failed, after trying for decades, to lure Grace.

Did Teddy know what he was doing? Grace felt certain Mallory did. She had grown up in a family with a history of things going their way. Families like that often possessed neither awareness of their privilege nor how that privilege played out on others. Grace had no reason to trust her.

Before she had a chance to check on breakfast activity, the phone rang. Grace took the front staircase and jogged to her office.

"Hello!" Sarah greeted her. "I've had such a week!"

Sarah launched into a detailed rundown of her activities, including her plan for an extended vacation in France. "It popped into my mind and I thought, 'Why not? There's nothing stopping you. Do it!' So I bought a ticket and made hotel reservations. I should be back in time to join you for that play you always have in June. Make it a funny one. The last one put me to sleep."

"Fran picks the plays," Grace said.

"Make Fran pick a funny one. Too much pain and drama in the world. I want to laugh!"

"Me, too," Grace said.

"Grace, you sound glum. Why don't you join me? You've said more than once you want to see Paris before you die. I'll spring for airfare and accommodations."

Grace slumped into her office chair. "You can't be serious. You do remember that Nick's left me in a total panic here."

"Can you work out a deal with Nick's granddaughter to let you all stay there for a year? I'll help with money if you need it."

Grace knew she would never be able to pay back a loan and she didn't want to simply take Sarah's money, which really came from Donald. That would only prove him right. The Donald who lived in Grace's mind would always see her as a failure. "Sweet of you to offer, but I have to work this out some other way."

"Talking to someone might help."

"Therapy is your thing, Sarah. My thing is…." Grace looked up. "My vision is a world where art creates collaboration. My mission is to bring people together to find common purpose through artistic activities."

"You're reading that sign on your wall," Sarah said. "Your vision and mission statements."

"I'm not giving up, Sarah."

"A vacation is not giving up. The France offer stands."

"Thanks, but I have work to do." She'd spent the last week reading about cooperative ownership of property. They would have to establish a corporation. There would be huge upfront costs. Some could pay, but not all, including Grace. She'd gone for years without paying herself in order to keep things going. She was nearly broke.

"By the way," Sarah said. "Teddy left a message on my answering machine last night. He invited me to a party on the 18th. Send my regrets. I'm already booked."

"Teddy invited you to the party?"

"He said that neighbor of yours, Sam, would be there. Where have you been hiding him? I am definitely interested. When I get back from France, I think I'll make a habit of visiting on a more regular basis."

Grace froze. Sam and Sarah?

"Grace? Are you still there?"

"You met Sam?"

"At the memorial. He's divine. Why haven't you mentioned him before?"

"Never crossed my mind." But, really, why hadn't she told Sarah about Sam? Maybe because there had never been anything to tell? Maybe because she feared what might happen if Sarah met the most tempting and eligible bachelor in Wood Grove? "When do you leave?" she asked.

"Next week! I'm so excited. I need to buy new luggage so I can carry home all the clothes I intend to buy. Who said that money can't buy happiness?"

"Someone without money." Sarah and Sam? The idea stung. "Call before you go?"

"Of course, darling, and I'll check in while I'm there. Kiss kiss. I feel so French already."

After the call ended, Grace hung up the phone and sat back in her chair.

Maybe they would be perfect for each other. Grace shook the image out of her head and looked at the statement on the wall again. She didn't have time to think about Sam and Sarah. Grace turned on her computer and waited for it boot up. That proposal wouldn't write itself. She was nearly done.

Chapter Twenty-Four

SAM DROPPED THE LITTER he'd collected from the ditch into his garbage can. One 7-Up can, two wine bottles, a Dire Straits CD, a maroon knit hat, and two plastic bags. He'd already been on the treadmill and knocked out five pages on the computer. He had no other Saturday plans. He washed his hands and took his second cup of coffee for a walk.

Cutting through a break in the fence at the back of his property, he entered the semi-shade of the woods. Sunlight broke through the trees in patches creating a play of light and shadow. Here he could wander without interruption. He needed that.

Now that he'd met Mallory, he would talk to her about her family's intentions regarding Nick's property. Sam had no interest in having the land sold to a developer who would cut down the larger trees and bulldoze the rest for a subdivision, complete with retention pond and Bradford Pears in every yard.

If need be, he would buy all of Nick's property, including the house. Perhaps he should talk to Grace about the idea, or maybe not. She might not like renting from him. He could always set up a corporation to hide his identity. Sometimes that was the easiest way to go.

Sam wound around until he came to the rock where he'd encountered Grace so many times in the past. He decided to sit for a while, finish off the coffee, and listen to the water burble past. No sooner had he settled himself on the edge of the rock, when he heard a rustling sound. Across the stream, a doe and her fawn grazed not ten feet from where he sat.

Now this was magical.

He had often seen deer from his kitchen window but rarely on his walks in the woods, and never this close. He sat very still, almost afraid to breathe. The doe stopped and looked in his direction, then bounded off, her fawn following close behind.

"Did you see that?" Grace asked.

She appeared at his side carrying a large bag over her shoulder.

"I did," he said.

"She was a beauty."

No more so than the woman standing by his side. Her bag was made of roughly woven cloth and had a colorful pattern that made Sam think of Central America. She placed the bag on the ground and asked, "Mind if I sit down?"

"Plenty of room," he said.

She sat beside him, crossed her legs, and faced the water. "Sorry I scared them off."

"Deer scare easy," Sam said.

"Keeps 'em alive."

"Sometimes it keeps them from being in safe places."

"Are we still talking about the deer?" Grace asked.

"Maybe not," Sam answered.

The leaves rustled, birds called from tree to tree, and the water sang. "What's in the bag?" Sam asked.

"Nick," she answered. She picked up the bag and pulled out a large silver urn which she cradled in her lap.

"His ashes?"

"Yep."

"Do you want to be alone?"

She looked at him. "Not really."

Grace turned back to the water.

They sat in silence until the questions in Sam's mind settled and he didn't need to ask any more. He stopped wondering about her and noticed the thoughts floating through his own mind.

Randi would be moving in soon. He should have a key made. Did they still do that at the small hardware store? Otherwise he'd have to drive over to Chillicothe. He heard Grace take a deep breath. He relaxed into the moment and listened to the water until Grace startled him by saying, "Thanks for the flowers. They were lovely."

"Glad you liked them."

More silence. He noticed that her hands cupped the urn with a prayer pose. He wondered why she was there. He didn't care. He only wanted to sit beside her and enjoy the day.

"I heard you were invited to the birthday party for Phil and Larry," she said.

"I was invited to a party on the 18th. Didn't know it was for them. Will they mind?"

"Not at all." She paused. "Sarah won't be there."

"Who?" he asked.

"My sister."

"That's too bad." Grace must want her sister there or she wouldn't have mentioned it. Sam wondered about their relationship. Were they close?

He would sit with her for hours if she stayed, but he had to admit that the longer he sat, the more gravity seemed to pull the weight of his body against the rock. His hips would feel this tomorrow.

"Nick and I used to swim here," Grace said.

"Yeah?" he asked. She needed to talk about Nick. Of course she did. She had him sitting in her lap. How odd it must feel to hold the ashes of someone you've known for over half of your life. Sam could stand the pressure on his bones for a bit longer.

"One morning we stripped the wallpaper off his bedroom walls," she said. "It was August, one of the hottest days of the year. We'd come out here to cool off. After swimming, we lay down on this rock to let the sun dry us off. I remember feeling safe and happy and relaxed."

She paused.

"What happened?" Sam asked.

"He kissed me—," she looked at Sam, "—and I didn't try to stop him."

"And?"

She turned back to face the stream. "I never told Richard. I hated that secret, Sam. Secrets can destroy a relationship."

Sam's experience was different, but he kept the thought to himself. Some relationships require secrets.

"Somehow I don't think Nick's indiscretion destroyed your marriage," he said.

"It was my indiscretion, too," She looked at Sam again. "I told you, I didn't stop him."

"Okay," he said. "You made a mistake. Can you forgive yourself?"

"For the kiss? I suppose so. But I'm not sure that I can forgive myself for not telling Richard."

"What difference would it have made?" Sam asked.

Grace sighed. "If I'd been honest with him, I wouldn't have to wonder if he could feel me holding something back. I feel guilty about that."

"You're too hard on yourself, Grace. It was only a kiss."

"Not for me," she said. "Maybe kisses are like that for you, for Nick, for all men, but that kiss meant something to me. It was dangerous, desirable, but also dishonorable."

What could he say? That he wasn't like that? But what she said was true. He'd kissed many women and often the kisses meant very little to him.

Grace uncurled her legs, moved to the edge of the boulder, kicked off her shoes, peeled off her socks, and stepped over to the water, hugging the urn in one arm. Water swallowed her feet and ankles. She unscrewed the top of the urn and looked back. "You can come in with me," she said.

After removing his shoes and socks, Sam rolled up his pant legs and waded in.

With Sam standing beside her, Grace poured out the contents of the urn. Together, they watched all that remained of Nick's physical presence float away with the current, some particles sticking to the edges of almost-submerged rocks, some dispersing to the shore to form a gray line on the brown mud.

"That's Nick," Grace said, pointing. "He could never make a clean break."

"Sooner or later it'll rain and the rest of him will be swept away," Sam said.

They waded out of the stream. Sam sat down on the rock and dried his feet with his socks.

"Grace," he said, as he put his shoes back on. "I'm only going to ask you this one more time."

She put her hand up. "Don't ask me today, Sam. Please."

"Okay." He tied his shoelaces. "I won't." He wouldn't ask her again forever, if that's what she wanted, though the thought pushed him down harder than gravity pulled at him.

"Thanks for being with me," she said. "I didn't realize how much I wanted to not be alone until I saw you sitting here."

"My pleasure." He could have been anybody. She simply hadn't wanted to be alone. "I'll see you later, Grace."

Sam put his hands in his pockets and walked toward the path he'd worn down over the years.

"Sam," Grace said.

"Yeah?" He stopped and turned around.

"Ask me again another day."

"Okay," he said and smiled. "I can do that."

Chapter Twenty-Five

"YOU DON'T THINK it's too tight?" The new jade silk dress hanging upstairs on her armoire snugged Grace's figure from the square neck down past her thighs. Slits on both sides ran between her knees and ankles.

"Wear the dress," Loretta said. She had followed Grace into the pantry. The caterers scurried around the kitchen. "If you come downstairs in anything but that dress, I will haul you back up myself and make you change."

All week Grace had anticipated the party. She'd told Sam to ask again. She'd shown her hand. He'd be at the party.

"You wear the dress," Grace said. This moment defined the essence of "chickening out."

"Grace Baxter. Go upstairs and put that dress on. I am telling you this for your own good." Loretta pointed up and refused to back down.

Grace put her foot on the first step.

"Go," Loretta ordered.

At six forty-five, Grace emerged from the door to the pantry and smoothed the dress over her hips.

One of the caterers, a young man with a blonde ponytail, put his fingers in his mouth and blew a loud whistle. All four of the workers stopped, looked at Grace, and clapped.

Loretta put her hands together, fingers pointed up and under her chin. "My dear, you look stunning."

"You paid them to do that," Grace said.

"Yes, I did." Loretta said. "Thanks, boys. Now get back to work."

The young men resumed their duties. Grace shook her head and walked with Loretta through the door to the dining room.

"Everything's ready," Loretta said. "Teddy called. He and Mallory will be late. He asked that you put a tray of food in his room so they can eat when they arrive."

"Why not eat down here?"

"He said something about needing to shower and being famished and I didn't question the boy, Grace. Do you want me to do it?" Loretta seemed a bit cranky.

"You feeling okay?" Grace asked.

"My arthritis is acting up."

"Don't worry about Teddy. I'll take care of him."

"And Mallory, too?" Loretta asked.

"Yes." Grace leaned forward and wagged her head rapidly. "Mallory, too."

Everybody seemed taken with the young woman. Grace was only too happy her son kept Nick's granddaughter busy on weekends. Who knew what Mallory did during the week? She showed up for meals randomly, stayed in Nick's room a good deal, and drove her BMW to parts unknown the rest of the time. As long as she stayed out of sight, Grace had the good fortune to keep the girl out of her mind.

Loretta returned to the kitchen. Grace wandered into the great room to survey the preparations. The drink cart and snack table were in place. The rest of the food would be served from the dining room. Grace retreated to her office to tie up a few loose ends and stayed there until the doorbell rang at seven.

Of course Sam would be the first to arrive.

"You look beautiful tonight, Grace." He stepped over the threshold, his black Western suit worn over a pale blue shirt with a leather string tie impressive. Polished black cowboy boots completed the ensemble.

"You look nice, too," she said. He looked like he'd stepped out off a cover of GQ for Seniors. She tamped down her response. The feelings encased in her tight green dress threatened to burst the seams.

"Let's start the party," Sam said. He seemed different, more sure of himself with her. Was that a good thing?

He held out his arm. She took it, but before they could take a step, the doorbell rang again.

Grace opened the door and was surprised to find Ed Turnbull in his usual attire, a conservative gray suit, white shirt, and tie with slanted stripes. He smoothed the sparse outcropping of hair. Who invited him?

Sam moved around her to greet Ed with enthusiasm. "Glad you could make it. Why don't you go on into the living room and we'll join you in a minute?" As Ed walked away, Sam whispered in her ear, "I'm sure you're aware his wife died last year. He's been terribly lonely. I thought he might do for Elizabeth."

The awkward funeral director walked with tentative steps into the great room. "Thoughtful of you," Grace said. "For both Ed and Elizabeth."

His eyes acknowledged her appreciation. She held his gaze, determined to not flinch, until loud voices coming through the door to the kitchen pulled her back to her duty as temporary hostess.

Everyone from the dorm arrived en masse. Sam left her side to join Ed. Grace strode, with shorter than usual steps, down the hall to greet the other community members.

First in line, Grant pressed his cheek to Grace's cheek. Norma wore a spectacular African dress, magenta and yellow and turquoise and white. A band of the same print wound around her head. She hugged Grace and bit both of her lips as she made a sound in her throat. "Mm Mm. I have never seen you looking so good."

Grace could not help being swept up by Norma's compliment. "And you look gorgeous, as usual." This was the function of a party, to abandon petty differences and dislikes and join with others on the common ground of enjoying life.

Fran and Peter followed, arm in arm. Fran kissed Grace's cheek, but Peter didn't seem to hear when she shouted a greeting.

Elizabeth, Polly, and Ben, their arms linked, came next. Grace could hear Elizabeth talking about the day she married Max. Polly leaned away from Elizabeth long enough to plant a kiss on Grace's cheek, then attended once again to her companion's description of flower, song, and ceremony. Ben smiled as he passed.

Grace heard a loud laugh from across the room and looked over to see Norma already entertaining Sam and Ed. Grant sat in a corner, opening a book.

Loretta entered on Judy's arm. Raven followed close behind, never far from Judy's heel. Grace stood with them and surveyed the group.

"Who invited Sam?" Judy asked.

"Teddy did," Arthur said. He had come through from the door to the kitchen. "But he's going to be late. He asked me to check on Sam, make sure he's doing okay." Arthur skirted the threesome and continued into the room to join Sam.

Of course Teddy had taken care of Sam. Grace had raised her son to be thoughtful.

"And Ed Turnbull?" Loretta asked.

"Sam invited him," Grace said.

"Norma's in rare form," Loretta said.

Norma stood between Sam, Peter, and Arthur, the center of the universe, telling a story with all of the energy that her well-trained body could rally. Fran glowered from one of the chairs.

"Maybe I should go talk to Fran," Judy said.

"Good call, Judy." Grace watched the young woman move across the room to sit on the arm of the chair beside Fran. Soon, Fran followed Judy toward the dining room where they encountered new arrivals Deirdre and her partner, Daphne. The four women stood together talking and laughing. Grace watched until she felt satisfied all was well.

Sam seemed fine without her, always in the middle of three or four people. Laughing. Talking. Not hanging on her every move. Should she join him? Not yet. Better to allow time for him to connect with the others first, which he seemed to be doing in a way she'd never witnessed before, almost like he belonged.

Forty-seven out-of-town guests filtered in throughout the next hour. Phil and Larry arrived late to assume their roles as hosts and raison d'être for the gathering. The musical trio also arrived late, but nobody seemed to notice except Grace. As the trio set up to play, the high-pitched hum of human voices highlighted how downhearted they'd all been since Nick's death. Like the water that carried away his ashes, the flow of conversation, handshakes and hugs, and traffic around the buffet table and drink cart carried away the sense of everything coming to an end. Life existed here and might go on, for a long time. And then the music began.

"Need something?" Sam put his hand on her arm. His touch sent a pleasant buzz up her arm, like the first time they touched.

Her head swam and she stepped backward to ground herself. "Maybe a little air."

He grasped her elbow, guiding her through the maze of people and out the front door. Cool air hit her skin and she collected her wits. "Thanks. I'm fine now. I only needed a breath out here."

She started to go back in the house, but Sam led her to one of the rocking chairs on the porch. "Sit down. You need a break." He removed his jacket and put it around her shoulders.

She tried to shrug it off. "No, really, I'm okay..."

He insisted. "Keep it on. Your dress will pick up dirt from the chair." He guided her into the chair and pulled another chair close to sit beside her.

"What about your clothes?" she asked.

"I can have them dry cleaned."

"I can have my dress dry cleaned." She sat up straighter in the chair and looked out to the dark lawn beyond the line of cars parked along the driveway.

Last week she'd encouraged him; when he arrived, she could only think of passing him off to Teddy; thirty minutes ago she'd calculated how soon to go to him; and now she acted petulant again. What about Sam discombobulated her so?

"I was trying to be gallant," he said.

"I don't appreciate gallantry." What must he think of her inconsistency? Sometimes she annoyed the hell out of herself.

Sam pulled his chair a little closer and leaned toward her. "What do you appreciate?"

She bit the inside of her cheek. "Reliable cars, good writing, and well-mannered dogs. How about you, Sam? What do you appreciate?" If only he didn't make her feel so darned vulnerable.

He looked at her without answering for too long. She couldn't stand his eyes on her like that. "Well?" she asked.

"I appreciate you telling me to ask again."

"Yes, well, wait a little longer." She pushed herself out of the chair.

Another car turned into the driveway. The driver honked and rolled down the window.

"Hey, Mom!" Teddy called.

"I forgot to take up the food," Grace said, to herself but aloud. She left Sam on the porch as she hurried, again with short strides, to the kitchen.

Having loaded a tray with plates that included a sampling of every hors d'oeuvre, she headed to the pantry to take the back stairwell. Not three steps up, she realized it would be impossible to keep going forward. Neither was she confident that she could negotiate a turn to go back down. She considered whether the step was deep enough to hold the tray so she could free her hands to hike up her dress.

"Need some help?" asked a familiar voice behind her.

"I do. I need help." She needed help in so many ways.

Sam stepped up beside her, unable because of the narrowness of the stairs to avoid brushing against the entire left side of her body. She held her breath. He put his hands under the tray, lifted it away from her, and climbed the steps until he was past her. "Coming?"

Grace released the air in her lungs and lifted her dress up far enough to move freely. She followed up the stairs, smoothed her dress back down when she arrived at the top, and tried to take back the tray. He resisted, so she directed him to Teddy's room.

She knocked. Teddy called out, "Come in."

Sam waited in the hall while she delivered the tray. Her son still had on jeans and hiking boots but stood in front of the closet, pulling out a pair of pants and a black shirt.

"Thanks, Mom. I'll be down as soon I shower." He glanced at the food. "That looks great. I'm so hungry." He took a brie and mushroom pastry and popped it into his mouth, whole.

"There's a plate for Mallory," Grace said.

"Thanks." He sat on the bed and untied his boots. "She's in her room, dressing."

"Where were you two all day?" Grace asked.

"I took her to Hocking Hills to hike."

"You're spending a lot of time with her."

"Did Sam make it?" he asked.

"Yes," she said.

"I'm so bummed Aunt Sarah couldn't come. They'd be per—"

"You get in the shower and come down to the party," she interrupted. No more talk about Sam and Sarah. The idea made her stomach queasy. Grace slipped out the door and shut it behind her.

Sam stood at the end of the hall, facing a window. He turned as she approached. "I've never been on this floor. The wood is beautiful."

"John refinished it." She led the way to the back stairwell.

"Still miss him?" Sam asked.

"Always."

When they reached the top of the stairs, Sam said, "You look stunning in that dress, Grace, but it doesn't allow you much room to move, does it?"

"I can move," she said, the lie so obvious she laughed.

"Keep it on until I have a chance to dance with you in it." Had he meant to say it like that? An image of both of them trying to squeeze into the silk sheath flashed through her mind. He touched her elbow and another electric hum ran up her arm. Would that keep happening?

She lifted her arm away from him. "You have to go first so I can hold my dress up.

Sam stepped in front of her and she followed, hiking up the dress so she could move, amazed and apprehensive about what lay ahead. Each step took her further away from the comfort and ease of the black stirrup pants and oversized blouse hung on the clothes tree in her room on the third floor.

Grace knew it was a leap of faith, a flying jump over the heads of all the women who had burned their bras, held their own doors, and insisted on paying half the bill, but for the first time in a long time, maybe ever, she didn't want to ignore the seductive attention of a man who utterly attracted her.

She'd never been good at romance, in part because she had never cared to learn, and in part because certain men scared her. Men like Sam. Men who made her heart race. Richard had never appealed to her in the same way. She loved him, but he'd always offered protection more than passion.

This thing with Sam had been brewing for a long time.

When they reached the bottom of the steps, she smoothed the fabric down her hips, took Sam's arm and let him guide her into the community room.

The musical trio, their instruments and sheet music packed in brown and black cases, exited through the front door. Larry stationed himself behind a table with a sound system and a stack of CD's. He held a microphone and spoke into it softly. "This one goes out to Nick, wherever he is. We miss you, buddy."

The song began, a sultry version of *Someone to Watch Over Me.* Phil and Larry took to the floor first. Ed and Elizabeth joined them, followed by other pairs of partners, male and female, male and male, female and female.

"Ready?" Sam looked down at her.

"Yes," she answered with a pretense of self-assurance. Was allowing oneself to be with a man who made your mind go fuzzy ever a good idea? Sarah would have known how to respond in a situation like this. Grace felt awkward, inadequate, and badly trained.

Sam opened his arms. The only sensible thing to do was relax. She took a deep breath, put one hand on his shoulder, the other in his hand, and stepped forward into the swaying couples

Warmth swept through her. No wonder he enjoyed phenomenal success with women. Grace felt an aura of such acceptance that it made her want to weep. She thought of how sweet he'd been when she poured out Nick's ashes. Teddy thought Sarah and Sam would make a good couple. Grace couldn't, would not let herself, see that happening.

Larry's song dedication merged into her memory of dancing with Nick last New Year's Eve and sadness enveloped her. Nick loved a good party.

Sam pulled her closer. All thoughts of Nick faded away. Consumed by this moment, by this man holding her, she turned her head sideways and allowed her cheek to touch the lapel of his jacket. She could smell his aftershave and wanted to scrub it away, to see what he smelled like underneath the manufactured scent. She could almost make him out. She closed her eyes and tried to separate out the olfactory sensations but then she noticed something else, a sound. Could it be his heartbeat? She pressed her ear to his chest and tried to listen closer.

Conscious of her actions, she pulled back slightly. Sam slid his hand up the silk dress until his fingertips rested on the skin of her upper back. She wanted to melt. This was delicious and decadent and more desirable than anything she had experienced in years. His chest warmed her like lying on the heat of her rock on a summer day, but here there was something yielding, something alive, not a huge chunk of mineral. She might have had the joy of lying on this chest repeatedly over the years.

The song ended. Grace pulled away from Sam and touched the top of her head, pretending to smooth her hair back but keenly aware that every strand was still in place.

"Thank you, Grace." His voice slid down her body and mingled with the silk of her dress. She yearned to move back into his arms, but the feeling was cut short by a wolf-like whistle from the other end of the room.

Everybody turned to see what it signaled. Phil disengaged from the crowd and walked to the door, his arms outstretched. "What have we here?" he asked loud enough to be heard by everybody present.

Grace couldn't see the object of his attention until Teddy stepped through the door with Mallory blushing on his arm and looking like the handmaiden of Bacchus. She wore a skin-tight, red dress with spaghetti straps that showed cleavage in the front and as much thigh as possible on the bottom. Nearly every man in the room, and a few women, lit up, including Sam.

"Long live the legacy of Nicholas Mason!" Ben raised his glass.

"Here, here," chorused those who could remember the old days and those who wished they had been around then, too.

Larry dedicated the next song to Ben and Polly. The attention settled away from Mallory as couples retook the dance floor.

"Would you like to dance again?" Sam asked.

"No, thanks." Grace walked out of the room without looking back. She had seen the way Sam looked at Mallory.

Memories flooded her mind as she climbed the two flights of steps to her room. Sam had looked at Mallory like Nick had looked at Norma when he brought her home, and at any number of other young women over the years.

Grace unzipped her dress as she crossed the third floor to her room.

Why in the world was she having such a strong reaction to what she could easily have foreseen? Of course Sam would have a greater appreciation for someone like Mallory.

She kicked off the dress and slid into her pants and shirt.

A relationship with Sam that went beyond friendship would always include the possibility that someone more desirable would come along, someone younger, like Mallory, someone more his type, like Sarah.

Grace plopped onto the edge of her mattress.

"Can I come in?" accompanied a knock at the top of the stairs.

He'd followed her up?

"Grace?" Footsteps approached her screened off corner. "You okay?"

"Yes," she said.

"Can I come in?" he asked.

"Well, I suppose you can, since you're already here." Her skin vibrated with heat in spite of the chill in the air.

Sam's face appeared around the edge of the screen. "This is your room? It's cold up here."

"I like it cold."

He walked in. "Mind if I sit for a minute?"

She moved to the head of the bed and gestured to the foot. "Have at it."

Why was she so angry? She wanted to tell him to get lost, but she knew Sam hadn't done anything wrong.

"What happened?"

Grace breathed out and sank into herself. "I can't do this Sam. I simply can't."

"Can't do what?"

She looked at him. "We tried it once, remember? And you blew me off after only a few dates." Drat the tears that filled her eyes. She didn't want him to know how much he'd hurt her.

"I am so sorry, Grace." He looked at his hands. "I count that as one of the biggest mistakes of my life."

"Well, you might do it again, so let's not go there."

Sam chuckled. "I can guarantee I will not do that again."

She listened to his version of what happened. He'd made a foolish mistake when he was young. Right when he and Grace started dating, he'd found out he had a daughter. The news upended his life. He'd come back to Grace months later and tried to start over, but she refused him every time.

"Do you remember?" he asked.

Of course she did.

"And then I thought you were with Nick, so I accepted my loss and moved on."

"To dozens of others," she said.

"There weren't that many, and they never lasted long. I'm interested in you, Grace. If I'd known you weren't with Nick…."

"Why does everybody assume I was with Nick?" The idea irritated her. Couldn't a woman have a relationship with a man without everyone assuming they were sexual?

"It doesn't matter now," Sam said. "Could we spend some time together, get to know each other?"

"We do know each other, Sam. We've known each other for forty-three years."

"No, we don't. I want to spend time with you. I want to court you."

"You want to *court* me?" Grace raised her eyebrows, poking fun at his word choice, which made Sam laugh.

"You know what I mean," he said.

She bit her lips, noticing the ease in her body now. The ambivalence had left her. She took a deep breath and dove into the future. "Okay, I accept."

They made plans to meet for dinner at Handels on Monday night.

Sam kissed her cheek before he left.

When his departing footsteps were no longer audible, Grace fell backwards on her mattress.

What if Teddy had already raised Sarah's interest in Sam? Grace would have to tell her sister sooner or later, but Sarah would be gone for six weeks. No need to break the news until she returned. By then, Grace might have discovered her interest in Sam had no depth.

That could happen.

But she didn't think so.

Chapter Twenty-Six

FINALLY, HELL HAD FROZEN OVER. Grace had agreed to give him another chance. The workday seemed endless. Sam had another client coming in at three thirty. That would absorb some of his excitement about meeting Grace for dinner.

More and more, Sam's interest in maintaining his law practice waned. He had called Teddy in the early afternoon to ask, again, if Teddy might consider moving back to Wood Grove to take over. Teddy was interested, but asked Sam not to say anything to Grace. Sam could respect that. Probably the young man didn't want to disappoint his mother if he decided to decline the offer.

At the end of the phone conversation, Teddy had gone into a rather long description of his aunt. Teddy thought she and Sam might have a lot in common. Would he consider having dinner with her when she returned from France in June? Grace must have already told her son about their date this evening. Was Teddy letting him know the sister approved and wanted to meet him? Sam was thrilled. This was going better than expected.

The phone rang. Ruby was out on an errand. Sam answered and a familiar voice said, "Hello, Sam."

He sat back in his chair. "Hello, Elena."

"How's the weather in Ohio?" she asked.

Though they had spoken only a few times since her big reveal, he had learned she was slow to come to the point, always starting with the least intimate. They exchanged more pleasantries about the weather.

"Thank you for the flowers. They were beautiful, Sam."

"I received your thank-you note." Sam had asked Ruby to send flowers a few months ago, when Elena's husband died.

"Randi called last night. She told me she's planning to move to Ohio, to live with you."

"She is." Did that bother Elena? Sam hadn't thought about that. Maybe he should have consulted her feelings first, but Randi was his daughter, too, and also an adult. He didn't need to ask her mother for permission, but he did anyway. "You okay with that?"

"More than okay."

That came as a relief.

"I worry about her, Sam. She's over forty years old and she still doesn't seem to have found her place in the world."

"Maybe she takes after me in that regard, Elena. I'm not sure I've found my place yet, either."

Elena's laughter tumbled over the phone line. "You have always known your place in the world, Sam."

Her laughter still warmed him inside, like a good shot of bourbon. He hadn't heard it for a long time.

"It'll be good to spend time with her." He picked up a pen and doodled on a notepad.

"I'm happy to hear you feel that way." Elena's voice dropped in tone. "Randi's going to need you more than ever."

"Is she okay?" he asked.

"She's wonderful. I couldn't imagine a better daughter and you've been so good to her. Thank you for everything, Sam."

"Everything" amounted to a sperm donation and stepping up when Elena's narrow-minded husband couldn't move beyond his love affair with his own version of morality. How could Sam reply to that?

"I'd like to see you sometime," Elena said.

"You're always welcome here." Damn. That came out like a reflex. He back-pedaled. "I'll be in Denver in July to visit my parents. Let's make plans for dinner then."

"That sounds lovely, Sam. I'll be in touch." She hung up the phone before he had a chance to say good-bye.

Sam leaned up to replace the receiver and settled back into his chair.

"What was that all about?" Ruby had wheeled her chair to his door.

"When did you get back?" he asked.

"I came in when the phone was ringing. You picked up before I had a chance."

"I'm not sure what that was all about," he answered.

"Is this the first time you've talked to her since her husband died?"

"Yes." He looked down at the doodling on the notepad. *Grace. Grace. Grace.*

"Why do you think she called?" Ruby asked.

Sam looked up. Soft, gray curls hugged her head like the brown wool skirt embraced the girth of her belly. He'd given Ruby the right to ask questions like that. Several years ago, he had divulged the details of his relationship with Elena, including the fact that Randi was his daughter.

"I don't know," he said. "There's something she's not telling me."

"Maybe she wants to get to know you again, now that her husband's dead."

"I don't think so." Sam looked down as he rolled his pen between his fingers and the surface of the desk. At least he hoped that wasn't the case. Elena had been his first. And she had given him a child. History had a way of mucking up the present. He wanted this time in his life to be all about Grace.

"This whole thing drives you nuts, doesn't it?" Ruby crossed her thick legs, put her hands behind her head, and leaned back in the five-hundred-dollar chair Sam purchased when her back started aching.

"What do you mean?" he asked.

"You like to be in control, Sam. You're a neat freak." She brought one hand out from behind her head and put her index finger in the air. "First you slip up and have sex with Elena." She added her middle finger. "Then you find out, twenty years later, you have a daughter." She raised her ring finger. "Then you learn this daughter you never knew about is a lesbian." She poked up her pinky. "For another twenty-plus years you avoid talking to the mother of your daughter because there's a stepfather who objects." She extended her thumb. "And now that the stepfather is dead, you don't know where you fit into the whole picture." She clutched her hand, massaging the air. "You can't get a handle on it. It's out of your control. You hate that, don't you?"

She put her hand behind her head and pushed the chair back, smirking.

"You know me so well." Sam peeled the doodled note from the pad, wadded it up, and tossed it into the trash. "Why don't you knock off early, Ruby? Go pester Hal with your mordant analyses of other peoples' lives."

Ruby didn't know everything. He had never confessed the full depth of his feelings for Grace, and Ruby didn't know Grace had finally agreed to have dinner with him again.

"You can't put me off with rarely used words," Ruby said. "You know I'm right."

He heard her wheel away from his doorway. Five minutes later, she poked her head back in his door. "I'm leaving now."

"Have a good night, Ruby. Give my regards to Hal."

"You have a good night, Sam. Have a little fun." Her voice exuded warmth, caring.

"I will," he replied without looking up.

Again, the phone rang.

He heard Ruby answer and say, "Hello, Randi." He waited until Ruby put her on hold.

"Got it," he called out. The outside door closed and he knew Ruby had left.

Sam picked up the receiver. "Hello, Randi. I just got off the phone with your mother."

"You called her?" Randi asked.

"She called me," he answered.

"You know, you could call her now that Dad's gone."

"Yes, I could." As far as Sam knew, Elena's husband had never known that Sam was back in the picture with Randi. Elena had a unique talent for orchestrating life to suit her. She'd turned lying-by-omission into an art form.

"How'd she sound?" Randi asked.

"She sounded good," he answered. "Concerned about you."

"She worries too much."

"Don't all mothers?" he asked.

"I wouldn't know," Randi answered. "She's the only one I ever had."

Sam liked his daughter. He hoped their mutual regard would withstand the friction of daily interaction. Toaster crumbs, messy bedrooms, and dishes left unwashed were okay for a visit, but not full time. She would have to make a few changes. Sam supposed he might have to make a few, too.

"What's your ETA for Wood Grove?" he asked.

"My lease runs out at the end of May, but the new tenants are willing to pay my May rent if I leave by the thirteenth. I'll stay with friends in Pennsylvania for a few days and arrive in Ohio by the fifteenth."

"I'll have your room ready and waiting. Hope the change of scenery does you good."

"I need more than a change of scene." She paused. "I'm thinking of an entirely new direction."

"What do you mean?" Sam asked.

"I appreciate everything you've done for me, but I think I want a real career path, one with health insurance, a pension. Think it's too late for that?"

Sam had been paying for private health insurance and helping her build a retirement portfolio for years. Besides that, someday she would inherit from him. Randi had no real money worries, but he understood the need for independence.

"It's never too late. Let's talk when you get here."

"Thanks for letting me chill in Ohio. I need a break from New York."

"And I need a break from not seeing you."

They said their goodbyes. Sam sat back in his chair. New York probably reminded her of Barb. They'd been together for a long time. Randi ended their relationship, but she hadn't offered details about why and he hadn't asked.

If she wanted out of the book contract, that would be the end of the Randi Flemming novels. He wasn't ready to let go of his ties to the publishing industry altogether. He would continue to act as agent to several other writers he represented. He would consult and offer education programs, as he had for decades. But losing the Randi Flemming novels would be a big change. Sam wasn't sure he was ready for that. Maybe Randi would reconsider. Maybe he could drive a bargain she couldn't refuse.

Grace might be a good person to talk to about this. He'd told her he had a daughter, but he hadn't gone into details. Maybe he should tell her Randi was his daughter.

Only a few more hours and he'd be with Grace.

Only a few more weeks and he'd be living with Randi.

What a difference a few weeks can make.

Chapter Twenty-Seven

THIS TIME, GRACE DIDN'T obsess about what to wear for her first date with Sam. She decided to go as herself, frayed edges and all. He met her at Handels as she'd expected, on time, with a shirt still crisp from ironing and a stunning suit. After he let the jacket slip off, loosened his tie, and rolled up his sleeves, Grace began to relax.

"Been here long?" he asked.

"A few minutes." She picked up a menu and looked over the fare. "When did they switch to pizza?"

"Not long ago. They have salads, too." Sam sat back in the booth and put his hands on his thighs. "Thanks for coming."

Grace looked up from the menu. "Why wouldn't I come? I said I'd be here."

"I know," he said. "I'm happy to see you."

A peanut landed on the table between them and bounced a few times before landing in Grace's lap.

"Oops." The waitress positioned herself at the end of table. "I meant that for Sam."

"Have you met Mandy?" Sam asked. "Skip McKay's niece. Mandy, this is Grace Baxter."

Grace held out her hand. "Nice to meet you Mandy. I think we've probably seen each other in town a time or two." The girl couldn't be more than sixteen. Long brown hair tied back from her round unblemished face. She resembled her mother, with a look less hardened.

"My ninth-grade art class had a show in your hallway two years ago," Mandy said. "My picture was a collage of lips and eyes."

"I remember that," Grace said. "You paired Rock Hudson with Hitler, Madonna with a Dalmatian, and Alanis Morrisette with an eagle."

"You have a good memory!" Mandy said.

"I framed all of the art," Grace said. "You have a good eye."

"Thanks," Mandy said, standing a bit taller. "Can I take your order?"

"Yes, you *may*," Sam said.

Mandy rolled her eyes before looking at Grace. "He's always correcting my grammar."

"How irritating," Grace said.

Mandy smiled. "See Sam? She's on my side."

"So am I."

The sternness in Sam's voice sounded like concern, not judgment, but Grace considered that grammar was probably the least of the girl's worries at this point in time. Sixteen, or thereabouts, could be a challenging age, even more so than when she was a young girl.

They ordered a pizza to share and two salads. Sam asked for a beer. Grace requested water.

After Mandy left, Sam said, "You were great with her."

Grace brushed off the compliment. "She seems like a good girl. By the way, if you drink more than one beer, I'll drive you home. Rule number one, no driving under the influence."

"I can—"

Grace held up her hand and he stopped talking. "Rule number two," she said. "There's no arguing with my rules. I have very few. Each one is meant to keep everybody safe and whole."

"Fair enough," Sam said.

And so the date began.

He asked about GraceHaven. Grace spoke about her fears and hopes. Sam listened with few interruptions. He asked questions more than made comments. When he did comment, his words were thoughtful, supportive. She could tell he didn't want to stumble right out of the gate.

She asked him about his day. He started to answer, but a peanut landed in his lap, diverting his attention to Mandy who stood behind the bar, holding up two fingers and mouthing, "Two points." He acknowledged the girl with an unsmiling nod and turned back to Grace.

He talked about his gardening plans and his appreciation for Judy.

"I didn't know you two knew each other," she said.

He talked about meeting the young groundskeeper when she moved to GraceHaven, how she'd helped him choose plants for the south side of his garage. Grace hadn't realized how connected he was to people living at GraceHaven. But then she remembered his friendship with John. Now she understood Loretta's mild disgust with Grace's attitude about Sam. She had been so very wrong about him.

"And what are your ties to the authors you've brought to town?" she asked. She'd always wondered. Sam had acted as host for any number of book signings at the used bookstore downtown. Grace had never gone to one, but she'd seen lines of women snaking down the sidewalk, brand new novels clutched in their hands.

"I act as their agent," Sam said.

"I had no idea you were an agent." How had she missed that? She could have referred any number of promising writers to him over the years.

"I have a little business on the side," he said. "I act as agent for writers who might not be published elsewhere. Not every book needs to be a bestseller."

This was a new side to Sam, but then she remembered. When they'd first met he'd talked about reading cheesy romance novels. She liked seeing him as a hero for hard-to-publish authors. She'd met so many over the years, good writers who would never fit into the typical market.

"In fact," —Sam unzipped his brief case and brought out a book— "I have a copy of one my most prolific authors. Have you read any by Randi Flemming?"

"Guilty." Grace laughed.

Another peanut landed in Sam's lap. He again looked toward the bar. Mandy raised her hand and announced her victory in silence. Sam shook his head and mouthed, "Stop."

"Where were we?" he asked.

"Randi Flemming," Grace said.

"Right," he said. "You've read her. What did you think?"

"It was about what I expected," Grace said. "Novels like that put me to sleep with no discernible side effects, so I'd have to say I'm a fan, for health reasons." She tidied up her portion of the table, using her napkin to dry the ring on the table left by the bottom of her water glass.

"So—" Sam scratched his chin. "You liked it?"

"You want an honest answer?" Grace asked.

"Of course," Sam said. "Say what you think."

Should she say what she thought? Why not? Her feet rested in her favorite tennis shoes with the worn soles. She might as well let go of all pretense. "It's not a question of liking, Sam. People like their addictions."

"Her novels are addictive?" he asked. "Sounds like you do like them."

"'Like' is relative term. I like wine, but I don't recommend it as a dietary staple." She'd never forget that headache the day after Nick's funeral.

"Go on," Sam said.

"Okay," she said and smiled. "Remember you asked for it."

Sam hand-signaled her to continue.

"The truth is, I've read several." The truth was, she'd read them all. "The earlier novels are like so many others of that genre written fifteen years ago, one long infomercial for sexism. Twenty-something women are girls with 'pert breasts' and the men all suffer from priapism."

"Priapism?" Sam asked.

"An abnormal condition that results in a persistent erection."

"I know what the word means." He put his hands in his lap. "Go on."

"Her later books don't penetrate to that place where you can lose yourself in the story. They're boring, vapid, lack intimacy. She's trying to move into the mainstream market by creating more intricate plots, but her novels don't work."

"What do you mean they don't work?" he asked.

"You know her better than I do, but I'd say she's scared of letting the world know who she really is."

"Everybody's scared to let the world know who they really are," he said. "Aren't you?"

"I think you're defending Randi Flemming because you're her agent. You know as well as I do that her novels are trite. Her characters are roadkill and the plots barely limp along."

"Ouch." Sam sat against the back of the booth. Another peanut landed in his lap. Sam scowled toward the bar.

He was irritated and Grace was to blame, at least in part. She'd gone too far. The snobby part of her that read the New Yorker cover-to-cover had discredited what appeared to be significant to him. "I'm sorry," she said, awkward and unsure again. However did men and women manage to survive more than the first few dates?

"It's okay," he said. "I asked for honesty."

"They're not that bad," she said, committing herself to damage control. "They do put me to sleep, but an occasional phrase is extraordinary and in her latest, the heroine actually has a gay brother. Two points for moving toward the twenty-first century."

"You liked that one?" he asked, a slow smile returning to his face.

"I think they might be getting better." She smiled at being able to end with a positive spin on her critique.

"How many have you actually read?" he asked, his eyes twinkling.

"More than I'm willing to admit to," she said.

He reached across the table and gave her hand a quick, gentle squeeze.

They moved on to other topics; salad and pizza arrived together. Grace noticed she was happy, devoid of concern about whether or not she had salad in her teeth, and becoming less interested in how he felt about her and more in how she felt about him, which seemed to fall somewhere in the range of mildly to madly "falling in love with."

After a series of direct peanut hits that elicited more scowls from Sam, Mandy stopped throwing them. He explained their relationship and Grace remembered the time on the boulder, after Stephen and John died, when she'd almost said, "Yes," right before Sam was called away to attend a birth.

"I apologize for her behavior tonight," he said. "Gloria told me that she can be persistently irritating, but this is the first I've seen it."

"Don't be too hard on her," Grace said. "Sounds like she needs to have you on her side."

"She has me on her side," Sam said. "She needs discipline."

"Raising kids is a challenge," she said.

"Especially when you're not the parent."

Grace knew that non-custodial parents and even grandparents sometimes struggled to assert their rights. Though Sam had a stake in Mandy's life, he wasn't even related. She admired his commitment to the girl.

After Sam paid, and Grace insisted on leaving the tip, they walked out to the sidewalk.

Sam apologized again for Mandy's behavior.

"No worries," Grace said. "I had a good time."

"You did?"

"Yes, I did." Why was he surprised? Hadn't she smiled enough? Ugh. She had no clue about how to be a proper date.

"So you'll do it again?"

"Of course." He had to ask? Sam had so much to learn about her.

"Okay," he said. "How about Friday night? I'll cook."

"Okay." She remembered to smile and started to walk away.

"Want a lift?" he asked. "I only had one beer."

She didn't have to remember to smile this time. "Thanks, but I'll walk."

Five more steps and he asked, "Favorite dish?"

She stepped back to him. "Did you know some people are genetically predisposed to not liking the taste of cilantro? To them, the herb tastes like soap."

"You're kidding," Sam said. "Poor them!"

"Well, I am one of them. So I'd say my favorite dish is anything without that herb."

"Poor you." He overplayed the regret with charm. Someday she would rope him into performing on stage, if she could manage to keep GraceHaven going. Her stomach clenched. She'd forgotten to worry about that for the past few hours.

"Rule number three," he said. "No cilantro."

Her face and stomach relaxed. Amazing how the body, given the right cues, remembers to trust.

On the walk home, Grace noticed flowers, children, a dog, and recalled that the world offered unexpected joys every day. Sam said that dumping her after their first few dates had been one of the biggest mistakes of his life. Her mistake had been stubbornly hanging on to the hurt of being dumped.

Chapter Twenty-Eight

INSTEAD OF WAKING to sleep fog on Tuesday morning, Sam's mind snapped to attention. He had another date with Grace on Friday night. After his usual stints on the treadmill and keyboard, he whistled through his shower, skipped his second cup of coffee, and headed downtown, on foot. He hadn't walked to work in years.

Misty haze hung low on the fields. Birds called to each other and swooped down to alight on tree branches and bushes. He caught sight of a doe on the edge of the woods. Life was good.

In town, Sam smiled and said, "Hello," to everybody he passed. Even the dour new guy who ran the doughnut shop, his teeth crooked and his jacket worn at the cuffs, returned a smile. Everybody needed a sweet start to the morning. Sam preferred some*body* to some*thing*.

The office door held fast when Sam tried to push it open. He looked at his watch. Ruby wouldn't be there for another thirty minutes. He could let himself in, but his schedule was light today. No need to start early. Sam jogged back to the doughnut shop for another cup of coffee.

Seating himself at the counter, he reached for a newspaper. "Just a cup, black, please," he said to the counter girl. Someone touched him on the back. Sam turned around to a familiar face.

"Hey, old buddy," Skip said. "Mind if I sit with you?"

"Have a seat." Sam had run into him a few times lately. Skip seemed calmer, less abrasive.

Skip ordered a cup of coffee. When the counter girl placed it in front of him, he thanked her and cradled the cup between his hands.

Sam skimmed the business section of the newspaper.

"I want to thank you," Skip said.

"What for?" Sam asked. He folded the newspaper and shoved it to the next spot at the counter.

"For helping out Gloria all these years. She and I had a heart-to-heart last night. I was doing this thing, you know, about making amends, and I felt like I needed to apologize for not being there for her all these years." The words came with effort.

Though buried under years of bad behavior, Skip appeared to be coming to life again. This was Sam's old roommate from college, the guy who dug a little deeper and questioned authority just enough to find alternate perspectives. Sam reached out and grasped Skip's shoulder. "No problem," Sam said. "And you're welcome."

They spent the next hour talking about their lives. Skip's mother had passed a few years back, and though Sam had attended the funeral, he and Skip had never talked about her death. Skip spoke about watching her waste away and how he developed a new respect for Mary Sue as she cared for her mother-in-law. That started him down a new road, but a direction of sobriety took time to discover and maintain. He had relapsed many times.

"I hear that's common," Sam said. "Glad you keep getting back on the right path."

They moved on to other topics, covering community changes, sports, and politics. When Sam looked at his watch, the time surprised him. "Skip, I enjoyed talking with you, but if I don't leave now, Ruby'll have Hal checking to see if I'm still alive." He stood.

"Before you go—" Skip stood beside him, "—Gloria told me she saw you last night with that Grace Baxter." Skip looked down at his feet. "I'm not trying to tell you what to do, but I'd be careful." He looked back up.

"You're a good guy, Sam. I don't want to see you get hurt, and well, she's a fast one."

Sam receded without taking a step back. "What do you mean?"

"Well, I never cheated on Mary Sue, but if I'd wanted to, I knew where to go, if you know what I mean."

Memories flooded. Skip's cheap flirtation at the soda counter when Sam met Grace for the first time. Running into her in the woods when he moved to Wood Grove and noticing the way she shrank from Skip. Hearing Skip talk about her at the dining table that night. He had no use for his old friend. "Goodbye, Skip."

Sam walked out of the shop and past the door that led to his old apartment. When he'd first moved to Wood Grove, his dreams had run into a brick wall of reality. He had that same jarring feeling now. What Skip had implied about Grace wasn't surprising. Sam had been swayed for decades by similar, foolish notions.

By the time he'd walked to the office, his mood lightened. Skip McKay could go to hell. Sam had a chance with Grace and he wasn't going to screw it up this time.

"Where have you been?" Ruby asked.

"Shooting the breeze with Skip McKay," he answered as he sailed past her and into his office. He tossed his jacket onto his chair and leaned back on his desk to face the door. Ruby appeared as expected.

"Ahh!" She jumped back. "I didn't expect you to be standing there."

"Where else would I be, Ruby?" He crossed his arms.

She leaned against the doorframe and crossed her arms. "You usually wait until I get here."

"After thirty-six years, I think I know the drill."

"Why are you smiling like that, Sam?" She smiled back. "You're positively contagious this morning."

"I'm in a good mood," he said.

Ruby waited two beats and then asked, "Are you dating Grace Baxter? Mavis Bradley called last night and told me that she saw you two at Handels. Said you looked pretty cozy."

"I had dinner with Grace last night." Sam uncrossed his arms and put his hands on the desk behind him.

"And are you going out with her again?" she asked.

"Yes."

"Do you think you'll have sex with her?"

"Do you really expect me to answer that?" he asked.

"Are you smoking pot?"

"What?" Why was she asking these questions?

"You're acting like Hal Jr. did when he started having sex with that Haney girl and smoking pot. It really is a gateway drug. We're so lucky that he couldn't afford a cocaine habit and he was smart enough to not do crack. Also, my prayers were answered when that girl did not get pregnant. Are you using protection, Sam?"

"What?" he asked again. Skip's behavior had been obnoxious, but not a complete surprise. Ruby's behavior floored him.

"You really have to protect yourself these days," Ruby said. "Even older people are getting AIDS, and God knows who she's slept with over the years. That place is a magnet for all kinds, if you know what I mean."

"That's enough!" Sam said. He walked to his chair, put his coat on the back, and sat down. "I'll let you know if I need anything. Shut the door when you leave."

Ruby's eyes widened and filled with tears. She backed out of his office and shut the door.

He had never spoken to her like that.

The rest of the morning was very quiet.

At noon, Ruby paged him for a phone call. She said that she was leaving for lunch.

Sam thanked her and picked up the call.

"What's going on with you, Sam?" Gloria McKay asked. "Mandy came home from work last night in tears. She said you yelled at her."

"I didn't yell at her," Sam said. He'd gone back into Handels to address Mandy's behavior after Grace left. He'd told Mandy she'd been inappropriate. He expected her to behave better than that.

"She said you yelled," Gloria yelled.

"I was having pizza last night with a friend and Mandy threw one too many peanuts. I had to talk to her. She's never acted like that before. Grace and I could barely have a conversation."

"Grace? Grace Baxter? Mandy told me you were with that woman, but I didn't believe her. What are you doing?"

"What do you mean?" Sam asked. What right did Gloria have to even ask the question? "I had a date. We were talking."

"Well, you are old enough to date whoever you want," Gloria sputtered, "but you can't yell at my daughter."

"I didn't yell at her," Sam said, his voice rising in volume. "She was out of line. I talked to her about it. If you and Jasper had ever tried to discipline her, maybe I wouldn't have to."

The phone line clicked. Sam hung up the handset.

Instead of going to lunch, Sam sat at his desk thinking for the next hour.

He'd never imagined his decision to date Grace would be such a challenge for others.

When Ruby returned, Sam went to her desk. She looked up, her face emotionless. "Yes?" she asked. "What can I do for you?"

Sam sat in a reception chair. "Come with us this weekend. If Grace agrees to attend a concert with me on Saturday night, come with us. I have extra tickets. I want you and Hal to join us. I think you'll like her, Ruby. Give her a chance."

Tears brimmed in Ruby's eyes. "I'm sorry," she said. "I shouldn't have said what I did."

"I'm only asking you to give her a chance, Ruby."

She nodded. "Okay. I'll ask Hal."

"Thank you," Sam said. He returned to his desk. This time he left the door open.

Chapter Twenty-Nine

"WHAT DO YOU DO for a living, Hal?" Grace asked. They were twenty minutes into their trip to Columbus. Sam had picked her up promptly at six followed by Hal and Ruby at six fifteen. Grace couldn't see Ruby's face since she sat directly behind, but she'd looked none too enthused when she'd walked to the car. Hal, on the other, beamed interest. Grace had seen him around town a few times but they'd never spoken. She hadn't known he and Ruby were married.

"Toolmaker," Hal said. "Started in high school."

"That's a changing industry." She sat half turned so she could see him as he answered.

"You bet. Now it's all computerized." Hal described the long process of learning a new way to do his job.

"Almost sounds like a career change," Sam said.

"I guess," Hal said. "But it's still a shop, so that makes it feel like home."

His wife remained silent.

"Ruby," Grace said, facing forward again. "Sam said you have two children."

A quiet, "Yes," floated over the headrest.

Grace started to ask another question, but Hal jumped in.

"Boys," he said. "They're both married. Hal Jr. lives down in Cincinnati. Works for an insurance company. He got married last fall. Our youngest, Hank, already has three kids. One boy and twin girls. He and his wife have their hands full."

"Do they live close?" Grace asked.

"Right in Wood Grove. They come over every Sunday for dinner. Gathering them around the table is like herding cats."

"I'll bet you love every minute of it," Grace said.

"You bet I do," Hal said.

Grace tried a few more times to engage Ruby in conversation during the drive to the concert. Ruby's responses were brief and polite. Finally, Grace let it rest. Maybe Ruby and Hal had a fight earlier. Maybe she and Sam had some work difficulty. Maybe she just didn't like talking, but that seemed unlikely. Grace had seen Ruby around town many times over the years and the woman rarely kept silence. Words seemed to spill out of her. But not tonight.

The four of them sat through the string quartet without talking. Halfway through, Sam reached out to hold Grace's hand and she let him. Though they'd touched in the past, this felt different, more significant, reliable.

After the concert, Sam suggested a club down the street. The four of them walked to the door and looked inside. The women wore cocktail dresses. The men had on suits. Grace suggested something a little less upscale. They agreed on a Mexican restaurant near the edge of the city. There, the four of them settled into a colorful booth.

When the others ordered beer, Grace asked for a glass of water.

"You don't drink?" Ruby asked.

"Rarely, mostly at funerals," Grace said. "If I'd been born in the early 1900s, I might have formed a chapter of the Women's Christian Temperance Union."

"She's serious," Sam said. "When we ate at Handels, she told me that if I had more than one beer, she was driving."

Ruby loosened up after that.

When Grace went to the bathroom, Ruby followed and began to quiz her.

"Where did you grow up?" she asked.

"Dayton," Grace said. "Born and raised there. Went to Catholic school."

"I had a friend who went to Catholic school in Cincinnati. She said the nuns rapped knuckles with a ruler if anyone stepped out of line. Did that ever happen to you?"

"I saw that happen a few times," Grace said. "Never had the experience myself. I was probably too scared to act up when I was young, and clever enough to act up without being caught when I was older."

Ruby laughed. "I was like that, too."

Grace washed her hands.

"I don't think kids should ever be hit in school, by anybody, for any reason," Ruby said. "Discipline is the parents' job."

"My son didn't have trouble in school, but if he had, I would have expected his teacher to talk to him. If anybody had ever hit Teddy, they would have had me to contend with."

Ruby nodded, making eye contact with Grace in the mirror over the sinks.

"How did you come to work for Sam?" Grace asked.

Ruby told her the story about the blind date.

"You were very lucky to have found Hal early in life."

Ruby lit up.

When Grace started to open the door to return to the booth, Ruby stopped her. "Sam's been my hero," she said. "Tall, dark, handsome, smart, kind, out there saving people. You can't imagine the way he steps in to help people, even people he doesn't know well."

"That doesn't surprise me," Grace said.

"I can't say too much, but I know you'd be impressed."

Another woman entered the restroom. Grace moved away from the door. Ruby didn't seem in any hurry to leave.

"I'm surprised I didn't see this before," Ruby said. "I remember the first time he asked you out. He never seemed interested in other women after that. I thought it was because of, well, something else, but now I see it was you.

The thing is," she continued, her expression thoughtful. "I want him to have everything he deserves, a happy ending, if you know what I mean." She paused. "If you're his happy ending, Grace, I'm happy for both of you."

Grace wanted to say what she thought—that she had given up on happy endings when Richard left—but she liked the change in Ruby so chose a more benign response. "Thanks for the vote of confidence. When Sam needed to hire someone, he certainly found the right person in you."

Ruby lit up again. She opened the door and ushered Grace through.

Back in the booth, Hal sipped his second beer.

"I'm sticking to one," Sam said. "I'll go with water the rest of the evening."

Grace patted his knee. Sam grasped her hand under the table.

"Have you met Randi yet?" Ruby asked.

"Randi Flemming? The author?" Grace asked.

"Yes, the author," Ruby said, shifting her eyes to Sam in a way that implied something unspoken.

Hal was no actor. The muscles in his face froze and his eyes shifted from Ruby to Sam.

"No," Grace said. Why was Randi Flemming coming up now? She looked at Sam.

He let go of her hand and tugged at his collar before clasping his hands on the table. "Ruby assists in my role as literary agent."

"Do you edit?" Grace asked, turning back to Ruby.

"I act as copy editor after Sam and the author have made all their revisions," Ruby said. "I don't think readers appreciate all the work that goes into producing the final product."

"I like reading Calvin and Hobbes," Hal said.

"So do I." Grace liked Hal.

"Oh, hon. You don't have to humor him," Ruby said, patting Grace's arm. "He's kidding."

The moment of awkward glances evaporated. Sam's hand returned to hers. Grace noticed how much she felt at home.

After dropping Hal and Ruby at their house, Sam pulled out of the driveway and headed for GraceHaven. They rode in silence past the edge of town.

"I had a great evening," Sam said as he pulled into the driveway. "You won over Ruby."

"Didn't know I had to win her over," Grace said.

He parked the car, removed the key from the ignition, put it in the console, and turned to Grace. "Ruby's important to me," he said. "I knew you'd like each other."

He reached across the console and caressed her hand.

"There's something I need to tell you," he said.

That sounded ominous. Grace took a breath, steeling herself.

"Remember the daughter I told you about?"

"Yes."

"I should have told you before we talked about the novels." He let go of her hand and shifted toward his door, opened it, and turned back to say, "Randi Flemming is my daughter."

Her face flared with heat. "That wasn't fair, Sam," she said as he moved out of the car. "You should've told me."

"You're right," he said. He left his door open and walked around the back of the car.

Her cheeks burned. She'd been so harsh.

Sam opened her door. "That wasn't fair. I wanted to hear what you thought without knowing about my relationship with Randi."

Grace waited a moment before stepping out. Sam closed the door behind her.

"The novels aren't that bad," she said. "I enjoyed parts of them."

"You don't have to say that."

"I'm not. There are moments of real humor, sensitivity. She has potential."

"Potential?" Sam asked. He stood close, taking her hands, teasing her with his eyes.

"I'm not saying another word." She couldn't stop the blood rushing to her face.

Sam smiled and stroked a lock of hair across her cheek, tucking it behind her ear.

"I'll call tomorrow." He let go of her hands and walked around the car.

"You should have told me!" she said.

He smiled across the top of the car.

"Rule number four. Full disclosure on relationship status before eliciting feedback of any kind."

Sam laughed and eased himself behind the wheel. She stood in the driveway watching the lights go on when he started the car, listening to the tires move down the asphalt, feeling even more ashamed that she'd slammed the books with such force.

"Grace!"

Judy left her apartment door and crossed the driveway. "Peter had to drive Fran to the hospital in Chillicothe. She fell at the grocery store. Her leg is broken in two places."

Sam's car hummed onto the road and moved the short distance to his driveway. "Is she okay?" His headlights shown through the tree line, moving toward his house.

"Pete said they gave her pretty strong meds. She's not feeling any pain right now."

His garage door lifted. "Do they need anything?" Grace could drive to the hospital now, if necessary, or in the morning.

"No, but Fran is concerned about the play. She must have known how bad her leg was. Even before Peter drove her to the hospital, she said Mallory might have to take over."

"Mallory?" What did Mallory know about directing a play?

"Don't shoot the messenger," Judy held up her hands. "Mallory's in there with Loretta." She gestured to the back of the main house. "I wanted to give you a heads up."

"Thanks." Grace walked to the back door.

Mallory and Loretta sat at the kitchen table, a pot of tea between them.

"Fran broke her leg," Loretta said.

"I heard."

"She wants Mallory to take over the play."

"I heard." Grace looked at Mallory. Her face was set with no expression, at least not one that Grace could read. "Do you want to do that?" she asked.

"Yes," Mallory said.

"What makes you think you can direct?" In her mind, she was the better option to replace Fran at the helm. Why was Mallory even being considered?

"My undergraduate degree was a dual major in English and performance art," Mallory said. "I ran a community theatre in Minneapolis for an internship and worked there for a year after graduation. I have worked in every capacity, as a stagehand, set designer, lighting tech, actor, and director. I even sold tickets, collected them at the door, and ushered when necessary. That was before I went back for my MBA."

Nick's granddaughter was full of surprises. "Okay." Mallory had more experience. Mallory was the better choice. "Do it. Let me know what you need." Grace looked at the clock. Past midnight. "Loretta, we're going to have to serve meals to Fran and Peter in the dorm until Fran can handle steps again."

"Or," Mallory said. When Grace looked at her, the young woman continued. "You could have the carpenters come back and put in a ramp to the back door. They did a great job on the stage."

"We didn't budget money for that," Grace said.

"You haven't turned over that checkbook yet," Mallory said. "I'm guessing you have enough in there to pay for a ramp."

"Are you authorizing me to build a ramp to the back door?" Asking for permission took a slice of her ego, but the money was no longer hers to manage.

"Do it," Mallory said.

Grace walked to the pantry, waving behind without looking back.

As she trudged up the steps, she considered that, first impressions aside, Mallory's similarity to her grandmother, Natalie, seemed uncertain. Perhaps the young woman was not the committed community destroyer after all. Teddy seemed to approve, and he had high standards. And now, Mallory, a young woman with no shortage of surprises, would direct the play.

Nick's granddaughter better not screw it up.

Grace pushed through the door opening to the third floor. A faint glow from her night light shone through the screens around her space. She rounded the screen, dropping clothes as she went. She hadn't even brushed her teeth, but she rarely slept through the night anyway. She'd do it later.

"Ugh," she groaned as she lifted the sheet and blankets to fall underneath them. Randi Flemming was Sam's daughter. Grace burrowed between the cold fabric. Sam had set her up to be honest without restraint when he asked for her opinion about the books, but he'd taken the feedback well. She would be more careful next time, or maybe not. Being careful circumvented closeness. "Ugh," she groaned again. Dating exhausted her.

Chapter Thirty

SAM KNOCKED ON THE back door. He'd have to ask Grace about the protocol for entering.

Was knocking required or did one simply walk into the house? Neither the main house nor the gray building behind were typical homes. In Sam's mind, they were more like his college dorm, the kind of place where nearly anybody had access to main halls and gathering areas.

Mallory opened the door. "You don't have to knock," she said.

Sam stepped into the kitchen.

"Ben and Arthur are in their rooms. You do have to knock on those doors. Grace isn't here."

Mallory returned to her seat at the kitchen table and sat down, one foot tucked underneath the opposite hip. Hunching over a sheath of papers, she made notes with a pen and drew a yellow highlighter across a line.

"Working on the estate?" Sam asked.

"The play," she answered without looking up. "No time for the estate until I feel confident about directing this play."

"What play?" Sam asked.

"The Solstice play."

"That's a big deal." He'd attended several over the years.

"I know." Mallory looked up from what Sam could now see was a script. "Loretta and Teddy said those exact words, ending with, 'and you'd better not screw it up.' Apparently, Grace has made that clear."

“Any chance of that happening?” Sam asked.

“I don’t know how anybody could make this play any worse than it is already.”

“That bad?” he asked.

“Fran only picked it because my grandfather wrote it. I can see why he never made it as a playwright. Clearly, he was a better novelist.” She went back to marking and highlighting.

“Mind if I have a seat?” he asked.

“Be my guest. Mind if I keep reading?”

“Be my guest,” Sam said.

He sat in the chair across from Mallory. He’d only been in the kitchen one other time, when he followed Grace up the back stairs. He’d barely noticed the setup. The table and chairs appeared to be antique, glossy paint not quite filling small holes and nicks. In the middle of the white table, a bowl loaded with fruit sat on a woven mat made of reed that had been dyed the colors of the chairs: banana yellow, bright orange, lime green, fuchsia, turquoise, and purple.

The gas stove had six burners and two large ovens. The stainless-steel refrigerator had side-by-side doors. Sam guessed that the other upright appliance with one door was an additional freezer. The commercial sink had three basins and a gooseneck faucet. Wall cabinets on either side of the sink probably held everyday dishes. Floor-to-ceiling cabinets covered the wall behind him, also painted in high gloss white, but newer, unmarked. He knew he was already in love with Grace, but when he took in the beauty of her kitchen, he fell in love all over again. He had to get her in his life, on a permanent basis.

“Do you know when Grace will return?” he asked. He’d taken a chance by coming by unannounced. When he didn’t run into Grace in the woods, which had been his hope, he decided to drop by.

Mallory looked up. “Fran actually broke her hip and her leg. She had to have surgery. Grace is hanging out at the hospital today.”

"What about Fran's husband?" Sam asked.

"Peter can barely hear. Grace drove over to make sure information is conveyed accurately."

"Seems like everybody around here relies on Grace," Sam said.

"I've noticed that." Mallory closed the cover of the play and leaned forward. "This place is pretty amazing, Sam."

"What do you mean?"

"I mean, all these people living together for decades, making a family out of nothing. I'm quite inspired." She sat back in the chair.

"How do you feel about being the one to end it?" Sam asked.

"Honestly?" She sank deeper into her chair. "I feel pretty crappy about that."

Happy to hear that, Sam asked. "What are you going to do?"

"I have no idea. I've been reading my grandfather's journals."

"Nick kept journals?"

The clock above the sink, a black cat with a tail that swished the seconds, meowed five times.

"Teddy was right, Sam. It's all in my grandfather's journals. Morally, this place belongs to Grace."

"How so?"

"Let me show you." She picked up the play and led him up the back staircase to the second floor.

When they reached her room, she waved her hand over an array of notebooks on her bed. Different shapes, sizes, and colors, most of the covers were worn around the edges.

"These are all of his journals," Mallory said. "I found them in the basement. My grandfather was obsessed with Grace, but she never gave in to him. My grandmother was so wrong about her."

Sam thought about Grace's confession regarding the one time she did give in. Maybe Nick forgot to write about that one, or maybe the man had a small portion of discretion in that self-serving soul of his.

“Mind if I read these?” Immersing himself in Nick’s unedited mind held little appeal, but maybe Sam could learn something useful.

“Be my guest,” she said. “I’ve been through them all at least once. Even if he didn’t sign the most recent will, at least he updated an earlier one that would have cut everybody out of his estate.”

Sam’s hand dropped. “What do you mean?”

“There’s the one he didn’t sign that left some of the estate to Grace, the valid one leaving his estate to my father, and one from earlier in his life that left everything to an organization that works to protect authors’ rights. I found that one in his journals.”

“Do you have copies of all the wills?”

“Yes, I mean I have a copy of the valid one, and the originals of the other two.”

“Could you make copies of all three and give me a set?”

“Do you think there’s a way we can make it right for Grace? Or at least fix it so that the community can go on?” Mallory asked.

“I don’t know. How soon can you get that set to me?”

Mallory gathered the journals into one neat, tall pile. “Tomorrow soon enough?”

“That would be great.”

“Thanks, Sam.” She hefted the stack of journals and deposited them in Sam’s waiting arms. “It’s good to have you on my side.”

A mild scent of mildew wafted up from the books.

“Yours is a good side to be on, Mallory.”

Sam carried the stack of journals down the stairs, out the back door, and across the lawn. By the time he cut through the tree line, his shoulders ached. Once in the house, he carried them into the living room and set them on the floor beside the couch, then went back to the kitchen to throw together a turkey-on-rye and turn on the tea kettle.

It was going to be a long night.

AFTER READING FOR HOURS, and long after the sun had set, Sam heard a knock on his front door. When he opened the front door, he found Grace waiting there.

"Mind if I come in?" she asked.

"Of course." He welcomed her into the house.

"Cup of tea?" she asked.

He guided her down the hallway and into the kitchen. "Have a seat."

Grace sat with her leg tucked under her hip, as Mallory had done earlier in the day. "I heard you stopped by."

"I did." Sam turned on the burner under the kettle. He'd already gone through a pot by himself. He'd be sorry tomorrow, but he wanted to finish reading the journals tonight.

"Any special reason?" she asked.

"You." Sam took two mugs from the cabinet and set them on the table.

"Thanks," Grace said.

"For the mug?"

"For saying I'm special."

Sam took the chair beside her. "How are things going?"

"First, let's talk about not setting each other up for embarrassment."

"I should have told you Randi was my daughter," Sam said.

"Promise me you won't do that again."

Sam laughed. "As far as I know, I have no other surprise children wandering the Earth." He put his hand on her arm. "How are things going over there? I heard about Fran."

"Fran is in pain." Grace sighed. "Peter is confused. Ben needs to move down to the dorm; the stairs might do him in. Arthur's kids are pressuring him to move in with them. Elizabeth needs constant supervision; Polly is tired of being her overseer. Phil and Larry want to know if they should start looking for a place to stay. Grant seems fine. Norma annoys me, as usual. Loretta's arthritis bothers her more every day, and Judy is the only one about whom I have no worries. We're in great shape."

She folded her hands and put them on the table in front of her.

Sam covered her hands with his own. “You left out Teddy and Mallory.”

“Teddy’s good,” she said. “Mallory surprises me and you’re right; I should include her. Having her in Nick’s room is like having the Mason I always wanted. She’s sharp, reliable, present, and cares.”

“Thanks for coming over,” Sam said. “I missed you today.”

“I was too busy to miss you.” She pulled her hands away and massaged her palms with her thumbs.

The teapot whistled.

Sam moved out of his chair and gathered a variety of teas, sugar, honey, and spoons. Was he going too fast? Touching her too much? He didn’t want to push, but he was ready, all in. How long would she take to decide?

“Thanks.” Grace picked a non-caffeine herbal concoction with chicory.

Sam hadn’t tried that one. It had been in his cabinet since that bank teller from Columbus, a friend of a friend’s sister. He’d dated her enough to have her over for dinner a few times. How long ago had that been? Surely not so long ago that the stuff would be outdated.

Grace held the cup to her nose and inhaled. “Smells heavenly. Thanks, Sam.”

“Thanks for coming to visit.”

“Actually, I came for more than a visit.”

That sounded promising.

“I want you to help me with something.”

“I’ll do what I can.”

“I’m formulating a plan for the residents to buy GraceHaven,” Grace said. “I’d like you to sit in on the meeting when I present it to the others.”

“Do you want help with the—”

“No,” she said, holding up her hands in the universal posture that means, “Stop.” She continued. “I want to write the proposal on my own. I want your feedback after the meeting.”

His help writing the proposal made more sense, but Sam didn't argue. He was sure there was a rule in there and he didn't need to have it spelled out this time. "I'll do whatever you want."

Grace sipped her tea and placed the cup back on the table. "Thanks for being here." She stood. "And thanks for the tea. I have to go home. Last night was lovely, but I am not a late-night person."

"I'll have you in bed by nine from now on," he said, standing to face her.

Her cheeks flushed. She'd misunderstood his words.

"Not in bed with me. That's not what I meant," he said.

She put her hands on his arms and laughed. "I'm too tired to worry about it, Sam." She laughed again, that punchy laugh that accompanies sleep deprivation. "God, I am so tired."

Sam took her elbow. "Come on. Let's get you to bed. Your bed."

She laughed again and linked her arm in his as he led her down the hall.

"Can you make it home on your own?"

"Yes, I can make it home."

Before she walked out the door, Grace put her arms around him and hugged him in a way that he hadn't been hugged since… maybe ever. As he put his arms around her, gently pulling her in, he realized that he had been hugged like that, by Mandy, before she reached adolescence. She used to run at him and wrap her arms around him, without reservation, with full trust and innocence. Mandy's mother, Gloria, had hugged him like that, too, when she was young. And his own sister, Maria. And he used to hug his mother and father like that, but he stopped when he was five, because he'd heard a kid at school say it was "weird."

Grace let go first. "Thanks, Sam. See you tomorrow?"

"Of course." His voice caught. He cleared his throat. "I'd love to see you tomorrow."

He closed the door behind her and walked back to clean up the kitchen table. A tear slipped down his cheek. What was he getting himself into?

Chapter Thirty-One

"I LOOK FORWARD TO meeting Randi tonight," she said into the phone receiver. Grace glanced at the clock on her desk. She had hours before dinner at Sam's. "I guess I could stand seeing you again, too."

His laugh came through the earpiece. "I feel warm inside every time you say something like that."

Except for some out-of-town travel days to lead workshops with Loretta, Grace had seen him every day of the last three weeks, since she'd gone to his house for tea.

"What did you decide about Sarah's offer?" he asked.

Though she'd only asked him to sit in on the meeting, every minute of every day had been focused on the proposal. She couldn't help but include him in the process and when Sarah offered an interest-free loan as a down payment for the property, she'd gone straight to Sam for his thoughts.

"I said, 'Yes!'" She'd moved past the need to do it all on her own and the money no longer came tainted with Donald's insults. Sarah had convinced her it came with only blessings and a sense of pride in a sister's life work.

"Good for you!" Sam said. "Looks to me like you're close to pulling off your plan."

If all went well, Grace hoped to save enough in ten years to pay back Sarah and finance a mortgage. All going well would include reasonable interest rates when the time came to apply for a mortgage, and at least twelve stable, paying residents. Grace expected that Norma and Grant would leave. Phil and Larry seemed solid. Elizabeth was up in the air, in so many ways. Ben, Polly, Fran, Peter, and Arthur seemed content. Grace would need to bring in new people. She might have to move permanent residents into the second floor of the dorm. Sacrifices would be made.

"You're welcome to come over early and hang out while I cook," Sam said.

"I think I'll take a few hours for myself here." She could take a walk, practice yoga, read a novel.

"Okay. See you at six."

As she hung up the phone, Grace realized that more than anything, she wanted a nap.

She flopped down on the loveseat, resting her head on a pillow. Her sleep patterns had changed. She went to bed later and woke up earlier, her mind turning over the proposal again and again, planning, anticipating difficulties, thinking through possible solutions. She needed to rest, so she tried a round of deep breathing and curled up facing the cushioned back. Dream images formed in her mind. The ringer on the phone startled her. She rolled out of her fetal position and went to the desk to answer the call.

"GraceHaven," she said. "This is Grace. How may I help you?"

"Hey, Mom."

"Hey, Teddy." Grace settled into her chair, one knee up to her chest, ready to engage in a long conversation.

"I only have a minute," Teddy said, rekindling Grace's hope for a nap. "I wanted to run something by you."

"I'm all ears." Grace yawned.

"Could I move back into my old room?"

"Why?" she asked, waking up. That made no sense. In Columbus, he had a ten-minute commute to work, lived in a friendly neighborhood, and his housing costs were reasonable.

"I'm moving back to Wood Grove and there's no place I'd rather be than with you. But listen, if that's inconvenient, I can find a place in town."

"Why?" she asked again. Teddy had created a life for himself. Grace could think of no reason for the move. "Commuting to work in the winter can be a challenge. Fran still struggles with that. That's why Larry and Phil shifted part of their office time to working at home."

"My job won't be in Columbus after September first."

"Where are you going to work?" Maybe he'd taken a position in Chillicothe. That was the only nearby city that made sense.

"Sam wants me to take over his practice when he retires."

"He what?" Sam hadn't mentioned anything to her, not the idea of retirement, and certainly not the idea of luring her son back to a place that held no promise of career development.

"We've been talking about it for a few months. I called him last week and we both took a step deeper into the idea. He said if I want to do it, he's in."

"But you've always talked about moving on to positions of leadership so that you can make changes at the policy level." Teddy had been talking about that for years. What was going on?

"I can live in Wood Grove and still make change happen on a larger scale. Look at you and Loretta. You do it."

Loretta, maybe, but Grace took no credit for any positive change related to their anti-racism workshops. During their weekends away, Grace was happy to go to bed without having made a mess of things. White people, she had learned, can be clumsy, unaware, and, well, racist, when it comes to addressing issues of racism. All white people, including her.

Teddy pressed on. "I made a list of—"

"Pros and cons." Grace finished his statement.

"The pros won," he said.

She sighed. "If that's what you want, okay. You living in the house is more than acceptable. Or you could live in the dorm. Whatever you choose, I'll have to charge rent."

She filled him in on the highlights of her plan. Teddy approved. He wanted to pay his own way. They both agreed that if Grace's plan failed and GraceHaven disbanded, they would find a place in Wood Grove to accommodate all three of them, Teddy, Grace, and Loretta.

The phone call ended and her mind spun. Why hadn't Sam talked to her about his interactions with her son? His lack of transparency left her confused, reminded her of how he'd induced her honest critique before telling her the author was his daughter.

Back on the couch, she curled her body into a tight fist. Men were difficult. She thought about Norma. Women were difficult, too. Had anybody in her life not been difficult at some point? Maybe she should find a nice dog to keep her company.

SAM HAD THE SALADS on the dining room table when Grace arrived. He bustled around the kitchen, assuring her that all was under control. "Go have a seat and pour some wine. Randi will be down in a minute."

Now wasn't the time to initiate a tete-a-tete about his plans with Teddy and how she felt about being left out. Grace wandered into the dining room and kept going, ending up at the front of the living room. She surveyed Sam's perfect front lawn and manicured hedges. Large pots overflowed with begonias. Boston ferns hung suspended from the porch roof. Everything glistened from the afternoon rain. A car sped by on the road.

"You must be Grace."

Sam's daughter stood in the doorway to the hall. Put some points on those ears and a pair of gossamer wings and she would have been queen of the Fairies. Luminous eyes closed the gap between them in three strides of her long, slender legs.

"I'm Randi. So nice to meet you." She shook Grace's hand and didn't let go as she led her to the couch. "Let's sit in here and talk for a few minutes. I've learned to stay out of Sam's way when he's in the kitchen." She smiled and Grace saw the resemblance between her and her father, but something more that must have come from her mother. Inbred confidence, sophistication. Suddenly Grace could see the imprint of Sam's childhood in what his daughter lacked— any cracks in her self-assurance.

"I'm happy to meet you, too," Grace said.

Randi Flemming looked like the back cover of her books, only better. Hair cut to frame her face with silky black waves, high cheekbones, a perfect slim nose, and a full mouth that revealed even, white teeth when she smiled. Grace had always assumed those pictures were airbrushed. Nobody could be that perfect. Randi was.

"Sam's been telling me about GraceHaven. I'm dying to come over and hear more from you."

Randi's voice was deep, alluring. Grace wondered again about her mother. She must be beyond beautiful, too. "You're welcome to come over tomorrow. I'll introduce you around."

"Wonderful."

"Sam's been telling me about you, too," Grace said. "And I've read your novels."

"Don't judge me by those." Randi laughed. "Would have been better if we'd met first. The novels might lead you to all sorts of false assumptions."

"It's a living," Grace said.

Randi huffed. "I guess."

Sam's daughter intrigued Grace. She wanted to sit down and have a long talk, but her father came through the door at the far end of the room, wiping his hands on his apron. "Come on down here and have a seat. Dinner's ready!"

He seated Grace on the longer side of the table, two empty spots on each side, which put her facing the back wall of the living room. Randi sat at the short end to her right and Sam at the head of the table, on her left, closest to the kitchen.

"So," he said. "How are you two getting along?"

"Fine," Grace and Randi both said at once.

They all laughed and Sam served the food. Baked salmon with butternut squash risotto and steamed broccoli.

Conversation gave way to enjoying the food, but between bites they managed to cover Randi's recent travel adventures, Sam's current reading choice, and Grace's misadventure with the lock on the bathroom door. She'd been stuck in there for an hour this afternoon, until Mallory happened by.

"That could be dangerous," Sam said. "What if there had been a fire?"

"Never crossed my mind," Grace said. "I used the time to clean out the linen closet."

"Wish you'd been locked in with me while I was moving out of my apartment," Randi said. "I could have used the help."

Sam's daughter was charming.

"Maybe you should have someone check all of the locks in the house," Sam said.

"Killjoy." Randi poked Sam's arm. "Sounds like she knows how to turn a challenge into an opportunity. Maybe someone should use Grace as a model for a character in a novel."

"I don't think Grace wants to be cast as a damsel in distress," Sam said.

They both looked at her. Grace shrugged her shoulders. "Never thought of myself as any kind of damsel."

The conversation lulled as Sam poured more wine for Randi. Grace watched their interaction. They liked each other, though Sam seemed a bit formal. He treated his daughter like a colleague more than a family member. Sam had said he'd met Randi in 1975. That was over twenty years ago. Seems like he'd be a little more relaxed by now.

"How did you start writing?" Grace asked.

"That is a very long story." Randi stood and stacked her empty dishes. "Much more interesting is the story of how I'm going to stop." She looked at Sam, raised her eyebrows, and moved around the table to collect Grace's dishes.

"You're not going to write any more?" Grace asked. "Why end a successful career?"

"As careers go, I don't find much substance there. I've been thinking that I'd like to go back to school and finish my engineering degree."

"What a shift!" Grace said.

"That's what I said." Sam jumped in. "I told her to go slow. She could take a few classes to see if engineering makes sense." He looked at his daughter. "It's been over twenty years, Randi. What if you still don't like it?"

Now he sounded more like a father, but his timing was off. That was something one would say to a teenager or younger adult, not to a woman in her forties with a successful career.

"You misunderstood, Sam," Grace said. "I didn't mean to be discouraging. I think if Randi wants to return to school, she should do it." Turning to Randi, she asked, "How old are you?"

"Forty-two."

"You have plenty of time to develop a career. I still think of finishing my degree and I'm sixty-two."

"Thanks!" Randi said. She carried the stack of dishes to the kitchen.

"You're thinking of going to school?" Sam asked.

"I think I've mentioned that to you before," Grace answered. Those 'in love' feelings gave way to the annoyance that had been building since her phone call with Teddy.

"What would you study?"

She didn't like the look on his face or the tone of his voice.

"Whatever I want to study," she said and stood up. "But it probably won't be engineering." She winked at him and walked into the kitchen to help Randi clean up.

They worked together at the sink, Randi rinsing and Grace placing the plates and glasses and utensils in the dishwasher. Sam worked behind and beside them, clearing counters and bringing pans to Randi, who filled the sink with hot, soapy water.

"I appreciate your support, Grace," Randi said, running a cloth over the inside of a saucepan. "Going back at forty-two is scary."

"Do you remember the first day of college when you were eighteen?" Grace asked.

"I do," Randi answered. "I watched Mom and Dad drive away and I felt absolutely alone."

"Were you scared?" Grace asked.

"I was!" Randi answered.

"What happened after that?"

"I met my roommate, and started classes, and made friends."

"And felt less afraid?"

"Oh, absolutely. I found myself that year."

"You are your own role model," Grace said. "Do what you've already done. If you find you don't like it, then find something else. What is life anyway but a series of choices?"

"You should write self-help books." Randi bowed. "That was brilliant."

Grace bowed. Randi made her feel good about herself.

"And what happens if you do quit again?" Sam asked. "And you've thrown away the stability of a career that is already working for you?"

Grace and Randi both turned to him. "She starts something else," Grace said. "She can always go back to writing romance."

"Doesn't work that way," Sam said. "Publishers move on, find fresh voices."

"C'mon, Sam. Have a little faith." Randi tossed a towel at Sam and he caught it. "Thanks for dinner. I'm going up to my room." Turning to Grace, she said, "Really loved meeting you."

Grace extended her hand. Randi grasped it and pulled her in for a hug. "Thanks so much," she whispered in Grace's ear. "I needed to have someone on my side." She stepped back and smiled. "See you tomorrow."

After Randi left the room, Sam sat down at the kitchen table. "You don't understand," he said. "She's been through so much and the book deal has been good for her."

"Sounds like she wants a change." Grace leaned back against the counter, the width of the kitchen between them.

"You don't understand," he repeated. "You don't know her."

Grace looked at the floor. She wasn't going to say it, because it would sound like retaliation. Sam could turn her son's life upside down, but Grace wasn't allowed to have an opinion regarding his daughter. Double standards like that never failed to amaze her. Was he completely unaware of what he was saying, what he was doing?

"Thanks for dinner," she said. "Randi's wonderful."

"She is." He looked up. Grace couldn't read what was in his face.

"I need to go." She moved toward the door.

"We'll talk later," Sam said.

Grace walked home, sobered by how the evening ended. She could have told Sam she was irritated about his interference with Teddy. Was she using that as an excuse to create distance? She stopped in the middle of the lawn beside the stage. Something else was bothering her.

Sarah would be home in a few weeks. They'd had a few international calls. In an earlier one, Grace had sidestepped Sarah's questions about GraceHaven's "delicious neighbor." In a more recent call, she'd said she couldn't wait to visit Wood Grove again. She'd never been that excited about visiting before. Grace hadn't really done anything wrong, but every day the guilt grew stronger. How would Sarah feel about Grace stepping in ahead of her? Over sixty was a godawful age to start competing for boyfriends with her sister.

She continued on to the house, unsure, unsettled.

Mallory waited for her at the kitchen table. "Grace, I need to talk to you."

"Now?"

"Please."

Grace sat down. "Play problems?"

"The play is what it is, horrible. I wouldn't have chosen it."

"I know," Grace said. "Fran insisted."

"Well, I'm doing the best that can be done with the play." Mallory rolled a glass of water between her palms. "The thing is, I want to know if I can stay here, after the play. I want to live here."

More surprises from the young woman who no longer wore pumps and pearls. Mallory had settled into daily jeans and t-shirts, many with small holes. Grace liked the new style. "That will be up to your father, if he refuses my offer."

"If everything works out, would I be welcome here?"

"You'll have to pay rent," Grace said.

"No problem. Is that a yes?"

"Sure." Grace hadn't heard any objections to the young woman from the others, and Mallory seemed to be committed to the play, in spite of difficulties with the play itself, the awareness of which demonstrated standards higher than Nick's. "Is that all?"

"Yes!" Mallory said.

Grace left the chair and took the back staircase up to the second floor. Too tired to try to think of something distracting to do, she locked herself in the bathroom and drew a hot tub.

"No more for today," she said out loud before sinking into steaming bubbles. "No more people or problems or thinking or talking."

She might arrange to have herself locked in here for the next week.

Chapter Thirty-Two

HE'D HAD ENOUGH of her silence. He'd called the day after the dinner with Randi and Grace said she would be gone for a few days. She hadn't left a number where she could be reached, and she hadn't answered the message he left this morning. He walked out of his house earlier than necessary for the six-thirty meeting she'd invited him to weeks ago, determined to have it out with her, whatever "it" was. He let himself in the back door, went to her office, and knocked on the inside frame of the open door.

Chairs had been arranged in two semi-circles.

Grace looked up from her desk.

"Why so early?" she asked.

"You didn't return my call," Sam said. He pulled one of the chairs closer to her desk and sat down.

"Yeah, sorry," she said. "I had to make copies of the prospectus and all of the copiers within ten miles seem to be out of order." She smiled up at him. "Took all day."

"What's going on, Grace?" he asked. "Where have you been?"

"I just told you. I've been busy with the…."

"I mean since the weekend."

"I went to my sister's house and holed up for a few days of uninterrupted peace and quiet. Had a lovely time."

"Not good enough," Sam said. "If we're going to make this happen between us, I need more than that. I was worried."

Grace put down her pen and swiveled her chair to face him. "Could we talk about this later?"

"I think that now is the later that's been happening all week." He'd never initiated, let alone insisted on, a conversation like this with a woman, but he'd been on the receiving end plenty of times. If their roles had been reversed, he would have taken what he just said as his cue to end the relationship.

Grace screwed up her mouth. Sam waited, uncomfortable with his wanting her to want him as much as he wanted her.

"Why didn't you tell me you'd invited Teddy to take over your practice?" she asked.

"Is that what this is all about?" he asked, relief blown out with a sigh. "Teddy asked me not to talk to you about it."

"He did?" she asked, looking down, her cheeks becoming rosier. "I hadn't considered that."

"Is that why you've been avoiding me?" He sounded so much like the voices from his past.

"I needed time to myself."

"Is that the most honest answer?"

She took a breath. "Well, yeah, maybe."

He waited.

"Okay, yes. You seemed to not want me to even comment on Randi's life after you'd made a life-changing offer to my son."

"Wow. You must have been angrier than I thought."

"A bit," she said. "Yeah, fairly irked."

"Are we okay now? You're not going to take off for days or dodge my calls?"

"I'm sorry," she said.

"Stand up," Sam said.

They stood up together.

Sam opened his arms. "Now come here."

She moved into him.

He wrapped his arms around her and kissed the top of her head. "Don't do that again, Grace. If you're mad at me, tell me. We're too old to waste time on petty misunderstandings."

She hugged him around the waist and he felt her take a deep breath. "There's something else," she said. "But I really don't want to talk about it right now. Please?" She gave a deeper hug and pulled away to look up at him. "Can we get ready for the meeting now?"

"In a minute." He pulled her back in and kissed her on top of the head again. What else was bothering her? He wanted to know, but she'd said, 'Please,' and her embrace felt real. He released her from his arms.

"Come on," she said, walking to the door. "Help me with the water."

In the kitchen, Grace gave him two large pitchers to fill with ice water as she muttered to herself. "I have the chairs set up, the copies ready, water…"

"What else can I do to help?" He stood at the sink, holding a pitcher under the faucet, careful to leave room for ice.

"Glasses." She pointed to a cabinet to the left of the sink.

She gave him a tray. After putting ice in both pitchers, he placed glasses upside down on the tray.

Grace picked up the tray with glasses, carried it to the door, turned to push open the door with her hip, and backed into the hallway. Sam followed with the pitchers.

"I want you here, but don't interrupt," Grace said, resuming her forward movement. "If you have any ideas, wait until after the meeting. Share them with me in private."

"Aye aye, captain," he said.

They placed the water and glasses on the seat of the bay window.

Grace handed him the stack of proposals and said, "One on each chair, and I'll be back in a minute."

Before Sam could distribute the papers, Ben and Polly came in. Sam welcomed them and handed each a copy.

"Are you our new office boy?" Ben asked.

"Thanks for helping," Polly said.

They sat down. Sam stationed himself at the door to greet each person and hand over a copy. When all were seated, Grace appeared at the door, her hair brushed and a hint of lipstick brightening her mouth. She crossed the room to the bay window.

The other residents talked among themselves, commenting on the unusually high temperatures and the health of the plants in the window. Sam took a seat by the door and watched as Grace poured water into each of the glasses, her hands shaking, and passed them to her audience. She poured the last bit for herself, took a sip, set it on her desk, and picked up her copy of the document. Everybody stopped talking and looked at her.

"Thanks for coming. As you all know, I've been working on a proposal to secure our place here at GraceHaven. You each have a copy, but I wanted to give you an overview in person, in case you have any questions before you read it."

"That was thoughtful," Arthur said.

The rustling of papers occurred as fourteen first pages turned.

"The first section outlines the history of the community and the current situation," Grace said. "The second section breaks down the financial picture: how much it costs to run the place, how much money comes in annually. The third section goes through some of my ideas about how to improve the finances by making changes in our daily operations. Section four describes a strategy for us, as a group, to buy the property. It includes a plan for acquiring the real estate and running our community as a cooperative business."

Sam kept the document on his lap and his eyes on the people.

Polly tried to turn the papers back over to Grace. "Oh my, I'm afraid I don't know too much about the business end of life. I hand my money over to my nephew and he invests it for me."

Grace pushed the document into Polly's hands. "That's okay. Have your nephew look it over or you and I can sit down together and take it a section at a time until you understand."

Arthur leafed through the pages. "What I want to know, Grace, is what's in it for me? I mean, if I invest a chunk of my money in owning this place, what kind of profit am I going to make?"

Leaning her hips back on the desk, clutching her papers, Grace answered, "Honestly, Arthur, I can't guarantee much of a financial profit in the short run, but the biggest benefit is we'll all be able to live here. Long term, a portion of your monthly fee will be an investment, rather than rent. But again, biggest benefit? Your life will not be disrupted by moving to a new community, leaving all your friends, and trying to establish new relationships."

"I don't know." Arthur looked at Ben. "Think I ought to risk money on being with you? You might kick the bucket any day."

"Arthur! Don't say that. He can't die until he marries me." Polly smacked Arthur's knee with the papers.

Ben straightened in his chair and spoke in a dignified tone. "As long as I am vertical and above room temperature, I think I can be thought of as a solid investment."

"I don't like this idea," Norma said.

Norma scared Sam a little. She was one of those women who would not mince words for the sake of social capital. She would have been a good prosecutor.

"You haven't had time to read it." Grace leveled her eyes at Norma before looking away. "Listen, why don't you each take the prospectus and read through it? We can meet again in a few days and discuss any questions you have."

"Okay." Ben rose and Polly followed him.

"I'll do that," Arthur said. He followed Ben and Polly out of the office, leafing through the pages. "See you later, Sam," he said as he passed by.

Sam nodded back.

"This cooperative idea will never work," Norma said. She put the proposal on Grace's desk. "You have to face reality. Nobody wants this place as badly as you do. You're the only one who can keep it alive. You're the only one who ever could." She turned and walked to the door.

Larry and Phil walked out with their copies hanging off the ends of their fingertips. “Bye, Sam,” Larry said.

“Larry, Phil,” Sam said.

Loretta approached Grace’s desk. “For once I have to agree with Norma. You’ve got to do it, Grace.”

“We’ll back you up,” Judy said.

“I don’t want backup,” Grace said. “I want you to work with me on this. I’m tired of doing it alone.” Even from a distance, Sam could see the tears that welled up in her eyes.

“You’ll do it, honey. You always do. I’ll be praying for you.” Loretta kissed Grace’s cheek and walked out the door with Judy.

Loretta smiled at Sam as she passed. “Nice to see you, Loretta, Judy,” Sam said.

He stayed in his seat until everyone else, including Fran on a walker, had cleared the room.

Grace put her face in her hands.

Sam stood and walked to her side. “Without having read this, I can’t say much, but your presentation was excellent. I’m impressed.”

“Impressed? Why?” She looked up.

“That took courage,” he said. “I saw a woman who’s spent most of her life managing from the sidelines step forward and act on her dreams.”

“For me, it’s not much of a dream if I have to do it on my own.” She let the papers in her hand fall into the wastebasket.

“Come home with me,” Sam said. “We’ll talk about it over tea.”

“That sounds nice.” She fished the proposal out of the trash and put it on her desk. “I guess I can’t let a little resistance kill my enthusiasm for the overall plan.”

“I didn’t.” Sam slipped his hand into hers.

He could tell by the look on her face she understood him.

“No,” she said. “You didn’t.”

Chapter Thirty-Three

"THIS PLAY IS HORRIBLE," Sarah said. "I should have stayed in Paris."

Grace's sister had arrived late, and Sam had given up his seat to her. He moved to the end of the aisle, which was all the better for Grace. The flirtatious greeting Sarah threw Sam's way forewarned of possible discord when she found out he and Grace were unofficially a couple now.

They sat in the front row with Loretta, behind the director's chair. For Grace, the debut of the new stage outshone the production, but Mallory had done the best she could. By including the Wood Grove high school drama club, she had created a collaboration that exceeded any past efforts by Grace to join GraceHaven with the greater community.

A cloudless blue sky provided perfect lighting. The new bushes and ornamental trees were small enough to not intrude on the otherwise drab setting for the story, a 1960s look at a proletariat protest against out-of-control profit and greed. The play still stank, but the acting, costumes, and set were more than adequate.

Mallory had done well. Grace was pleased.

"I can't wait until you open the present," Sarah said. She had stowed a wrapped box under her seat upon arrival. "That Sam is so scrumptious-looking." She leaned forward and looked down the row.

Grace pulled her bare foot into her lap and dug her thumb into the spot for her solar plexus.

"Feeling a wee bit nervous there?" Loretta asked.

Grace side-eyed her best friend.

Loretta shook her head and chuckled, her smug face I-told-you-so-ing.

Yes, she should have told Sarah about her relationship with Sam. Yes, she should have at least warned Sam so he could be discrete until she had a chance to talk to her sister. And why didn't she tell Sam? Because if he'd known about Sarah's interest he might have been less interested in Grace? She didn't think so, but she'd never given him the chance to choose.

The closer they came to the end of the play, the closer the awkward moment when she had to orchestrate the big reveal. Who should she tell first? How could she keep them separate long enough to avoid having it blow up in her face, in front of both of them? She'd cast herself as the other-woman, Sam's second choice. Nearly the entire town sat in the audience this year. Public humiliation loomed.

Focus on the play, Grace ordered herself. Focus on the play ahead. Not the one *in* her head.

A flash of pink—homecoming queen Tina McKay in a tutu— bounded across the stage and stopped in front of Ben. Ben portrayed worker-as-hero, a family man who strove to model virtue, dedication, morality. Tina portrayed the paragon of temptation, easy fixes marketed by thoughtless corporations, overconsumption, a decaying capitalist system.

Ben raised a plastic bat above his head as if to smite Tina. This was meant to be the climax. Grace couldn't wait for the applause to begin but she dreaded what came after the applause, a full confession and assuaging Sarah's disappointment.

Peripherally, Grace saw Mallory put her hand inside her blouse and brush something away from her side. Suddenly she cried out, leapt from her chair, whipped her blouse over her head, and twisted her torso to look down at the skin over her ribs. Her breasts threatened to pour out of their lacy bra.

Teddy rushed to her. Mallory said something to him, and Teddy retrieved Mallory's blouse, shook it out, then handed it over to Mallory who quickly slipped it back on. Grace followed Mallory's horrified gaze as she looked at the stage.

All action had stopped. The actors displayed bafflement, which was not in the script.

After that, everything began to go in slow motion. Deirdre, two seats from Loretta, stood and applauded, shouting, "Bravo! Encore!" Deirdre's partner, Daphne, joined her.

The cast remained frozen in place, all except Elizabeth. She unbuttoned the front of her work shirt. Gyrating her hips, she pulled the shirt open to reveal the lace teddy underneath as she walked to the front of the stage yelling, "Shed your oppressive ways! Reveal your inner beauty!"

Never before had Elizabeth's voice been so strong, her posture so proud as she strutted across the stage, sliding the shirt off her shoulders when she lost her balance and bumped into Tina McKay who, laughing so hard she could barely stand up, bumped into Polly.

Raven, who had been sitting peacefully beside Judy throughout the performance, jumped up, growled, and raced toward the stage.

In the row behind Grace, Phil gasped. "Raven thinks Tina is trying to hurt Polly!" Judy barked an order and the dog stopped short of sinking her teeth into Tina's frilly pink bottom.

Raven's lunge and Judy's sharp command startled the children in the audience and several began to howl. Others followed suit. Within seconds, most of the children in the audience under five were hysterical.

Judy whistled again and Raven returned to sit at the groundskeeper's feet.

Norma picked up the plastic ball bat dropped by Ben. Her voice rang out to the back row of the audience as she bopped Elizabeth on the head and said, "Nobody wants to have your limp old breasts paraded across the stage, Lizzy. Now keep your clothes on."

Mallory appeared to be in shock. Elizabeth strutted back to her place on stage, buttoning her shirt, turning to wink over her shoulder at the audience.

Polly marched to center stage and announced, "The End."

Teddy escorted Mallory to the back door of the main house.

The audience seemed divided in their response. Half clapped and cheered as if this was the best entertainment they'd seen in years. Half shook their heads as they rose from their chairs, muttering, "Damned nudists," "Communists," and "Old hippies."

Ed, seated on the other side of Sarah, stood in front of his chair clapping louder and longer than anybody. "Isn't my Elizabeth the most amazing woman you've ever seen in your life?"

Randi, seated on the other side of Grace, pushed herself out of her chair. "I have to go check on Mallory." Randi and Mallory had struck up a quick friendship in the past month.

Phil and Larry stood together. "That was weird," Larry said.

"Very strange," Phil agreed. They walked away arm in arm.

"Was that supposed to happen?"

Grace turned to Sam who now stood by her side.

"Hello, Sam," Sarah said. "So nice to see you again."

"Um, no," Grace said. "That was improvised." Turning to Sarah, she said, "Come sit with me in the gazebo. We haven't had a chance to talk."

"Nice seeing you again, Sarah. See you later, Grace?" He asked.

"Yeah, sure. Thanks for coming." She could see the confusion on his face.

He walked away, turning back once, which gave Sarah the opportunity to blow a kiss.

"I like him!" Sarah said.

"I do, too," Loretta said, eyeing Grace.

Teddy trotted up, hugged Sarah, and said, "Mallory wants to apologize. A bee stung her. She said to tell you that she feels, 'mortified.'" He finger-quoted the last word.

"Tell her the revised ending was perfect," Grace said. "Couldn't have done it better myself."

"Thanks, Mom." Teddy kissed her on the cheek and trotted back to the house.

The two sisters headed toward the gazebo, leaving behind the buzz of conversations crisscrossing through what remained of the audience and cast.

"What's up with Teddy?" Sarah asked. "He's been acting mysterious, rather like the Cheshire Cat."

"He's thinking about some big changes in his life," Grace said.

"So he's told you about Mallory?"

They climbed the two steps into the gazebo together.

"What about Mallory?"

"To what big changes do you refer?" Sarah asked.

"What about Mallory?"

"Oh, shoot!" Sarah threw her hands up. "I know nothing."

Sarah took the end of the swing furthest from the road and Grace the opposite end.

"Teddy said he's moving back here to take over Sam's practice," Grace said.

"That sounds lovely! Much better than what he's doing now." Sarah tapped the box Grace had placed in the middle of the swing. Open your present."

"What about Mallory?" Grace asked.

"I don't know," Sarah said. "He may have called while I was in Paris. He may have mentioned meeting Nick's granddaughter. He may have said he liked her. I mean *really* liked her, maybe."

Grace noticed a butterfly as it landed on the railing of the gazebo. She knew Teddy spent time with Mallory. Grace thought he was being kind. And the fact that he took up so much of the young woman's time, interrupting her ability to address business with the estate had only been a benefit to Grace. She hadn't thought to question the nature of their relationship.

He was an adult, she reasoned. If he wanted to date Nick's granddaughter, it was none of Grace's business. The only glitch might be the impact on Grace's ability to work with Mallory's father on a plan to keep GraceHaven alive, whole. Teddy's romance better not interfere with his mother's plans.

"Love is grand," Sarah said. "I might have a new beau."

Loretta walked out the back door.

Sarah waved and called out, "Come sit with us and see what I brought for Grace from Paris."

Loretta headed for the gazebo. Grace knew she needed to tell Sarah about Sam now, right now.

"Well, that's the thing," Grace began. "I think your new beau is not available."

"Why not?" Sarah asked.

"Because he's, well, he's my beau." She stumbled on the word, but had no better way to explain her relationship with Sam at the moment.

"How is he your beau?" Sarah asked.

"It's been a very slow process, but Sam and I have been seeing each other quite a lot since you went to France."

"That's wonderful!"

"It is?" Grace asked.

"Well, isn't it?"

Grace turned more fully to her sister. "Sarah, are you interested in Sam?"

"No!" Sarah said. "Did you think that I was sweet on Sam?"

"Maybe. Yes."

Loretta had made it to the gazebo. "What did you get for Grace?"

"Clarity!" Sarah laughed. "She thought I had my eye on Sam."

Loretta raised her eyebrows.

"What new beau are you talking about?" Grace asked.

"Jean Pierre," Sarah said. "He's French, but he lives in New York. He was visiting his parents, who are also lovely, while I was in Paris, and he's coming to Ohio for a visit this summer."

"So you're not interested in Sam?"

"No, silly. Open your present!" Sarah gave up her seat on the swing to Loretta.

Relieved, Grace tore off the silver paper and opened the box. A book lay on top of white tissue paper. She read the title out loud. "Sex is better after Sixty." She dropped her head and looked up at Sarah.

"Sex Is Better After Sixty." Sarah pointed her finger at Grace. "Yes!"

Grace shook her head and peeled back the tissue paper. Lifting the silk and lace she found lying there, she let it unfold to reveal a diaphanous negligee. "Really, Sarah? Like I'm going to wear this?"

"Live a little!" Sarah coached. "Wear it tonight with Sam."

Grace blushed.

Loretta crossed her arms. "They haven't even kissed yet."

"We only started seeing each other in April."

"What are you waiting for?" Sarah asked. "Life is short. More amour."

"She's right." Loretta said. "Anybody with any sense at all can see that Sam Cielo's been in love with you for longer than I care to remember. I feel it's my Christian duty to tell you you've had your head up your behind. It's about time you came around and gave the man a chance, a real chance, not this maybe-yes, maybe-no game you've been playing."

Grace looked from her sister to her best friend, speechless.

Turning to Sarah, Loretta drew herself up and asked, "Do other people in your family have this difficulty?"

"Trust me," Sarah said. "It's not genetic. Come on, Loretta. I'll walk you back to your cottage. After dinner, we'll catch a movie on TV or go out to a bar and find an eligible man for you." She extended her arm and helped Loretta out of the swing.

Loretta laughed. "How about coming to the church carry-in with me later?"

"What do we carry in?" Sarah asked.

"Mostly, we carry in our old pitiful selves."

"Sounds like a wonderful place to stir up some trouble," Sarah said.

Loretta laughed and the two of them walked out of the gazebo, leaving Grace alone.

She watched them walk away before opening the book and reading the highlights of each chapter. The information seemed fairly straightforward. No surprises. She closed the book and returned it to the box, placing it on top of the negligee which covered another item she had chosen to ignore earlier. That might come in handy later.

Patting the lid in place, Grace pushed herself out of the swing.

"Okay," she said, walking out of the gazebo, the box under her arm. "Let's do this."

"COME IN!" SAM ANSWERED her knock on the back door.

Grace walked into the kitchen. Sam stood at the kitchen sink washing lettuce. He turned off the faucet and took the towel from his shoulder to dry his hands.

"I thought that you and Sarah had dinner plans," he said.

"Are you in love with me?" Grace walked to the table and set the box down.

"Yes, I am," he said slowly.

Grace folded her arms and cocked her hip to one side. "What does that mean to you?"

Sam rubbed the back of his neck. "I guess when I say I'm in love with you, I mean I like you. I want to be close to you. I want to touch you."

She nodded her head.

He continued as he walked toward her. "I find myself walking in the woods more, worrying less about my lawn. I want you in my life, Grace. My life is better with you in it."

Satisfied with his answers, she asked, "Do you want to see what's in here?" She glanced at the box.

"Sure," he answered.

She took the lid off. "I skimmed it so I can tell you what's in it if you're curious, not that I think you need instruction."

"I've read it," he said.

"Of course you have." She drew out the negligee, draping it down the front of her body by holding it up to both shoulders. "Sarah seems to need special costumes that fit the occasion. I've never been much of a lingerie person myself. Do you want me to wear the nightie?"

"That won't be necessary." A silly grin distorted Sam's facial muscles.

"Okay." She palmed the third item and dropped the nightgown back into the box. "Let's go."

She took his hand and led him down the hallway. He followed her up the stairs to the second floor where she headed straight to his room.

"How did you know which one's mine?" he asked.

"Randi gave me a tour last week." The push from Loretta and Sarah was probably unnecessary. Sam's workout room had already convinced her. He even had a massage table.

Once inside his bedroom, Grace closed the door behind them. She felt unsure about the timing, not knowing when Randi might show up, but telling Sam she'd changed her mind, that they could wait until later, was not an option.

Sam stood at the end of his bed. Grace stood a few feet away, facing him as she unbuttoned her blouse and let it fall off her arms. Her heart sped up as he looked at her standing in front of him, her silky tank revealing she was braless. She emptied her pocket and tossed the tube of KY jelly onto Sam's bed, then unzipped her pants and pushed them to the floor, stepping out of them and her shoes at the same time, standing before him in her underwear.

Sam touched his chest.

"Are you okay?" she asked.

"Absolutely," he said, dropping his hands to his sides.

Grace clasped her hands and held them in front of her.

"Do you want me to take my clothes off now?" he asked.

"If you don't, I'll take them off for you," she said. If he wanted to be with her, he was going to have to meet her on her terms. Her terms were: she would decide where, when, and how. This was the place and now was the time. She wanted him without any silly seduction. That was how she had always operated with Richard. She wasn't going to change now.

He walked toward his bathroom.

"Where are you going?" Grace asked.

"I always undress in here," he said.

Grace followed him through the bathroom and into his large, walk-in closet. She watched as he removed his shoes, socks, pants, and shirt, putting his shoes on the rack, his pants on a hanger, and his socks and shirt in the laundry basket.

"I have to be honest with you." He stood before her in his undershirt and boxers. "I don't know if this is going to work for me."

"Why not?" she asked.

"I'm used to a little more action on my part."

"We'll make it work." She took his hand and led him back to the bed.

Grace sat cross-legged in the middle of the bed and Sam sat down on the edge.

"How do you get your legs to do that?" he asked.

"Yoga. Every day for over thirty years."

"My body doesn't work like that," he said.

"I know." Grace smiled at him.

He raised his eyebrows, obviously waiting for her to make the next move.

She took a deep breath, knowing she only had to touch Sam and he would be there, for her, with her, at least for now. But would he be there in the long run? Because if she went through with this, everything would change, at least for her it would. Once more she screwed up her courage so tight it gave way like a spring in a blind wound too many times.

"Oh, I can't do this." She buried her face in her hands.

"It's okay." Sam put his hand on her knee. "Let's get dressed and go have dinner."

"What?" She dropped her hands, puzzled.

"Let's take it slow. We can wait until you're ready."

Grace sat up straight. "I'll never be ready for this, Sam. I can't have casual sex. It means something to me."

"It means something to me, too," he said.

She studied his face for a moment, deciding whether or not to trust him, then nodded her head. "Okay. We need to get a few things straight."

"Okay."

"If we have sex, then I'm going to expect you to be my exclusive lover until death do us part, and I plan to outlive you, so that means that you'll never have sex with anybody else. Can you live with that?"

"I'd be happy to live with that."

She furrowed her eyebrows. "I don't go in for kinky stuff. You wouldn't expect me to do anything strange?" she asked.

"You mean like props, pornography, third parties?" he asked.

She nodded her head.

"No, I don't go for stuff like that," he assured her. "Grace, I haven't had sex with anybody in four or five years."

"What about the condoms in your bathroom?" she asked.

"You snooped in my drawers?"

Grace blushed. “I did. The day Randi showed me around. She got a phone call. I toured solo, deeply. Why condoms?”

“I have many safety devices in my house which I never use,” Sam moved closer. “I have a fire extinguisher under my kitchen sink, smoke alarms on all three levels, and carbon monoxide detectors in every bedroom.” He ran his hand through her hair, stroking it away from her face. She leaned into his palm. “Once a year I go around and check to replace batteries. I’m a safety-conscious guy. Why not have condoms on hand? You never know when you’re going to get lucky with the girl next door.” He touched her cheek.

She wanted to kiss him, but had more questions.

“You’ve been tested for AIDS?” she asked.

“I always use a condom.”

“Always?”

“Grace, except for my first time, with Elena, I have never failed to use a condom. I have even used condoms with women who swore they had hysterectomies. I told you, I’m a safety-minded guy.”

Grace took another deep breath. “I’m old, Sam. My breasts sag and, according to the book, my vagina may not provide adequate lubrication for comfortable intercourse.” She picked up the tube on the bedspread, held it up to illustrate her point, and dropped it beside her leg. “I haven’t had sex since Teddy’s father left. I am neither embarrassed by that nor particularly proud of it. The point is, I’m scared, and I want you to know I don’t do this lightly or without reservation.” She stared at a place in the middle of his abdomen.

Sam raised her chin with his finger and looked in her eyes. “I want you to know that I’ve been in love with you since the first day we met. If I’d known you and Nick weren’t lovers, we would have started this a long time ago.”

She smiled and a tear slipped down her cheek. “I don’t want to wait. I want to make love with you now.”

Sam put his arms around her and hugged gently. When he let go, he moved to the edge of the bed as if to leave it. "Where are you going?" Grace asked.

"To get a condom."

"Why? I think we can safely assume neither of us has a sexually transmitted disease and I'm not going to get pregnant. I don't think we need a condom."

"Okay." He didn't look like he meant okay, but he sat back down on the bed.

Grace stood on the mattress and removed her undershirt and panties. When she sat back down, Sam reached out and touched her breast. "You're beautiful, Grace."

She tugged on the strap of his undershirt. He pulled it over his head and then slipped out of his boxers. When he sat down on the edge of the bed again, Grace crawled into his lap. "You're beautiful, too, Sam." She touched the sides of his face while she feathered her lips across his mouth.

He let her touch him, her hands trailing up and down his torso, weaving across his back, rising to his scalp.

"I still can't believe how flexible you are," he said.

She straddled him. "Yoga," she whispered in his ear, moving to the other side of his head. "What are you thinking?" she whispered in his other ear.

"I'm thinking I want to take yoga, starting forty years ago."

"It's never too late." She ran her hands up and down the outsides of his thighs while pressing her torso against his chest. "You're in good shape, Sam."

"Not like you." He lifted her off his lap and laid her on the bed. Bracing himself above her, he looked in her face. "Why did we wait so long?"

"I don't know, but let's not wait any longer."

Sam lowered himself on her as he reached out to grab the tube of KY jelly. Grace took it from him and removed the cap. Within seconds, she grasped and massaged him while looking in his eyes. Any fear still remaining left her as she saw no hesitation, no guile, nothing but clear light coming from his eyes.

"Do you want me inside you?" he asked.

"Yes, I want you inside me." She guided him to her, and he eased himself inside.

She contracted her muscles and he groaned. "Don't. I don't think I can stop myself."

"Don't hold back, Sam. Let yourself go."

He leveraged himself above her. She wrapped her legs around him, smiling as he began to thrust himself deep inside. She wanted him to go further, all the way to her soul. She could feel her eyes grow hazy. He closed his eyes and exploded. She shuddered.

He lowered himself on top of her again. "God, that happened so fast. I'm sorry."

"Don't be." Grace put her arms around his shoulders and hugged him. "That was wonderful." He raised his head to look in her eyes, then rolled to the side, pulling her close to him. He kissed the top of her head, her forehead, her nose, and finally her mouth.

They spent the next several hours exploring each other's bodies, first without talking and then with animated conversation about their romantic histories, or lack thereof. Laughter accompanied the many misperceptions. He was not the detached seducer she had imagined. He said she was far more traditional than he would have guessed. Grace drifted to sleep in his arms, aware of his coarse hair against her skin, snuggling into the smell of him.

Footsteps on the stairs and water running in the hallway bathroom stirred Grace from her dreams. She looked at the clock. Two a.m. She moved against Sam and he woke.

"You're still here," he said, pulling her close and kissing her hair. "I keep waking up and thinking I've been dreaming, but every time you're still in my bed. I'm not dreaming, am I?"

She ran her hand from his chest downward.

He groaned, pushed her onto her back and kissed her.

She knew he had the stamina to start all over again, but she couldn't let herself do that with Randi in the house. "I think I'd better go home. Randi's back."

"Is she? I didn't hear her."

"I did. I'm going home." She heard the bathroom door open and another door shut. Grace pulled away and slipped out of bed. Using the light from the bathroom, she found her clothes. Sam pushed himself out of bed and reached for his underwear. "What are you doing?" she asked.

"I'm going to walk you home."

"Why?"

"It's dark out. You shouldn't be out walking by yourself at night."

She put her hand on her hip. "Sam, I've lived next door for over forty years. I've taken more night hikes than you have, I'm sure. I will not allow you to accompany me home. I'll be fine."

"Okay, okay." He threw his hands up and crawled back into bed.

She went to him, kissed the middle of his chest, and moved up his neck to his mouth.

"When do we get to do this again?" he asked between kisses.

"I'll call you this afternoon." Grace buried her face in the side of his neck.

"I have to tell you, it won't always be like last night."

She pulled her head back and looked in his eyes. "You mean it gets better?"

"I mean it gets less frequent and sometimes it doesn't happen at all."

"I was counting on that. I told you. I skimmed the book." She kissed him again and rolled off the bed. "Goodnight, Sam."

"Goodnight, Grace. Oh, wait." He sat up and the sheet slid down to his waist. "I fly to Denver in the morning, remember? I fly back on the fourth."

"Right." He had mentioned a few days ago he needed to help out his parents. Disappointment tugged at Grace's heart. How could she become so dependent in one night? With Richard, she'd learned to feel relaxed about their time apart. With Sam, she felt bereft because she faced two weeks without him.

"Okay. Call me," she said.

Sam tossed the sheet aside and moved out of the bed so fast Grace backed up in surprise. He pulled her into his arms and held her close. "Of course I'll call you. Every day. I want to wake up with you every morning and go to bed with you every night. If I could cancel the Denver trip, I would. Do you want to come with me?"

"No, but thanks for asking." She pushed him back to the bed. "Call me every day. I'm expecting it now, so you better do it."

Sam saluted and she smiled as she left his room. She tiptoed down the stairs, stopping in Sam's office to draft a quick poem.

Your nibbling lips move
from peak to peak of my warm
moonlight-becalmed breasts.

She folded the paper and wrote Sam's name on it before propping it against the keyboard.

Grace headed out the back door, glowing. Sarah was right. Sex *was* better after sixty.

Chapter Thirty-Four

SAM STOOD ON THE porch of Elena's house and rang the bell. He would be flying home tomorrow. He looked at the flagstone under his feet and the glass blocks on either side of the wide door. Seeing his family had been wonderful, but he only wanted to return to Ohio, to be with Grace.

He rang the bell again. Elena had said to come at seven. He looked at his watch. It was five after.

The door opened and a tall woman stood in the doorway. Her unadorned dark blue dress hung below her knees. Sturdy black shoes covered her large feet. She was thinner than he remembered. The skin on her face sagged below her jaw, but he recognized Elena's companion immediately.

"Hello, Marguerite. I've come for dinner with Elena," Sam said.

"She's expecting you." Stone-faced, Marguerite stepped aside to allow entrance and shut the door behind him. She led him through the two-story foyer into a room on the right. Elena sat on the couch, a phone pressed to her ear. A fire blazed in the soapstone fireplace. Elena took the phone from her ear and set it beside her.

Forty-three years faded away. Except for a few wrinkles and a pale cast to her skin, Sam saw the young woman with whom he had studied, slept, and conceived.

"Sam! Come in."

He moved forward to receive her offered hand, noting the soft, warm touch of her skin. She gestured to a chair facing her and he sat down, memories rising up with the familiar way she lounged on the couch, stockinged feet curled beneath her hips, shoes lying on the carpet.

"Would you like a drink?" she asked.

"Sure." A drink might help. Even at her advanced age, Marguerite inspired a bit of fear and seeing Elena again produced more anxiety than he had anticipated.

Elena moved off the couch to a cart that sat by the wall. "Scotch?"

"Sure," he said.

"It's good to see you. You haven't changed much."

"I've changed, Elena. We all have."

"You know what I mean." She handed the glass to him and sat back down on the couch.

He knew what she meant. They had both changed on the outside. On the inside, they were the essence of who they had been, who they would always be.

"Thanks for inviting me." He tipped the snifter to swallow a mouthful of courage.

"Marguerite's going out after she serves dinner," Elena said. "It's you and me tonight."

"Like old times." Sam sat back in the chair considering the prospect of an evening alone with Elena. What had he been expecting? Something not as— dare he think it— romantic?

Elena laughed. "Don't worry. I won't try to seduce you again."

"Thanks for that, but to be on the safe side, I think I'll stick to one drink."

She laughed again, her low, throaty sound that rumbled in his chest as the alcohol burned going down.

"How do you like the old homestead?" she asked.

"It's nice." That was an understatement. From the outside he'd guessed her modern mansion, tucked at the end of a long drive, sprawled for as much as six thousand square feet. "Did Randi grow up in this house?"

"She was two when we moved here, into everything. Leo purchased the house for its presentation value, the ability to entertain business associates. He didn't think about how the design would work for a child. He felt terrible and offered to move, but I modified as needed, blocking the stairs at both ends. We kept a barrier in front of the fireplace for several years. We made do."

Anybody who could afford a house like this could afford to "make do" when it came to modifications. Sam thought of his parents, now in their late eighties, and their need to "make do" with the small house that had served them for almost seven decades. For the past two weeks, he and his brother had worked together to design an accessible bathroom and kitchen. Over and over, his mother and father had thanked him. It was the least he could do.

"So he was a good father to Randi?" Sam asked.

"He was wonderful," Elena purred. "Nobody could have asked for better. He made up games every night. I don't think any child ever laughed more than Randi when she was young. It was only later he changed."

Sam began to have a deeper understanding of what Randi had lost when the man who raised her shut her out. They had been a loving, playful family. Sam was happy to learn that, but sad, too, because it put a spotlight on his absence and he wished he had been included somehow. Selfish of him, probably.

Elena began asking about Sam's life, his law practice, his hobbies, and his plans for the future.

He answered all of her questions, wondering if he should mention Grace. She was part of everything now. How could he leave her out? And yet, it was all so new, what would he say?

Marguerite strode into the room and announced dinner.

Elena stumbled while slipping into her shoes. Sam caught her arm and held on until she regained her balance. He hadn't noticed before how frail she seemed, almost brittle.

"Maybe I had a little too much to drink before dinner," she said.

Sam didn't think so.

He followed her through a door at the end of the room and entered a formal dining room. The long table had two places set at the far end, under a family portrait in which Randi looked like a teenager. Elena's image seemed wooden, her husband's gaze passive.

Marguerite pushed through a swinging door and carried a round tray into the room. She served two large salads and put a tray of dressings on the table between them. "Will there be anything else?"

"That will be all for now. Thank you, dear," Elena said.

Sam shook out the cloth napkin and placed it on his knee. When Marguerite was gone, he asked, "Is she the only help around here?"

"Oh, no," Elena laughed. "Usually Anna serves meals and takes care of my laundry. Emily cleans. Berta cooks. James does the maintenance and Bernard drives me around when I need to go places. Marguerite is more of a friend these days, but she fills in when needed. Leo took very good care of me."

"I can see that." Sam picked a dressing and poured some on his salad. He wouldn't have been able to keep her in such comfort. It seemed to justify her decision to keep him out of her life, out of Randi's early life.

Sam asked about Elena's activities. She spoke about her charity work as they ate their salads. After Marguerite's return, they worked their way through the main course.

After a conversation lull, during which Sam dedicated himself to the sirloin cooked to perfection, Elena said, "Sam, I want to talk to you about Randi."

Sam lay his fork across his almost empty plate and noticed that the food on Elena's plate seemed barely touched.

"You know Leo wrote Randi out of his will?" she asked.

"You've mentioned that."

"He wouldn't leave anything for her. He had two children from a previous marriage. They will inherit everything, including this house, when I die." She put her head down.

"Go on," Sam said. If Elena was driving at whether or not Sam would claim his daughter in his will, he already had. But he wasn't going to volunteer the information, unless Elena asked.

"He was a good man, in all other ways, but when she came out to us at eighteen, he was devastated. I felt so alone. I knew you'd be able to handle it. That's why I told Randi about you."

They had been over that before, but Sam had never shared his own feelings.

"You should have told me you were pregnant, Elena. I would have handled that, too." Not the elegant opening he might have planned, but the words were on the table.

Elena shrugged and sipped her wine. "I did the best I could. Leo took care of me." She sipped her wine again and looked over the glass. "Do you hate me?"

"No, I don't hate you." He sat back in his chair. "Of course I don't hate you." She looked so vulnerable sitting by herself, seven empty chairs to her left.

Elena put the glass on the table and ran her finger around the rim. "I've sometimes wondered if I married the wrong man." She rested her chin on her hands. A huge diamond sat on the ring finger of her left hand; a diamond tennis bracelet dangled on her left wrist.

Marguerite arrived and asked if they were ready for dessert.

"Sam?" Elena asked.

"I'm full."

"We won't be having dessert," Elena said. "You can go now, Marguerite. Thank you for helping out tonight. I'll see you in the morning."

Marguerite glowered at Sam, nodded to Elena, and left the room.

"She really doesn't like me," Sam said, starting to rise from his chair.

Elena laughed. "You're her only failure, Sam. The main reason you're still alive is that Marguerite adores Randi."

Sam stopped midway up and looked at Elena.

She laughed so hard that she spilled her wine. "Still gullible after all these years."

Sam stepped behind her and gently pulled her chair away from the table, his eyes falling again on the glittering diamonds. "You married the right man, Elena."

She laughed. "Of course I did."

He escorted her back to the living room.

"I thought you might want to look at Randi's life," Elena said. She went to a side table and took a large, leather-bound album from a stack of similar albums and delivered it to the couch. "Bring the others, will you?" She lowered herself to the carpet in front of the couch.

Sam ferried the albums to her, three at time, in three trips, adding up to ten with the one she had carried over.

They sat in front of the fire for hours, looking at photos of Elena pregnant, Randi as an infant, a toddler, a grade schooler, and an adolescent. There were birthdays, vacations, family gatherings, Christmases, Easters, and graduations.

Sam's mind teemed with the images of what had transpired without him, how it might have looked had he been on the scene.

When Elena closed the last album, she said, "I have to tell you something. Something Randi doesn't know yet." She looked down at her hands and rolled the bracelet around her wrist. "About a year ago I found a lump in my breast. My doctor assured me it was nothing, but she biopsied it anyway…." She hesitated.

"It was more than nothing?" Sam asked.

"I managed to have treatments when Randi wasn't around. She eventually found out, but by then the treatments were over and I told her I was cured."

"She never mentioned it to me," Sam said.

"I asked her not to," Elena said. "I hate seeing myself as someone to be pitied."

"Sometimes telling others can help."

"I'm telling you now, Sam. And I do need your help."

He waited as she seemed to gather her courage.

"The cancer was much worse than expected. It's gone everywhere. There are small lesions in my liver and brain now."

Sam tensed. He didn't know why. Whether Elena lived or died would have very little impact on his life, and yet he wanted her to live, for the young woman she had been, for Randi, for the possibility planted as they sat together tonight. He already felt more connected to her than when he had walked in the door. And now he would lose her all over again.

"I went to Mexico for cancer treatment. The doctors here don't give me much hope."

"What do the people in Mexico say?"

"They say, 'Eat this. Don't eat that. See what happens.'" She shrugged. "They don't know. It's in God's hands."

"Why haven't you told Randi?"

"I wanted you to know first. She's going to need you even more now. She doesn't really have anybody else. She always comes to me with her problems. Nobody else has ever loved her the way I do."

"Everybody needs somebody who will love them completely, no matter what." Sam thought of Grace, thought of the possibility he might be able to finally share that kind of love with her.

"I want you to be that person for Randi, Sam. It won't be easy. I'm sure Randi hasn't shown you her struggles. Does she ever talk about Leo?"

"She called and told me when Leo died, sounded pretty calm."

“She’s still in mourning, Sam. We talked on the phone yesterday and she cried. Can you imagine how it’s going to be when I die? You’re going to have to be there for her.”

Sam knew what it was like to hide one’s own pain. Hell, he couldn’t remember crying in front of another person for the past sixty years. In spite of his own limitations, he would find a way to help his daughter. “I’ll be there for her, Elena. I’ll always be there.”

The sun had been down for a long time when Elena put her hand on Sam’s knee and said, “I never could have imagined that we’d be able to be so comfortable with each other again.”

“Why not? We parted on fairly good terms. Of course I had no idea you were carrying my child at the time. I wouldn’t have let you go so easily if I’d known.”

“Would you have married me?”

“You know I would have.”

They sat together in silence for several minutes. Aware of her hand on his knee, Sam smelled her perfume. He noticed the way she tucked her feet under her hips, and he remembered Grace sitting like that on his couch many times. Thinking about Grace stirred up the blood in his groin.

“Sam, I feel a little funny asking you this, but would you stay here tonight? I never sleep through the night anymore. I think I’d feel so much safer if you were here.”

His musing about Grace hardened into a knot in his gut. If Elena had asked him that three months ago, he wouldn’t have hesitated. He’d have drawn her into his arms and held her there all night. Three months ago he hadn’t been dating Grace, slept with Grace, made a promise to Grace.

He looked at Elena, thought about all she’d gone through to raise his child, the pain of losing her husband, the terror of dealing with cancer. A conversation with his younger brother from earlier in the day replayed in his head.

"I love you, Sam," Hector had said. "But you gotta know there's some resentment about how you left here and abandoned us for your perfect life in Ohio. Mom and Dad missed you. I missed you. Did you ever miss us?"

Sam couldn't remember missing them; something had been missing in him. If not for Grace, Sam might never again have known the comfort of family, someone he could count on. Here, in front of him, sat a woman whose life reflected his own, a life with sacrifice, loneliness. He couldn't deny Elena's simple request. Putting his hand over hers, he said, "I'll stay."

She took him to her room and pulled back the covers on the king-sized bed.

Sam dropped his jacket on a chair, pulled off his belt, untied his shoes, and stepped out of them. Elena lay down with her clothes on and Sam joined her, knowing his pants and shirt would be utterly wrinkled in the morning, embarrassed that it even mattered to him. Tugging the blankets around both of them, he thought about the comfort of lying close to someone and pulled Elena into his arms, spooning her from behind.

"You can sleep now," he said. She felt so small, almost like a child.

As her breathing eased and Sam felt her grip on his arm loosen, he thought of Grace, of their lovemaking, and realized that he had left more than one body part unprotected that night. For the first time in his life, at the age of sixty-seven, he had made love without a protective barrier around his heart. He tried to send some of that love to Elena now, hoping she would find comfort in the days ahead. He silently promised her over and over that he would care for Randi. And he prayed that Grace would understand.

Chapter Thirty-Five

GRACE BENT AT THE WAIST, head down, brushing out her hair. She wore a black skirt, tights, and tunic gifted by Sarah years ago, coral-colored and trimmed with beaded luminescence symbolic of celebration. It matched her mood. Sam would return today.

He had called every night he was gone, except last night, but Grace had been out late with Randi and Judy. Maybe he had called and someone had forgotten to give her the message, or maybe he didn't call because he knew he would see her today. Anyway, it didn't matter. He might be landing in Columbus right now.

Grace couldn't believe how much she had missed him, how excited she was to see him again.

Through the open doors in the stairwell, she could hear the house phone ringing on and on. The ringing stopped. The answering machine must have kicked in.

Thirty more strokes to her hair and she stood, looking at herself in the mirror, wanting to look good for Sam, wondering what he saw in her. Lust reflected back in her eyes. Her gaze dropped to the two statues of the Virgin Mary on her dresser.

"Stop telling me there's something wrong with this," she said to the blown-glass icons. "Anything this heavenly must have the hand of God in it."

Her mother had gifted one of the statues when Grace was confirmed. Mallory had given her the other one last night. A late birthday present.

She and Mallory were on very good terms now. Much had changed in the past two weeks. Grace had learned Mallory was lobbying for her father to accept Grace's proposal to buy GraceHaven. Even before that, Grace had re-gifted the negligee to Nick's granddaughter with the result of a proposal of marriage from Teddy. He'd fallen fast and hard, but Grace wasn't worried. The Mallory she knew now fit for her son. If Nick hadn't been the young woman's grandfather, Grace would have seen that from the start.

Life was good, so very good.

Grace dropped the brush and walked away from the dresser, humming an old hymn she'd heard Loretta sing. She danced down the two flights of steps, passed through the kitchen, picked up an apple, and headed for her office. Nobody else was around. Not unusual for this time of day. She had stayed in bed late, reading another Randi Flemming novel. As prosaic as they were, she still couldn't stop reading them. Was there a twelve-step program for people who read too many love stories?

"Hello. My name is Grace and I am a romance addict." Chuckling, she strode over to the desk, bit into the apple, and flipped the switch on the answering machine to replay the message.

"*Hello, Grace. This is Thomas Mason. I received your proposal a few weeks ago and while I admit there may be some moral value in supporting your idea of a land contract, I do not wish to extend my involvement with my late father's estate. However, I must say my judgment was swayed heavily by the fact I'd already received the proposal submitted by Mallory and Mr. Cielo. I've decided to go with that offer. They told me things probably won't change much around there. It seems like it'll work out best for everyone all around. I'll be in touch. Bye, now.*"

Grace flipped off the message, spit the apple into the trashcan, and fell into her chair, stunned.

Sam and Mallory bought GraceHaven out from under her? The would-be heiress had turned out to be a conniving bitch after all. Grace couldn't believe she had lectured her son only last week to not let Mallory get away.

And when did Mr. Cielo plan to tell her about this proposal? How could he possibly have made love to her and failed to mention this detail about his dealings with her livelihood?

Thomas had said their proposal had arrived before hers. That meant Sam had sent it before she slept with him, and he hadn't even bothered to tell her.

Grace took a pad from the side of her desk and started writing down every single step she would need to take in order to disengage herself from the community. Sam and Mallory could run or dismantle GraceHaven without her. She wouldn't serve them. She had had over forty years of making the place a success for somebody else. She was getting out.

Hours later, she still sat at her desk, filling computer documents with information about the day-to-day operation of the community, when Sam walked into her office.

"Hello," he said.

Without looking up, she said, "I'm kind of busy here."

"I don't even get a hello hug?"

"You'll have to get that from somebody else. That shouldn't be a problem for you. You've had lots of practice."

"Grace, what's wrong?" He sounded tired.

"Nothing."

"Then why are you acting like this?"

"This is not an act. This is me." She hit the computer keys steadily, adding another name to the list of electricians, plumbers, heating and cooling technicians, roofers, carpenters, and painters from the address book on her desk. She had underlined her first choice in each category and made a notation about why she preferred their services above the others. She also had made notations about some unsatisfactory transactions she'd had with a few of the others. She perused the list as she typed in another name, satisfied she was being mature about the whole thing.

"I think that I deserve an explanation."

She looked up, ready to fling a vile insult, but stopped when she saw his face. She looked back at her computer, holding tight to tears. "You don't deserve anything from me. I wish I'd never slept with you."

"I'm sorry, Grace."

"You can't possibly be sorry enough. I want you to leave now. I have work to do."

When she heard the front door close, Grace went to her office door and slammed it. Her chest had the oddest feeling in it. She wondered if she was having a heart attack. In a way, she didn't care.

She looked at the picture of Nick on the wall and breathed in the arrogant esteem thrown her way. Why did she fall under the influence of men like him? She should have moved to New Jersey with Richard, but she probably never deserved someone as stable and kind. He was better off with Donna.

Less intense but still present, the feeling in her chest gave way to hollow emptiness. She took the picture of Nick off the wall. She had an overwhelming urge to hurl it through the window, but put it face down on her desk. Other violent actions came to mind: smashing the clay plant pots on the window seat, ripping the pages from every book in the room, clawing through the fabric on the love seat until it was nothing but shreds.

She sat down hard on the floor and hit the love seat with her fist. "It's not fair," she said as she hit the cushion. "It's not fair," she said again, louder. "It's not fair," she said a third time and the most powerful feeling she had ever known surged up from her belly.

A mighty wail erupted from her throat. She buried it in the cushion because she couldn't hold it back and she knew if anybody heard her they would think she was dying. Maybe she was.

The sound would not stop. Wave after wave of anguish tore from her gut. She cried about seeing the pain on Sam's face not five minutes ago. She cried about seeing the death mask on Nick's face when she found him in his bed. She cried about seeing her parents' faces battered beyond recognition. She cried about being deceived by Mallory, and losing Teddy when he moved to New Jersey, and hearing from Richard that he wanted a divorce, and being rejected by Sarah and Donald when she started dating Richard, and hearing Stephen had died in prison, and John on the stretcher, and Loretta's grief after he died, and Nick introducing her to Norma.

The images flew through her mind in no apparent order. She cried until she felt like she was going to vomit. She grabbed the trashcan and threw up.

When the heaving subsided, she lay in the middle of her rug, sweaty, breathless, and strangely at peace. For some odd reason, she thought of Deirdre at the Solstice play shouting, "Bravo!" after Mallory pulled her top off. Grace started giggling and then she was laughing and she couldn't stop. Was she going insane? Like the possibility of having a heart attack, insanity did not scare her anymore. She laughed until she thought she might pee her pants. Remembering the episode of throwing up in the trashcan, she hoisted herself off the floor and made it down the hall in time to keep her dignity intact.

When she stood at the sink to wash her hands, she looked in the mirror, amazed at her reflection. She looked ten years younger and she felt the way she used to feel when her parents took her to mass, serene and in awe of life, like nothing could mar her connection to everything.

Tears filled her eyes again, but this time they were the tears that came with reawakening, a coming home to the life of her soul. She would survive this loss. Maybe she would go back to school. She and Loretta would find a place to live in town. Grace knew she would be okay.

She went back to her office, cleaned out the trashcan, and pulled out her yoga mat. As she settled into her meditation pose, the phone rang. She waited for the machine to pick up.

"*Grace, this is Mallory.*" Hers was not a voice Grace wanted to hear. She started to reach for the volume control. "*I called to say congratulations. Can you believe you're actually going to own the place?*"

Grace bounded off the floor and picked up the phone.

"*I can't wait to get back and celebrate….*"

"Hello?"

"Hello? Grace? You're there! Isn't it great news?"

"Isn't what great news?"

"About the estate. I thought Daddy told you."

"Not really." She wasn't going to commit to knowing anything since, obviously, what she thought she knew didn't seem to be correct. "Fill me in on the details."

"Daddy's signing the buildings and five acres over to you."

Grace was flummoxed. "Why would he do that?"

"Because I told him I would contest the will leaving the estate to Daddy if he didn't sign it over to you."

Grace's mouth went dry. "I need more information, Mallory."

"It's a bit complicated, but we've been operating on the assumption that the 1961 will, the one my father wrote after he and my grandmother divorced, is the last valid one signed."

"It's not?" Grace asked.

"The 1961 will left nearly all of the estate to my father, but it also gives my brother, Mark, a small portion. He was the only grandchild alive at that time. My sister and I were born later."

"Okay," Grace said.

"According to his journals," Mallory continued, "my grandfather was experimenting with hallucinogenic drugs and had dropped some acid when he wrote and signed the 1961 will. One could effectively argue that his mind was unsound at the time. Are you following this?"

"I'm with you." The top of her head felt like it might come off any minute, but Grace wanted to hear it all.

"Because Mark is a beneficiary, he could contest the will and then the estate would have been passed on according to an earlier will I found in my grandfather's journals. That one was written in 1958. He left the estate to PEN, you know, the organization dedicated to freedom for authors. He wrote in his journal he wanted to support the organization. He also wrote he was angry with my grandmother at the time."

Typical Nick behavior. Support the cause with no thought for the needs of the people who should matter most in your life.

"Why would your brother contest the will?" Grace asked.

"I have a little dirt on my brother. It didn't take much to convince him this was the right thing to do."

"Tell me how you worked it out," Grace said.

"Mark's not going to contest the will. Daddy's going to sign the buildings and five acres over to you. Sam's going buy the rest of the land at an inflated price to make up for Daddy's loss."

"You and Sam worked together on this?"

"Actually, most of it was Sam's idea."

"Why didn't you include me?"

"Sam wasn't sure if Daddy would go for the idea and he didn't want to get your hopes up."

Dear God. What must Sam be thinking right now? "What do you get out of this?" Grace asked.

Mallory hesitated and then spoke as if the answer was so obvious Grace shouldn't have had to ask. "You know, it was the right thing to do."

Grace wanted to apologize to the young woman on the other end of the line, but to do so would have been to inflict the pain of communicating how little Grace had trusted her in the first place. She simply said, "Thank you, Mallory."

"You don't have to thank me. It's what should have happened in the first place, if my grandfather had been more thoughtful and thorough. So congratulations! Teddy and I are shopping for an engagement ring today. I'll show you tonight."

Grace rushed through the good-byes and hung up the phone. Not bothering to look in the mirror, she walked out the back door. She needed to talk to Sam. Her mother had often said her youngest daughter's temper ran too hot. Still so many things to outgrow.

Sam didn't answer her knock on the back door, so Grace walked into the kitchen and called his name. Still, no answer. She went to the stairs, climbed to the second floor, and entered his bedroom where she could hear the shower running in his bathroom.

Pushing open the bathroom door, she saw Sam through the mist billowing out of the shower stall. He stood with his hands against the wall, leaning into the water, his back to her. Grace walked out of her sandals and opened the steel-framed glass door. She closed it behind her and slipped her arms around his waist.

Sam didn't move. She laid her cheek on his hot, wet back. She moved her hands up to his chest until she could feel the hair under her fingertips. Taking his hands off the wall, he stepped forward, then gently brought his arms down and caressed Grace's hands. A few minutes passed in stillness. Finally she could feel his chest heaving as he silently sobbed. She hugged him a little closer and tears ran down her cheeks.

She turned her face to his back and kissed it softly. "I'm sorry. I was angry. I was confused. I'm so sorry."

Sam took a slow deep breath and exhaled fully. "I should have told you right away."

Hot water splashed her arms and steam swirled in her face, until she slipped out of the shower stall and closed the door. He didn't turn around. Cool air hit her skin. The wet clothes clung to her. She unbuttoned her shirt and dropped it on the floor, adding her sopping skirt, tights, and underwear as quickly as she could. She grabbed a towel, dried her arms and legs, left the bathroom, and crawled into Sam's bed.

The water shut off minutes later. Sam stepped out of the bathroom, a towel secured around his waist. "You're still here," he said.

"Do you want me to be here?" she asked.

"Yes."

"Then come in." She held up the blankets. He crossed the room, dropped the towel, and slid into her arms.

She settled the sheet and blanket over his back as she kissed him. It all seemed warm and right and comforting. He pulled his head away and they settled their bodies so that they could lie together, holding each other.

"Not telling me about your plan was a mistake," Grace said. "I don't want you to do that ever again. Don't protect me from the possibility of disappointment. It's patronizing. Promise me you won't do that again."

"Do what?"

"What you did about the will."

"You were upset about the will? Did Thomas turn down the proposal?"

"He turned down mine, but not yours. He's signing the building and five acres over to me."

Sam hugged her tighter. "That's great. Congratulations."

"What did you think I was angry about?"

"I thought Randi told you I slept with Elena."

"What?" She reared her head back.

"Relax, Grace. When I say, 'slept,' I didn't mean it as a euphemism. We slept together. Both of us had our clothes on. Nothing happened. I didn't even kiss her." Grace listened while he told the story. By the end of it, her breathing had calmed.

"I understand," she said.

"You're not upset?"

"No. I think you did the right thing."

He kissed her head. "I love you, Grace Baxter."

"I love you, Sam Cielo."

Grace moved to lie on top of him and started kissing him but he stopped her. "I have to tell you something else," he said. "I did lie to you about something. Or I let you believe something that wasn't true."

"What now?" She glared at him with a menacing look.

"Randi doesn't write the books. I do."

"No!" She stared at him in disbelief, then moved inches closer, clutching the sheet and blanket above her breasts. "Why are they published in her name?"

"I started writing in college and never stopped. When Randi came along, I proposed we write together and try to publish. He put his arm behind his head and settled back against his pillow with a smug smile.

"She worked with me on a few, but lost interest in the writing part. Being the face on the back cover, however, appealed to her. We established a mutually satisfying arrangement. I write. She handles everything else: book signings, photo shoots, fan mail. It was a win-win."

Grace whispered in his ear. "*You* write those novels?"

"Yes."

"They're terrible." She started laughing and fell onto her back.

"So you've said."

Grace laughed harder and Sam started laughing, maybe in reaction to her. When the laughter subsided, he moved closer and kissed her hair. "Randi doesn't want to do it anymore. I have to find a new image. Ever want to be a published author?"

"Only if you let me write them with you."

"I was counting on that."

"Lie on your back," she said. He moved to the middle of the bed and she crawled on top of him.

He pulled the blanket over her shoulders. "There's one more thing I have to tell you," he said.

"Can't it wait?" She rubbed her breasts against his chest.

"I can't make love to you."

She stopped what she was doing and reached down until she found evidence to the contrary. "I think you can."

"That's not what I mean. Something happened in Denver."

"What now?" she asked.

"I decided to hold out for marriage."

"You're kidding." She was astonished.

"I'm not kidding. You know what happens in my novels. When the hero finds the woman of his dreams, he won't have sex with her until after they're married. That's part of the reason the books sell so well."

"But we already had sex."

"That was before I knew I had it in me to be a hero." He kissed her again. "Will you marry me?"

Grace flopped on her back and moaned. "Do I have to?"

"Only if you want to."

"But is that the only way you'll have sex with me again?"

"What's so repulsive about the idea of marrying me?" he asked.

"It's so—" she searched for the right word and settled on "—Catholic. I'm used to thinking of myself as a liberated woman."

"Liberation is a process, Grace, not a permanent state of being. Let's get married and liberate each other for as long as we live."

"I'll think about it." She crawled back on top of him and settled her ear against his chest to listen to his heartbeat.

Chapter Thirty-Six

"MARRIAGE IS A HOLY UNION, entered into by two people who have decided to forsake all others, no matter how good one of those others might look in a pair of shorts." Laughter rippled through the rows of seated wedding guests. Even the bride and groom laughed. Polly was resplendent in her flowered cocktail dress, a lovely bride, and Ben even more debonair than usual.

A gray sky threatened rain, but so far, no drops, so the wedding had commenced as planned on the outdoor stage.

Sam shifted in the folding chair, trying to ignore the achiness. Grace's bed, where they'd been sleeping every other night for over a month, was too small and too soft. That, and the fact he held himself back sexually, had resulted in unrelenting lower back pain.

Ruby had lectured him on his insatiable need for control and how Grace was probably his last chance to let go. For once, Sam was ready to take Ruby's advice with no argument. He had to give up on the idea of holding out for marriage.

"I like this guy," Teddy whispered. "I wonder if rabbis ever officiate at the weddings of people who aren't Jewish?"

"My family would love that," Mallory said.

"Shush," Grace said. "Pay attention to the ceremony."

The stage had been turned into a church-like setting with panels of stained glass, large containers of plants and flowers, and a satin-draped altar. A rather serious Baptist minister stood by the funny Jewish rabbi to bless the union of Polly and Ben and to make it official from both the Christian and Judeo perspectives.

A gentle breeze moved through open panels on all four sides of the tent covering both the stage and the congregation seated in rows on the lawn. Ed and Elizabeth served as attendants but could easily have been the bride and groom, the looks on their faces revealing how close they were to exchanging their own vows.

"Did Ruby agree to continue working in the office?" Mallory asked.

"She agreed to stay on until Mandy finishes paralegal school," Teddy said.

Mallory leaned over Grace, "Sam, that was so nice of you to offer to put Mandy through school."

"Shush!" Grace said.

While Ben recited his wedding vows, Sam calculated the number of hours until he could take Grace to bed. He knew she would not want to make love at his house with Randi sleeping down the hall. Maybe they could sleep in her bed again, or maybe he could ask Randi to stay over at Grace's.

He and his daughter had gotten closer since his return from Denver. Sam remembered Randi's surprise when he hugged her the day after his return. Since then, they had become more like family members than business associates. Sam had told her he expected her to wipe up her bread crumbs around the toaster and Randi had made fun of him for keeping the sidewalk edged to perfection. "Grace likes a little 'outside-the-lines,'" she had said. "You'd better get used to that." Sam had to admit his daughter was right.

He leaned over and whispered in Grace's ear. "Let's write a novel about this place. Make it a romance where there's a happy ending for everybody."

Grace whispered back, "Nobody would believe it."

"You're not supposed to believe romance, Grace. The purpose of romance is to open you up to the possibilities, to remind you of how life could be."

The woman sitting in front of them turned around and said, "Shush!"

"Right?" Grace said, leaning forward and not whispering. "I keep telling them that."

The minister asked everyone to stand and greet the newly wed Mr. and Mrs. Benjamin Sollinger. Applause and cheers rose up. When it died down, the neat rows of people dispersed in a variety of directions, some to the stage area to congratulate Ben and Polly, some toward the house, others in small groups, making the air come alive with words and laughter.

Grace tugged on Sam's sleeve and he followed her to a quieter place a few yards away from the stragglers on the outer rim of the crowd.

"Listen, Sam. I've been thinking," Grace said. "I want to finish school."

He remembered Grace's support for Randi's return to school and knew not to argue. "Good for you," he said. "What are you going to study?"

"Thanks for not debating." She cuffed his arm. "I'm going to study history, to have a better understanding of where we've been; sociology, to better understand where we are; and art, to better understand what we might become. I have so much more to learn from Loretta, but I want to offer something back to her, too."

Sam flashed on a phone call with Hector earlier in the day. They had been talking since Sam's return from Denver. Hector had insinuated Sam liked white people more than his "own kind." Sam had felt insulted, and intrigued.

"Are you on board?" Grace asked.

"When did you decide all of that?" he asked.

"I've been thinking a lot lately."

Sam considered he might point out Grace never seemed to stop thinking, but she sailed on without pause.

"I might need to travel," she said.

"Am I invited?" he asked.

"I'm counting on that."

He pulled her in and kissed the top of her head. Someday soon he would take her to Denver to meet his family. Being with Grace opened the door to so many parts of himself, forgotten and abandoned parts.

"And Sam?" she said.

"Yes?"

"We're getting married next Wednesday. I asked the priest from the local parish to officiate but there were too many rules, so I asked Loretta's minister, instead. Are you okay with that?"

Sam registered his surprise, then deep relief as he hugged her tighter, the muscle tension in his back already starting to melt away.

"I checked with Ruby," she said. "You're free on Monday afternoon. I made an appointment with an attorney to go over end-of-life documents. If you want a premarital agreement, she can do that, too."

Ruby hadn't said a word. "A revised will can take care of anything that would go in a premarital agreement," he said. "Unless you're thinking we could end up divorced."

"No more divorces for me," Grace said. "If we marry, you're stuck with me."

"Sounds good." He brushed a wisp of hair from her face. "What changed your mind?"

"I'm embarrassed to tell you."

"Go on," he said.

"I kept having this urge to go to confession after we had sex. I don't want to have to put up with that for the rest of my life."

He chuckled and pulled her toward him one more time.

"I thought we could invite all the people who live here, of course, Teddy, Sarah, Randi, and Ed."

"Gloria and Mandy should be there," he said. He and Gloria had made peace weeks ago. "And Ruby and Hal."

"If you want something with your family, we can go to Denver later."

Tears came to his eyes. She offered everything he could imagine wanting, and more. "Whenever you say, Grace," he said. "You're in charge."

THE WORDS STARTLED HER. That's what Nick had said over forty years ago, right before he left her to make all of the decisions and to do all of the work, too.

"We're both in charge," Grace said. "I'm counting on you to remind me of that."

"Of course, mi amor," he said, voice calm, deep, reassuring.

She looked up into Sam's eyes, choosing trust, embodied armor melting away from her head and shoulders. She knew the tension, the resistance, would come back, love not determined by one happily-ever-after moment. She prayed to keep letting go, to keep trusting, to keep loving.

Sam kissed the top of her head once more. Grace led him back to the people milling about the stage area and gathered around the newlyweds. Elizabeth hung on Ed's arm, smiling up at him, pirouetting now and again. Teddy had his arm around Mallory. Fran and Peter, and Phil and Larry stood in line to congratulate Ben and Polly. Loretta sat in the front row of chairs on the lawn, fanning herself, receiving those who walked by or stopped to chat.

Loretta continued to heartily approve of Sam. She had offered to move into the main house, to free up the cottage, but Grace had insisted she stay put. That was Loretta's home, for as long as she needed it.

Grace nudged Sam and directed his attention to the right side of the stage. "They look cozy," she said.

"Randi and Judy?" he asked. "Is that possible?"

She started to answer but Mallory interrupted.

"I have something for you, Grace," Mallory said.

Grace turned toward her future daughter-in-law. "What is it?"

"Open your hand."

Grace opened her right hand.

Mallory pressed a key to Grace's palm.

"What's this?" Grace asked.

"The key to my grandfather's Paris apartment. It's yours until the end of the year, whenever you want to stay there. Daddy agreed he wouldn't sell it for a few years and I'm giving you first dibs."

Grace thanked and hugged Mallory. The young woman left to rejoin Teddy.

"You really think something might be going on with Judy and Randi?" Sam asked.

Grace started to answer but Deirdre interrupted.

"I have to thank you again, Grace, for deciding to give ownership of the buildings to the foundation. Great plan. You own the land and pay the foundation for use of the buildings. Beautiful!"

"When did you decide that, Grace?" Sam asked.

She started to answer but Teddy called from the stage. "Hey, Mom! Ben and Polly want you to come up here for a picture with them."

"I'll be right back." She started to walk toward the stage.

"Grace?" Sam called.

Grace turned to look over her shoulder. Sam stood alone, confusion knitting his forehead into worried wrinkles above his eyes.

Deirdre came up from behind and clapped him on the back. "Welcome to your new life, Sam!"

His face registered surprise.

Grace ran back and took his hand. "Please come with me. I want us to be in this picture together."

Made in the USA
Coppell, TX
24 February 2021

50721889R00206